BOOKS BY TOBSHA LEARNER
from TOM DOHERTY ASSOCIATES

Soul

The Witch of Cologne

SOUL

TOBSHA LEARNER

TOR®

A TOM DOHERTY ASSOCIATES BOOK
NEW YORK

Author's Note: This is a work of fiction written to entertain, inspire, and intrigue, and should be read as such—any similarity to a living person or institute is entirely coincidental

SOUL

Copyright © 2006 by Tobsha Learner

First published in 2006 by HarperCollins *Publishers* Australia Pty Limited

Reader's Guide copyright © 2008 by Tobsha Learner

A Tor Book
Published by Tom Doherty Associates, LLC
175 Fifth Avenue
New York, NY 10010

www.tor-forge.com

Tor® is a registered trademark of Tom Doherty Associates, LLC.

ISBN 978-0-7653-5975-9

First U.S. Edition: May 2008
First U.S. Mass Market Edition: February 2010

Printed in the United States of America

0 9 8 7 6 5 4 3 2 1

For my father,
Dr. Arnold Learner, mathematician
(1934–1975)

As natural selection works solely by and for the good of each being, all corporeal and mental endowments will tend to progress toward perfection.

—CHARLES DARWIN, *On the Origin of Species*

We still dream what Adam dreamt.

—VICTOR HUGO

PART ONE

THE APPLE

1

Ireland, 1849

The housekeeper had brought Lavinia to the remote place before, to this gully south of the village where the peat bog finished in a sharp edge, sliced away like a layer cake. The housekeeper's sister had married a peatcutter whose stone and peat hut crouched resolute against the unforgiving elements. They were Catholics, now suffering under the great famine.

It was spring and the squares of turf sitting in piles on the new grass of the returning bog exuded a rich smell that was somehow exciting. The nine-year-old girl glanced back at the hut. The housekeeper, her wispy gray hair tucked firmly under a woolen bonnet, was in intense conversation with her sister, pushing the bound food parcels into her clawlike hands. Starvation had reduced the woman's femininity to a series of sharp corners beneath her ragged dress.

Behind her, Lavinia heard the thud of a slean, then ringing as the iron turf-spade found a hidden rock. She knew it was the boy. He looked to be a good three or four years older than her, with a fudge of curling black hair over the wind-burnt oval of his solemn face. She'd noticed him as they were driving toward the small outpost: a skinny, shadowy parody of a man standing by the split peat, scowling at the approaching cart. Here was mystery, and Lavinia had felt her power as she caught him staring at her long loose hair, the ribbons of her bonnet, the extraordinary whiteness of her clean hands, her fresh face.

Without thinking, Lavinia ran toward him while the boy, feigning indifference, knelt to carve a rectangle with the slean.

"Do you like it here?" She kicked at the soil beside him.

Squinting up, he paused, watching the play of her fingers against the scarlet wool of her cloak.

"It's a living . . . but you wouldn't know anything about that, a flash missy like yourself."

She skipped around to the other side of his patch of peat, turning the word "flash" around in her mind until she imagined she could taste it, like the sugar plums her father had brought her from Dublin for Christmas. The idea made her heart and stomach flutter.

"You think me flash?"

"Flash and pretty, like the sun, like a golden statue that belongs in church." He sat back, surprised at how the observation had suddenly made him feel demeaned, unclean. He knew her to be the daughter of a Protestant vicar, near gentry, and now he found that he resented the pristine naivety of the child, the plumpness of her forearms visible beyond the sleeves of her pinafore. It was almost as if he could eat the child herself.

Picking up a sod of peat, he threw it at a crow—the bird's cawing scribbled across the pewter sky as the black wings lifted it high into the air. Standing, the boy wiped his muddy hands across his thighs, then looked back to where the two women were still engrossed in conversation.

"If you like, I can show you some magic—an elvin's cave."

Lavinia hesitated. She knew it was wrong to walk off unescorted, but he looked harmless enough, his adolescent wrists dangling, his face as mournful as a donkey's. Besides, she liked the burning feeling she had when he looked at her.

"We cannot be long. Mrs. O'Brien will worry if I am not in sight."

But he was already leading her away from the field, his cutter swinging from a notch in his belt. She followed him, clambering down a hidden ravine beyond the bog.

Looking around, Lavinia panicked at their isolation. "Where is the cave?"

The boy walked across to a clump of low bush and pulled it aside to reveal the darkened mouth of a small burrow. Most likely an abandoned badger's den, Lavinia thought, annoyed that he could believe her so gullible; but she still wanted to see it, just in case—against all the logic her father had taught her—elvins might really exist. Then, later, back at the vicarage, she would be able to tell the story to her whispering box, so that her mother could hear her up there in Paradise.

She hoisted her skirt above her knickerbockers and dropped to the spongy heather to crawl into the cave.

"If you get closer you will see their wee purple eyes glinting in the dark."

Lavinia peered into the darkness. Behind her, suddenly, she felt the strangeness of his hands under her petticoats, up between her legs. Kicking, she pushed herself back into the light as she tried to fight him off.

To her amazement, she was not so much afraid as surprised when he pinned her against the bracken. As he held her there he supported his weight with one hand while reaching down with the other to his breeches. The glint of his cutter hanging from his belt pulled at her consciousness. Before she had time to think, she'd grabbed it and, with a strange, soft tearing sound, plunged it into the boy's thigh.

He screamed once like an animal. She rolled from under him and for a minute, they both stared down at the buried knife. Fascinated, Lavinia watched as blood began to well around the lip of the wound, staining his thin burlap breeches.

"You have fallen on your own knife, understand?" she said softly. Her cool demeanor sent a shiver through the injured boy. "If I hear mention of any other explanation, I shall have you whipped."

Lavinia waited until the boy nodded, his ruddy face now ashen. Then she ran, filled with a wild, thumping exhilaration that she intuitively knew she would have to keep secret, perhaps for her whole life.

2

Afghanistan, March 2002

The grandeur of the looming mountains and the clear sky above contrasted sharply with the hillside where the Humvee wound its way up a dirt track.

The rotors of the Black Hawk helicopter beat the air above. As it swooped down, it reminded Julia of a huge angered wasp, a sinister danger glinting off the hardened cockpit window.

Two door gunners hung out of it, their M60 machine guns aimed straight down at the ground. Julia, sitting in the back of the Humvee, caught view of the soldiers squatting behind the gunners, their faces camouflaged—striped in green and black paint. One of them blew her a kiss.

The lieutenant escorting Julia followed her gaze.

"Greenhorns," he said. "War's one long glorious computer game until it's like—oh wow, real blood, real death."

The Humvee tilted as it took a corner. Julia grasped the strap of her seat belt; the flak jacket she wore under her sweater was a dead weight pressed against her breasts and chest, but it was comforting all the same.

"Colonel told me you were on some kind of field trip, so I guess you're not one of them bleeding heart journos?" Yelling over the sound of the engine, he bent toward her, his breath acrid even in the cold air, and squinted at the name tag bouncing on her chest. "Professor Huntington," he read aloud. "You a medic?"

"I'm a scientist. I'm out here testing adrenaline and hormonal levels immediately after conflict."

"They let you do that?"

"Special clearance."

He looked at her strangely then spat out the open window. "You think we like being here?"

She looked away. On the side of the road, two Afghani boys—their heads wrapped in traditional tribal scarfs, skinny ankles thrusting out of split Reeboks, old sweatshirts pulled over their kaftans—sat in a burnt-out BMW. Although they waved at the Humvee, their eyes were hostile.

"Some do, some don't."

It was true. Many soldiers secretly—or openly—enjoyed the adrenaline-fueled challenge of a risky environment, even among those few who had endured the most brutal conflict. In actuality, an average of two out of every one hundred combat soldiers never suffered post-traumatic stress disorder—and it was this two percent that fascinated Julia. The geneticist had spent the past three months in the Middle East on a research grant from Harvard, testing and interviewing such men: Israelis, Pakistanis, Americans, and Brits. Julia didn't take sides—her agenda was scientific not political. This was her last day; she was booked on a flight back to California the following morning.

The Humvee bounced over a pothole in the dirt track. Ahead, the hillside fell away to reveal a staggering view. They turned a sharp corner, only to be blocked by a flock of long-haired black goats being herded across the road by a wizened old man in a dusty, stained robe and a pale blue turban. He waved his staff at the bleating animals, seemingly impervious to the vehicle. Julia wondered why the driver didn't blast his horn, then realized he was trying not to attract unnecessary attention. She sensed the driver and the soldier tensing up. Five miles from the combat zone, and theoretically inside friendly terrain, an ambush was still possible.

Her companion glanced at the driver, who shrugged. "I hate this bullshit!"

Muttering darkly, the lieutenant clambered out of the Humvee and yelled at the goat herder. The old man's wrinkled visage stared back at him without a glimmer of comprehension.

In an instant, the old man dropped to the ground. The lieutenant spun on his heels, looking around wildly for a possible sniper, but before he had a chance to react, Julia heard the rhythmic pop-pop-pop of automatic gunfire. The soldier's body thudded against the Humvee, smearing blood as it slid down the window.

The driver accelerated straight toward the startled goats, which scattered, bleating, across the path. Julia ducked, huddled against the seat. Glass rained down as bullets shattered the front window and the tires were shot out. Swerving wildly, the Humvee bumped across the stony ground and skidded to a halt.

Julia could hear the dying driver groaning. Then silence, filled only by the bleating goats and a bird cry Julia imagined to be from an eagle. Suddenly there came the chanting of their assailant: *Allahu akbar, Allah is great, Allah is all powerful*. The Arabic words were defiant, hypnotic, and horribly musical. Although her senses were taut with panic, Julia gleaned that there was one voice, one set of footsteps. She waited, amazed by the clarity with which she seemed to be functioning—her single objective, survival.

The Humvee door was wrenched open and a dark face materialized: brown eyes, beard, skin peppered with acne. There was the incongruous smell of chewing gum and, faintly, hashish. Grabbing her by the shoulder, he pulled her out of the car then wrapped one arm around her neck.

"Scream and I kill you."

Julia said nothing, her heart pounding now from anger not

fear. Her legs scrabbled against the rocky ground as he dragged her backwards. He was smaller than she was, she estimated, about five foot six to her five foot ten, and slight, his arm bony and sharp around her neck.

In the corner of her vision she saw he carried a *jambaya*—the traditional Arabic knife, curved and embossed—in his belt. With a sudden sideways lurch, she forced him to trip and allowed her full weight to fall directly on top of him, pushing them both to the ground. She jabbed her fingers into his eyes. He screeched. The AK–47 he'd been holding rattled against the stony ground as it rolled away. In the split second he lay there stunned, his arm still circling her neck, Julia reached down and pulled out the *jambaya*, then plunged it deep into his side. It sank without resistance as his screaming battered her eardrums. Vaguely remembering a briefing on the mechanics of close combat, Julia tried to pull the knife up through his body. He groaned deeply, his grip on her neck slackening.

Julia rolled to the side and scrambled to her knees. The AK–47 lay on the ground beside her. The man clutched at the hilt of the knife in his side, his face already gray. She picked up the gun and pointed it at his torso. The calm voice of the briefing instructor returned to her in an instant: "Squeeze the trigger . . . don't pull."

She flicked the safety catch and fired directly into the man's chest. Then she waited—what for she wasn't sure. The precision with which she saw and heard everything around her stretched time and space with a razor sharp clarity. There was no thought; just the listening, and the smell of pine cones and goats' dung, and now the faint metallic tinge of blood on the breeze rolling down from the mountains.

A clatter of stones falling down the slope of the hillside caused her to swing round, but the old goat herder was nowhere in sight.

Julia got to her feet, still holding the gun, and walked a few steps away from her dead assailant. Turning her back on him, she looked down across the ravine to the ancient pine trees still frosted with snow, indifferent and timeless. She was suddenly overtaken by nausea, a clutching at her womb—not delayed shock or disgust, but something else, something Julia had suspected ever since she'd bought a pregnancy test in Kabul. Watched by two doubtful goats, she doubled over and vomited.

Afterwards, she was horrified to discover that she felt relief but nothing more—no fear, no repulsion at her own actions. Above her, she could hear the rotating blades of the returning helicopter.

3

Los Angeles, 2002

As she pushed the trolley loaded with her old leather suitcase, the battered rucksack covered with stickers from obscure hotels in obscure destinations, the steel case marked "Scientific Specimens" balanced on top, Julia tried to control the growing excitement drumming at the pit of her stomach. There's always that moment of apprehension, she thought, as you walk through the customs exit and onto the ramp leading to the arrivals lounge. Anticipation tainted with apprehension—will you recognize him? Will you feel the same jolt of intimacy and love you've imagined night after night during the weeks apart? Or will estrangement betray you?

The spectators leaning over the rails came into sight. Children, their faces mobile with trepidation, clutching the long strings of silver helium balloons painted with hearts saying "I love you"; an aged father holding up a home-made sign painfully restrained in its controlled emotion—"Welcome Emilio!"; a mother, dressed as if for a party, bright blue eye shadow folded into optimistic creases as she tried not to cry. These were the moments that made up the mythology of families, Julia observed—arrival, departure, birth, death. She wondered why she was always so uncomfortable at such events, as if her nature kept her one step apart, defined her as the commentator.

It was crowded at the bottom of the ramp. The flight had been delayed, security at customs unusually tight, and Julia sensed restlessness in the anxious spectators.

She scanned the crowd, looking for her husband. A large man, Klaus was always visible. She found him standing back, watching her looking for him. Their gaze fused and there it was, that jolt Julia was always so afraid would one day vanish. Abandoning the trolley, she ran into his arms.

"Welcome home," he murmured into her hair.

At six foot five, Klaus was taller than Julia by almost a head and was the first man who had been able to envelop her entirely. Every other lover had made her feel ungainly and awkwardly unfeminine because of her height. This feeling of being cradled had been an unexpected revelation: a liberating sensation that made Julia—a woman who preferred to be in control—finally surrender.

She buried her face in his shoulder and breathed him in. Afghanistan had already started to recede as the normalcy of the L.A. airport and her husband's touch anchored her. There and then, she decided she would never tell him about the ambush and her reaction. Leveling her eyes with his, she kissed him.

"I was going to ask you to marry me but I seem to vaguely remember we're married already," she whispered. Forgetting they were in a public space, she slipped her hands in his trouser pocket to rub against the blind bulge of his penis: the lucky talisman of their love.

He groaned softly then extracted her hands. "So that's what this is for," he said, grinning and holding up his left hand to indicate his wedding ring. Turning, he started pushing her trolley to the exit. She followed reluctantly. "Where's the car?"

Two men came into sight—a limousine driver and another individual Julia recognized immediately. Colonel Hank Smith-Royston was head of the psychology division of the Department of Defense—the official who had originally authorized her research trip. Why were they here, she wondered nervously. Had she violated some protocol she wasn't aware of? A report of the ambush in Afghanistan had been filed, and, after assessing her for trauma, they had debriefed her in Kabul and reassured her that any account of her behavior was both confidential and sealed. So why the escort now?

Reading her face, Klaus squeezed her hand reassuringly. "Sorry, but the DOD insisted—apparently they have a proposal that can't wait, and I couldn't resist the prospect of a stretch limo. But don't worry, I'll sit in the front seat like a good boy."

"We *are* going straight home?"

"That's what the big boys promised."

※

Rain splattered against the windows of the limousine. Julia stared out at the miniature oil wells that stood at the edge of the La Brea freeway; the scaled-down mechanisms with the one metal arm ceaselessly pumping had always fascinated her. Colonel Smith-Royston sat beside her. A muscular man in his forties, radiating a humorous irony that Julia suspected helped keep him both buoyant and optimistic in a job that was often grim. He had an empathetic air that allowed one to be comfortably silent in his company.

"It's nice to see you again, Professor," he said smiling.

"You, too, Colonel, but I'm kind of surprised."

"Indeed. I apologize for my audacity." He checked his watch. "I promise we'll have you and your husband home within the hour."

"You're forgiven. Anyhow, it's good to know my tax dollar now stretches to a military chauffeur service."

He laughed. Julia glanced across at Klaus, who was sitting with the driver in the front, behind the glass partition. She couldn't hear a word he was saying, but from his animated gestures she guessed he was probably engaging the driver in one of his endless anecdotes about the entertainment industry. Klaus loved an audience, and he also loved extracting stories from lay people—gardeners, chauffeurs, cable technicians— the hidden nuggets of suburban fables.

The colonel spoke again, lowering his voice. "I know this is a little unorthodox, but there is some urgency involved, as well as high security."

Julia looked at the briefcase resting next to her companion. "If it's about the ambush . . ."

"Professor Huntington, we're in Los Angeles now. Whatever happened over there stays over there."

"I don't want anyone to know." She indicated Klaus. "Not even my husband."

"I understand."

Relieved, Julia relaxed into the plush leather seat. Why was she so ashamed of how she had reacted in the ambush? What was she—some kind of aberration? She examined her psychology with a forensic objectivity: she had acted in self-defense and therefore there was some moral justification to the killing. But what she found so disturbing was the very private acknowledgment that she had experienced a complete lack of remorse, or any other emotion.

"Trust me, Professor, the whole incident is buried. I'm here on an entirely different matter. As you're aware, the DOD has followed your work for a good decade now, and certainly in my division we're all big fans."

"Thank you." She replied cautiously, slightly suspicious about where all this flattery was leading to.

"To put it bluntly, we're offering you a job. A commission.

We want you to establish whether there is any possible link between genetic makeup and violence that we could use to identify potential crack combat soldiers specifically to recruit for our Delta force. We're looking for people with a genetic propensity for close combat without emotional engagement, who will not, and I repeat not, suffer from PTSD. In other words, the two percent you are so obsessed with, Professor. Now I know genetic profiling is currently illegal, but we're looking to the future here, when everyone will be profiled at birth, and we will be allowed to approach those natural born soldiers. Look at it this way: we're offering to finance—and finance generously—the natural trajectory of your current research."

Julia struggled to conceal her excitement. To discover such a gene function would ensure her own scientific legacy, and would secure enough funding to keep the small laboratory she ran at the University of California going for decades. Yet she was aware of the potential pitfalls: the scientific complexity of the research, as well as the ethical questions surrounding the location of such a gene function. Indeed, some research indicated that a gene could lie dormant for generations until an external event—occurring either in utero or in the developing adult—triggered it into activity. Julia's work involved eliminating the obvious candidate genes, whose various functions were already known, and isolating new genes that might be linked to a psychological and emotional predisposition for close combat. If such a gene function could be identified, Julia knew the army would be quick to capitalize on it.

The colonel opened his briefcase and pulled out a large brown file. He pushed it across the seat toward her.

"Five hundred twins from the veterans' database—all potential subjects for the research. Thought a little groundwork might make it easier for you."

She waited for a moment, watching him lean forward. She knew he was anxious for her to jump at the opportunity.

"Professor, we both know the terrible cost of post-traumatic

stress disorder on ex-soldiers, their families, and society itself. If we can locate the men who don't *ever* suffer from it,
we'll be doing society and humanity an immense favor."

In the ensuing pause while Julia contemplated the offer,
the sound of the rain against the windows seemed to grow
louder. The colonel glanced out of the window, Julia looked
down at his hands; one of them was clenched, betraying his
casual façade.

"You don't have to make a decision now. Sleep on it," he
murmured.

The limousine turned into Los Feliz Boulevard, then drove
past Julia's local diner. She lifted the file and rested it on
her lap.

"I don't have to. I'll take the commission."

4

"It took over an hour to get through customs. I'm amazed
they didn't confiscate my samples."

"Homeland security," Klaus said wryly. "The getting of
wisdom for this land fair and free."

Since the lethal attack on the twin towers of the World
Trade Center the previous September, security had become
terrifyingly rigorous. Fear laced the air like a sudden chill in
every public space, from car parks to baseball grounds.

Klaus, his black hair sprinkled with sawdust, picked up a
chisel and continued his woodcarving. "America is like a
woman who has lost her virginity in a gang bang. I'm still
surprised it's taken this long for the United States to experience a serious terrorist attack within its borders."

"Blame our foreign policy. Besides, we've had serious terrorist attacks before."

Julia, showered and unpacked, caffeine pounding the last of her energy into a jittery wakefulness, felt herself being drawn into a reluctant discussion when all she wanted was to make love. But after she'd told Klaus about the job offer, he'd been uncharacteristically unsupportive.

"You have got no idea," he said, looking up from his work. "Europe is made from war. Look at the Balkans, the Basque movement, Northern Ireland. My parents still remember famine under the German occupation. Europeans wade through centuries of vendettas, racism, and battles over sovereignty every day on the way to the bus stop. A European can't escape, unless he goes to the New World, and now it's here, too. You know you can't take this commission," he concluded grimly.

Julia kissed him across the wood vise, hoping to defuse his darkening mood. The sawdust slipping from his hair showered her cheeks.

"Yeah, and I love you, too. But if you can think of another way of making the mortgage, I'm open to suggestions."

Klaus frowned. "Wonderful, you've been back for two hours and we're already arguing about my inability to match your income."

"I have to take the job, baby, it's a huge opportunity."

"Sweetheart, you always get so swept up you never see the broader implications. This *will* lead to genetic profiling."

"Not necessarily."

"Yes necessarily."

Julia stood at the workbench that ran along one side of the tool shed Klaus had redesigned as his writing studio. Built at the back of the yard in the 1950s for a previous resident's wayward teenage son, the small hut was made from pale pine that still exuded a sweet scent in the summer. It was Klaus's sanctuary, an inherently masculine domain hung with icons from his Belgian adolescence: Anderlecht football club posters, a photo from a drunken student reunion, a battered hockey stick, a picture of an ex-girlfriend, blonde and toothy, on a horse.

Above the desk was a shelf packed with books on script writing; next to that stood a metal cabinet filled with television screenplays filed meticulously, the labels winking hopefully: *sci-fi, crime, supernatural, comedy*—all unproduced.

The workbench was where Klaus relieved his frustration with his career by constructing things—from small carvings to cabinetmaking. It was a form of meditation for him, this rhythm of the wood rasp, the tattoo and swing of the hammer. It was how the writer stopped thinking, and also how he assuaged his aggravation at the precariousness of the entertainment industry by smashing the occasional object he had created.

"If there is a mutant gene function, and I don't find it, you realize another geneticist will—eventually. So why not me?" Julia caressed his shoulder. "Please, let's not argue. I missed you, honey bear."

Klaus turned back to his work without responding.

A half carved head was clamped in the vise attached to the bench, powdery with shavings. Watching the chisel bite into the rose-tinged wood, Julia tried unsuccessfully to stop her mind crowding with the overwhelming myriad of ethical questions that always swirled around her research. How did her colleagues survive? They all held wildly different opinions. Craig Venter, the maverick who had shocked the scientific community by using a large percentage of his own genome as the first generic prototype, was an agnostic who believed all research was valid. His nemesis, Francis Collins, a born-again Christian, believed in strict ethical codes on research, but still alleged that the discovery and mapping of the genome fell under God's plan. Then there was the actual pioneer of the genome, James Watson, whose original motivation was to prove that there was no God, no grand designer of man and nature.

Where did Julia stand among these three schools of thought? The ache of jet lag burned behind her eyes. She sank into a chair and stared over Klaus's shoulder at the small window framing the sky. A blimp advertising Dunlop tires floated across a corner of the blue canvas. For a moment the ground seemed to tilt slightly with it, as if Julia was still on the airplane, terra firma as insubstantial as the falling air beneath the jet.

The wood shavings curling back like thick locks of auburn hair, Klaus's mallet tapping down onto the end of the carving tool in a ceaseless beat—both converged into a seductively familiar rhythm that pressed Julia's recent experiences in the Middle East into a surreal pastiche that suddenly seemed to belong to somebody else's memory. You're home now, she reassured herself. Relax, this is where you belong; no more strange hotel rooms, 4 a.m. drives through collapsed, war-torn suburbs, the gallows humor of bored soldiers, no more ambushes.

Outside, the rain had stopped and the afternoon sun caught the top of the bench, transforming the wood shaving into a fine golden powder. Julia traced an outline in it with her finger—a small stick figure, a primitive man with a spear in his hand. She looked at the back of her husband's neck, the soft feathering of his hairline, the tangible presence of him bringing back the sharp sense of missing him when she was away. Two months. They hadn't made love for two months.

She moved behind him and gently bit the back of his neck. The beating of the mallet stopped as, groaning softly despite his irritation, Klaus arched his neck in response. Then, pushing back the work chair, he wrapped his long arms around her.

They kissed and he bit her lower lip playfully. Even after ten years of marriage, Julia still felt that tug of desire, as if Klaus were a new lover with each seduction. Nevertheless, they did not make love enough, and she had often puzzled over the awkward balance between domesticity and desire. She was a workaholic, and both of them were cerebral animals, easily distracted by anxiety. Sometimes Julia fantasized about a life where they could be more spontaneous. She'd even contemplated renting a room to recreate the excitement of a clandestine encounter, to eroticize the familiar.

Sliding her hand around Klaus's growing erection, she slipped her tongue into his mouth, curling one leg around him. He kissed her back passionately, all annoyance evaporating.

He hauled her skirt up over her hips, his fingers between her legs, playing her. Groaning, she propelled him toward the dusty old couch against the wall. Pushing him down, she sank to her knees and took him into her mouth.

How she loved the scent of him. It was like coming home; the familiar rich buttery concoction, tinged with sweat and something a little darker, was overwhelmingly sexual to her, flooding her with a pungent masculinity that was completely his—his individual pheromone fingerprint.

He weaved his fingers through her long hair and she felt him growing harder, tremors of pleasure running up his cock, his thighs quivering under her hands. He pulled her face up to his and she mounted him, easing him into her, filling with a delicious sense of recognition as both their bodies relaxed into each other. She paused, the thickness of him causing her to gasp. Searching his face, she could find nothing but affection and the history of all their couplings reflected in his irises, a chronology of moments like these, their time together, their intimacy.

And then, their lovemaking grew more frenzied, the images of Afghanistan, of the spinning wheel of the Humvee, the blood on the stones, the eyes of the startled goats, all started to leave her as—with each gasp—she was drawn into the moment, into this homecoming, this union that was the core of the two of them.

Her swollen breasts brushed the stubble on his unshaven chin, his lips tugged at her nipples, as, closing her legs, she drew the ecstasy between them into a tight ambiguity, mounting higher and higher until both of them came—he, buried in the black wave of her hair, she screaming out loud in a tremendous release of grief and deliverance.

Afterwards, as she lay in the crook of his armpit, Klaus ran his hands thoughtfully across her breasts and down to her belly.

"You're bigger. Your nipples are darker."

She buried her eyes in the underside of his arms, not wanting him to read them.

"Julia?"

She said nothing but he felt her heart accelerate under his palm.

"You're pregnant, aren't you?"

She nodded, her hair brushing his skin. Klaus sat up, instantly pulling away from her. "Great."

She looked up to see his face buried in his hands.

"It's what we've always wanted, isn't it?"

"It's just that the timing's so wrong. You have this commission; I have this possible television series."

"When is it ever right?"

He looked at her then, and smiled uncertainly.

"Klaus, I want this baby."

Kneeling, he placed his head against her belly. "*Uwl moeder is een genie*," he murmured to the unborn child.

"I'm not sure that's going to make him bilingual. But it's a good beginning. And no, I'm not a genius."

"Your Flemish is improving. How do you know it's a boy?"

"Feminine intuition. What do you think of the name Aidan James—after my grandfather and great-grandfather? James Huntington."

"Okay, my love, Aidan James Huntington-Dumont it is. Julia, Klaus, and Aidan—fantastic. Life is good. It's all going to be okay."

For one small moment Julia wondered whether he wasn't just trying to convince himself.

5

The Amazon, 1856

Colonel James Huntington stood taller than the men around him, a good foot taller. Gilo, his assistant and translator, adjusted the large box camera that perched awkwardly at the edge of the clearing. Amid the plumes of white curling smoke and against the thick green jungle foliage it looked absurdly incongruous: an icon of a modern world set in a primordial landscape. The anthropologist worried whether Gilo would be able to capture a clear image. The Bakairi had agreed to allow the Colonel to be photographed during the ritual but not themselves. After the Colonel had explained the workings of the camera and assured them it would not steal their spirit—which seemed to be their prevailing fear— and that the instrument would carry their story around the world, the shaman had reluctantly allowed the photography of the villagers in all other practices, but not this—the conjuring up of Evaki, their goddess of day and night.

The tribesmen had insisted that the Colonel be near naked for the ceremony, his white skin smeared with ochre. He felt as though he were now in the skin of another man—a creature of instinct, despite his scientific bent, his bare feet anchored against the spongy moss and undergrowth, the earth throbbing beneath him as the hallucinogenic trickled through his veins like a thick honey. Already, the branches above him writhed and the sky had begun to turn.

He was to be initiated as the twenty-second in a group of shamans, and, in keeping with the tribal laws, had fasted the day before to purify his spirit. There was little James

Huntington wanted more than this—to be invited to partici-
pate in an ancient ritual no white man had been involved in
before. The lure of both experience and knowledge was irresistible. The anthropologist's knees trembled, and his stomach clenched in rhythm with the drums that four young
boys—no older than ten—played beside the fire that burned
in a shallow pit in the center of the cleared arena. The other
twenty-one initiates stood around him, forming a circle. In
the center stood the chief shaman, his broad wizened face
solemn with concentration, the band of red ochre across his
cheekbones highlighting the piercing intelligence of his black
eyes.

The shaman—the wise man of the village—sensed conflict within the Colonel. Awed by the age and muscularity of
the veteran soldier, he perceived the white man had a valuable
soul. As he traced the facial scar the Colonel had received in
the Crimea, he promised that the half of the soldier's soul that
had been torn away from him in battle would come back to
him if he had the strength to face the Goddess.

With the help of two boys, the shaman lifted the ritual
mask—an elongated face with huge lidded eyes, a streak of
yellow ochre for a nose, a screaming circle for a mouth, and
fringed by reeds that hung to the ground—and solemnly
placed it over the white man's head and body.

The heavy scent of the oiled wood mixed with the smell of
the pungent soil, filling the Colonel's nostrils. The mask
hung heavily; it felt as if it were fused to his skin. His heart
thumped as he mimicked the movements of the dancers
around him: arms arching up to the heavens, evoking the
spirit of each of the Gods their masks represented—the
earth, the river, and the rising moon, a pale coin suspended
above them. The dancers' arms whirled about him faster and
faster, until they transformed into feathered limbs and he felt
the Goddess becoming him, he becoming her—the great
bird that delivered man at birth and took him up at death.
And now, infused with the drug, the Colonel saw how Time

could be broken down into a series of moments, each layered upon the next, and how those moments need not be linear. "I am Evaki!" he screamed out, encouraged by the shaman who whirled a torch around and around, creating a spiral of trailing embers and light that seemed to arch up to the very heavens. At the center of that burning helix Huntington suddenly saw himself as a child, then at the age he was now, and finally the terrible specter of his own death. The panting breath of his fear filled his eardrums, as, stumbling, he struggled to stay in rhythm with his companions, the dancing messengers, their shiny legs and arms making a cradle for his terror as the Goddess rose from the smoke of the fire with nothing but her eyes—vast and recognizably human, floating like leaves swept up in the heat.

Where there is death there must be life, she whispered and the Colonel felt the words through the rattling cage of his ribs, through his very bones, and knew then that he must beget an heir, a son, and that within this revelation lay his deliverance.

6

Ireland, 1858

The carved ivory head of the walking stick was in the form of a snarling gorilla and had a ferocity that, privately, Colonel James Huntington found comforting. Just as Moses had held up the golden calf, he could hold up the stick and wave it at the indifferent gods in righteous indignation, the monkey sneering for him. But the Colonel was not a righteous man. In all his soldiering, all his travels, he was yet to find a reason to believe in anything but the relentlessness of Nature, that onward grind called life—the grimacing ape.

He flicked a ribbon of seaweed across the pooling sand. The tide was on its way out and the foreshore was broken by a ridge of rock pools, each glassy pond a still, tepid eye beyond which the Irish Sea thrashed. I should like to be a better man. Would marriage make me so? It was a rhetorical question. He had already made up his mind, sometime in the early hours, having examined his options from every angle, turning them over like an hourglass, calculating the various ways the sand might trickle, finally concluding that whichever way the instrument was turned, the sand did indeed travel grain by grain. Time ran only one way.

At forty-seven, the Colonel was haunted by his own mortality. Arthritis beat hollowly in his left shin—a battle wound from Sebastopol—and there was more gray in his whiskers than he cared to acknowledge. He had arrived at that time of life when a man is confronted with the legacy of his conquests; in his case, a series of unsatisfactory liaisons that he regarded as a festering collection of regrettable memories. A libertine, whose sensual pleasures transcended the notion of gender, James Huntington was, naturally, intensely private about his pursuits. Recently, old diversions had ceased to excite and he was now driven to extremes to experience any stimulation—intellectual, emotional, sexual, or otherwise. Consequently, his erotic expeditions had of late become increasingly perilous, as if propelled by an unconscious compulsion to destroy his social standing. He was at a crossroads: the path he was on could lead to social disgrace, or worse, but all the future seemed to hold was further decadence and an erosion of the primary morals he, at least mentally, subscribed to—truth, honor, fidelity.

A bubble broke in the sand ahead and he wondered about the sandworm beneath. Did such creatures mate? Or did they reproduce asexually? The answer escaped him but his resolution rushed back anew. The epiphany he had experienced in the Amazon held true: he must procreate, and the seventeen-year-old girl approaching him was a destiny any hedonist might wish for.

"It is an uncommonly beautiful day, do you not think, Colonel Huntington? It is early for the west coast to experience sunshine as glorious as this."

The Colonel looked up from his sandworm and smiled, amusement crinkling around the eyes that Lavinia could never quite decide on as blue or green; they seemed to change with the emotions of their owner.

Lavinia glanced back to where the gray stone and wood of the cottages and fishermen's shacks followed the mouth of the river to where it spilled into the sea. She knew that Maggie O'Dowell, the postmistress, would be spying on her, tutting like a parrot as she fantasized about all kinds of immoral behavior that she could report to the four local widows who sat in judgment on every young woman this side of Killarney. Lavinia knew she was already damned: for her arrogance, for her youth, and for the worst sin of all—ambition. *Lord help me if I am also to be condemned as whore, a woman who walks hatless and chaperoneless with a man.*

Laughing at her own irreverence, Lavinia pulled off the straw bonnet, letting her hair fall to her waist. Her neck, bared, burned under the Colonel's gaze and, tilting her head at an angle that she knew would flatter the strong planes of her face, she prayed silently, *Ask me, ask me now, you must. You will be my husband, and I your wife, and you shall lift me high like the wind and carry me away from this atrocious backwater that is a murder for my spirit.* The silent invocation bubbled under the crashing waves.

Colonel James Huntington was the first man—aside from her father—who had taken her aspirations seriously and she had decided to love him for it. He was also the only man she'd met who wore spats and a velvet waistcoat and had an expensive gold pocket watch with his name inscribed on the back. The Colonel was the epitome of the cultured English gentleman, inhabiting a world he had described to her as a fascinating paradox of ambition and greed, beauty and terror; a world Lavinia was now convinced would be her salvation.

The cottage chimneys were smoking and under the fecund odor of burning peat, she imagined she could detect the very smell of the prejudices and fears that shackled all of the village's one hundred and fifty-six inhabitants, censoring even their dreams. It was a stench composed of body grime, the blistered ink of fading postcards from relatives in faraway places and other people's infidelities slipped like whispers between the billowing laundry—rags worn for so long they had become threads.

Lavinia skipped a few paces on the sand, then waved her hat defiantly at a clump of seagulls that threw themselves into the air screaming. Even the birds sound disapproving, she thought. A pox on them all; she was determined that Lavinia Elspeth Kane was destined for bigger things, for a life that would leave an indentation on the world, even if it were less than a chicken's scratching.

❧

Watching her dance the Colonel lifted his head to breathe in the breeze. The fresh salt air chased the exhaustion from his bones. The young woman standing before him, so charmingly seductive in her violet smock and buttoned leather boots, the heels of which were now splattered with wet sand, her inky hair loosened like a shimmering waterfall, was from an entirely different class altogether. In fact, it was only by a capricious and wondrous synchronicity that the two individuals there on the strand, buffeted by the Gaelic wind, knew each other at all, brought together by a coincidence of events that pivoted entirely upon the very humble *Liparis liparis*, otherwise known as the common sea snail.

The Reverend Augustus Kane—Lavinia's father—was a widower Presbyterian minister whose lack of passion for the sermon was matched only by his passion for the study of all things natural, including Man himself. In Nature, he had told his daughter more than once, lies God and in Nature alone.

Blasphemous words, particularly in that part of the world where the apostles, the moneyed landowners, and the English had abandoned the ordinary man during the terrible years of the famine. Perhaps it was this profanity, and the Reverend Kane's noticeable want of enthusiasm for the theatrical, that had caused his parishioners to dwindle to a mere loyal seven.

The patronage of Lord Lahmont, the local landowner, kept the small church open as its graveyard, packed with tombstones jammed like playing cards, was the only Protestant cemetery within a fifty-mile radius.

One blustery damp morning, the minister had made a minor discovery about the gender and sexuality of the *Liparis liparis*. Elated, he had danced in the churchyard in the rain, wearing just his dressing gown and Wellington boots—an act that set many of the local Catholics to muttering about the powerful disrespect of the Protestants for all things sacred.

Despite a subsequent heavy cold, the reverend wrote up his findings and they were published in the London, Edinburgh, and Dublin *Philosophical Magazine* and the *Journal of Science*. His florid and compellingly graphic prose had caught the attention of Colonel Huntington—himself an amateur naturalist—and a correspondence had been fostered upon this commonality of interests. The letters had blossomed into a friendship of sorts, and the Colonel became a regular visitor to the Kane household.

Now, Colonel Huntington walked alongside to the next rock pool. A small crab scuttled from under a piece of seaweed and threw itself with endearing desperation into the glassy shadows of the stilled seawater. Catching a glimpse of Lavinia's narrow ankle as she negotiated the uneven terrain, he was reminded of the first time he had set eyes on the young woman—then a shy pubescent, whose swelling curves were just beginning to soften her birdlike frame.

A slim figure lipped with a crescent of sunlight, Lavinia had stood before her father's desk, a huge conch shell held deferentially in her hands as she recited first the definition of the creature then a précis of its habitat, both in fluent Latin, to the proud delight of the reverend.

Despite the recent additions of frills and petticoats, the young woman relished still the dissection of specimens and could converse easily about the distinctions of various plant life and the manner in which species varied and mutated. The promise of mentoring such innocence was dangerously tempting to the Colonel. He needed a wife to relieve him of the increasing stress of compartmentalizing his private life from his public life, and he needed a child. With the detached eye of a scientist he assessed that Lavinia had three major assets: intelligence, youth, and, most enticing of all, anonymity. Her lineage was so mundane that Society would not be able to place her. Inherently a provocateur and a maverick, the Colonel was excited by the audacity of introducing such a creature into his circle. As his wife, Lavinia would be entirely his creation.

❧

When Colonel Huntington had arrived unexpectedly from London the month before, Lavinia, whose notions of love were informed solely by copious readings of Victor Hugo, Stendhal, and George Sand, had assumed that the long walks they took along the shores of the Irish Sea must be a form of courtship. But after weeks of convoluted small talk, she had begun to fear that his only interest might genuinely be her education.

Then one evening, after her father had discreetly retired, the Colonel had lifted her mouth to his and slipped his hand inside her bodice. Shocked, she had stood there frozen, with his warm hand over her breast, astounded by the trickling excitement that ran from her nipples to the very core of her.

But that was a week ago and the Colonel still had not proposed. Could he be exploiting her status? After all, Lavinia was the penniless daughter of a Presbyterian minister with no dowry and few marriage prospects, and he was the son of a Viscountess, independently wealthy with a town house in Mayfair and a country house in West Scotland. There was little but the gossip of the village to stop him from making her his mistress.

It was this anxiety that had kept Lavinia up most of the night. At the very least, respect for her father would surely prevent him considering such an arrangement. But the Colonel was a worldly individual who could afford anything and anyone he wanted.

Today, however, he appeared nervous, unexpectedly formal—like a noble predator, normally so in control of its territory, suddenly cornered and befuddled by an unforeseen change of locale. Lavinia would have found it amusing except for her own fears. He *must* ask her; any delay now would endanger her reputation.

The Colonel took her arm and together they peered into the rock pool.

"These habitats are a microcosm of the greater world, my dear," he said. "A miniature metropolis filled with predators, prey, scavengers and those individuals who cling to the edge of life and simply observe, praying that today will not be the day they are eaten. Lavinia, London society is far more ruthless, far crueller, particularly toward a species it cannot place."

Lavinia peeled off her glove and wove her fingers through his. Her skin felt deliciously cool and, to his surprise, the Colonel felt the stirrings of genuine emotion.

"Yes." The girl's voice was confident, determined.

He looked sideways, trying to read the blue band of her eyes, dazzling in the sun.

"Yes what, my dear?"

"Yes, I will marry you."

7

Los Angeles, 2002

Carla waited in the lounge room, tapping her foot nervously. Unable to keep still, she walked over to the fireplace. A frenetic energy seemed to beat beneath her translucent skin, a restlessness—some might call it unhappiness.

She ran her finger along the mantelpiece, past the pictures of Klaus and Julia—the wedding photo, the holiday in Cuba, Julia receiving her doctorate. As Julia's closest friend, Carla knew the history of each of the pictures intimately, almost as if they were her own memories.

Her finger paused at the photograph of Klaus in Antwerp, posing outside his university. Taken when he was twenty, it was one of the few images that pre-dated the marriage. His face appeared optimistic, as yet unlined by disappointment. Carla traced his mouth. Do not make judgment, do not, she caught herself thinking, before glancing away. I love both of them—that's the terrible paradox.

A large portrait hung over the fireplace. It was of a young woman dressed as the goddess Diana and sitting in a mossy glen, a quiver slung over her shoulder. A baby boy played at her feet. In the foreground lolled the majestic head of a huge stag the goddess had just shot down, the arrow still impaled in his rust-colored hide. An engraved brass plaque set into the bottom center of the frame read: *Mrs. Lavinia Huntington as Diana. Darcy Quinn, Dublin 1860.*

The young woman looked no older than about seventeen, and was clothed in a draped tunic that provocatively displayed one naked shoulder, her hair incongruously coiffed in elaborate coils. But it was her expression—the direct gaze that stretched beyond the canvas and the artifice of her setting—that was most captivating. An unnerving intelligence shone in the blue eyes. Carla stared back at her, and found that the realism of the young woman's stare made it difficult not to feel, as a spectator, that one was both an impostor and a voyeur.

Despite the summer heat beating in through the windows Carla shivered. She turned at the sound of her friend entering the room.

"I've never seen this painting before," Carla said.

"An inheritance from my father, I had it hung just before my trip. It's my paternal great-grandmother, Lavinia Huntington, painted in the early days of her marriage to my great-grandfather, James. He was an eminent explorer and gentleman soldier and wanted her painted as Diana as a tribute to his own exploits. The child at her feet is my grandfather, Aidan. See the dead stag? That was weirdly prophetic—Lavinia stood trial for her husband's murder just a year later."

"Jesus, Julia, did she do it?"

"My grandfather always claimed that she was innocent." Julia held out the wrapped present. "Sorry, it took a while to get through all the boxes, but here it is. Don't get your expectations up too high—it's sort of humorous."

"Thanks."

Carla submitted reluctantly to Julia's embrace and the two women held each other briefly, the sunlight slanting in through the low windows throwing their melted shadows into stark relief. The blonde-haired television producer was ten years younger than Julia and a good deal slighter in frame and in height. If Julia had been an observer, she would have seen Carla staring emotionlessly over her shoulder, but, holding her friend in her arms, she was oblivious.

Pulling the paper free, Carla glanced down at a set of DVDs, the cover showing a cheap Xeroxed image of a man holding a gun to a woman's head, then laughed as she recognized the title beneath—a TV series she'd worked on.

Julia smiled. "I found them on this tiny stall on the West Bank—counterfeited copies, subtitled in Arabic. I couldn't resist."

"I guess that makes me an internationally renowned producer," Carla remarked ironically as Julia sat down beside her. "You look amazing. Two months striding through the killing fields of the Middle East suits you."

"Well, I'm definitely changed, but I'm not sure I like what I'm turning into. It's the Minotaur syndrome—the monster within. There's a definite danger of becoming politically cynical—the disease of the morally bereft."

"Let me guess: you don't believe in free will and Democrats anymore?"

"Try secular democracy, capitalism, and satellite technology . . ."

"Wow, is there anything left?"

Julia smiled. "I dunno—reproduction, white picket fences, escapist television?"

"You *are* changed. Next thing I know we'll be doing baby showers and the outlet malls."

They had slipped into their particular banter—a humorous shorthand developed over the years. Julia loved this breezy word play; it was a grounding distraction from the pressures of her work. Apart from Klaus, Carla was Julia's closest companion, the friend who had counseled her through the bouts of professional insecurity that, at times, had threatened to overwhelm the geneticist. Julia regularly discussed her more private and lateral theories with Carla, spilling them in an impassioned stream across the warm afternoons spent together on the back porch, margaritas in hand. The two friends functioned as emotional ballast for each other; in a city as transient and disseminated as Los Angeles, one needed such camaraderie to survive.

"Unconditional friendship, it's a hell of a burden," Julia joked, but Carla averted her eyes. Julia wondered what was troubling her normally resilient friend. Despite the armor of her professionalism, Carla had a tenderness that shimmered at unexpected moments—an aspect of her personality Julia had always found redeeming. But now, sensing Carla was in one of her morose moods, she decided to wait before telling her she was pregnant.

The bleeping of Carla's pager cut through the sun-laced air.

"Great, the spa's confirmed. We have fifteen minutes to get there."

As she followed Carla out of the room, Julia noticed that the portrait of Lavinia Huntington was askew. While straightening it, she caught the reflection of fingerprints glistening on the brass frame.

❧

They lay opposite each other in the small pine-lined sauna, so tightly wrapped in towels that Julia felt as if she had been spun into a cocoon. The steamy heat sent rivulets of sweat down her body to pool in the hollows of her collarbone, between her breasts, in her navel.

The dim light and the scent of orange and jasmine—the droplets of oil sizzling on the grid of the steamer—gave the room a confessional intimacy, as if there would be no consequences of words spoken behind the thick pine door.

Julia closed her eyes and felt two more large drops of sweat form and then run down either side of her face.

Restless, Carla sat up and moved to the lower shelf. Across the room Julia's long pale form looked like a languid marble statue. She spoke out into the steam.

"It's funny, you can feel your physical self diminishing. Heat really strips us right back to essentials."

Carla didn't answer. Worried, Julia opened her eyes. "You still with me?"

"I'm here. I'm just concentrating on sweating."

"So what's new on your emotional horizon?"

"Nothing."

"C'mon, something must have happened in two months?"

Fearing she might betray herself, Carla stared at the light above the door until a small red dot danced in front of her retinas.

"I've resigned myself to a kind of self-indulgent single-dom. I mean, I've done the usual dates but nothing's really grabbed me . . ." She paused, waiting for Julia to detect the disingenuous tone she herself heard in every word. To her amazement (and strange dismay), her friend believed her.

"Don't give up. You'll find someone, I know you will."

Sudden tears welling, Carla turned her face to the pine wall. "I should get out now." As she started to stand, the heat of the wooden floors burned the soles of her feet.

Julia rolled onto her front. "Carla, I killed a man." The words leapt out of the misty steam, incongruous and unbelievable. "In Afghanistan. It was in self-defense, but it was a killing nevertheless."

Stunned, Carla sat back on the bench. "Oh, Julia."

"I haven't even told Klaus. But I need to tell someone, here in Los Angeles, just to make it real."

"How? How did it happen?"

"There was this ambush, my escort and driver were killed, he pulled me out of the car . . ."

"He?"

"The assailant—he was just a kid. God knows who he thought I was—maybe some VIP he could use to trade with. He had his arm around my neck, we stumbled and I managed to wrench his knife out . . ."

"Jesus. I would've been petrified with terror."

"Somehow I wasn't—everything slowed right down, into an emotionless clarity. I did what I had to do to survive."

"Are you okay now?"

"That's the obscene part—I actually feel guilty about not being more affected. It's frightening . . ."

"What's frightening?"

"To know I'm capable of such detachment. I feel so ashamed,

like some kind of freak. Promise you won't tell anyone. I just want to bury the whole thing, Carla. I need to."

Now that Julia had actually said the words, confided the terrible truth, she felt a tremendous sense of relief. It wasn't absolution—that, she knew she would never find.

❧

The snow that shimmered on the peaks of the San Gabriel mountain was a rare sight and always surprised Julia. Originally from San Francisco, she still found it hard to credit Los Angeles with any innate beauty, though in reality the sprawling metropolis was veined with canyon walks that, in summer, were pungent with the scent of eucalyptus and pine, while the indigenous scrub peppered the landscaped hills with a sparse beauty. And there was a splendor to the tall palms that lined even the seediest of the downtown boulevards; their languid swaying made Julia think of seaweed undulating in an invisible sea. *Mi ciudad hermosa.* Julia liked to think of the city as an aging actress, whose loveliness still glimmered beneath the paint and surgery.

Several shopping bags sat next to her in the passenger seat. They were filled with baby clothes; three cotton jumper suits, two bonnets, and a tiny silver rattle. She also bought a book on pregnancy her gynecologist had recommended; ironically she felt, as a geneticist, she knew everything scientific there was to know about the developing embryo, but little as a woman. She'd even been amazed to find herself outside a baby clothing store in the Beverly Center shopping mall. She knew it was rash to buy such things when she hadn't quite finished her first trimester, but she hadn't been able to resist the temptation. Walking in and purchasing the clothes had felt like a public declaration of her pregnancy, and her exhilaration, standing there holding the small pale blue suit, the empty feet impossibly tiny, had astounded her.

Julia reached across and caressed the bags, the sense of her future comforting under her hand. She turned back to the road.

The Lexus swept past a huge poster of the latest celebrity actor with political ambitions. His resolute jaw and gunmetal eyes made it impossible to separate the man from the action hero. None of Julia's friends—typically nonchalant Democrats—viewed his campaign as a real threat. It all seemed too bizarre—especially the rumors that he might run for Senate the following year. Julia took him seriously, however. A secondhand comprehension of the film industry made her aware of the existence of a parallel world, a universe where the slavish worship of celebrity underpinned an aberrant pecking order. Could a man who had played a robotic killing machine run for Governor? At the dawn of the twenty-first century the cult of celebrity made anything possible and the Actor/Candidate himself embodied the great dream. Darwin would have approved, Julia observed wryly.

Lights spluttered then glowed as the local cinema switched its sign on; while on the opposite side of the street the usual line of tourists and moviegoers queued in front of Pink's, the famous frankfurter stall that had been in existence since the 1930s, with its hand-painted signs reading "Polish Dog," "Hotdog," "Chili Dog" swinging from the white wooden frame beneath which three Latinos labored over boiling pots.

La Brea—a wide boulevard lined with furniture stores, antique shops, and the occasional shopfront with "Psychic" scrawled across the glass—was imbued with the same impermanency like many of the blocks south of Hollywood, where brick veneer mixed with a frontier-town sensibility. It was as if the ever-present awareness of catastrophe, natural or otherwise, made it impossible for the Los Angelino to ever really relax into the landscape.

The geography of Hollywood was also an atlas of Julia's marriage. She drove past the tapas bar where she and Klaus had had their first date and remembered how he'd given off the jittery aura of the recently arrived, defiantly un-American in his formal dress pants and linen jacket.

Tall and big-boned, Klaus was a combination of French

and German ancestry—his physique northern European; his high cheekbones, black eyes, and black hair a throwback to the ancient Celts who had settled the cities of Flanders. Attractive in a feline, eagle-eyed manner, Klaus seemed to be both awed and revolted by the insatiable appetites of the entertainment industry. The son of a retired Belgian diplomat, he was fluent in English and had arrived in L.A. as a stringer for a small Belgian online magazine, which had recently been consumed by an international publishing house and was now compelled to extend its market and take a more popularist direction. Sending Klaus—popular for his satirical dissections of the big blockbusters—to L.A. had been their first strategy.

By the time Julia met him, Klaus had managed, through both his natural charm and aloofness, to make himself a commodity at the press conferences held by the Foreign Press Club. However, his degree in philosophy and his left-wing leanings soon made him too sardonic a critic for the machinations of the promotion of celebrity; besides, Klaus had his own ambitions. Julia remembered her secret dismay when, over tapas, Klaus had confessed all of this.

"I would like to be a real writer—a novelist, or failing that, a writer on one of those TV series about lawyers and crime. Maybe set in Antwerp," he confided in his curious Flemish accent, which made Julia imagine the consonants being ironed flat as they fell out of his mouth.

Regardless of her reluctance to become involved with someone who appeared so directionless at thirty, Julia had smiled encouragingly, then drunk another two glasses of chardonnay, while secretly trying to fathom whether there was a girlfriend back in Europe, and, if not, what hidden (and potentially horrendous) emotional debris could this very attractive single man be carrying? Despite her reservations, Klaus made her laugh and his attentions were flattering. Having just won her first laboratory appointment, she was swept away by optimism and so, buoyed by this, their courtship continued.

Nevertheless, her ambivalence lingered for several weeks, but only seemed to fuel Klaus's advances. He was, she suspected, a man not used to being refused and her hesitancy appeared to both perplex and excite him. In reality, the situation could have gone either way, Julia now reflected. But then, didn't the most profound relationships often start in a deceptively arbitrary fashion? Two strangers waiting to board a plane, a man reading the same article as a woman in a doctor's surgery, a car denting the bumper of another. And events that seemed initially portentous often dwindled away into meaninglessness she concluded ironically, as she accelerated through a traffic light.

The arbitrary event that propelled her and Klaus's relationship forward was a surprise trip to the planetarium at the Los Angeles observatory for her birthday. It was a week night and the auditorium was almost empty—a Texan family and a row of giggling Korean schoolgirls were the only other visitors. They had sat in the front row to watch the light show of the Milky Way, the guide's pre-recorded voice sounding out in the darkness like a narrator from the 1950s, from an epoch when, somehow, stars had seemed more fixed. Suddenly, another tiny beam of light had appeared on the Sagittarius–Carina arm of the galaxy.

"See that?" Klaus had whispered, concealing the torch with his sleeve. "That's the Huntington star, found on the tattooed arm of the impossible-to-seduce Huntress planet formation . . ."

By this time the Texan father was hushing them. Julia had broken into laughter, but to her further surprise Klaus had reached into his jacket and pulled out a certificate, which he placed onto her lap. "No, really—the star exists and you own it. Happy birthday."

Their kiss had them falling onto the empty seats alongside, and to Julia's acute embarrassment the Korean schoolgirls broke into applause.

That night they had slept together for the first time. There was something unnaturally familiar about Klaus's scent and skin and, intuitively, Julia had sensed this would be a long-lasting relationship. They had a questioning intelligence in common; Klaus's thinking skipped across disciplines in a similar manner to her own. Julia's first degree had been psychology, her second genetics, and they shared a fascination for behavior—human or otherwise. However his physical beauty initially made her question her own motives: his rugged masculinity had an authenticity that made people turn and stare, even in a town where physical beauty wasn't just a commodity, it was commonplace. Julia had found it hard not to be suspicious and judgmental of his good looks, even a little intimidated. But Klaus's own indifference to his beauty, and his deliberate negation of that power, had convinced her not only of his sincerity and monogamy but also that he, like herself, valued intellect above everything else.

Julia placed her left hand over her womb. Aidan: her son, their child. She was determined to be a good mother, an attentive mother in a way her own had never been. She had calculated that her research would be concluded by the time she was due to give birth, and after that she planned to take a year's maternity leave. It was going to be her year for consolidating both her career and her marriage, she decided, vowing that she would be more thoughtful of Klaus's ambitions in the future.

A car hooted behind her; the lights had changed to green. She swung the car into the parking lot.

8

The Rhineland, 1859

He entered the hotel bedroom unexpectedly, catching her preparing to wash, her chemise unbuttoned to the waist, her hair pinned up and flat against her scalp. Startled, Lavinia froze, staring at her new husband in the mirror, her tiny breasts and boyish figure elongated and pale in the candlelight.

They had not yet made love. It was an act Lavinia had been anticipating ever since they had arrived by boat the night before, but sensing a delicacy, a certain ritualized timing to his courtship, she had decided to wait for his caress.

Her excitement fluttered wildly at her throat. I have imagined this for so long, she thought, trying to guess at the unawoken lovemaking that lay under her skin like an exotic language, waiting to be translated. I am so ignorant of what is to be expected; will I know how to pleasure him? Despite her anxieties she knew she had begun to love him, her initial infatuation deepening first to admiration then to this fierce desire to please him.

Lavinia had discovered she did not like the way other women noticed her husband; his upright handsome figure attracted glances wherever they went. She wanted him to see her only; to treat her as a peer but also as someone he could learn from, rather than always having to play the mentor. But how, when their life experience was so unequal?

The idea that he should be as preoccupied with her as she had secretly become with him now possessed her completely. Sitting there, her skin sharpened in anticipation of his touch. But now, as their gaze met, it was not how she had imagined.

His eyes held just to her face as he moved toward her. She began to turn.

"Don't move," he said.

Now behind her, stroking her shoulders, he lifted her to her feet, her bony back rippling out of the silk top of the undergarment. He ran his fingers lightly down her spine, over the fabric, and to her narrow buttocks, as firm and rotund as a young boy's.

Shivering, she watched his face in the looking glass, saw his eyes half-close. The caress of his fingertips—the lightest of touches—sent waves of bliss down her back and into the very nucleus of her, tantalizing her, promising so much more. She wanted him—she wanted him to take her, to exercise his authority over her.

His hands encircled her buttocks, then his fingers moved over to her hips and to her sex.

The Colonel closed his eyes fully as he touched her, dreaming of an earlier time in his life, a less complicated time. *I will love this girl; I will.* The sound of her quickening breath encouraged his fingers, making him forget who he was with and what he was.

When he judged the moment to be right, he freed himself and, bending her over the chair, took her roughly and swiftly. His mind full of another scenario, he made love to a specter of his own imaginings, but to his astonishment Lavinia cried out in ecstasy—an uninhibited sound of delight that triggered his own orgasm.

Afterwards, with the eagerness of a child, she covered him with kisses, murmuring over and over how she loved him. The earrings he had purchased as a gift remained hidden in his trouser pocket—three gold hoops strung with pearls.

❧

Mama, we have been back in Ireland for six months now, in Dublin. I seem to remember Father telling me of relatives of yours in this fair city. I wish I could make their acquaintance

*now. But still, it has not been too lonely and you should see
this place—I have my very own town house. To be sure, it's a
rented accommodation but James has given me permission
to decorate it how I desire, allowing his foolish wife much
expenditure. And what a folly I have made of it! It is full of
feminine indulgence, with all manner of flowers and lace.
More importantly, he has sanctioned a room for my own use,
where I have erected a small desk for my note-taking. It is
an indulgence I have only dreamed of!*

*In the evenings, when he has returned from the university,
James often shares his lecture papers with me and allows me
to contribute. What more could a wife desire? I am most
deeply in love with my husband. Oh, I know he can be a formal and cold sort of creature, but this I believe is the legacy
of his intelligence. It cannot be easy carrying the experiences and weight of such a life, and I am determined to support him in whatever manner I can.*

*Daily my womb grows. If only you were here to see the
woman I have become and now to become a mother myself!
I shall have to learn by example and look to the women
around me. James is so joyful over this event and is ridiculously solicitous; he must think me made of porcelain!*

Lavinia paused, the plain wooden lid smooth against her
fingertips. Since the age of five she had whispered daily into
the undistinguished container, the only object she had inherited from her mother. Despite its humble appearance, Lavinia had never doubted the alchemy of the whispering box.
Even now there was part of her that believed that the benign
spirit of her mother was sitting beside her, watching and listening, as she whispered against the sandalwood.

❧

Lavinia stood on a chair, hooking curtains onto a rail. The
newly sewn drapes were painted with small red peonies, and
she had placed a vase with the same flowers on the side table
that stood against the wall of the drawing room.

She paused for a moment to rub the small of her back, her pregnancy, almost full term, weighing against her frame. She had a strong sense it was a male child; she had dreamt of a small boy standing on a jetty in front of a steamer ship—an isolated and strangely poignant figure. If it was a boy she had decided to call him Aidan.

"Are you all right, ma'am? I really think it should be me up on that chair, what with you so big." Rosie, the maid the Colonel had insisted on hiring, held the tin of curtain hooks up to her mistress.

"I shall live. Besides, they have to be hung exactly so."

Lavinia attached the last hook and, with Rosie's assistance, clambered down from the chair, then pulled the curtains open, letting in the sunlight and the view of the walled garden. Positioned on a secluded bank of the Liffey, the dwelling was small but had its own orchard and land that ran down to the water's edge.

Their sojourn in Dublin was an indulgence, but the Colonel had wanted his wife's confinement to take place where she would have the support of both her father and his housekeeper, who in many ways was Lavinia's de facto mother. The Colonel had passed the time with a short guest lectureship at the university, having several colleagues on the staff there.

Lavinia rested against the chair and examined her handiwork. Fabric matching the curtains covered the legs of the small upright piano in the corner and was also used in the tablecloth. A photographic wedding portrait hung on the wall, as well as a small picture of the young Queen Victoria. Apart from a walnut console table with gilded legs, which Lavinia had purchased herself from an auction house, there was little else in the drawing room. But Lavinia was comfortable; here she was mistress of her own existence and already she had managed to establish a small salon composed of some elderly scholars—peers of the Colonel—and one minor painter, a Darcy Quinn, whom the Colonel had commissioned to paint Lavinia as soon as the baby was born. They all visited once a month, attracted by the outspoken views of the charismatic young wife and the possible patronage of her husband.

I have come into my own, Lavinia concluded, experiencing a happiness that stemmed from both a contented domesticity and the inspiration she found in assisting the Colonel with his study. I am a fortunate woman: my husband is both affectionate and indulgent. At last I have achieved the social status that allows me the freedom of conversation and a social mobility that is truly stimulating. And now, on top of all this serendipity, I am to have a child!

The sound of the front door opening broke her reverie. Lavinia pulled herself to her feet.

The Colonel entered, still dressed in his herringbone cape and hat. Lavinia watched as he removed them and handed them to the maid, fighting the desire to rush over and embrace him. It was still a source of wonder to her that she was married at all, especially to a man she had desired for so long. Sometimes she felt as if she were living in a delightful daydream of her own construction—a thought that disturbed her greatly, as she was of a questioning and doubtful disposition.

"Lavinia, there are more peonies in here than on a flower seller's cart."

"Do you not like my decorations?"

The Colonel maneuvered past the console table, appalled by the overly ornate décor. It was hard not to feel claustrophobic, particularly as his own aesthetic was of a more ordered nature. "It is both refreshing and delightful," he lied.

She is so young, so gauche—will she survive the demands and protocol of Mayfair, he wondered. It was such a bohemian existence, this idyllic retreat of theirs, a fool's sanctuary. Initially, the chaotic nature of the days had been a liberation, but now the Colonel found himself longing for the order of London society.

"Lavinia, I beg you, do not become too attached to this place. As soon as the babe is strong enough to travel we shall

return to London. By my reckoning, that should be late
October—if all goes to plan."

"As you wish."

Hiding her disappointment at his lack of enthusiasm, Lavinia stood to rearrange the flowers in the large crystal vase
in the middle of the table. As she did, a flood of dampness
ran down her thighs, followed by a sharp cramping across
her midriff. Smiling, she turned.

"My love, I believe my confinement has begun."

9

Los Angeles, 2002

The five of them sat around the circular lacquered table, a
paper lantern hanging low over the polished surface in silence as a Japanese waitress placed a platter of sushi on the
table's revolving center.

An unknowing observer might imagine them to be two
couples and a single, free-floating female—attractive, middle-
class Americans, affluently dressed in an understated way,
in the prime of their lives. Klaus, in jeans and a cashmere
sweater, his arm casually thrown around Julia's shoulders,
was the embodiment of the happy husband. The younger man
sitting opposite, thickly muscular, dressed in an expensive
suit as if he had just come from the office, could be taken as
partner to the middle-aged woman next to him. Naomi was
not his wife, however, nor even his lover, but an old friend of
Julia's from San Francisco. A frustrated potter, Naomi had
outraged her conservative Jewish parents by marrying one of
her fellow art students, an intense Latino sculptor, but the

marriage hadn't lasted and, when they were finally divorced, Naomi had been left with the custody of their son, Gabriel.

The man, Andrew, was a homosexual colleague of Julia's, also a geneticist, who liked to imagine he belonged to the corporate world and dressed accordingly.

The fifth of the group, Carla, seemed distanced from the others; she sat on the edge of her seat, methodically shredding her paper napkin. She had already drunk most of the hot sake in front of her and emanated an alcohol-induced air of confrontation—an attitude the others were trying to ignore.

"This must seem so civilized after Afghanistan," Naomi said, balancing a bead of golden cod's roe delicately between two chopsticks.

"Actually the hotel in Kabul was quite comfortable and the food surprisingly edible." Out of the corner of her eye, Julia watched Carla anxiously.

"So did you find the data you were looking for?" Andrew's laconic manner infused every gesture he made.

"I'm optimistic." Julia was careful, knowing that her colleague would be fishing for any new discovery that could influence his own research on genetics and viruses.

Carla leaned forward. "Julia's got a new commission, with the Department of Defense, top secret, very hush hush."

Julia glanced back at her, worried. It was uncharacteristic for her to be so indiscreet. Was there some secret unhappiness in the producer's life, some new liaison she hadn't told her about?

"So I guess the DOD have you working on the next big thing in biological warfare?" Andrew joked.

"It's an extension of my own research on combat soldiers who don't suffer post-traumatic stress disorder."

"Ah, the famous two percent you're so fond of." Andrew reached for the tempura.

Carla laughed. "I don't believe it exists. I think we can all kill given the right circumstances."

Terrified Carla would reveal the ambush incident to the

others, Julia moved the sake bottle out of her friend's reach. "Actually, historical research indicates that most soldiers avoided hand-to-hand combat—particularly killing with bayonets. The data shows that it's just a small proportion of soldiers who do most of the killing."

"But what *is* the army going to *do* with this research?" Carla pulled the sake bottle back toward her and poured herself another cup. Julia had never seen her so aggressive.

"I've signed an agreement preventing me from talking about this in public," Julia replied. "That includes friends."

"You see, this is what happens when we turn thirty-five," Klaus intervened. "We become establishment. We're told we've become respectable citizens, but in fact we become unquestioning citizens."

"That's simplistic, Klaus, and you know it!"

There was an awkward silence. Julia looked into the faces of her friends. Did fear make unquestioning citizens? Life had certainly changed profoundly since the attack on the twin towers; it felt as if the insularity and arrogance of the western world had been shattered forever. Suddenly, politics and culture had become more complex, and the traditional humanist assumptions that everyone wanted the same things— equality for employer and employee, man and woman—didn't seem to apply anymore. Had they been laboring under the old philosophical illusion that all people were the same under the skin? Did religious and cultural differences profoundly shift the way one experienced reality?

"Any more problems with the pro-lifers?" Klaus asked.

"They weren't pro-lifers, they were animal liberationists," Julia corrected him.

"Just be thankful it wasn't the creationists," Andrew piped up. "Do you know that in Atlanta there's a movement to get a warning sticker put on biology books reading, 'This textbook contains material on evolution. Evolution is a theory, not a fact' etc. etc. etc. Welcome to the twenty-first century! I swear, between the cowboy in the White House and the Religious

Right, America is on the brink of plunging into a new Dark Age. So help me God." In frustration, Andrew disemboweled his meticulously constructed tuna sushi roll.

"You've also had trouble with them?" Julia leaned forward.

"Trouble? We stay unlisted and receive all correspondence through a post office box. As much as I believe in the Enlightenment, I refuse to be martyred for it. Crucifixion is such a bad look."

"Amen to that," Julia agreed, grinning.

"So hands up—who did vote for the cowboy in the White House?" Carla interjected drunkenly.

"Not I said the fly with my little eye, although I confess I was once a Gay Republican, but only for eight weeks," Andrew retorted archly, then winked at Klaus. "I was dating a senator at the time. He, of course, was still in the closet."

The atmosphere suddenly turned leaden. Determined to lift the mood, Julia looked across at Klaus. "We have something else to celebrate."

"Not now," Klaus murmured, looking panicked.

"Why not? I'm past the first trimester."

Paling, Carla turned to Julia. "You're pregnant?"

Julia smiled tentatively, suddenly nervous at her friend's ambivalent tone.

Lifting the sake bottle with a violent jerk, Carla held it over the table. "Wow! That's far more important than some kooky defense department gig." She swung around to Klaus. "Wouldn't you say?"

Klaus laid his hand on her wrist. "Carla . . ."

Ignoring him, she banged the bottle against Julia's cup.

"The geneticist is pregnant!" She turned to the others. "Isn't that just so poetic?"

Outside, a police car headed downtown, its siren screaming.

❧

Klaus stood in the bathroom door, his wet hair crowning his head in a halo of curls, his chin plastered with shaving cream. "She's just stressed."

"Evidently. The last time I saw Carla that intoxicated was at the Sony Academy Awards party, when she was dating that B-grade actor, and that was eight years ago. She was really weird about the pregnancy." Julia, already between the sheets of their brass bed, looked up at her husband.

"She was just surprised. I think a lot of people are going to be surprised."

"Why? Aren't I allowed to be a mother?"

"Sure, it's just that everyone sees you as so career oriented." He finished toweling his hair. "You should really invest more in your other friends, not be so much of a hermit."

"I have Naomi."

"You tend to have colleagues rather than friends. Women need friends; they need that support system in case of sudden disaster."

"Sudden disaster? You're really uplifting tonight."

Klaus covered his eyes with the towel for a second.

Julia sat back. "Okay, from now on I promise it'll be nothing but antenatal classes, and then picketing the local kindergarten with the rest of the careerist mothers," she joked.

Shrugging, Klaus retreated into the bathroom.

Julia gazed up at the hand-finished roof beams of the bedroom. The second largest room in the California Craftsman bungalow, it looked out onto a large backyard planted with jasmine and bougainvillea. They'd got the house five years into their marriage, and had been clever enough to buy into Silver Lake—an area that was on the brink of gentrification. It was an idiosyncratic suburb built on the side of a hill; developed in the '60s and '70s, the houses were an eclectic architectural mix of bungalows, apartments, and the occasional mock-Tudor cottage. Some of the houses were built on stilts sunk into the side of the valley to secure them against earthquake damage; others butted up against the hillside.

Their neighbors on one side were Latino—a retired postal worker and his wife, who often invited Klaus and Julia over for their huge family barbecues. On the other side lived Gerry, a young screenwriter who specialized in animation and never seemed to leave the house until after dark.

The rest of the street was occupied by young middle-class couples all eager to make their mark—actors, lawyers, and one director at the very end of the cul-de-sac, who was famous for a horror film everyone had forgotten but which still played late on cable.

Julia and Klaus had decorated the house with vintage furnishings that reflected the era it was built in, Klaus carefully restoring the pieces they found in markets. The walls were pine, the beamed ceiling cedar and the two fireplaces—one in the lounge and one in the bedroom—were both original. There was a ground-floor bathroom, a small study, a sitting room and a dining room off the kitchen, and a small staircase leading to the bedroom, which was a converted attic.

When Julia first met Klaus, all she owned was a shoebox of her mother's photos, an old passport shot of her first boyfriend, and several rolls of unprocessed film. She had no furniture, preferring to rent furnished accommodation. Horrified by this lack of material possessions, Klaus had called her a barbarian, attributing her lack of enthusiasm for history as inherently New World.

"But it's my history to immortalize or discard as I please," she'd exclaimed, offended by his European sensibility.

"Okay, my love, we will rewrite it together, both present and past. And maybe, if we're lucky, there will be a little fiction left over for the future," he'd replied teasingly.

For the first twenty-five years of her life Julia had an aversion to collecting anything that reminded her of the past—even the recent past—a revulsion that had sprung from her mother's passion for amateur photography. Her mother was a vivacious woman with extraordinary drive, who never appeared to live in the present tense, her ferocious intellect pushing her comprehension several seconds in front of everyone else. She frantically photographed every possible family event, as if by documenting the moment it negated her own responsibility for actually participating in it. The experience had left Julia with a hatred of being photographed, and a dread of collecting memories in any shape or form. Part of her even feared that a photograph of a lover would curse the rapport, jinx the relationship, and set it on a course of separation. It was a fatalistic superstition but one that Julia hadn't been able to shake until her marriage.

Her mother had suddenly died when she was twelve—an event that had transformed her emotional lexicon. Frenetically energetic, her mother's thick curly hair had been a beacon for the young girl, an image that later, as an adult, Julia would catch herself searching for over and over. Her father, already in his sixties, took over her parenting. A quietly spoken biologist, he would tell her stories about his own father—Aidan Huntington—who had emigrated when he was twelve from Ireland with a mysterious guardian. And how the old gentleman had convinced him—in the educated Irish accent of his childhood—that his mother, Lavinia Huntington, was innocent of the murder of her husband, Colonel James Huntington—stories that ballooned in the young girl's imagination.

Ignoring Julia's horror of investing in the material, Klaus had arranged for a linen cupboard that had belonged to his grandmother to be shipped over from Antwerp, followed by the purchase of a video camera which he used to faithfully record the minutiae of their relationship. Once, Julia had come back from a conference early and found him watching a tape of her sleeping. Other times he filmed her lacing up her climbing boots, putting on her makeup, taking a bath—every mundane gesture seem to fascinate him. There was a whole shelf dedicated to these videos labeled with his crablike scrawl, *Mijn Vrouw 1,2,3* . . . Julia had always regarded such details as unimportant, until finally she realized that Klaus regarded them as the very cement of marriage, the pauses between arguments, negotiations, lovemaking.

She also began to see it as a way of Klaus securing himself geographically, as if the immigrant was trying to anchor himself in a sea of images that viscerally linked him to America.

Then suddenly, after five years of marriage, Julia began to take her own photos. At last, she herself had come home.

❈

The ultrasound image was propped up against the bedside lamp. The embryo was an amorphous bundle of sudden twitches, kicks, and alien sensations that Julia struggled against to maintain her own hormonal equilibrium. But there he was: flesh made into logic; chemicals, genes, all twisted up into living structure—a child, a male child. It was the final jigsaw piece of their marriage. Touching the slippery surface of the scan she whispered out loud. "Aidan."

"What are you muttering?" Klaus walked across the room naked, his heavy sex lolling against his thigh, his skin peppered with soft brown-blond hair. His limbs retained the slender musculature of a younger man while his hips and stomach had just begun to thicken into maturity. But he was most handsome in his hands. Finely chiseled, long-fingered, with arched bones, they fanned out from his wrist like white coral. Both hands constantly caressed the air whenever he spoke, as if he were unable to prevent a gestural rendering of his sentences shooting to the tips of his fingers. It had been his hands and his height that she had first noticed—a streak of a masculine presence across the room at a party. He had two physical defects: his torso and his feet. His torso was too long for his legs. This imperfection made him human; made him more like her. And his feet were wide and long, the feet of a peasant. They had become her private metaphor for what she saw as his innocence—a trait she associated with his unquestioning enthusiasm for life.

Klaus started to climb into the bed.

"Baby, can you just walk around some more?"

"Julia! I'm cold."

"Please, you know how I like to watch you."

Grumbling, but with a lopsided grin, he did two laps of the television at the foot of the bed, as naturally and unselfconsciously as he could.

Klaus didn't like to be looked at, resenting the assumptions made about him because of his physical beauty. Nevertheless, his penis began to harden under Julia's scrutiny.

"Satiated, you pervert?" He stopped and stood before her, his hips and groin level with the edge of the bed. She glanced down; he was now almost fully erect. It was a sight she had always found a paradox—the way a penis, erect or otherwise, somehow rendered a man defenseless.

"You enjoy it, admit it. I can see that it's turning you on."

"Because I think you're objectifying me, and I can feel myself morphing into a beautiful stranger who happens to be standing naked in your bedroom ready to fulfil your every fantasy." He placed his hands ironically but provocatively on his hips.

"Liar. Besides, it would only be the male gaze that found such a scenario erotic. I find your nudity erotic because it's you and you happen to be the man I wisely or unwisely publicly pledged eternal love to."

Walking over to his side of the bed, he climbed in between the sheets. "Husband, Julia. Remember—we're married."

"And that means I can't define you as my lover?"

"Perhaps," he answered ambiguously as she reached over to take his mouth.

Groaning, he kissed his way across her body, then pulled her thighs over the sides of his head like a veil, his lips taking her sex into his mouth, while she ran her tongue down, tracing a path to his belly button. His long torso was an undulating panorama of hair, skin, and scent. She gently bit the inside of his thighs, caressing him, teasing him, knowing that with each indirect stroke his sensitivity heightened, aching for the direct touch, the moment she would fasten her mouth over his cock.

And as she arched over him, his mouth sending tremors of intense pleasure up and down her thighs, his cock hard against his belly as his hands cupped her breasts, the astounding revelation that she had never been happier flooded her body a second before her own orgasm.

~

The beating of the helicopter pounds through Julia and seems to push her view of the mountain further and further away. The soldier sitting next to her in the Humvee turns and smiles. Something vitally significant tugs at the edge of her mind. They bounce over the pothole, Julia's flak jacket jarring against her stomach. She knows now what she has to say. She shouts a warning but the two men—the driver and the soldier—can't hear over the noise.

In a magical instant the Humvee is full of bleating, terrified goats. Their hooves tear into the canvas seat covers; Julia is pushed against the window. From the corner of her eye she sees the dying soldier, now outside, slide down the glass, leaving a filter of red.

Now she is outside herself and the dead Afghani convulses at her feet. A drop of blood hits her boot, menstrual blood, a thin trickle from between her legs. Touching it, she is deeply ashamed; ashamed at the killing, ashamed that she feels nothing.

~

Julia woke. Stretching her legs across to Klaus's side of the bed, she curled her toes, searching for him. The bed was empty. She lay there for a moment, dawn saturating the bedroom as the sounds around her gathered into an audible mass.

The low murmuring of her husband's voice emerged from

beneath the early morning birdsong. Still half-asleep, Julia walked to the window. Klaus stood in the garden, his muscular calves flexed, his bare feet white against the sandstone paving, the pale blue toweling robe wrapped loosely around his body. The small cell phone was tucked against his shoulder, his neck and head bent over it as if he were protecting an intimacy. Sensing a movement he glanced blindly at the bedroom window, then, not seeing Julia, stepped into the growing sunlight.

Blearily, she tried to ascertain whether he was speaking Flemish or English until a wave of morning sickness forced her to run to the bathroom. Surprised to be nauseous this late in the pregnancy, she wondered whether she should contact her gynecologist, then decided she was probably overreacting.

10

Mayfair, London, November 1860

Lavinia paused at the top of the staircase, reveling in rare solitude. Smoothing down the silk of her skirts, she took courage, breathed in deeply, then moved toward the banister. For a moment she lost her balance. Her dress—the latest crinoline from Paris—was a cumbersome instrument of physical limitation. The huge circumference of quilted silk arched from her narrow waist to bump and rustle against every possible surface—such a ridiculous fashion and thoroughly impractical she concluded, irritated by her own clumsiness.

Steadying herself, Lavinia looked down the staircase to the palatial entrance hall. She still found it hard to believe she was actually there, surrounded by such opulence. Beneath her, the stairs cascaded in a semi-spiral of marble and gilt. An arched glass canopy in the ceiling above allowed natural light to filter in, illuminating the whole stairwell during the daylight hours. It reminded Lavinia of the delicate inner compartments of the sea snail, but on a grandiose scale. The neo-classical staircase was the spine of the whole house, dominating the large entrance hall. At the foot of the stairs stood a bronze statue of Mars, commissioned by the Colonel's grandfather.

A service staircase was located at the side of the house, solely for the use of the servants and house staff. Its access doors were hidden behind mirrors on each floor, thus allowing the staff to discreetly appear and disappear.

On the top floor were the bedrooms, the nursery, and the Colonel's study. The second floor had six reception rooms: the library, a second study, two drawing rooms, the dining room, and a gallery which doubled as a ballroom. The ground floor contained the entrance hall and an inner hall, used as a small waiting room to receive less important guests. The kitchen, wine cellar, laundry, and all other domestic necessities were located in the basement, while behind the mansion lay a landscaped courtyard backed by stables that led onto mews cottages and a lane.

The Georgian mansion had been designed by Robert Adams in the early part of the century, and built by the Colonel's grandfather—an army general. The Colonel's mother, the Viscountess, had imagined she would live out the rest of her widowed years in the family residence, in defiant ostentation, but to her surprise—and that of much of Mayfair—the Viscountess had found herself dying of influenza at the age of thirty-eight.

After her death, the Colonel had had gas lamps installed— the first in the square. The ornate brass and glass fittings flung light into the darkest corners, illuminating the depths of the many paintings he had inherited.

A portrait of the Viscountess in her youth hung on the wall opposite. Handsome rather than beautiful, with a pronounced chin and sweeping jawline, she posed in pale cream silk, a pair of greyhounds—restlessly thin and eyes bulging—at her feet.

Lavinia glanced at her own portrait, which her husband had commissioned in Dublin, insisting that Lavinia should pose as the huntress Diana despite the goddess's legendary virginity. "How are you to explain the presence of a baby?" Lavinia had asked him, smiling at the time, indicating her pregnancy. "We shall place him into the composition and disguise him as an infant wood sprite," he'd replied, determined to incorporate a personal symbolism into the painting that embodied his own love of adventure and hunting.

She had completely escaped the village, Lavinia thought to herself, smiling at her own image, proof of her success. She had freed herself of the claustrophobia of the place and all that went with it. She had *arrived*. Even now she was incredulous at her achievement. Most of all she had the freedom of study, the opportunity to indulge her intellectual curiosity. For that alone she would love her husband.

As if in answer, his melodious voice boomed out of the half-opened dining room doors.

"My studies have convinced me there is a natural hierarchy—even in the animal kingdom. After all, what is a human being? We display the same tendencies as our animal cousins."

"Speak for yourself, James. I like to think of myself as slightly more advanced."

Lady Frances Morgan's alto voice was distinctive and decidedly flirtatious, Lavinia observed unhappily. She had not yet fathomed the nature of the intimacy between her husband and the aristocrat described as an "old dear friend."

"I entirely agree with the Colonel. As far as I am concerned, many of our politicians are hardly more than baboons. Disraeli himself has often displayed behavior in the house which could more properly be ascribed to an ape." Lavinia recognized the voice as belonging to a cartoonist for *Punch* magazine—a gentleman of forty with the most protruding forehead.

"As you have so sensitively illustrated on many an occasion," the Colonel retorted smugly.

"Whig!" shouted Mr. Hamish Campbell—Lady Morgan's latest prodigy—in mock accusation. The party erupted into laughter.

One sole voice remained stern. "Come now, I do believe some politicians have transcended their more bestial impulses. Abraham Lincoln, for example—any humane person would support his campaign against slavery . . ." the Colonel replied before Lady Morgan interjected.

"Lincoln fights for cotton not the Negro. You may wish to assume otherwise, especially if you have the advantage of youth and naivety, like the Colonel's sweet wife. But the rest of us must be pragmatic and look to our investments as Mr. Lincoln does. He needs to impose his export cotton tax to prevent the Lancashire mills from undercutting the cost of manufacturing cloth. The north of the United States is the manufacturing center, and so he naturally wishes to bring prosperity to those States. I believe this means that our sympathies may more naturally lie with the southern States, *n'est-ce pas*?"

Now anxious she might eavesdrop upon a conversation that could prove compromising, Lavinia stepped into the flurried atmosphere of the dining room.

The Colonel, sensing her presence before the others, turned. Lavinia radiated a warmth that had initially made him believe she would serve as the ideal counterbalance to his own compulsively critical eye. The young Irishwoman was naturally generous, whereas he was not. Misanthropy was one of the Colonel's natural tendencies and one he tried to conceal. He stood, followed by the other male guests, as one of the footmen pulled out a red velvet-covered oak chair for Lavinia.

The female guests turned toward the hesitant young woman in the doorway. The coiled plaits visible under a filigree of black lace and seed pearls—a little too ornate for the season, Lady Morgan noted spitefully—gave her the air of a Medusa. The young Irish girl reminded her of a Ford Madox Brown model with her chalk-white skin and disproportionately large eyes. A common look, Lady Morgan observed ungenerously. London's streets were awash with such women.

It was true that Lavinia Huntington's most startling feature was her eyes; aquamarine ringed by yellow, they gave her a feline quality. Over the years, fascinated, the Colonel had watched those eyes mature, shifting in light like the mist over a distant lake, a burgeoning intelligence behind the beauty.

Impervious to Lady Morgan's scrutiny, Lavinia concentrated on gliding with grace across the room, guiding her crinoline with both hands. To her relief, she successfully navigated her way into her seat at the table.

"Please forgive my absence, but my child required my attention."

"My wife insists on feeding the babe herself," the Colonel ventured.

"How quaint." Lady Morgan did not bother to disguise her disapproving tone.

"I believe it to be healthier, but perhaps in the present company such a belief might be considered naive?"

The other guests laughed politely, while Lady Morgan broke a piece of bread with her fingers.

"Not at all," she responded. "And in any case, there is nothing whatsoever wrong with naivety. It allows one to get away with the most outrageous of behaviors—at least for a short time. Is that not true, James?"

The Colonel was determined to rescue his wife from Lady Morgan's sarcasm. "Indeed, in battle it is often the quality that underpins the greatest acts of courage," he counteracted.

Lavinia turned to Lady Morgan. "I believe you were talking of Lincoln. I am a great supporter of his ambitions. How else to unite a nation in the face of such conflicting interests?"

"Ah, my dear, but is it a nation or merely a gaggle of colonies of disparate refugees?" Lady Morgan curled her fingers around the stem of her wine glass; a small gesture that indicated much.

There was a pause, as if the room itself had inhaled. Aware that a starting pistol of sorts had been fired, the diners turned toward Lavinia.

"If it is not a nation now, it certainly will be if there is a civil war. For what else defines sovereignty so aptly—a bill of rights, a war of independence, and perhaps now a civil war? The Irish could learn much from the Americans."

A half-smile flitted across the mouth of the cartoonist sitting opposite and Lavinia's diatribe faltered as she suddenly became aware that her intensity did not suit the timbre of the evening. After all, she reminded herself, these were people who took art more seriously than politics.

"And no doubt they will." Hamish Campbell smiled at the young wife; the smile of a co-conspirator in youth. Judging by the softness of his whiskers, Lady Morgan's companion couldn't have been much older than Lavinia herself.

"Your wife has strong opinions for her age." Lady Morgan turned to the Colonel.

James Huntington's betrothal had been a source of surprise to many of his circle. There had always been a swirl of mystery and speculation around the Colonel and his perennial bachelorhood. There had been rumors of various liaisons over the years—including one with Lady Morgan—but those who called themselves friends (and there were not many) had concluded that Huntington had become too addicted to his private pleasures to marry. His sudden change of status was a cause of some irritation, disrupting as it did the delicately balanced equilibrium of those unspoken strictures by which the wealthy aristocracy lived. Not one of them approved of the Colonel's unexpected union with one so apparently unsuitable in terms of class, and the concept of marrying for love was preposterous, dangerously modern, and vaguely obscene.

Huntington's young wife was annoyingly "earnest," Lady Morgan observed, a characteristic she could only just tolerate in younger men, and then only when they were particularly beautiful or particularly wealthy. Furthermore, she subscribed to some bizarre political ideas. Obviously the Irish Question was one of them—rather peculiar considering the girl was a Protestant. What was her maiden name? Kane. Lady Morgan tried to recall the names of all the Irish aristocrats she knew, but Kane was not among them.

Plucking a gooseberry from the bowl of fruit on the table, she furtively studied the couple. Hamish Campbell, noting her scrutiny, smiled—a gesture Lady Morgan found irritatingly insincere. She glanced back across the table. The Colonel no longer appeared in a hurry to rescue his young wife from the political quagmire she seemed so determined to mire herself in; perhaps a certain heartlessness had replaced his original intrigue? Lady Morgan had herself fallen victim to his caprices in the past.

"Are you not Church of Ireland, dear?" she asked Lavinia patronizingly.

"I am, but as a child I witnessed the horrors of the great Famine. Those people were human, not the sub-human caricatures portrayed in your English newspapers."

"James, darling, you must introduce your wife to the honorable Mr. Hennessy," Lady Morgan declared. "You must know him from the Carlton Club? I hear he is doing some wonderful things for our Celtic friends."

"Indeed, I have met the gentleman in Dublin, but I fear my opinions were too Whiggish for his Tory tastes." Lavinia, her face now ablaze, was having trouble controlling the tremor in her voice.

"My wife, the revolutionary. You see I married her for the idealistic fervor which has evaporated in myself." Nevertheless, the Colonel, pinching a piece of bread between his fingers, was secretly disturbed by Lavinia's obstinate pursuit of the Irish Question. Lord, did the child not know when enough was enough?

"Poppycock and tosh, James, you were never idealistic nor fervent—unless it came to war, a good claret, or an adventure of a dubious nature," called out Charles Sutton, a gentleman of fifty and an associate of the Colonel's since his days at Sandhurst Military Academy.

"Not at all, sir! I have always been passionate about Nature and Science."

Charles tapped his wine glass. "We can thank Darwin for the current national obsession with such matters, and perhaps the explosion of industry. Together they threaten to dissect Nature and give us an anatomy of Beauty that will exorcise all spiritual mystery and quite ruin my morning walks."

"Science does not destroy the spirit, Charles; in fact it reveals it. There is God in evolution, just as there is God in a snowflake. We have just given him Reason," the Colonel parried.

⁓

Hamish Campbell, Lady Morgan's young companion, gestured to a footman who obliged him by pouring him another glass of claret. As the manservant poured, Hamish Campbell took the opportunity of the two military men's banter to observe his host. James Huntington was one of those fleshy, handsome men whose magnetism emanated from a sense of coiled power. In the Colonel's case, it was neither wealth nor a commercial understanding but intellectual amplitude. The Colonel was an interesting mixture of both soldier and scholar, his appearance and manner showing the controlled habits of the military man, while his easy wit and natural intelligence gave him a cosmopolitan demeanor.

The Colonel's ruby signet ring flashed in the candlelight as he lifted his wine glass, one eyebrow raised. He was the modern Renaissance man, the perfect embodiment of the Victorian intellectual. I shall endeavor to study him closely, Campbell vowed. James Huntington's life was one the young Hamish Campbell badly desired, and was now intent on emulating.

Still burning at Lady Morgan's patronizing manner, Lavinia barely heard the conversation that was propelled across the table in short bursts, filling the room with laughter one moment, emptying it the next, the hidden meaning beneath the clipped English consonants as thick as the glutinous liquorice jelly she watched falling from her spoon. It made her yearn for more frank and open conversation, in which emotions and intuitions could be freely expressed.

She examined the countenances of the individuals before her, and couldn't help wondering, as she observed Lady Morgan's twitching mouth, why they couldn't all just say what they mean? The pretense was so mannered that for a moment Lavinia imagined the guests had suddenly turned into figures from a commedia dell'arte. She was ill equipped to navigate the artifice of these people; even her accent—which would have been considered English in the drawing rooms of Dublin—sounded hideously provincial. As she sat there, contemplating the elegant dress of the other woman, she was suddenly horribly aware of the inappropriate elaborateness of her headdress.

"I remember a time when you were a very vocal detractor of Mr. Darwin, Colonel," the *Punch* cartoonist, ever the antagonist, interjected.

"We are allowed to change our minds. I believe it was *On the Origin of Species* that converted this soul."

"But to suggest we are related to the gorilla?" Lady Morgan shivered with disgust.

Lavinia leaned forward, seeing an opportunity open in the conversation.

"There seems to be a patent logic to the notion that form is affected by environment. As a river shapes a rock, so animals must adapt over time to their environments. And we ourselves must have sprung from somewhere. We are, after all, inherent to the Natural world."

Surprised by her eloquence, the other diners turned; at last they saw how this provincial young Irishwoman might have captivated the Colonel.

"Does this mean, Mrs. Huntington, that you are an atheist,"

Lady Morgan retorted. "For surely belief in Darwin must preclude a belief in God?"

The Colonel took Lavinia's hand, the first gesture of affection he had made toward his wife during the three hours they had been dining. "Frances, you are wrong. My wife is a practicing Christian. So there you are: it is possible to invest in both Science and the Spirit." He turned to Lavinia. "But be careful, my love, Frances has set a trap for you. One like the insect-eating plants of the Amazon, in which I, the fly, have been caught many a time."

"I am quite able to fend for myself, James. After all, have I not the naivety of youth on my side?" Lavinia replied.

Inwardly wincing at the barb, Lady Morgan made a mental note never to take the girl's ingenuousness for granted again. At forty-three, she was already depressed by the ever-increasing stratagem required to maintain the appearance of her own legendary beauty.

"My dear, I simply cannot believe that God did not have a hand in the development of Man. After all, there is such an extraordinary leap of physical and emotional development between a man and an ape; it seems preposterous to think that they might have shared the same mother. And so I can only conclude there must have been divine intervention." Lady Morgan's tone was finite, but Lavinia persisted.

"I agree; however, the rationalist in me also asks the question: Could it not have been simply a set of fortuitous circumstances that advanced Man over his ape cousin—the wielding of tools, the move to two feet?"

"Not to forget that most momentous event—the eradication of fleas?" the cartoonist added helpfully, an irreverent grin on his face. At which the whole room dissolved into laughter.

11

Three hoops strung with pearls. Lavinia held the earrings up to the candlelight remembering the occasion James first made love to her in the hotel room on the Rhine. She tried to recognize herself in that woman: it was impossible.

She still loved her husband; if anything, her desire had intensified as James had increasingly distanced himself. At first she had thought it due to the intrusion of the child, but Aidan was almost eighteen months now and James was an adoring father. No, it must be something else. A hidden dissatisfaction he had with her? But what? Back in Ireland he had loved her many times, professed desire for her, but since their arrival in London his attentions had waned. Increasingly, Lavinia felt as if she were absent to him; only at social events and in discussion of his work did he seemed appreciative of her presence. All of which would be tolerable if she were not in love with him.

After dismissing the maid, she unpinned her headdress and lay it carefully across the polished wood of James's dresser, taking care not to scratch the surface. The formality of the bedroom was intimidating; it was a territory that was very much the Colonel's. Heavy maroon velvet curtains, hung with a brocade, covered the windows, and the Louis XVI bed's ornate headboard was adorned with carvings of pine cones interwoven with garlands. Alongside the bed stood a Japanese porcelain and metal mounted cabinet—where James kept his secret papers and his pharmaceuticals. Opposite, beside the window, a walnut marquetry cabinet displayed James's medals, received for his service in the Crimea. The clasps were engraved with the names *Balaclava, Sebastopol, Inkerman,* and *Alma*, indicating he had fought in all four battles. Every surface radiated luxury in a manner Lavinia was unaccustomed to, and it was hard not to feel a little awed by the value of the objects that surrounded her.

The order of the room reflected her husband's soldierly habits. Lavinia knew it was also his way of dealing with his hidden terror of the uncontrollable. His dreams were often nightmares—of the battlefield, of a tribal sacrifice in a smoke-filled rainforest, of dying suddenly like his mother. Lavinia forgave him this foible, but within such a controlled environment there was no space for natural chaos, and certainly not the chaos she had been used to as a child.

She reached across to his pocket watch, which was sitting on the rosewood cabinet. The exquisitely crafted timepiece, its miniature springs and cogs marking off eternity, ticked loudly. It reminded her of the relentless heartbeat she heard when she lay with her head upon her husband's chest, drawing them closer with each subterranean thud. It had been months since they had lain together like that.

∼

"That was rather a success." The Colonel stood ready for bed in his Turkish robe, the silk of his nightshirt visible beneath. At six foot one he was a striking figure, despite the corpulence of middle age. His features boasted a luminous ferocity—people often took him for a statesman—and his eyes were large and heavy-lidded, conveying an intelligence that was penetrating and, at times, intimidating. Luxuriant eyebrows betrayed his Celtic heritage, and his upper lip, although on the thin side, was counterbalanced by a full lower companion that suggested a hidden sensuality. The shape of his face was oval, with fashionable sideburns and a beard serving to hide his jowls. It had the contours of both the optimist and the realist, the Colonel himself would have remarked if asked—regarding himself as an authority on such matters, having trained under the phrenologist George Combe.

Skull and face shape, he was convinced, were a strong indication of character.

Caught now in her husband's gaze, Lavinia felt she was being examined and judged.

"It was successful, except for my little disagreement with Lady Morgan."

"My dear, it is perfectly appropriate to call her Frances. She is, after all, a dear friend of mine."

Again, Lavinia wondered about her husband's association with Lady Morgan. Her father had made an oblique reference to some great disappointment in love when the Colonel was younger—an engagement that had been broken off, with no explanation—but the Reverend Kane had the delicacy not to press the Colonel for further information, and James himself had never mentioned such a thing. Was it a fiction? Or could his acquaintance with Lady Morgan have been more than mere friendship?

"What did you think about her young companion?" the Colonel asked. "He's another Etonian, I believe."

"The sycophantic Hamish Campbell? He seemed presentable enough."

"Sycophantic but charming, wouldn't you agree?"

"Is he Lady Morgan's consort?"

Irritated by the artlessness of the query, the Colonel pulled at his whiskers. "Frances has a weakness for the conversation of handsome young intellectuals, especially ambitious ones, but then she has some gifts of her own so it is a fair exchange of talents, one could say." He sat heavily on the edge of the bed and took off his slippers. "I think she took a liking to you, my dear."

"I think not."

"Come now, Frances adores an opinionated woman."

"She thinks I am an Irish heathen with unruly manners and she cannot fathom why you have married me. This makes her both curious and nervous."

"Succinctly observed; you have the callous eye of the

scientist. You do realize her father was a Jew and her mother's family are in the wool trade. It was sheer beauty and strength of character that propelled her into a profitable marriage. You must charm her; she will be your entry into society. It was Frances who introduced me to Darcy Quinn, the portraitist whom I commissioned to paint you as Diana. Frances knows everyone."

He leaned over to kiss the top of her head before slipping between the sheets. Lavinia watched as he picked up a copy of the latest newsletter from the Entomological Society and placed his spectacles on his nose.

"I sat for him myself once, when I was young—Icarus on the Mount, about to make his leap of faith. There was some rationale to it at the time—rash youth or something . . . Couldn't see it myself."

Lavinia knew the painting—it hung in the library above a desk the Colonel liked to work at, which was usually covered by his drawings of the various specimens he'd collected. Some specimens sat on the drawings themselves: outlandish seed pods that looked like bunches of withered grapes, the skin carefully peeled back to reveal the small yellow fruit nestled against the blackened leaves; plants with fronds so exotic in shape Lavinia found it impossible to imagine the landscape they could have been plucked from; exotic sea shells; desiccated ocean monsters—one he had once humorously described as the foot of a mermaid: a frail arched ivory bow that looked as if it had been carved by centuries of rushing undercurrents.

The painting, looming above, dominated this plethora of objects. Mounted in an ornate gilded frame, it displayed the heroic figure of Icarus—a pale-skinned youth of no more than twenty—entirely naked and standing on a boulder below which shimmered the outline of Crete, the columns of its temples and citadels a hazy blur in the afternoon sun. The boy's wings were spread as if he were about to plunge defiantly into the abyss, the evening sun streaking his sweaty face. The soft down of his cheeks, the faint shadow of a moustache, heightened the poignancy of his imminent demise.

Lavinia had gazed at it, transfixed. Recognizing the muscularity of the body, she'd initially wondered whether it was not in fact a portrait of some lost younger brother of her husband's, so youthful was the figure's stance—so different from the solid uprightness of the man she knew. But there was a look about the eyes that she recognized, the same gleam of inspired ambition Lavinia had seen in James as he worked on his illustrations and scribbled observations of the Bakairi, the Amazonian tribe he had studied, and other indigenous peoples.

In such moments, his inspiration transported her along with him into the fecund world of the Amazon, and provided an escape from the stifling atmosphere of the household—of dealing with Mrs. Beetle, the contemptuous housekeeper; the territorial struggles with her son's nursemaid; and the ennui of being trapped in the endless gray of the English winter.

She glanced over at the bed. The Colonel was propped up on the pillows peering through his reading spectacles.

"A woman like that does what she wants, does she not?" Lavinia asked.

"Within social protocol, Frances is happy to provide a modicum of scandal but she would never be foolish enough to risk ostracism."

"Would you?"

James looked at her over his paper, aggravated by her persistence. "Don't be absurd. What is it? You have that curve to your mouth that indicates disappointment."

Lavinia sat on the edge of the bed. The physical distance between them had mysteriously lengthened. Why was it so hard to broach such matters? When they were courting, she had assumed he would treat his wife as an equal, both intellectually and emotionally. It was an understandable delusion: James had been so respectful of her own ambitions, so attentive to her own amateur scientific hypotheses—even those absurd notions created from snippets of information she had gleaned from her father: how the starfish might have got its legs; why the anteater had a snout. But far from ridiculing her strange fusions of fact and fiction, James had gently pointed out biological truths without patronizing her.

He had also captivated her with his stories of the battle-field. He regarded heroism as residing in the small gestures: a medic entering no-man's-land to carry out an injured infantryman; a horse leading a blinded soldier to safety; a drummer boy who saved a brother. And yet he expressed heavy criticism for the blundering war strategies that had caused so much catastrophe and unnecessary bloodshed in the Crimea— commands he had often been forced to carry out. All these doubts and revelations he had shared with her before their marriage. But now here she was, her unspoken question a turning stone in her mouth.

Lavinia stared down at the lace counterpane. A wedding gift from her father, it had once belonged to her mother.

"You have not lain with me for over six months."

The Colonel took off his spectacles, folded them neatly, and placed them on the side table.

"Am I failing you as a husband?"

There was a peevish tone in his voice which angered Lavinia. An older cousin had once warned her: *Do not expect love in marriage. It is an illusion that does not fit with the pots and pans of domesticity. Besides, men only love you before they have had you. We are not the same as them, do not ever forget it.*

Shocked, the fourteen-year-old Lavinia had sworn she would never make such a compromise, and had every intention of expecting both passion and love, as much as any man, gentleman or otherwise. Smiling sadly, her cousin had accused her of trying to imitate the heroines in the French novels she read so avidly.

Later that same day, fearful that she might, indeed, be unnatural in her ideas, Lavinia had furtively perused the medical treatise of the great physician Dr. William Acton, a tome her father regarded as the ultimate authority on the human psyche. In a chapter headed "The Married Woman," the eminent doctor declared that the "proper female" lacked sexual feeling. The phrase had terrified Lavinia. Was she improper, then, to feel such sensations?

As her mother had died before she was two, Lavinia had received little feminine guidance, and the range of sensations that had invaded her adolescent body had been both bewildering and frightening. The only image she had ever stumbled across which seemed related to the curiously pleasurable sensations that threaded themselves through her nightly was an old woodcut of Eros and Psyche. Psyche was leaning over her lover, holding up an oil lamp so that she could see him for the first time. The disheveled abandonment of the beautiful sleeping naked youth and the look of awe and lust on the girl's face had intrigued Lavinia; she found herself wanting to be both in the body of the supine youth and in the skin of the excited girl.

"You were so attentive when we were first married," she answered softly.

"Lavinia, you are a mother now."

"And that precludes congress between man and wife?"

"It should not, but I thought it might be intelligent to wait before conceiving another child."

Lavinia reached across and lifted his large hand in her own. He kept the contact deliberately expressionless, his fingers a dull weight across her palm.

"Do you no longer desire me? I still want you." Her voice tightened in her throat. Why ask the obvious when she knew the answer? Her eyes traced the line of black hair that led down to his naked chest beneath the silk. James said nothing. So she waited, his scent drifting across the bedspread lulling her body into tumescent hope. If only she were a man, or as audacious as Lady Frances Morgan, then she would take him anyway.

"You must be patient," he said. "I think perhaps when the child is older."

In lieu of a reply, Lavinia leaned over and kissed him, the heavy veil of her hair temporarily eclipsing his face.

To his surprise, the Colonel found the assertiveness of her gesture arousing. Catching her tongue between his lips, he pulled her under him, but when his hands searched out her breasts, the unfamiliar protrusion of her nipples, altered by breast-feeding, instantly dampened his enthusiasm.

"Forgive me," he murmured as he extricated himself.

Smoothing down his ruffled hair, he reached again for his spectacles. Lavinia's optimism stumbled, then fell, like an ice skater who had miscalculated her pirouette.

12

He sits with his rifle across his knees. The shelling stops and the sudden silence makes him look up. He can even hear the faint cry of a circling hawk. White plumes of gunpowder smoke drifting across the sky part to reveal a gateway of azure. Heaven, oblivious of the Hell below, he thinks.

Stanley is sitting to his left. He always knows where Stanley is. He is James's talisman. Fused to him through the war, the blood and the shit and, most terrifying of all, the tedium of waiting. There is a faint vibration. Stanley must be whistling, he thinks; a tiny drumming James can feel in his own lips. He turns.

The sky turns white then red, fragmenting as he is thrown against the sandbags. A shattered portrait of the young Queen tumbles to the bottom of the trench while beside him Stanley's body shudders.

A moment later a Russian soldier hurls himself into the trench. James wrestles him to the ground. There is nothing but this: the shapeless mass of enemy, urine, fear, the stench of the young soldier's breath as they roll over and over. James's face presses against the mud of the trench, dirt filling his nostrils as the soldier reaches for his neck; James kicks out with his feet, twisting his body and jabbing with his elbow. The youth falls back, spread-eagled for a second. Lifting his bayonet, James thrusts it into his enemy's throat. For Stanley, he whispers, for Stanley. The Russian, lying there, his face draining to a ghostly pallor, looks up in amazement at the exact diamond of sky James had been staring at moments before. His helmet tips off and now James can see. Can see the sapphire eyes, the jutting Slavic cheekbones, the beardless chin, and the terrible youth of him.

❦

It was a wailing, the hollow moaning of a male banshee, that woke Lavinia. The gray of early dawn splattered across the insides of her closed eyelids as she buried her head further into the pillow, but the wailing continued. She climbed out of bed and, after pulling on her dressing gown, stumbled across the corridor to her husband's bedroom.

The bed sheets were twisted around his thrashing body; his lips were pulled back over his teeth, his skin taut to the skull. His eyes were open, the pupils dilated, and darted from one invisible opponent to another as he fought the blankets.

"James!"

His body stiffened; his eyes closed as he fell back onto the pillows. A second later he woke. "Again?" he murmured.

Lavinia nodded. James stared at her, shivering as the sweat dried on his skin. He looked utterly exhausted. "Oh God."

"I wish I could help you."

"I do not need help!"

Wanting to hold him, but knowing he was unpredictable when his night fears possessed him, she stayed her hand.

"It's just the disease of an old soldier, that's all. The dead stain our dreams, all of us who have fought and killed."

Swinging his legs over the edge of the bed, he felt blindly

for the hypodermic syringe he had purchased from Ferguson's a week ago at the recommendation of his doctor. The medic had promised that morphine injected into the muscle tissue would free the Colonel of his laudanum addiction. Bringing the needle down to his thigh, Huntington pushed the drug into his flesh. Loathing the sight of the thick spike breaking the skin, Lavinia looked away.

James lay back against the pillows and waited for the opiate to slither its caressing way through his body. It was like watching a cloud moving across the sun, Lavinia thought; the muscles in his face relaxing as the pain lifted like a veil.

Suddenly, she felt a dampness across the front of her nightdress—lactation. As if on cue a whimpering sounded from the adjoining room. Then the child began to scream.

"Go to him if you must," James muttered without opening his eyes.

❧

Slipping through the half-open door of the nursery, Lavinia felt in the dark for a candle. Her son's small fists gripped the top of the wooden rails, his screaming face a scrunched rag. After lifting him out of the cot, she collapsed into an armchair and freed her breast from the neck of her nightdress. The child, who had his mother's heavy mouth and pronounced chin and his father's deep-set eyes, reached for the nipple greedily.

As he suckled, Lavinia stared drowsily at a small portrait of James and his mother, dimly illuminated by the candle. The grim-faced young woman, in a riding outfit and brandishing a crop, sat on a poised black stallion. Beside them, the infant James, in an identical riding coat, perched solidly on a small pony—a diminutive patriarch. Even at the age of five he bristled with territorial masculinity.

It had been painted for James's father as a miniature to take with him when soldiering. Eduard Le Coneur had been a young naval officer—and a Huguenot refugee from the first wave of the French revolution. He had died prematurely after contracting rabies from a dog's bite—an inglorious death which had embittered his young wife. The Viscountess had reverted to her maiden name and had never married again.

She displayed little affection for her son, other than a paranoia that, like his father, Death might claim him in the most unexpected places. It was an obsession that caused the young boy much mortification during his time at Eton, resulting in a bombardment of letters to the house master about the school's sanitary conditions, the food, the dangers of the playing fields, and any other element that could bring about her child's untimely demise.

Upon leaving Eton, determined to rid himself of his mother's stifling protectiveness, James apprenticed himself to a distant cousin, a general in the army, who was happy to assist in the young man's promotion. James began his military career at twenty, enthusiastically accepting the most dangerous posts across the Empire. Then at thirty, blessed with a generous annual income and a fashionable residence in Mayfair, he resigned from the army and, inspired by the example of Lt. General Pitt Rivers, pursued a career as an anthropologist, joining expeditions into Australia, the Amazon, and Africa. In the manner of the French philosopher Rousseau, he adopted the belief that primitive man was pristine, free of evil and sin—a hypothesis that was essentially optimistic, and one that Lavinia subscribed to.

The Crimean War broke out in 1853 and James, now forty-two, volunteered. After surviving malaria, smallpox, and yellow fever, he had concluded that, thankfully, he had escaped his mother's fatalism. Deeming himself blessed and therefore invincible, the intrepid Colonel began to test his theory by placing himself in increasingly dangerous situations, both on the battlefield and off. When his second officer and closest friend, Stanley Dickenson, was killed, his conjecture was confirmed. He had told Lavinia, Death had chosen to ignore him over and over. He had convinced her that it had been both a sobering and an invigorating notion but one that had shook him from his inherent lassitude. In civilian life, it propelled him into the opium dens of Shanghai, the brothels of Buenos Aires and, finally, to the shamans of the Amazon.

The child stopped suckling and fell instantly asleep at the breast. Lavinia closed her eyes, not wanting to wake Aidan. The diminishing world shrank to the scent of her son's wispy hair and the sweetish smell of breast milk. She was woken from her doze by the click of the door.

"It has to stop, Lavinia." James stood over them, swaying slightly, his face puffy from sleep. "The breast-feeding is unbecoming for a woman of your status. Besides, the child is old enough to be weaned."

"But it's what all good mothers do."

"This is not Ireland and you are my wife!"

His raised voice woke the child who started grumbling. Shocked, Lavinia drew her son back to her breast. How dare he prevent her from raising her child the way she intended. Surely that was a mother's prerogative. Can he care more for social mores than plain instinctive sense, she wondered.

"I believe it to be better for the child," she began.

"Lavinia, we will not debate this. I have made myself clear."

Lavinia tried to control her fury. I refuse to poison my milk with anger, she thought. Her mind struggled impotently against her husband's authority, before she decided she had little choice. She was expected to obey him.

The Colonel looked down at Aidan pushing blindly against Lavinia's breast. He had been surprised at the magnitude of feeling he held for his son. Even now, at this early stage, he recognized traits in the child that he knew to be his own: Aidan's impatience; his fascination for anything natural—animals, plants; the shape of his eyes and mouth, the long thick fingers and broad palms. These were all his.

Reaching out, he lifted the sleeping child to his chest.

Immediately the boy's hand curled around his father's pajama collar, making a tiny fist.

This act of creation has made me a good man. This life is the payment for all the lives I have taken, the Colonel vowed silently, now determined to protect and nurture his child in a way that his own parents never had.

As he cradled his son in his arms, the opiate transformed his thoughts into grandiose declarations that seemed to wind around the pattern of the wallpaper.

13

California, 2002

Julia leaned against the railings, her hair a whirling furor that caught at her lips and snaked across her nose and eyes. The memory of their lovemaking suddenly spread throughout her body, the intensity of her orgasm resounding. The couple stood on the deck of the Catalina Express ferry, buffeted by the wind. Klaus had organized a surprise visit to a jazz concert at the Ballroom on the island. He had a habit of orchestrating mysterious events: the whole of their courtship and marriage had been peppered by such occasions—day visits to Napa Valley vineyards, rock concerts, picnics in unusual places, sailing trips, his proposal in the hot-air balloon, a tour of the haunted sites of Los Angeles, a night visit to William Randolph Hearst's castle; once he had even taken her on a tour of the city's sewers. These occasions had come to frame their relationship—emotional and geographical reference points that became mythologized by memory.

Julia loved him for it. It was as if she was discovering her own country again through his eyes. Klaus's childlike delight in astonishing her, as well as his sense of adventure and thirst for the unusual, kept her from complete absorption in her work. Without him, she suspected she might lose her sense of play altogether.

They had taken the ferry from Long Beach. It was one of those spring afternoons when the light seemed to cut a clear edge around everything. As the boat sliced through the water, Julia watched the frothing waves descending away from the prow, exciting ripples that raced across the surface of the turquoise bay. Mesmerized by the rhythm of this constant movement, she found herself wondering about nature and the continuous renewal and atrophy that made up the physical world.

"You have to grasp your own piece of time and ride it, ride the whole wave until it peters out onto the foreshore," she said out loud, forgetting herself.

Klaus, standing against her, his face turned into the wind, only caught every third word.

"What?" he asked, but, deafened by the boat engine and the sea, Julia only saw his lips move. Looking up, she smiled back reassuringly, then pressed herself against him. His arms curled around her, his face buried in her hair, a hidden swirl of confusion and sadness.

Oblivious, Julia leaned over the railing and was instantly reabsorbed in the submerged cosmos beneath the parting waves.

It was typical of Julia, Klaus thought, she had this rare capacity to be completely captivated by the act of observation and, like a chameleon, become an invisible watcher. He glanced at her profile: the strong nose that arched nobly, the jet-black straight hair that hung to her shoulders, the blue hunger of her eyes. Almost as tall as him, she had broad shoulders that could cradle a large man like him comfortably. She was everything he had wanted—intellectually stimulating, funny, ambitious, sexually adventurous—and yet here he was, torn between this moment and a parallel existence that pulled violently at his instinct. Where would he be at fifty, even sixty? He shut his eyes, trying to imagine the three of them as a family, his son's tiny hand linking the two of them—he couldn't visualize it. He should be able to know it, to see their future. He swallowed, fear bobbing in his throat like an apple in a barrel.

"There's something else . . ." he mouthed into the roaring wind, knowing Julia couldn't hear a word. He'd planned everything, and now he'd arrived at this junction, he found himself gripped by an irrational terror. Could he do it? Was he capable of such a finite decision?

The blasting horn of the ferry momentarily obliterated his anxieties as the boat swung toward the small harbor of Avalon.

⊷

They were standing right in front of the stage in the Catalina Ballroom—a circular neoclassical building positioned on a peninsula originally built as a small opera house by the chewing gum magnate Wrigley when the family owned the island in the 1920s. The building—now a ballroom and casino—was spectacular. A balcony, with pillars and arches, ran all the way around, providing a 360-degree panorama of L.A. harbor and the luxury yachts and boats twinkling and swaying in the small port of Avalon directly below.

Julia loved Catalina, the quaintness of its immaculately maintained small cottages and fishing shacks that ran up its slopes. A haven for celebrities during the 1920s and '30s, it had somehow retained its individuality. It had a fairy tale quality, an old-worldliness that seemed unimaginable given the bustling proximity of Los Angeles.

The band's saxophonist was dwarfed by the alto saxophone she was welded to; swaying, it was as if she was making love through the instrument itself, its rich tones spilling out into the treacly, humid night. She broke into the first notes of "My Funny Valentine"; as the double bass plucked at the backbone beneath, Julia's body thrilled to the music. A

Spanish guitar, keyboard, and drums joined in, building the refrain with a poignant tenderness.

Julia and Klaus were pressed between a group of four young girls and a middle-aged couple who sounded as if they might be from the Midwest. The wife, well over fifty and about two hundred and eighty pounds, began to sing along loudly. Determined to block her out, Julia stayed focused on the saxophonist, on the interweaving notes soaring up toward the chandeliers. The song ended and, turning, Julia suddenly noticed that Klaus had left her side.

She found him out on the balcony, leaning against one of the arches that framed the view. He was staring toward the city—now a twinkling mirage of distant lights set against the fading crimson of the sunset.

"You've been really quiet since I got back. Is everything okay?"

He glanced at her then back out to sea. "A lot changed while you were away. I guess I found the time to find myself."

Wondering at this sudden despondency, she wrapped her hand around his arm. "Am I that demanding?" she joked.

"Not demanding so much as all encompassing. Somehow you manage to fill a space completely. I guess it's like uneven magnetic fields—I am always in your orbit."

"Not from my axis: you're all that's on my horizon." She searched his eyes but found them vacant. Shivering, she nestled into his jacket. "You know, I used to think happiness was something dramatic, something that happened suddenly. Now I think it's like a constant note you're barely aware of until those rare and wonderful occasions when it suddenly intensifies and you find yourself standing on a balcony in some tiny opera house at the edge of the Pacific, and you think, wow, how did this happen?"

Now he looked at her. "Julia . . ."

She waited, wondering at the strange play of emotions that ran like scene changes across his face.

"What, sweetheart?"

He hesitated, then, shaking his head, pulled away from her. "Nothing. I have to go to the restroom. I'll see you back inside."

As he left, she turned back to the glittering skyline and vowed to take him with her on her next research trip.

Klaus stumbled into a cubicle and locked the door. Slamming the toilet lid down, he sat on it and buried his face in his hands, great silent sobs racking his whole frame. His cell phone, tucked in his jacket pocket, began to ring. Ignoring it, he held himself tighter.

14

Mayfair, 1861

The smell of hot lemon tea and porridge laced with whisky drifted up from the silver tray the maid had placed over Lavinia's lap. She sat in the four-poster bed, yawning, as the maid pulled open the curtains. Outside, the chestnut trees and windows of the Georgian houses were a wash of black, green, and pale gray. The winter light barely managed to tinge the park and the square.

"Would you like the *Queen*, madam? It is expected that you follow the events of the day."

Not much older than Lavinia, the maid had been hired specifically to address the shortcomings of the young wife's etiquette. Expecting a rebuff, she bravely held out a copy of the leading social broadsheet James had insisted his wife subscribe to.

"Why not, Daisy? Let's examine the glorious adventures

of the Upper Ten Thousand At Home and Abroad, a group to which, evidently, we do not belong."

The Upper Ten Thousand was a listing of the elite members of English society—a fiction invented by the broadsheet to fuel the ambitions of the middle-class matron, a recent social phenomenon desperate to mimic her aristocratic counterparts.

Lavinia began reading sarcastically.

"The Prince Consort attended a hunt at Finchley; surrounded by his attendants and several of the Royal children he was a fine and invigorating sight. Meanwhile, in the city, Lady Waldegrave held a late supper for many of the parliamentarian figures. It was said that Disraeli was in attendance. Hugh Lupus Grosvenor was seen at St. James's Park last week for the Changing of the Guard. The Queen will today receive the Viceroy of India in a reception to be held at Buckingham Palace . . ."

Lavinia faltered, wondering at her own lack of social credentials. James is right—I need to win Lady Morgan's patronage if I am to have any life outside these four walls, she thought, chastising herself, then took comfort in remembering that Lady Morgan's lineage was as insubstantial as her own.

The rustlings of the staff, already on their rounds of carpet sweeping, polishing, and general maintenance, floated in under the door. Lavinia's aching breasts suddenly reminded her of her son.

"Daisy, have I slept late?"

"It is past nine, madam."

"Past nine! Why wasn't I woken earlier? Does Aidan not need feeding?"

"The nursemaid has the child, madam. The Colonel insists that master Aidan must be completely weaned or take a wet nurse," the maid continued, sensing Lavinia's chagrin.

"I must speak to my husband at once!"

"Colonel Huntington is not in the house, madam, he is already off to a lecture then to the Carlton. He left instructions that you are to expect him back late tonight and should not wait up."

"Then I must be dressed and to my child as quickly as possible."

❧

The kitchen was situated in the basement. A huge room equipped with a large fireplace and vast stove, it was the domain of the cook, Mrs. Jobling, and the other servants: Mrs. Beetle, the housekeeper; Mr. Poole, the butler; four manservants and six maids. A small room adjacent to the kitchen served as the laundry, and on the other side was the chute that delivered coal directly to the cellar. There was also a cool room, lined with thick stone, that had once served as a dairy. Now it held the icebox, within which the ice man dropped his weekly delivery.

The water for the household came from the well at the back of Chesterfield house, a nearby mansion. The spring was famous for the purity of its water, which was brought in daily by the lowest-ranking footman.

The laundry looked out onto a landscaped courtyard that boasted a struggling lilac tree in its center. An old marble horse trough delineated the stables from the garden. There was a cobbled area in front of the coach house and stables, which fronted onto a mews lane, enabling easy access to the main street and square. These were also the living quarters of the head coachman, two grooms, and four young stable-hands who slept in a loft above the stables.

Next to the laundry was the butler's pantry, the command post of Mr. Poole, a sanctimonious Scottish misanthrope in his fifties, who had served James during his army years. The chamber was furnished with a plain wooden table, an armchair and a watercolor of Loch Fyne hanging on the wall. It also contained a large Dutch display cabinet in which the silver plate and fine china were kept locked when not in use.

There was also a safe built into the wall for the very expensive pieces, which Mr. Poole guarded jealously.

The kitchen was a terrain separate from the rest of the house. Since the recent installation of a dumbwaiter—of which James was fiercely proud—there was hardly an occasion to bring Lavinia down into this nether world of steam, meaty cooking smells and raucous robustness.

The hiss from the clothes press and the rattle of the immense boiler that dominated one corner of the laundry fractured the murmuring that drifted through the half-open kitchen door—a flurry of whispers that finished in a staccato of female laughter.

Pausing, Lavinia wondered whether to enter or not. Back in Ireland, she had never been excluded from life below the stairs. The minister kept only one housekeeper and a young scullery maid, who lived in the village, and Lavinia had helped with both the laundry and the cooking. Here, in this huge house with its hidden service stairs and quarters, the two worlds were carefully divided. Lavinia missed the earthy humor of the women she had grown up around, their easy direct speech and, most of all, the magic of their superstitions. The village mysteries had included the ghost of a young woman who had killed herself over a philandering sheep farmer some seventy years earlier, a forty-eight-year-old woman who had fallen miraculously pregnant after the Virgin Mary had appeared to her youngest in a cabbage patch, and the sinister possession of a chimney sweep in his death throes—a circumstance that had terrified even the priest as he leaned over him to administer the last rites.

This parallel world had fascinated the imaginative young girl, but there was one mystery that was never mentioned in the household, upstairs or down. When she was five, Lavinia asked why she could not remember her mother's funeral. The old housekeeper had pulled the child onto her lap and, letting her play with the rosary beads she kept in the pocket of her kitchen apron, explained that she herself had looked after her because at the age of one she had been too young to attend.

"But oh how your father wept. I have never seen a man more distressed, not since the first Famine. Whatever they tell you, Miss Lavinia, she was a loved woman, your mother."

Now, encouraged by the memory of the housekeeper's flour-dusted affection, Lavinia entered the kitchen.

Her son was strapped into a high chair as the nursemaid, a stoic young woman from Leeds, bent over him, spooning a thin stew into his mouth.

"So he's taken to the meal?"

The nursemaid paused, a guilty look on her face, then hastily wiped the babe's soiled chin with her apron as Lavinia bent down to kiss her son.

"The master instructed me, madam. I would have waited for you but he was most insistent."

The cook hurriedly cleared a place for Lavinia at the oak table. Mrs. Jobling was a laconic skinny creature, one of the few servants who had warmed to the young wife, correctly perceiving her abrasive arrogance as a way of masking her lack of confidence.

"You think me a fool for feeding my own child?" Lavinia sat down and took an apple from a pile waiting to be peeled and baked into a pie.

"No, madam," the nursemaid replied carefully, acutely aware of the dispute between husband and wife. "However, it is a most unconventional choice for a mother of your social standing. But the child is happy; it was time he started on more solid foods, madam."

"We all hate letting them go, madam," the cook interjected as she hovered over a scullery maid who was chopping fruit. "I had to let mine go to the baby farmer—'course she neglected them something terrible. My two newborns died of the colic and I had to send my son to work at six year old. It's hard for a mother, it is. But they grow so fast, and before you know it he's a rake with three bastards of his own."

As if in reply, Aidan belched loudly. All four women burst into laughter and a classless unity fell momentarily over the kitchen.

It was only when Lavinia noticed the nursemaid blushing and straightening her apron that she realized someone else—most likely a man—had entered the room. Then she smelt him; the sharp tang of horse manure interwoven with tobacco and saddle soap. It was a familiar aroma that she associated with Ireland and the farm of her childhood. Lavinia did not turn; instead, she waited for him to announce himself—as would be the protocol of servant to mistress. But the silence lengthened until it threatened to become sullen in its obstinacy. Finally, the nursemaid gestured toward the stranger.

"Madam, have you met the new coachman?"

Lavinia remained seated, her spine a ramrod. Coachmen were the Colonel's domain, and she was convinced the man's insolence was an indication of her husband's lack of support for her own authority with the servants.

"I have not."

"Please excuse my rudeness but I fear to tread mud around the kitchen."

The voice was young but mellow and Lavinia instantly recognized the accent. He stepped around the table to face her.

"You're from County Kerry?" she said.

"I am indeed, originally from the McGregor estate." He bowed, his hair a thick helmet of dark locks that tumbled almost to his shoulders. Beneath his riding coat he wore the vertically striped waistcoat that defined him as a coachman.

"Aloysius O'Malley of Dingle, at your service."

"We call him John, madam, as we do all the head coachmen here," the cook added, worried that the servant's manners might be considered audacious.

The young coachman looked down truculently. Lavinia guessed, correctly, that he resented the anonymity.

"Then you shall be the first coachman called Aloysius," she replied.

The young man grinned, a smile that entirely transformed his otherwise grim countenance.

The nursemaid looked sharply at Lavinia, then knowingly at the cook. Typical of the new mistress, she thought, not to know her own place and that of others.

Ignoring her disapproval, Lavinia turned back to the coachman. "I know Dingle well. There is an excellent blacksmith there."

"That would be my second cousin, madam."

"You are very young to be head coachman."

"My credentials are excellent, madam, and I have been in service since I was six years of age."

He looked directly at her now and she saw that he had barely reached manhood. The wizened cast to his features gave him a deceptively older appearance. A third of the indentured workers of the McGregor estate had starved to death and it had been one of many places that Lavinia had visited with her father, bearing paltry gifts of clothing and food. She recognized the aged appearance of the coachman's face as the legacy of childhood malnourishment—the stigma of the Famine.

The young Irishman's green eyes were set below a heavy brow and his slender face was a medley of angles placed crookedly above one another, thus creating a jaw, a chin, cheekbones and so forth. A thin mobile mouth twitched beneath a long broken nose, giving the tentative smile a certain vulnerability. His broad shoulders jutted out like awkward coat hangers from which the rest of his body fell like a cascade of bony planes. His livery—obviously inherited from his corpulent predecessor—was loose around his waist and hips, the wide leather belt buckled tight in an attempt to keep his trousers up.

"You're not long in England?" Lavinia asked, breaking into a brogue that made the cook's jaw drop.

The coachman, unwilling to be pulled into an intimacy that could compromise his position, stayed with his formal

English. "Madam, three months yesterday and I am mighty thankful for the job. I will not disappoint either you or the master."

"Good, in that case you may collect me at two o'clock this afternoon. I wish to attend church and then visit Bond Street, where there is a book I wish to purchase."

"Very good, madam." He tipped his cap and left.

Returning to the stables, he wondered if she was the daughter of the Protestant minister Reverend Augustus Kane, infamous for his outlandish scientific hypotheses and for fighting with his patron over the fate of his lordship's starving Catholic tenants. If she was Kane's daughter she must be a good woman, he thought, then remembered his grandfather mentioning some disreputable rumor involving the minister's wife. But that was years ago, and what did he, a Catholic, care about a Protestant scandal?

❖

Before leaving the house, Lavinia slipped quietly into the Colonel's study. It was a large room with ceiling-to-floor windows through which the English sun struggled periodically.

The pungent scent of dried plant specimens mixed with old tobacco, wood polish, and turpentine, reminded her of her father and his own study. In the middle of the room stood a magnificent circular table, the top inlaid with a marquetry of exotic flowers, the ornate border depicting all manner of tropical fruits—each section representing a part of the world James had explored. A commissioned piece, the table had been a gift from the Royal Society to celebrate the Colonel's achievements. Atop its varnished walnut surface were scattered various specimens and papers—the anthropologist's current work. Apart from the chair at the table, there was an alcove containing a cushioned window seat, and several green leather armchairs grouped around the fireplace.

A majestic mahogany bureau bookcase presided against one wall. Always locked, it held the Colonel's collection of skulls, which he had gathered in his youth when under the brief tutelage of the Scottish phrenologist George Combe. Behind the decoratively glazed glass doors, the shelves were stacked with a variety of tribal artefacts, a single skull on each ledge, representing the different tribes the Colonel had studied. Each was surrounded by the icons of its people—masks, small statues, hunting tools.

Smaller display cabinets lined the opposite wall, their shelves bursting with books, manuscripts, and bound note-books full of dried flowers, pressed insects, scribbled pencil sketches, each description illustrated with excited annotations in the margin. The enthusiasm of the younger man radiated from these pages, his fervor visible in the jittery handwriting.

The sun, breaking through the clouds, streamed in through the skylight, carved a thin arc across the parquet floor and fell over her head, warming her in one delicious lick. The Colonel's recent presence in the room had left an olfactory shadow of sandalwood soap, leather, and hair oil. The rustling leaves outside melted into the sound of the Liffey River as the scent drew Lavinia into the memory of one particular afternoon—the first time they had made love in daylight.

Kneeling, James had fumbled with her waistband, peeling each layer away—of silk, of damask, of lace—until she lay in her undergarments. Trembling with frustration, Lavinia had untied the ribbons at her side herself, then lifted his hand to that secret part of her she had now discovered for herself. Leaning into her, he had shut his eyes, his face inches from her own, as he let her guide him. Watching him, she wrestled with her own raising orgasm until the moment she felt herself clenching. Then she pulled him into her, begging him to take her.

"Look at me," she'd whispered, and in that moment when the Colonel opened his eyes, her bliss had become his and she had screamed, overwhelmed by a pounding rapture that drowned out the sound of the river outside.

Would they ever love like that again?

Lavinia walked over to the secretaire. Her husband's diary rested against a carved walnut lectern, open at its last entry.

> *The use of certain poisons during the initiation rituals of the Amazonian peoples and the Indians of the South Americas must not be underestimated. Belladonna, mescaline, Spanish Fly, Morning Glory, are just some of the flora used to enhance religious trances and often to communicate with the "Gods" themselves. I myself have experimented with ayahuasca, used by the Bakairi in their spiritual practices. Naturally, the administration of such dangerous substances is hazardous and it is only the shamans or wise men of the villages that have both the skill and the permission to wield this "sorcery" . . .*

Pinned next to the note was a curiously twisted root. Lavinia squeezed the spongy substance lightly between her fingers. Its toxicity was evident in the acrid scent.

15

Los Angeles, 2002

Julia drove up the wide tree-lined Westwood Boulevard and turned into Le Conte, where redbrick university buildings now dominated either side. There was a bland affluence to Westwood that she loathed. After the eclectic architecture of Haight-Ashbury in San Franciso, where she had grown up, the suburb appeared insipid with its relatively new shopping malls plastered with the generic consumerist icons that littered middle America—the movie house, the hamburger joint, the supermarket, the Mex-Tex restaurant. A district designed to service the student community and medical facilities, there was nothing to distinguish it from a thousand others across the country. As in much of Los Angeles, most of the historical landmarks had been torn down and with them any organically evolved sprawl. Why did rampant capitalism always reduce history to a bulldozed cliché, Julia wondered as she turned into the research center. Still, it was good to be back on her own territory, with all the necessities within reach—no more living out of a suitcase, packing samples in polystyrene coolers, going days without a shower.

Despite their disagreements it had been more profoundly emotional to return to Klaus than she had imagined. Sometimes when Julia went on field trips, she became so preoccupied she forgot that she missed him, really missed him.

Remembering their embrace before she left the house, she decided to ring him when she got to the office, then made a second mental note to check on Carla to see if she'd recovered from her drinking stint at the restaurant. Humming to the radio Julia parked the car.

The Neuroscience and Genetics Research Center was a redbrick and sandstone building constructed only two years before. At the front of the block was a small landscaped quadrangle with a futuristic bronze sculpture, an abstract representation of the double helix of DNA. Privately sponsored, the Center housed several cutting-edge research laboratories; Julia's laboratory was located on the first floor.

Clutching her briefcase, Julia ran up the granite stairs, past the eucalyptus trees and into the cool shadow of a stone arch leading into the building.

Her office was a small room removed from the bustle of the main laboratory, which was separated into a wet lab and a dry lab, with a low white partition dividing the two.

The dry lab consisted of two wooden benches facing one another, holding five computers that were constantly running.

Invariably, at least three of Julia's eight employees were using the space to work on their individual research projects as well as the larger commissions the lab took on as an entity.

The wet lab—where the hands-on experiments were carried out—was lined with benches stocked with equipment and bottles of various chemicals and reagents. All available floor space was occupied by fume hoods, huge freezers, and centrifuges plastered with instructions and warnings.

Down the corridor, in their own separate alcoves, were the electron microscope and the culture room. A photograph of someone's eighty-five-year-old grandmother suspended in a full lotus position smiled beatifically down on all the activity, and jazz played constantly from a CD player in the corner. Julia prided herself on creating an atmosphere that allowed the imagination of her employees to soar—the laboratory's record for innovation evidence of this.

Jennifer Bostock, a precocious young scientist from New York clad in a vintage velvet dress that gave her the appearance of a slightly aggrieved Gothic tragedienne, swung around from her desk.

"Julia, welcome back! Everything stored safely and shipped?"

"The samples arrive tomorrow. You got my e-mail about the commission?"

"Yeah, amazing. Congratulations! Whitehead must be so pissed."

"It's certainly one for the little guys."

Julia glanced at Jennifer's laptop. Jennifer's doctorate was on a link between dyslexia and genetics, but she was in her fourth year and Julia was beginning to suspect that she might be just another perpetual student.

"There's a position available—I'm looking for an assistant. Are you interested?" she asked.

"I'd love to, but the university's just issued an ultimatum—I have to have the doctorate finished by the summer. I'm really sorry, Julia."

Julia glanced around the office; another postgraduate was tucked into the corner, studiously avoiding her eye.

"Is anyone free?"

"Well, Hank's swept up with his slime molds and Phong's rushing to get an article published in the *Scientific* and Shawn's on sabbatical until April. You know how it is."

Swinging around on her swivel chair, Jennifer returned to her laptop. Grabbing the chair, Julia pulled it back to face her.

"Is this about working for the Defense Department, or is this about genuine commitment to our own individual pursuit? I mean, I'd love to think I had a lab full of potential Nobel prize winners, but I suspect not."

Jennifer looked sheepish. "Look, some of us have issues, and some of us are actually busy."

"Great."

"Don't worry, the goddess will provide. She always does," the student concluded philosophically.

Julia winced. Through her work she had come to the discomfiting conclusion that there was quite probably a gene for religion or spiritual faith and it was one she seemed to lack. It wasn't the concept of faith itself that irritated her, more the surrendering of control and determinism she felt it implied. Perhaps Marx was right: religion is the opium of the masses— and Buddhism the ecstasy of the middle classes, she concluded as she fought the temptation to slam her office door behind her. The room was a narrow rectangle lined with bookshelves, the large window at the end looking out over the university grounds. Facing the window was the desk; its black polished surface was impeccably neat, the state-of-the-art desktop computer—the nucleus of all her thinking. Against the wall opposite sat several locked filing cabinets, the files inside obsessively numbered and up to date.

Sitting at the desk, Julia retrieved the Defense Department file from her briefcase. It contained two computer disks. She slipped the first disk into the computer, then, as she waited for it to boot up, rang home.

The tone rang out; the answering machine had been switched off. That's odd, she thought. Klaus was usually writing by this time, having completed his eight-thirty morning run. He compensated for the unpredictable nature of his employment by structuring his days into a rigid timetable. Surprised, Julia decided to ring again in an hour.

She scanned the computer screen. The files contained a list of five hundred twins from the ex-veterans database. This was the most extensive database available to geneticists and one of the largest twin studies in the world. Half the men on the list were monozygotic or identical twins; the other half being dizygotic or nonidentical twins. Using twins in the study would make it easier to discern which traits were genetic and which were more likely to be environmental.

At least half of the twins were combat soldiers with experience of intensive frontline combat—Delta, rangers, special forces, soldiers who'd seen extreme service in places such as Afghanistan, South America, Rwanda, and Bosnia and all of the twins had been in the forces. Their age range ran between nineteen and sixty, which meant that many of the inherent genetic traits would have emerged by now. As Julia read down the list she began dividing the subjects into four main categories: Anglo–American, Latino–American, African–American, and Asian–American. This was for sociological uniformity only. External physical differences, including race, accounted for such minor changes in the overall genome sequence that they didn't count. *Homo sapiens* really were all the same under the skin—a fact Julia often considered advertising on the Internet to counteract racism.

The study's procedures involved testing the men's DNA (to ensure the exact status of the twins as well as screening for possible genetic determinants), a brain scan, and a series of tests to gauge physiological and psychological reactions to combat and violence. These consisted of measurement of heart rate, blood pressure, and particularly blood composition while the subject viewed images of violent combat.

There was also to be an interview to research the nurturing and other environmental influences on the twins' early life.

❧

When Julia looked up from the computer a couple of hours later, the sun was already high over the eucalyptus trees. Hating the incessant air conditioning and wanting fresh air, she pushed open one of the windows. Outside, she could hear the students milling around; snippets of conversations, bursts of young laughter, a guitar being strummed, the banally bright chorus of a cell phone and the smell of freshly mown grass, all drifted in. It made Julia remember her own student days: her exhilaration at her first discovery, her first published paper, the pride that infused her whole body the first time she walked into her own laboratory. Out of twenty graduates from Julia's year only eleven had stayed working in the field, and of the six female graduates she was the only one who had gone on to a career in science. The hours were long and the work highly competitive as well as extraordinarily tedious; great swathes of repetitious research stretched between moments of inspiration.

Julia's professor had always reminded the students as they started leaving for the day, sometimes as late as ten at night, "Scientists in France, Germany, and Japan are just starting their day, all striving to make the same discovery you're working on. Sleep on it."

It took resilience, obsession, obstinacy, and selfishness to make a good scientist—and maybe narcissism, Julia reflected guiltily.

Most of the young women she'd graduated with had given up research and laboratory work when they married. Even her nemesis, a young woman Julia knew was brighter than her, a scientist she had been convinced would have a meteoritic rise through the ranks, had retired at twenty-six to marry a British hedge-fund manager. Others had resorted to part-time commercial laboratory work or other mindless conveyor-belt-style research when they'd had families. The hours and the poor pay meant it was virtually impossible to have a family and a career in science.

Were there any role models for her as both a scientist and a mother? Julia had met one scientist at a seminar who'd taken eight weeks off work to have her baby before returning to complete her doctorate. "Motherhood actually sharpens your mind," she'd told Julia. "It's all the multi-tasking you have to do. It forces you to become a master of time management—at least, that's the delusion I function under. Otherwise forget it."

Julia reached for the phone again. There was still no answer at the house. She tried Klaus's cell phone. It was switched off. Strange, he never switched his phone off, ever. A nagging anxiety began to play at her mind as she tried to concentrate on the list of research subjects. The irrational notion that he might have had a car accident lurked beneath the written description of each case history. By the end of the chapter she had convinced herself that Klaus's corpse lay congealing on some mortuary slab.

She rang their neighbor Gerry, a scriptwriter who was inevitably home. Today he was attending to the vast collection of bonsai trees he kept on his deck, and murmured incoherently about a van.

"I thought you might be having a garage sale or something. I mean, I think I saw Klaus helping the guys out with something so I figured it wasn't, like, you know, a burglary."

Stoned again, Julia thought cynically. He was hardly ever lucid.

"Thanks, Gerry. I guess I'll see you later."

"You will. You know me—the dateless agoraphobic."

The phone clicked off. Again, premonition brushed across Julia's skin. Determined not to fall victim to the psychological tricks of her hormones, she dismissed her fear as irrational.

16

Mayfair, 1861

The coachman loitered at the stone entrance to St. George's. As an Irish Catholic at the door of one of London's most prestigious Protestant churches, it was impossible for him not to feel intimidated.

Smoothing down the lapels of his jacket, he pulled himself upright in an attempt to shake off an insidious sense of inferiority. A pox on the English, I'll not bend to their arrogance, he muttered as he peered through the darkened archway. He could see his young Irish mistress kneeling inside, the lilac brim of her bonnet sitting high amid the pews.

Despite her ambition, she seemed deeply uncomfortable with the authority foisted upon her, and there had been complaints in the servants' quarters about the way Mrs. Huntington contradicted her husband's commands and confused the senior staff with her over-familiar manner. "She should know her place," Mrs. Beetle had muttered more than once. There were only two servants who defended Mrs. Huntington's unorthodox ways—her own maid and the cook.

Aloysius pulled out a small clay pipe and packed it with tobacco, the besieged sunlight falling across the broken fingernails and mottled skin of his working hands.

A robin perched on the font stone looked at him quizzically. Feeling in his pocket, Aloysius found some oats and threw the bird a few flakes. At least the English birds are friendly, he consoled himself. Lavinia's mouth—that slightly wry curl of her lip—came to mind as he studied the bird's red plumage. Struggling to dismiss the image, Aloysius reluctantly acknowledged that he was partial to the young wife, whatever her politics, whatever her station, not just because she was unconventional but in the way a man likes a woman.

"Take the gifts God gives you and don't waste your life hankering after the unobtainable" had been the advice of his grandfather, who had adopted the small boy after his father, an itinerant farmhand, had disappeared from the village. Well, God had given him and his family nothing but grief and starvation. Everything Aloysius had, he'd earned through his own labor.

So he liked the woman, so what? Looking was not an offense. Could it be because she was Irish, a warm beacon in all this phlegmatic sensibility? Again, the coachman chastised himself—to imagine he could be anything but a servant in her eyes was an unforgivable vanity and most probably a sin. He held his hand out to the robin, who, after examining him with one beady eye, flew off as if to challenge his luck.

Aloysius then turned to watch several city gentlemen stride through Hanover Square. The sight of such industry was still a source of wonder to the village boy. The whole of London was a warren of frantic activity: hackneys taxiing merchants to and fro; the ragged army of children that lurked beneath tarpaulins, carts, archways, and in doorways—a river of grimy life all ambling toward the one grave. Three flower girls and a hurdy-gurdy man had set up on the pavement opposite the church; the girls' cries adding a curious lyric to the whirling music cranking out of the painted box.

It is an idyllic picture, this enclave of Mayfair, the coachman thought, all pomp and circumstance with its parks, its lamps blazing and footmen at the entrance of every grand house. But Aloysius knew that he would have to walk barely a mile to find himself in some typhoid-ridden slum lane. This is a metropolis of many cities, and I should be thankful to be living in a golden corner of it, he concluded, crossing himself for good luck.

Inside the church, Lavinia was conducting a conversation with her God. It was a dialogue in which her prayers were answered by a voice within herself; an alter ego whose pragmatism always provided a comforting but humorous counterbalance to her own idealism.

"May James desire me again," she prayed, before noting that it was both ridiculous and sacrilegious to be asking the Almighty for guidance on such earthly matters. Better to ask the music hall actress or the courtesan—the reply popped irreverently into her mind, prompting her to rise to her feet guiltily. By the time she had wrapped her cloak about her, the afternoon light was already fading.

She made her way to the imposing main doors, where the coachman was waiting.

"You do not worship yourself?" she asked, sensing Aloysius's reluctance to enter the church.

"Madam, I was born a Catholic so I've no love of the English steeple. Anyhow, I've not been inside a church for over four years." He lifted the edge of her cloak to prevent it dragging in the mud.

"Four years is a considerable lapse of faith for any denomination."

"I lost my faith while watching my mother starve, despite her prayers." His face tightened, deterring further inquiry.

Lavinia paused before stepping up into the carriage. "I also have found myself wondering about the value of faith when there appears to be no redemption."

"Not in this world, anyhow, madam," Aloysius added, trying not to notice her slender stockinged ankle, visible for a moment beneath her petticoats.

The lamplighters had begun their determined circuit, ushering in the evening with depressing swiftness. The coachman paused with his hand on the coach door, the chilly afternoon air making steam of his breath.

"Madam, forgive my impertinence, but it is now past four o'clock and it would be considered unseemly for a young woman such as yourself to be seen in Bond Street at this time."

"In that case we shall definitely make the visit, and I shall take you along as my valet."

Was this an example of her determination to shun convention and court controversy, or was it simply ignorance, Aloysius wondered as he swung himself up to the front of the carriage.

❦

The carriage wound its way past the elegant Georgian arcades of Regent Street, negotiating the omnibuses, carts, the mingling crowds, and on toward Piccadilly Circus. The evening's entertainment at the Princess Theatre was "M. Fechter's Hamlet," proudly advertised on a banner illuminated by burning gaslights, only just visible through the yellowish fog that had moved in from the Thames—as it did most afternoons.

An omnibus materialized out of the haze. It was filled with singing drunken men—a guild of journeymen from the north on an excursion to the big city. Their deep voices boomed out like an invisible chorus as Aloysius swerved to miss the vehicle with its heaving carthorses.

The brougham turned back into secluded Mayfair, where omnibuses were banned and only muffin-men, lavender-sellers and the occasional wandering musician with his barrow organ and monkey were allowed entry. Instantly it was quieter, and the smell of seclusion and money gave the insidious impression of safety. Lavinia, who had been staring out of the window, settled back against the leather upholstery.

They entered Bond Street, trotting past the booksellers and publishers and the gentlemen shoppers, several of whom tipped their hats at Lavinia—a woman strikingly alone at this hour of the day.

❦

Aloysius reined in the horses beside the covered entrance of the Burlington Arcade. Two beadles in distinctive black and red uniforms stood guard at the entrance to ensure that the Bond Street loungers—bored dandies and revellers who had emerged early from the gentlemen's clubs—did not enter the sedate and elegant arcade.

Above the entrance climbed a canopy of steel vines. Inside, gaslights illuminated the shops' displays of dresses, hats, jewelry, and all manner of frivolous objects craved by the very wealthy, creating an effect as seductive as Aladdin's cave.

Lavinia barely glanced at these treasures as she stepped out of the carriage. Instead, escorted by Aloysius through a milling group of curious male onlookers, one of whom whistled rudely, she made her way to John Brindley's bookstore at 29 Bond Street.

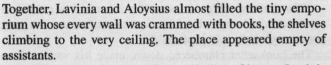

Together, Lavinia and Aloysius almost filled the tiny emporium whose every wall was crammed with books, the shelves climbing to the very ceiling. The place appeared empty of assistants.

Squeezing her way around several piles of boxes, Lavinia navigated a path to the high oak counter and peered over.

"I believe the American statesman Abraham Lincoln has published a volume of poetry?"

A diminutive man with a very large nose that divided his saturnine face into two distinct sides, sad and sadder, sat eclipsed by a large volume he held in his lap. He looked over his half-moon spectacles at her, then, shrugging indifferently, returned to his reading.

"I beg your pardon," Lavinia repeated, raising her voice in case the bookseller was hard of hearing, "I believe—"

"I heard you the first time, madam. And yes, Mr. Lincoln does write poetry, however he is a better politician than poet, therefore I suggest you save your pennies. Besides, you have the look of a Mrs. Gore reader." He sniffed contemptuously and pointed a long dirty fingernail to a pile of books on a table near the door.

"Appallingly prolific but salacious enough to sell; literature with the endurance of a gadfly. *Pin Money* is the one to read, or so they tell me."

Insulted, Lavinia placed her purse on the counter. "I detest Mrs. Gore's halfpenny scandals. I know what I wish to purchase and it is Mr. Lincoln's poetry. I am a great admirer of the statesman."

Sighing heavily, the bookseller slipped off his stool and, muttering, pushed a set of library steps along the sloping wooden floor at an excruciatingly slow pace. There, with surprising agility that reminded Lavinia of the bed bug she'd once seen under her father's microscope, he clawed his way up the steps and reached to a high shelf. He pulled out a book and shook it vigorously, releasing several dead moths that plummeted to the floor.

"*The Quincy Whig* journal—Mr. Lincoln has published several works in here, but I seem to remember there is only one of any merit. 'The Return.'"

The bookseller clambered down, made his way back to Lavinia, and placed the book firmly into her hands.

"One guinea. Outrageous exploitation on my behalf but literary stupidity, I find, is invariably expensive." He sounded irritated to make the sale at all.

As she reached for her money, Lavinia caught sight of a man outside. The familiarity of his profile drew her to the window where she peered through its grimy glass.

Colonel Huntington stood on the opposite curb, accompanied by a strikingly attractive young woman in an elegant overcoat and deep crimson satin crinoline. There was something exaggerated about the young woman's self-conscious gestures with her dramatically rouged cheeks and painted mouth. Pointing to a bonnet in a shop window, she laughed, then slipped her arm through the Colonel's and they continued their promenade.

Transfixed, Lavinia wondered for a moment whether it

actually was her husband, for she did not recognize the expression that transformed his face—a smile that suddenly rendered him ten years younger.

The coachman stepped in front of the window, blocking the mistress's view of the Colonel.

"This is no place for a gentlewoman at this time of day," he said. "Next thing, the Bond Street loungers will be taking pot shots at yer. I did try to warn yer." Moved by Lavinia's evident distress, Aloysius slipped into brogue.

Ignoring him, she continued to look blankly out the window. The girl could not be much older than herself. Could she be an old associate? A secret goddaughter? Perhaps the estranged child of a colleague? she thought, refusing to consider more obvious alternatives.

Aloysius gently tapped her on the arm. "Buy the pamphlet, madam. The gentleman is waiting."

Lavinia turned back to the bookseller. A supercilious expression played across his pinched features.

"A common doxie. They all float up from Curzon Street like there's no tomorrow, and not a literate one amongst them. Language of love? Language of the gutter more like. Do you know the Colonel?"

"I had assumed so," Lavinia replied coolly.

"My mistress is married to the gentleman," Aloysius said, wanting to protect her from further humiliation.

Shocked, the bookseller dropped the volume of poetry, now wrapped in butcher's paper, onto the counter. "The Colonel married, and to one so young? It wasn't announced in the *Gazette*."

Mortified, Aloysius stepped forward. "Mrs. Huntington, there are other bookstores."

The bookseller glanced at the coachman's livery then back at Lavinia. Suddenly he bowed, his long greasy locks falling toward his knees, his balding pate rendered visible.

"Forgive me, madam, I would not have insulted you with Mrs. Gore had I known. Perhaps I may interest you in George

Eliot's latest tome *Adam Bede*, or the *Rubaiyat* of Omar Khayyam—it is a fascinating read."

"I have got what I came for, and I cannot deny that it has been a most illuminating visit."

"We aim to please," he replied poker-faced, then pressed the guinea back into her hand. "It will give me great pleasure to charge the purchase directly to Colonel Huntington's account, madam."

17

James Huntington sat at the large center table, his papers scattered before him. His notebook—one of many—was open at a photograph of three Bakairi men involved in a dance ritual. He was immediately transported to that evening, the damp undergrowth of the rainforest scratching at his haunches, the smoke from the fires smarting his eyes, the hypnotic gyrations of the young men sending him into a trance. The wooden masks metamorphosed each of them into a god, and their hands carved stories from the smoky air about them, the beauty of their painted limbs transformed them into flying skeletons as the light faded between the trees.

This is my vocation, he thought, staring at the bound notebook, the edges of its pages stained faintly with smudges of red clay—a souvenir from his writing beside the Amazon river, the scent of the night still lingering on the paper. It is the only time I transcend my base nature, the only time my instincts are sharpened to the brink of survival. He looked over to the Indian leopard skin stretched in front of the fireplace—a hunting trophy. Of late he had felt his intellect deteriorating; he had slipped into the mannered wit and repartee of the gentleman, but craved the edge of danger that exploration brought. Such challenges kept him noble, and Lord knew he had been guilty of the most ignoble actions, he conceded, his mind returning to his recent encounter in Bond Street.

The Colonel reached for his snuffbox—a miniature silver casket in the shape of a traveling chest, an heirloom from his father—and placed a large pinch of the opiated tobacco into the crook of his thumb and forefinger. Lifting it to his nostrils, he inhaled deeply. An intoxicating wave swept through his sinuses and hit the back of his brain. The rustle of a skirt and the soft wash of lavender did not make him open his eyes.

"Thank you for visiting Aidan, his nanny told me you read him a story." Lavinia's voice broke his reverie, he smiled up at her.

"As any father would."

"I thought I might find you in here." She held her new book under one arm.

"Indeed, my dear. I am somewhat overwhelmed by the plethora of research that seems to stare at me more accusingly with every passing day. How was your church visit?"

"Attending St. George's is always an illuminating experience."

"As it should be: that building has sanctified more scandalous liaisons than a bordello."

Lavinia pulled off her kid gloves and observed her husband far more closely than her casual air suggested.

"You seem jovial," she said.

"And why not? I spent a pleasant morning with my accountant, lunched with several colleagues of the scientific persuasion, then ended the afternoon at the Athenaeum where I studied the *Times*, the *Daily Telegraph*, and the *Gazette* with much curiosity."

She wondered how he could lie with such panache, but then the possibility that his visit to Bond Street might have an innocent explanation occurred to her.

"I visited a bookshop after church." A questioning ran under the tone of her voice. "A bookshop on Bond Street."

The Colonel allowed the languid effect of the snuff to exorcise astonishment from his face. "So I gather from that dubious tome you are brandishing at me." Squinting, he could just see the title: *Quincy Whig*. More Irish politics, he thought, his heart sinking. "Rather late for shopping, Lavinia."

"Apparently so. Apparently it is an opprobrious time for a respectable married woman to be seen in Bond Street. Naturally, a different standard of decency applies for respectable married gentlemen."

The Colonel rose from his chair and strolled to the window. If there was anything he abhorred it was hypocrisy; besides, Lavinia's lack of sophistication was beginning to annoy him. He didn't want to argue; their confrontation of the night before had cast a gloom upon his entire day. In fact, it had been this ill humor that had compelled him to visit the brothel in the first place. The Colonel felt aggrieved; surely a gentleman's private actions should remain private?

Outside, it had begun to rain—a wet drizzle that transformed the lit trees into blurred gray-green infantrymen, reminding him of the harsh beauty of the Crimea.

"I trust the book was worth risking your reputation in such a way?" he asked his wife.

"Indeed. Without my even opening its pages, it has already proved to be educationally invaluable."

Determined to shift the conversation to safer ground, the Colonel walked back to his desk. Gazing down upon his notes, he couldn't help but envy the comparative ease of sexual and marital union in the Amazon.

Lavinia followed his gaze. "Are these your research notes?"

"I have finally begun to collate my work."

"You have organized the chapters?"

"I am uncertain whether to prioritize the habitat and customs of the natives, or begin with chapters describing the fauna and flora. It is altogether overwhelming."

The great collection of notes and illustrations stretched before him. Jumbled in a chaotic parody of order, it felt like a metaphor for his own life: a superficially organized façade concealing duplicitous pandemonium. It occurred to the Colonel that he no longer had the youth or the patience to contemplate the task of unraveling such confusion.

Folding back her long sleeves, Lavinia thumbed through the sketchbooks and their handwritten footnotes, scrawled in almost illegible fashion.

"Do you wish this to be a scientific treatise or to be perceived as a book for the layman?" she asked. She paused at a photographic portrait of a youth leaning upon his spear, his eyes and cheeks covered in red daub, bamboo sticks protruding from his cheeks like tiger whiskers. His direct gaze was a curious combination of intense interest and a complete lack of self-consciousness. This is Adam before the Fall, Lavinia thought, confrontational, defiant, yet hiding nothing. She realized the native reminded her of the young Irish coachman.

The Colonel looked over her shoulder and his scent drifted across her: a familiar musk with an undertone of something sharper—the sickening smell of cheap perfume. Lavinia continued to look at the notebook, concealing the uneasiness that played across her features.

"Naturally I aspire to reach many readers," James said, "although recognition of my work by the scientific community is of the utmost importance."

"Then I propose you structure the work as the journey of one man and describe the flora and the behaviors of the animals, insects, and birds as they play a role in his quest."

The Colonel was absentmindedly turning a seashell in his fingers. At Lavinia's suggestion, he sighed and sank heavily back into his chair.

"There are several notebooks telling of my time with the Indians, describing their family structures, their eating habits, their hunting, their rituals."

Momentarily forgetting her anger Lavinia placed her hand on his shoulder. "It would capture the imagination of the reader, James. Pagan practices are always of interest. The more barbaric the better; I think it must provide the illusion of moral superiority."

"Lavinia, please remember these are rituals not pagan practices."

He strolled over to a glass case and carefully lifted out a wooden mask. Long dried reeds hung from the carved face, trailing on the ground. "I was given this mask by the Bakairi, and a quantity of hallucinogen—ayahuasca—to evoke their gods whenever I might wish."

"And have you?"

"Not yet, but I will, once I have completed my studies."

He held the mask up to his face for a moment; by the time he dropped it, his expression had altered entirely. A youthful vigor had infused his features but his eyes appeared focused on a place far beyond the room.

"Their rituals invite their gods—river spirits—to visit and give them spiritual guidance for the following years. The shamans drink the brew of the ayahuasca to invoke the spirits. When the hallucinogen has taken hold of the body and the shaman begins a trance he dons a mask like this. The natives believe the spirit enters the mask and speaks through the shaman. It is quite frightening, and there were moments when I feared for my life. It was only due to the bravery of my young translator that I was allowed to attend at all."

"Then this shall be the climax of your narrative. To reach the gods, to communicate directly with these spirits—there can be nothing more extraordinary. Please, James, let me help you. You know your work is an inspiration to me."

"Would it make you more content, here in Mayfair? Where there is so much social engagement during the season?"

"For whose who are invited. I do not yet belong to any salon, nor do I have the female confidantes a young woman of my age requires . . ."

"This will change. Lady Morgan shall provide you with associates."

"Please, it would bring me great pleasure to work along-side you."

He looked at her, then pushed a pile of loose papers along the table. "These are the notes on each individual mask—each one represents a spirit. Now forgive me, I must take my leave. I am late for an early supper at the Carlton. Apparently Henry Smith is to join Lord Oswald and myself and you know how droll he can be. Don't wait up."

As the Colonel made his way down to the entrance hall, he reflected on his foolhardiness in allowing Lavinia entry into the last bastion of his bachelorhood. Still, the exercise would let her explore the nuances of the masculine mind, he concluded, which could only save her from further disappointment.

❦

The grandfather clock—an eighteenth-century pillar of wood, glass, and brass—chimed six. Lavinia, glancing down at the mask, thought how irrelevant social conventions became when set against the morals of other cultures. Nevertheless, she regretted losing her chance to confront her husband about the encounter she had witnessed earlier that afternoon.

She lifted the mask. It smelled of the earth, rich and pungent, a faint odor of burnt charcoal spiced with an undertone of something acrid. With a certain trepidation, she placed it over her face then glanced into a looking glass.

The primitive simplicity of its symmetry became a scream-ing caricature when framed by her black hair, and her lilac gown billowing out beneath created a carnival-like effect. Only this carnival character was not Venetian or Roman, but something far more primal; not a God to whom one prayed but a Goddess from whom one begged mercy.

❦

Tranquillity settled like thick pollen across the books and papers. It was an atmosphere in which Lavinia was quite comfortable;

a world of intellectual labor where the forays of a curious mind were expressed in an abundance of small details, each linked in an eccentric grammar of personal meaning and reference.

> *I arrived some fourteen days ago, after a long trek through forbidding jungle, a relentless swelter of insects and rampant fecundity. My guide, Gilo, an experienced hunter of both Portuguese and Mayan extraction, was patience itself, tolerating my naivety and my dark moods. He was constantly alert to every poisonous leaf or dangerous insect or reptile.*
>
> *It was a relief to reach the open cut in the forest, a clearing that indicated the presence of fellow human beings. At first I was unsure this was the place—there was little visible to the unpracticed eye, but Gilo, squatting down beside me, indicated the vine ropes hanging from trees that served as access to vantage points used to warn of danger.*
>
> *I will never forget the eerie sensation of being watched but seeing no evidence of the watcher. It is a sensation I have also experienced as a soldier; perhaps we humans have a sixth sense for it. I am convinced that a civilized person must depend upon his primitive instincts in such situations. I knew I was in extreme danger, and I could see from Gilo's expression that he felt the same, which was of no comfort.*
>
> *I cannot tell you how long we squatted there in the long grass waiting for some sort of signal of greeting, but it was long enough for the sun to have almost set.*

How did it feel to endanger your life like that? It must be exhilarating, an experience that brought all the trivialities of life into perspective, Lavinia concluded. How she craved to accompany James on such an expedition. How wonderful to be so sharply alive!

By the time she had finished arranging the first book of

notes into the semblance of a chapter, it was past midnight. James still hadn't returned. Wearily, she rested her head on the desk. Surely a man with such an insatiable lust for adventure and challenge was not of the nature to settle? Perhaps he had been inflicted with the kind of infatuation middle-aged men often felt for young girls. Or was it merely that he desired an heir? Her husband was an enigma, and, despite her new anxiety, one she still found fascinating.

She traced the outline of a dried blossom, a tropical flower James had discovered near the shaman's hut. He had named it *Luna albus*. Her husband was a collector: of beauty, of rarity, and of experience, she decided.

She began to consider how to resurrect their physical relationship, but before she reached a conclusion she fell into a light sleep, her head lolling against her arm. She dreamed she was running through a dark maze of corridors, running toward a figure she could barely see ahead. As he slipped around a corner, she caught sight of his shadow thrown against a wall—a huge bull's head with clearly delineated horns, and a thick neck that tapered into the slim torso of a man. The Minotaur, the lost chimera.

Why am I not afraid, Lavinia asked her dreaming self. Why am I drawn to him so irresistibly?

18

Los Angeles, 2002

Julia pulled the Lexus into the driveway and switched off the ignition. Everything appeared as it should: the sprinklers had automatically switched on at five; the cat next door, an overfed ginger animal, leapt down from the wall to greet her as he did every evening, twisting himself around her ankles; the chimes hanging off the jacaranda tree rang in the breeze. There was only one element that was disturbingly out of place—the mail protruding from the mailbox. Usually Klaus collected it in the morning.

If Julia had paused then, if she had stood immobilized on the lawn, her suede sandals sprayed every 20.8 seconds as the sprinklers continued their relentless rotation; if she had taken this crystallized instance to step out of her life and analyze the sequence of events that had already punctuated her week, she might have had a premonition. But she didn't. There was no reason to, for this is how we view the world, through the lens of our relationships—a perspective that is nearly always tragically subjective. It was a notion Julia herself subscribed to. She was a woman who had no cause to doubt the continuity of her life: a successful scientist, a contented wife, and an expectant mother. She reached the front door and, with her briefcase in one hand and the mail gripped between chin and neck, opened the door with her key.

Throwing the letters onto a side table, she noticed a thread of packing straw on the ground. She picked it up. Klaus must have received a package from Belgium, she deduced, pleased with her detective work.

"Klaus?"

Her voice fell flat against the walls, sounding pathetic and doubtful. It was only when she walked into the lounge room that Klaus's absence became achingly apparent.

"Presence doesn't just live in the material," Julia had once reasoned to Carla, pleasantly tipsy on the veranda one late summer afternoon. "We leave a whole stream of existence behind us, a constellation of evidence—invisible particles of skin, heat, breath, lingering sound, hair in plugholes. Then there are the stains, the dents, the scratches—the markers of passion, of arguments, of lovemaking, of the clumsy, stumbling move into a first embrace and the clumsy stumbling step backwards out of the last. If there is an afterlife, it must exist in how we are remembered. Our spirit can only live on in the others we have touched—those who have loved us and those who have hated us."

This was the hypothesis Julia had arrived at at the age of forty. An age when she assumed she would be safe, when she had known loss and thought that she would never have to know it again; would never dream of a parent or lover only to wake to the awful realization that they were now absent.

His chair's missing, she thought now, looking around wildly, terrified that they'd been burgled. Her mind spiraled as she tried to calculate what else had been stolen. The 1930s dentist's chair was one of the defining possessions Klaus had brought to their marriage, an icon from his student days in Brussels.

The portrait of Lavinia Huntington was still there, but around it were several blank spaces where prints had once been—a Van Gogh, an Aubrey Beardsley, a Chagall—all belonging to Klaus.

She stared at the wall; she knew it had changed but her brain wouldn't allow her to comprehend the enormity of what had happened. Suddenly other differences became clear. All her husband's books were gone from the shelves, leaving gaps like broken teeth in the dark oak, her own volumes left tilted and abandoned.

She ran outside, out into the evening sunshine that illuminated the fine smudge of smoke from someone's bonfire that filled the air. Someone whose world had not been inverted like a cheap paperweight so the snow was now falling upwards, against gravity, against all rationality.

Julia stumbled into the writing studio and a dusty emptiness. The stripped walls clasped the shadows of her husband's secrets like a faint tracing of fig leaves. The worktable was naked except for the abandoned wood vise, which now seemed to be yawning in sudden fear.

Julia's heartbeat hammered against her eardrums. Outside a cicada began to scream. Now desperate for clues, she raced back to the house and up to their bedroom, the last bastion of intimate terrain.

The door swung open; there was a new chip in the frame. The cupboard was ajar. All of Klaus's clothes had been taken except for a pair of trousers she'd given him which he'd never liked.

She flung herself on the bed, her hands clasping the mound of her womb. Rolling toward his side, she noticed the letter. Neatly folded into an envelope, her name printed on the front in her husband's distinctive left-handed scrawl: *Julia*.

Lifting herself onto her elbows, Julia stared at it, his handwriting an obscene point of normalcy in the emotional turmoil that pounded through her. Like a plot point in a fable she wondered what would happen if she didn't open the letter, if she acted as if she hadn't found it—would her life continue unchanged?

Taking a shuddering breath, she reached for the phone, the unopened letter sitting on her lap. She dialed his cell phone and waited until the dial tone finally cut any possible thread between them.

Dear Julia,

I don't know how many times I have started this letter. Too many times. It's like the thousand times I've tried to get the courage to begin this conversation, but have failed in the face of your happiness. Your blind belief. When I think back over our marriage I don't know how I got in so deep. You are so much more evolved than me. You're so lucky you know what you want. I never have really. I think for years I have allowed myself to be defined by your needs. How you see me. It's only now that I've finally woken up to my own potential—both the lack of it and the true extent of it. I have always been a secret coward. Forgive me.

I'm leaving you. Wish I'd had the bravery to wait for you and tell you to your face, but that moment has passed.

You're a survivor, you are so much stronger than me, you're going to be okay, you and the baby. I will always love you and maybe one day we can be friends.

Klaus.

Julia screamed, a wail that filled the house like blood, her husband's presence tearing away from her in the very anguish of the sound.

Doubling over, she vomited on the bed cover. Still retching, she gathered it up and ran to the bathroom where she dumped it into the bath. As she sat on the edge of the bathtub, a strange practicality possessed her. She walked back into the bedroom.

He'll come back. Just talk to him, talk to him.

She rang again. His cell phone was still switched off. Furious, she threw her phone. It bounced off the wall like a cartoon sequence.

Julia retrieved the phone and called Klaus's agent, keeping her voice as neutral as she could. The agent had no idea where Klaus was, nor that anything was wrong. She started dialing his parents, then realized it was 4 a.m. in Antwerp. It was then that she thought to call Carla.

❧

"Carla?"

Grief choked her instantly, as if verbalizing what had happened would make his absence final. *I have been left; he has gone.*

"Julia? I can hardly hear you."

"Klaus . . ."

"He's left you."

Carla sounded composed, detached. Julia stared into the receiver. Her reaction didn't make sense; it was as illogical as Klaus's empty cupboards.

"How do you know?"

"I know because he's here, with me."

"With you? Why?" Her voice sounded tinny and melodramatic even to herself. One hand pinched the skin of the other until it was white.

"Oh Julia . . . I wanted to tell you, I tried to tell you . . ."

"Have you and Klaus been having an affair?"

Beat. Outside the window, the sound of a lawnmower whipped up the air, an absurdly ordinary noise in the midst of a dissolving world.

"An affair implies that it's finite. But yes, Klaus and I are lovers."

Pain stabbed a path across Julia's midriff in short razorsharp jabs. Part of her refused to believe in the current reality; it was as if her closest friend and husband had decided, for whatever perverse reason, to test her affection.

She listened to Carla's breathing, this woman on the other end of the line to whom she had revealed all her emotional ambiguities, all of the information women trade and entrust in the binding intimacy men rarely experience. An intimacy Julia had imagined would be a constant factor in her future, no matter what, now profoundly betrayed.

"When did it happen? When I was away?"

"Julia, do we have to go over this now?"

"I have to know! I want to know exactly when and how it happened!"

"You're being irrational. The main thing is that it happened. We're lovers, we love each other."

"Is he there?"

"Stop screaming."

"Is he there? I want to speak to him. I want to speak to my husband!"

She could hear them conferring; his distinctive voice with its flattened phonetics made her heart rate quicken. A sharp cramp shot through her womb. When he came to the phone he was silent.

"Klaus, tell me that it's all a lie, a stupid mistake."

She could hear him struggling to find the words.

"You have the letter," he said at last. "I don't want to see you. I *can't* see you. This isn't only about you, Julia, you are not the only victim here. Try and understand."

Listening intently, she found it hard to reconcile the detached tone of his voice with the man she thought she knew.

"You're leaving me, that's all I understand at this moment. You're leaving me . . ." she gasped around the great hollow sobs that kept betraying her.

There was silence then the click of the receiver.

A sharp contraction toppled her—she fell back on the bed, clutching at herself. By the time she crawled on her hands and knees to the bathroom, her thighs were streaming with blood.

19

Julia lay in the hospital bed, floating on an analgesic balloon. It hovered, shiny, fleshy-pink and obscene, like a profane zeppelin, its great billowing circumference pushing everything of the outside world into irrelevance.

"Hey Julia, I know you're awake."

Naomi's voice echoed faintly in Julia's mind, each consonant falling upon the skin of the zeppelin and causing it to ripple like the surface of a pond. Regardless, Julia drifted along, her limbs deliciously leaden by a drug-induced torpor. A fruity scent reminiscent of oranges and violets floated across the bed.

"Julia?"

She opened her eyes reluctantly. Naomi was holding a vase crowded with lilies and freesias, waiting for Julia to catch the perfume. Satisfied her friend was now fully awake, Naomi placed the flowers onto the bedside table.

"So, you're back in the land of the living." Naomi studied

the geneticist. She looked truly dreadful: her eyes were puffy from crying; stress had etched a rigidity into the lower half of her face, giving the impression that she was perpetually clenching her jaw; her hair was unwashed and straggly; and she looked as if she'd lost at least seven pounds. But what was most devastating was the intense vulnerability that radiated from her. The layers Julia had carefully constructed over the years—irony, wariness, humor, curiosity—appeared to have been erased overnight, and the energetic professional had been replaced by an emaciated parody. It was as if Julia had relinquished her body entirely and now a wax effigy lay in her place, with huge rabbit eyes staring up out of a shrunken face.

"I lost the baby." Julia's voice was a monotone stripped of emotion.

"I'm so sorry, sweetie."

"I can't imagine life without Klaus. There is such a level of unreality about this."

"I'll take you away. We'll rent a house in Mexico and make voodoo dolls out of his clothes. I have the perfect hatpin. You'll recover. It doesn't feel like it now, but you will. It's not the end of the world."

Pushing Naomi's hand away, Julia flew into a rage.

"It *is* the end of the world. It's the end of *my* world. I love him, do you understand? I want him back. I want my child back, my life . . ." Her voice broke into harsh dry sobbing.

Undone by such grief, Naomi felt helpless. She stroked Julia's arm. "He's probably not coming back, Julia."

Julia swung back to her, suddenly frenetic. "You've seen him?"

"I've spoken to him."

"Does he know about the baby?"

Naomi nodded, then, finding it too painful to look into Julia's eyes, averted her gaze to the temperature chart pinned above the bed. "My ex-husband knows a great hit man," she joked. Again, the inappropriate comment rattled down to the floor.

"You know, I felt the baby move inside of me before . . ." her voice faltered again. "He was so real, so alive. . . . They've done all these tests, it could have been my uterus, my cervix, they just don't know. But I do. It was shock, Naomi. How could he? How could they?" Julia whispered.

A nurse passed by, wheeling an old woman whose drip preceded her like a victorious trident. As she caught sight of Julia and Naomi, she broke into a Yiddish lullaby in the clear childish voice of an eight year old. The two silently watched the old woman's progress, Julia with her eyes, Naomi with her smile stuttering brilliantly like a faulty fluorescent, both secretly interpreting her appearance as a bad omen.

"You know, the ironic thing is that they've put me on antidepressants but they take ten days to kick in. I could die of grief in that time."

She struggled to sit up, the sedatives still hazing her brain. Naomi squeezed her hand, but Julia's unhappiness continued to ooze out of her like a slow poison.

"But think of the benefits," Naomi replied. "A guilt-free medically justified selfishness during which you can indulge yourself outrageously and your friends will be expected to support you . . ."

Encouraged by what she thought was a faint gleam in Julia's eyes, she continued. "Seriously, though, they will help you prioritize what's really important."

Julia stared blankly at the wall, then suddenly her voice emerged, urgent, frantic. "He won't stay with her, you'll see, it's just a temporary thing. Fear maybe—or maybe the pressure was simply too much. He'll come to his senses."

"Julia, it was Klaus who rang to tell me what had happened. Sweetheart, I don't think he's coming back."

Julia's skin seemed to gray visibly, she leaned across and grasped Naomi's arm, her nails digging into her skin.

"It was a boy, tiny but perfectly formed. I'm going to fight. Do you understand? I'm going to fight to get my husband back."

20

Mayfair, 1861

"I regard matrimony in much the same manner as I regard the purchase of stock—there are risks involved and patience may be required, but, assuming I have researched the proposed investment thoroughly, I am usually confident that sooner or later my returns will justify the initial outlay." Colonel Huntington leaned back in the leather armchair, easing open a button of his paisley-printed waistcoat to aid the digestion of an excellent supper of jugged hare and claret.

"You're not as phlegmatic as you would like to appear, Huntington. I have to confess, up until this marriage of yours, you have been extraordinarily secretive about your trysts. Why, Charles and I had quite given up speculating what your pleasures might be." Henry Smith, a jovial man in his early fifties, retorted after belching loudly, spreading his weight a little more territorially than the younger man. He felt like pulling rank after the sanctimonious lecture the Colonel had bored them with throughout the meal—a treatise on the responsibility of the colonial powers, primarily the English. It was an issue Henry felt personally responsible for, given his involvement with Clive and the Colonial Office. "After all, I don't believe you married for money yourself. Nor beauty, I'm told. Youth, perhaps?"

An aggrieved expression clouded the Colonel's brow. The third member of the party, Charles Sutton, sensing the dismay that had temporarily floored the normally loquacious anthropologist, leaned forward and refilled his glass with more of the excellent port he had purchased for his friends.

"My dear fellow, that's a blow below the belt. Mrs. Huntington has her charms."

"Indeed she has," the valiant husband added, then fell awkwardly silent.

"She reminds me of an unbroken colt," Charles said. "A great deal of potential which simply necessitates some reining in." He turned to the still pained anthropologist. "Quite seriously, Huntington, she appears to possess an inherent sophistication that merely requires some tutoring."

"So you married for love?" Henry Smith snorted derisively. The idea was absurd.

"A manner of love, or perhaps affection might be the more apt term," the Colonel responded. "I will concede, however, that my initial impulse was emotional, believe it or not, Harry. I now realize that I was most certainly in the grip of that sentiment which affects gentlemen of a certain vintage. But I cannot tell you what it means to me to have a son. To see oneself in another, to know that one creates wealth and reputation for a reason other than sheer egotism."

Charles, English to the marrow, coughed politely and tried to diffuse the intensity of the moment by distracting himself with the color of the wine. Conversely, Henry concluded that this was a providential opportunity to gather some potential slander that could possibly prove useful in the future. He nodded encouragingly.

"But there was another influence," the Colonel continued, aware that his uncharacteristic revelations were leading him into a confession he would doubtless regret. "I had tired of the travel, of the battles, of having little but the maintenance of properties to hold me to Mayfair and Inverness. In short, I needed anchoring."

"Indeed, a wife and child will provide an anchor—and a short chain," Henry interjected, thinking of his own estranged wife and seven children.

"And there is the enthusiasm of youth. Lavinia has that at

the very least. And she also has a sharp intellect, and in relation to my work she is quite the inspiration."

"Ah, but do you love her?" Henry insisted, amused by the debating of such a nebulous subject.

Several men sitting nearby turned at his raised voice. One, immaculate in tails and a silk top hat, who looked as if he had come directly from the theater, glanced critically at the group through his monocle then turned to his companion and laughed.

The Colonel, ignoring the slight, drew heavily on his cigar before answering. "Love? Don't be ridiculous; you know as well as I that love is the domain of Lotharios under thirty."

"Come now, Huntington, however private you might be, I believe I'm correct in surmising that you have dedicated a good portion of your life thus far to the sensual pursuits?" Henry continued.

"I have been fortunate to have had the means to do so, indeed."

At which each of the three gentlemen fell into his own private reverie: Huntington reflecting on his past debaucheries and whether they had, as had been suggested, rendered him incapable of deeper emotion; Henry on his financial difficulties, the result of his inability to control his own baser passions; and Charles, suddenly overwhelmed by the epiphany that he had never loved and was, quite possibly, incapable of such an emotion. Was this fortunate or not? After glancing surreptitiously at his distracted companions, Charles consoled himself with the observation that at least he enjoyed a stable, if uneventful, existence and was probably the richest man at the table. The glum lull was broken by a reveller who drunkenly began a clumsy rendition of Beethoven's *Ode to Joy* on the club's piano.

"Bessemer's converter—what do you make of it?" the Colonel barked suddenly. Henry, for a moment completely disoriented, struggled to grasp the connection between love and the manufacture of steel.

"You mean the machine he has set up?"

"I do. What are the commercial advantages?"

"Well, it may be mere knives and forks now, but I dare say there shall be a greater industrial application in the future. The stocks will be floated, and when they are, I, for one, shall be buying." With what capital he had no idea, but, vindicated by the authority of his own declaration, Henry sat back, relieved that the conversation had moved to a more masculine theme.

"It's bound to have something to do with railways; that's the new world you know—to use industry to carve mystery up into small palatable pieces," Charles offered. "Soon there will be nowhere left where Man has not been, except for your Amazon, Huntington. That shall remain impenetrable for some time, I should imagine."

Charles's ironic tone left the Colonel pondering whether his friend meant the Amazon as a metaphor for his own impenetrable psyche.

"Colonel James Huntington?"

The trio looked up. A young man clad in a black evening coat with a white silk waistcoat, satin top hat in hand, bowed elegantly.

"Sir, allow me to introduce myself: Mr. Hamish Campbell. I was Lady Morgan's companion at that delightful supper at your home several weeks ago."

"No need to remind me, sir, you were quite memorable," the Colonel responded dryly.

Campbell indicated his companion, a tall, pencil-thin man of about thirty years, dressed in what appeared to be a Grecian-style smock with a dark purple velvet cap rakishly pulled over one ear. "My friend Lord Edward Valery, a painter of socialites and other dubious beauties."

The men laughed.

"Campbell, you do me a disservice," the painter complained in a booming baritone that almost had the others looking around for a more corpulent figure. "Trust me, my friends, I can make any wife ravishing under my brush."

"And not just under his brush," Campbell added, invoking more laughter and a coughing fit from Henry Smith. "I swear he's well worth the investment," Campbell finished, grinning broadly, "but we didn't come over to sell you Valery's services."

He pulled over a vacant chair and sat himself down. The Colonel, amused by his audacity, put it down to youth. On closer examination, Hamish Campbell looked far younger than he remembered.

"I have read several of your articles since that dinner, sir," Campbell declared loudly, "and I must say I am impressed."

The Colonel, not believing the student actually followed his work, stayed silent.

Undeterred, Campbell went on. "The article in *The Gentleman* magazine on the Amazon tribes' rite of initiation into manhood was wickedly intriguing, and I particularly enjoyed your treatise in *The Spectator* on the moral responsibility of the colonial powers."

The Colonel glanced at Henry, who smiled wryly.

"You are ambitious indeed, sir. At your age I was soldiering and chasing skirt," Huntington condescended, but the young scholar was not to be deterred.

In truth, he found the youth's praise a little intoxicating.

Sensing some influence, Campbell leaned forward, his eyes glinting. "I have aspirations myself, sir. It would be a great honor if you cared to show me your collection of artifacts. I am going up to Oxford next year and I would like to include reference to them in my studies."

There is no greater flattery than the informed admiration of one's achievements, and certainly the Colonel was aware of this as he noted the charms of the young man before him: the faint hue that colored his cheeks, and the depth of intelligence in his eyes. Eyes that were curiously almond in shape and sat beneath a dark brow that only served to heighten the illusion of light dancing around the youth's uncovered head. If he were to take on an acolyte, he could have not asked for a fairer one, the Colonel observed.

Before replying, he ordered another bottle of the fine port they were drinking. Hamish Campbell settled into the lounge chair, assuming that this was a signal that he and his associate had permission to linger at the table. But the Colonel had other ideas; the old sensation of sexual play had begun to rap at his veins and he did not care for the implications. Charles, recognizing the conflict behind the slight smile that now played across his oldest friend's lips, broke the uncomfortable pause.

"We were just discussing the idea of marrying for love. Such a modern concept."

Campbell tipped back his head and laughed, displaying a manly jaw—an agreeable counterbalance to the Byronic curls he affected. "I utterly agree. Marriage should be a cold-blooded economic exchange. For example, Valery here, who owns a small estate in Buckinghamshire, has been trying to hook a rich Jewess whose grandfather was a furrier, but she's decided not to have him! Why, the world is topsy-turvy and refuses to be righted. As for myself, I am young enough to relish the guidance of a mature, and preferably wealthy, woman."

"And Lady Morgan is the doyenne of such guidance. Trust me, you are in the hands of an expert," the Colonel parried.

Campbell blushed, momentarily losing his composure for the first time in the conversation, which led the Colonel to wonder whether he was in fact the aristocrat's lover.

"So you will allow me to view your collection, sir?" Campbell returned to his original quest, now more confident of his host's approval.

"The artifacts are of a suggestive and primitive nature. A man must have a full comprehension of the culture from whence they spring, otherwise the viewing of them is a wasted exercise."

"As I mentioned before, I have a burgeoning interest and am well-informed. But to learn from a man who has been there himself, who has surrendered all civilization in order to see through the eyes of another . . ."

Campbell's flattery threatened to become excessive. Glancing at his companions' wry expressions, the Colonel decided to save the boy from potential ridicule.

"Give me your card and I may send for you." And with that, Hamish Campbell was forced to be content.

～❦～

The moonlight glittered in the puddles, broken only by the sweep of the coach wheels. The night tribe of the homeless and itinerant workers had emerged, loitering around railway stations and the gin shops with their smoky crowded windows, hoping to beg a penny from the emerging carousers. The carriage swung into Regent Street and the Colonel watched a chestnut seller pushing his barrel wearily home. Nearby, a family of gypsies huddled around a fire; their distant expressions, those of a lost people, illuminated by the dancing flames.

If Colonel Huntington felt any empathy for the dispossessed it was this: that no one should suffer the chill of an English winter's night. Like many members of his class, he saw no inherent nobility in the impoverished. He had been educated to believe such disparity was inherent. He did not regard the poor as his equals in intellect or humanity, witnessing, as he had often described, the great wash of human degradation pouring daily into London: the country fieldworkers; the swathes of Eastern European Jews that arrived, swarthy and exotic, at the docks; the thousands trying their luck at the new industries with only a lucky few pushing their way up through the rigid social strata.

It would have never occurred to the anthropologist to apply his studies to his own race and the inequalities it perpetuated. Instead, he chose to believe that those who ruled were born to rule. Yet, paradoxically, the Colonel was tolerant of the mercantile class whose ingenuity had begun to erode centuries of order, even as he was aware that individuals like himself—the landed gentry whose own work ethic had been destroyed—were slowly but inevitably heading toward extinction. This was the decay of the natural order, of this he was certain.

As a representative of this brave new order, young Hamish Campbell held a fascination for Colonel Huntington. The son of an industrialist, who surely had not foreseen his son would aspire to the lofty ambitions of science, Hamish Campbell was energy, he was the future. Unlike himself, the Colonel observed, with his own decadent breeding.

Perhaps this was the real natural order, he pondered, an evolution that favored adaptation, that favored the creature who dared, fought, and schemed successfully. He had observed this phenomenon in the Crimea, in the Amazon, and in the Guildhall, and nothing he had seen in his travels and in the lives around him had encouraged him to question his growing conviction.

The coach passed an infamous molly house, one the Colonel had visited before his marriage. Through the mist he made out two young men loitering outside. One glanced over at the passing brougham, seeming to sense its occupant's interest across the square.

How did he know? Do I give out some invisible signal? the Colonel wondered as he moved away from the carriage window, frightened the youth might be some past furtive conquest. Perhaps I am denying my own sensibility, he thought bleakly. The uniqueness of individuals and their desires was an issue that had occupied him much of late. It wasn't just his studies of other cultures that had led him to such musings, but also the manner in which many of his peers lived and loved, often exploiting others. And what was morality other than the order of the day when set against a broader canvas? Why, he had even read of tribes that defined sexuality in terms of three groupings.

This and other dilemmas coursed through him, churning up nostalgia for a simpler time when he would, without hesitation, have knocked twice on the carriage to direct the coachman to Leicester Square and Kate Hamilton's infamous brothel where his predilections would be catered for without judgment.

Lavinia was asleep, her head and torso slumped over his papers. The Colonel watched her. There was a defenselessness about her that was arousing. Her cheek rested awkwardly on her wrist, the pagoda-embroidered sleeve bunched beneath. Her eyelashes fluttered slightly with each inhalation: ebony against marble. Lavinia's skin was so pale one could almost see the blue of her blood flowing beneath it. He marveled at how the demarcations of adulthood could be suspended in sleep. Now, before him, he could see the child he had first met—her skirts swirling in the wind outside the vicarage, her curious gaze.

He thought that he would like to make love to her now, but knew there would come a point during their caresses when his detachment would erase his desire completely. He could not help himself. I have disappointed her, he thought, profoundly saddened. And placing her sleeping arms around his neck, he carried her up to her bed.

21

Los Angeles, 2002

At her gynecologist's insistence, Julia took two weeks' leave. During the first seven days of her husband's absence, she couldn't bear to think at all. The depth of her despair surprised her. She simply didn't want to confront the realities of her changed life. I'm in shock, she kept telling herself, soon

I will be angry. At least anger will be better than this bleak, flat sensation.

Between bouts of uncontrollable weeping, she watched endless cartoons on the Disney Channel. She didn't just watch; she became the cartoon characters; mouthing the simplistic dialogue, driving in the cartoon car through the cartoon world, with its postcard reds, lime greens, and acid yellows. Willing herself into a fictional character was a comforting sensation; it transported her into an acerbic two-dimensional parody of all that she knew. Julia didn't want to be human any longer. More exactly, she didn't want to be.

Meanwhile, the frantic sensation of missing Klaus deceived her into thinking he must be feeling the same bereavement. It was the habit of intimacy that Julia pined for: sharing observations of their respective days; his body at night; the innate expectation of being able to turn around and sound out an idea, make a joke, tell him about her work. It was as if she'd lost a limb and yet the shadow image of that limb stayed fatally glued to her. It was a searing loss amplified by the miscarriage.

❧

"Whatever I did, consciously or unconsciously, I can change, I know I can. Klaus? Are you still there?"

Sitting in the yard, watching a determined troop of ants dragging the twitching body of a dying beetle into the grass, Julia tried to read her husband's emotions through the sound of his breath down the phone. His silence seemed to echo the great space that yawned between them.

"Julia, look, I'm really sorry you had a miscarriage, but the dynamic between us has been skewed for years."

"I thought we were happy. How was I meant to know when you never said anything?"

"That's the point I'm making. You should have known; you should have had the time and the empathy to realize—"

"I'm not a mind-reader."

"It was always about you and your career. Half the time I couldn't tell you how disempowered I felt; I was frightened to burden you with yet another problem to solve."

"But I supported you, so you could stay at home and write . . ."

"There you go, undermining me again."

"Klaus, come home, please. I need you."

"Haven't you heard a word I've said? Carla's my chance at having a full life, my chance at functioning as a complete person. Even my work has started to take off . . . I'm sorry."

The line clicked then went dead. Frantically, Julia redialed the number but Klaus had switched off his cell. She lay curled up on the grass, the sun burning her skin, phoning again and again until finally he answered.

⁂

They sat awkwardly at the kitchen table, the three of them: Klaus on one side, Naomi at the head of the table, Julia facing Klaus.

Julia had put on a dress for the occasion, the first she'd worn for weeks, and painted her eyes and lips. Somehow the desire to appear beautiful was important—to make him realize what he'd lost. It was the strategy that had propelled her through the morning—albeit a perilous one—and now her stomach clenched with increasing nervousness.

She was unable to stop herself from staring at her husband, who couldn't look back. He appears so unchanged, Julia thought, still believing that if she could only reach out and take his hand everything would miraculously revert to how it was before.

"Klaus, this is ridiculous. I mean—look at us. This is us—me and you." She tried smiling, but instead a grimace cracked her face. "I forgive you and Carla," she went on. "I was away, you were both left alone, these things happen. But nothing's irreversible. We have so much . . ." Julia faltered, loathing her wheedling tone, her bargaining, when she knew that there was a border beyond which emotions could not be negotiated.

"How long?" She almost whispered the question. She didn't really want an answer—a confirmation of long-term betrayal would turn her instantly into a pillar of salt—but the litany of clues that she had begun obsessively to string together compelled her to ask.

"That's irrelevant." Averting his gaze, Klaus turned to Naomi. "I want to keep this to practical arrangements, things that need addressing immediately. I've started divorce proceedings."

The table began to slide away from Julia. "You can't be serious?"

On the other side of the kitchen, the fridge kicked into action, the mundane humming slicing through her despair.

Klaus continued to look fixedly at Naomi. "Julia will be served papers in the next week or so. In terms of the estate, I'm happy for Julia to buy me out of my half of the house as soon as she can raise the money—"

"Your half of the house? I paid for the house!"

Julia stood, her hands now bolted into fists, her face pounding red. Stepping around the table, Naomi placed an arm protectively around her shoulders.

Klaus moved toward the door. "I knew this was a mistake."

"Klaus, wait! We can't just separate like this. At least let's go to a therapist—surely you'd do that for me?"

He looked directly at her for the first time.

"You don't understand. I'm not prepared to give up my future."

"Klaus, don't go! Don't . . ."

As she crumpled into silence, the front door slammed.

22

Mayfair, 1861

Over the winter, Lavinia spent her afternoons in the study collating the notes for each chapter, which James then used as reference for the writing itself. And so the two of them worked together, marking their labor by the lengthening shadows.

Promptly at three, announcing his arrival with a distinctive little cough, Mr. Poole would light the gas lamps, then kneel and stir up the embers of the fire with the poker before throwing fresh coal into the grate. Lavinia would then hear the characteristic wheezing of the leather and copper bellows as the servant encouraged the flames.

Tea was brought on a tray at five and left carefully beside the table, the maid not daring to disturb the couple as they sat side by side. The mantelpiece clock under the domed glass would chime and, for a moment, both the Colonel and Lavinia would glance up from the rainforest, the savannah, the rocking hull of a river steamship, or whichever landscape lay described on the page and then look down again.

A symbiosis developed. Lavinia found that she could deduce the next piece of research James needed, handing over the page before he even asked. The need to communicate verbally evaporated as quickly as the words manifested beneath James's furiously scratching pen. It was an inspired dialogue that gave new hope to Lavinia, who decided she would attempt to seduce her husband anew. But opportunity proved elusive. Most evenings, he excused himself to attend a science lecture, a late supper at his club, a theater opening.

Sometimes Lavinia went with him, but on many occasions he insisted on going alone.

It was on one such evening in February that Lavinia received a card informing her that Lady Morgan would be visiting the following Sunday.

❧

"It is not my custom to be this familiar, my dear, but there it is and here I am. You are, after all, the wife of one of my *dearest* friends." Lady Morgan turned from Lavinia to hand her ermine and velvet cape to the maid. "Your husband has wanted me to make this visit for several weeks and you must forgive my tardiness. I entirely blame the distraction of the oncoming season. It must be difficult for you, my dear, to be so alone amidst such social activity. This will be your first London season, will it not?"

Lavinia smiled, a slight tic under one eyelid her only sign of discomfort. "I am content to work by my husband's side."

"Mrs. Huntington, you may be a good bluestocking, but you are a bad actress." Lady Morgan pulled off her kid gloves. "I am positive the season must hold a certain fascination, particularly to a peculiar creature like yourself. You have to understand: society is to the daughters of a family what business is to the sons. I cannot believe your father has been so neglectful in this area of your education. We have a steep climb ahead of us, but fortunately for you, I have no fear of heights."

The aristocrat perched carefully on the edge of a chaise longue and took Lavinia's limp hand into her own. "A wife is a reflection of both a gentleman's taste and his estate. The Huntingtons are an old and respected family. Impeccable lineage. You, as James's wife, are the family's current frontispiece. As you know, the official season begins in June and finishes by mid-August. By that time, we aim to have you firmly established in the upper echelons. After all, James has been known to hunt with the Prince Consort himself."

"Twelve weeks is not long."

"In my first season, I attended fifty balls, sixty parties, thirty dinners, twenty-five breakfasts, and received five marriage proposals. But then, my dear, I was on a quest, whereas you, with your extraordinary good fortune . . ." Here she faltered, suddenly realizing such a line of conversation might lead to the topic of her own questionable lineage, a subject Lady Morgan considered strictly taboo. "Well, at least your *treasure hunt* is over. Still, even a young wife needs female companionship and social mobility. We must make sure you attend one of Lady Waldegrave's famous Friday to Monday parties—both Gladstone and Disraeli have been known to breakfast at Strawberry Hill and an interesting Celt is always welcome. Then in May we have the annual exhibition at the Royal Academy of the Arts—always an opportunity to display one's latest Paris acquisition. Oh, how could I forget! You must be presented to the Queen at St. James's Palace. I believe you have not yet undergone that momentous experience?"

"I have not. I will need a sponsor."

"Say no more, my dear girl, St. James's Palace in August it will be. I shall have it arranged in a flash. After that, of course, it will be *de rigeur* to attend one of the royal soirées— you wait and see." Lady Morgan continued relentlessly, counting the months off with her fingers. "The Derby is May also. June is Ascot—by far the more desirable event, but one must put in an appearance at the Derby, the hoi polloi does expect it. The end of June brings the Henley Regatta, and then there are the cricket matches at Lord's. Personally, I always favor Oxford versus Cambridge over Eton versus Harrow. Yachting at Cowes in August, not to mention the obligatory morning ride along Rotten Row. And, of course, by now, what with the balls, the fetes, the charity galas, the whole of society is *completely exhausted*, so by the twelfth of August, when Parliament adjourns, all and sundry vanish to the north. Suddenly Mayfair is *fini*. Why, you could hear a sparrow expire, it is so deathly quiet. Luckily for you, your husband has a lovely estate just south of Inverness, and some fine grouse, if my memory serves me. Shooting continues through September and October—partridges, then pheasants— and foxhunting begins on the first Monday of November. And then the whole merry cycle begins all over again. You will be so *terribly* busy."

"And I shall resolve to enjoy myself terribly." Lavinia tried to sound enthusiastic.

"Poppycock! No one cares about enjoyment; like nuptial rights, it is one's duty."

Lady Morgan accepted the glass of sherry handed to her by the maid then leaned toward Lavinia as if she were about to impart some great secret.

"The Colonel is, of course, a complicated individual, that we both know. If I may speak candidly . . ."

"I would not expect less from you, Lady Morgan."

Lady Morgan glanced at the girl sharply; she couldn't tell whether Lavinia was insulting her or not, but this was the confusing audacity of young women, she noted, they were all so contemporary in their directness.

"Then candid I will be. James is an individual who is used to certain pleasures. A man of his status may enjoy freedoms we women, married or otherwise, cannot begin to imagine." Here Lady Morgan faltered, distracted by the ambition of her own imagination. A polite cough from Lavinia drew her back to the demure setting of the drawing room.

"I was saying?"

" 'We cannot begin to imagine . . .' "

"Quite." The aristocrat relaunched into a lecture Lavinia suspected she had uttered more than once. "It is the unspoken understanding between a man and his wife that contributes to the success of such a union. This is the sacrifice we women have to make. Do you understand my meaning?"

"Concisely, you wish me to ignore certain behaviors?"

"My dear, like many before you, it has been your fate to marry a multifarious man. But I have concluded that the only worthy asset in a man—apart from an income of at least two thousand guineas per annum—is complexity. It is the one asset that improves with age, and will never bore. Trust me, beauty does become somewhat predictable the older one gets."

Lady Morgan sat back, reflecting on the aesthetic contribution Hamish Campbell had made to her own salon; a contribution she had lately begun to miss.

"But I have a great and natural affection for my husband."

"In that case, I trust you will be sensible and turn a blind eye when appropriate."

"A blind eye, Lady Morgan?"

Sighing meaningfully, Lady Morgan studied the stuffed parrot that sat on a branch in the corner of the room—one of the Colonel's Amazonian companions, which he had had immortalized out of sentiment. The quizzical expression in its glass eyes irritated her. It was as if the parrot embodied the obtuse nature of the young wife. If only Lavinia had a comprehension of the innate struggle between man and woman, the nuances upon which society turned; if only she were a pragmatist and not the deluded fantasist she appeared to be.

"I blame the French," Lady Morgan said, "and those dreadful novels they write. They have reduced love to a malady of victimhood, and suffering is so bad for the complexion."

"I suppose you hate Hugo too?"

"Stendhal, George Sand—all charlatans. *Protéges-moi de cette bêtise nôble.* (Protect me from this well-intended folly.) You must appreciate that love is the last reason for which a man marries, Mrs. Huntington. He might think it so at the time, but men . . ." She leaned forward, fixing Lavinia with her black eyes, "men do not think with their *brains*, even gentlemen, except in matters of money."

Lavinia did not break her gaze. "Is it truly naive to believe in passion, honesty, and integrity?"

"In sophisticated circles, it is not only naive, it is positively hazardous."

Lady Morgan had come out of friendship, but the girl was trying in that willful way that was typical of the Irish. Sensing Lavinia's rising ire, she feigned interest in several Japanese artifacts in the room. Lavinia leaned forward.

"My dear Lady Morgan, I was taught to believe that the relations between a man and his wife were a private matter. But because I respect the lengthy friendship between yourself and my husband, I forgive you your indiscretion."

Horrified by the young woman's impertinence, Lady Morgan spluttered madeira down her dress. Lavinia handed her a napkin.

"With regard to the season," she continued with enforced cheer, "James informs me that you are able to engineer invitations to the Holly Ball on the twenty-first?"

Appalled at Lavinia's further presumption, Lady Morgan broke into a stammer. "He di-di-did?"

"And I think it would be most Christian of you to invite James and myself as your guests," Lavinia insisted, deliberately oblivious. "No doubt the occasion will provide an excellent opportunity to introduce me to society and for my husband to engender support for his next publishing venture."

23

The parcel sat on the nursery floor, a huge mass of brown paper and string, a small card tied to one corner.

"Look, Aidan! A present from your grandpapa in Ireland!"

The child clung to her, eyes wide, as Lavinia carried him

across the room and placed him onto wobbly feet beside the parcel. She pulled the card off—her father's formal handwriting made her instantly homesick. She pictured him bent over his desk, his arthritic fingers twisted around the quill.

Lavinia opened the card then knelt beside her son. "*To my dearest grandson, so that he may grow up to be the bravest dragoon in the world!*"

She pushed the wrapped parcel and watched Aidan's face light up with delight as it swayed on its rockers.

"I wonder what it could be?"

Tearing off the paper, she encouraged Aidan to do the same, until, both laughing, they sat in a swirl of flying brown paper and the rocking horse was revealed. It stood shiny with red and black paint, gold embellishing its saddle, a mane of real black horsehair hanging over one shoulder.

"Horsey! Horsey!" Aidan clapped his hands with impatience as Lavinia lifted him into the saddle. To her surprise, he instinctively grasped the miniature leather reins and began riding. Leaning down, she kissed him. "My wee man, your ma is so proud of you."

"Bravo! Aidan, you are a natural horseman."

The Colonel stood at the nursery door, dressed in his evening clothes.

"Papa!" Aidan held up his arms. Immediately, the Colonel came over and took Lavinia's place beside the child.

"Now isn't this grand? Your very own horse and a fine stallion at that!"

Lavinia watched as Aidan, keen to impress his father, galloped faster and faster.

"It's an expensive gift, Lavinia, and very kind of your father."

"Aidan is his only grandchild."

"And look at our son, our beautiful boy—isn't he a wonder?"

Lavinia, seeing James's loving look, softened. Placing her hand on his shoulder, she kissed the back of his neck.

He did not look up from the child. "I have to leave for the

Carlton shortly—a regrettable business meeting. You must not wait up for me, Lavinia."

⟡

After a solitary dinner, Lavinia wound her way through the corridor to the music room. She sat at the piano and began a piece her father had taught her—the memory of which now felt as if it were from a different life belonging to a different woman. A knock at the door disturbed her playing.

"Madam, would you care to study the menu I have prepared for tomorrow?" The housekeeper stood in the doorway holding a piece of card.

"Not at the moment, thank you, Mrs. Beetle."

"But it is customary for the head of the household—"

"Do we have guests tomorrow?"

"No, madam."

"Then I shall trust that Cook will prepare her usual excellent cuisine."

"Madam, I think I should point out that the Colonel expects—"

"Mrs. Beetle, I am perfectly aware of my duties. I just wish, at this moment, to be allowed some reflection on my own. Is that too much to expect?"

"No, madam." After the smallest of curtsies, Mrs. Beetle backed out of the room. Sighing, Lavinia returned to her playing, only to be interrupted five minutes later by a maid sent in by Mrs. Beetle to draw the curtains.

Exasperated, Lavinia left the music room and, craving solitude, made her way to the courtyard. Before she realized it she found herself in the stables.

The shivering flanks of the horses gleamed. Each stood in its own stall, some with their noses thrust into buckets, chewing meditatively; others glancing hopefully over their glossy backs at Lavinia. Seeing she was not their keeper, they turned back to their feed.

A lantern blazed overhead, and in the far stall an extra lamp burned to warm a recently born foal and its mare. Lifting her skirts, Lavinia walked over and reached across to caress the mare. Its skin was warm and coarse to touch, but of immediate comfort. Lavinia felt like a young girl again, hiding in a secret haven, relishing her escape from the sense of being constantly observed: by the servants, by Lady Morgan, by her husband . . .

"That letter there is a J. I swear on it. That much I do know."

A voice, male, deep, and American, rumbled from the other side of the stables. Lavinia walked along the row of horses. Aloysius the coachman sat in an empty stall, his back against the door, a lantern in one hand.

Sitting next to him was a Negro boy of about eighteen, dressed in a riding coat and breeches. Lavinia did not recognize his livery. The two were examining a piece of paper Aloysius was holding up to the lantern's light.

"Samuel, that is no J; that would be a T, as in Tattle."

"I know a J when I sees one!"

"Aloysius?"

Upon seeing Lavinia the two men immediately hid the jug of stout they'd been drinking from. Throwing on their caps and dusting the straw from their clothes, they jumped to their feet.

"Madam, you be after something?"

"No, I just came to visit the horses. It's always been a refuge to me, the stables."

She smiled to reassure them, but Aloysius, disconcerted by the impropriety of the moment, was staring at the floor, his large hands pawing the paper apprehensively. He indicated the youth next to him.

"This is Samuel, he's the coachman over at the embassy."

A smile broke like a white streak across the other man's face. Lavinia saw he had one front tooth missing.

"Ma'am, at your service. Begging your pardon, but the master's visiting number forty and so while I'm waiting I've put the footman in charge of the coach and taken the opportunity to visit my friend Aloysius—with my master's permission, ma'am, I swear." Samuel tipped his cap.

Lavinia had only ever seen one black man before and she tried to conceal her wonder. He was a well-made youth, with large slightly bulbous brown eyes, a nose that looked as if it might have seen a few fights, and a mass of tight oiled curls framing his round face.

"Which embassy?" Lavinia settled herself on a work bench. "And please, sit again and enjoy your tobacco and ale. I had not intended to disturb you."

Samuel waited until Aloysius nodded permission and then the two of them settled awkwardly back down. As the Irishman snubbed out a smoking piece of straw that had been ignited by the embers of his hidden clay pipe, Samuel took off his cap and polished the insignia.

"The embassy of the Confederate States of America, ma'am. I belong to Mr. Dudley Hunt; he's the ambassador and I am his coachman," he said proudly.

"Samuel does himself a disservice," Aloysius interrupted. "He's the best horseman I know. This laddie can calm the jumpiest stallion, and guide a panicked team through a flood as if it were a meadow, madam."

"Mr. Hunt is lucky to have you in his employment."

"Ma'am, I'm not employed. Mr. Dudley Hunt owns me, and my papa and the rest of us. That's the way it is in the South."

"And that's why there is a war on, Mr. Samuel."

"So they say, ma'am, so they say." Samuel, anxious about the introduction of political matters, looked from Lavinia to Aloysius.

"Samuel has brought me a letter from America," Aloysius interjected, thinking it would be wise to change the topic of conversation.

Samuel held up the envelope, the address stained and faded on the front. "There was a Union postal cart captured by the Confederate forces, and they finds this letter and sends it to Mr. Dudley Hunt Esquire, who throws it out. But I knows the word 'coachman' and the word 'Mayfair,' so I finds Aloysius myself and now I have myself an Irishman as a true friend, now ain't I a huckleberry above a persimmon?"

Aloysius put his hand up to silence the coachman.

"I believe the letter is from my brother, madam."

"And what is his news?"

A slow flush inched its way from under Aloysius's woollen collar and up to his large ears. "I can't properly say. Being the fifth child I wasn't sent to school as such. But Seamus, he was the fortunate one. Fortunate to have left and fortunate to have got to America alive."

"You cannot read?"

Now the coachman's face was scarlet. He looked down at his riding boots. Lavinia stretched out her hand and Aloysius handed the letter to her over the gate. As he did, she noticed that the tips of two fingers were missing and his hands were scarred.

She examined the parchment under the light of the lantern Aloysius had placed on the wooden doorpost. The handwriting was labored and the spelling dreadful. It appeared Seamus had received little more of an education than his brother.

"It is dated the seventeenth of February and begins, *My dear brother Aloysius*—"

"Well, even I knew that much," Aloysius grumbled, determined to win back some dignity. Ignoring him, and Samuel's sudden grin, Lavinia continued.

"I hope this letter finds you in good health and in good employment. Brother, I write to tell you that I am now a soldier with President Lincoln's Union Army. We are a worthy bunch of Irishmen with the 69th New York State militia regiment. I have volunteered and they have given me my own horse, saddle, and supplies. It will be food and a roof over my head, and I am hoping we will be fighting in Virginia by the spring. I will try and write you during the campaign, and

I have chosen you as next of kin should I perish. Yours in good grace, your brother Seamus."

In the ensuing silence, Samuel let out a long slow whistle and slapped his thigh. "Goddamn! I am all chawed up. If I could, I would be fighting with him my own sweet self! The Good Lord knows I would!"

Forgetting himself, Aloysius reached across and took the letter from Lavinia, then stared blindly at the page as if the face of his brother were printed there.

"Seamus won't make a good soldier," he declared. "He's barely five foot, and that's in his shoes."

"Surely you agree that fighting for the end of slavery is a just cause?" Lavinia interjected, surprised by the coachman's reservations.

"I'm not saying it's not; it's just that my brother and I—we've only survived this far by the grace of God himself, so I'm thinking it's mighty foolish of Seamus to voluntarily put his life in danger, for anyone." He turned to Samuel. "Forgive me, Samuel."

"I understand, my friend. I've been told the Irish are little better than slaves themselves under their English masters."

"A working man has no time to think on ideals, madam, you must know that," Aloysius replied.

"Which makes your brother's choice even more admirable, surely?"

But the coachman stood there in silence, his heavy brow knotting and unknotting. Finally, a crooked smile spread slowly across his face.

"Perhaps you're right, madam. Besides, he could be the first general in the O'Malley clan yet. They say anything is possible in the New World."

"It is for the white man," Samuel muttered gloomily.

The three of them stood silent for a moment, contemplating their own providence and the immense differences between them.

Lavinia broke the silence. "Would you like to reply?"

Again, Aloysius found himself angry at her insensitivity. Could she not see that would be out of the question? Shrugging, he refilled his pipe and, using a small wax wick to catch a flame from the lantern, lit the bowl. He exhaled; a small white cloud hung in the air before dispersing.

"I think not. No, my brother would not expect me to reply." His gruff words betrayed the frustration he felt at his own inadequacy.

"We could compose them together. There is a return address—the postmaster . . ."

Suspicious, he stared at the soft whiteness of her hands. What did she want with a lowly coachman? Was she one of those rich Christian ladies who sought redemption through good works? Was that how she saw him—as a charity? An ignorant young man she intended to educate? An irksome thought indeed, and a position Aloysius had no intention of adopting.

"What's in it for you then?" he blurted out.

"Aloysius, the young mistress just wants to help!" Samuel exclaimed, shocked at the Irishman's irreverent tone of voice.

"It would please me to be of some use to a fellow countryman. And, as a great admirer of Mr. Lincoln, I would welcome the chance to assist his war effort in any way I can."

"Oh Lordy! Now I really have seen the elephant!" Samuel interjected, grinning. "No one must ever know I visited this house. The ambassador will ride me out on a rail!"

"Fear not, Samuel, the name Huntington will stand well with your master," Lavinia smiled back. "My husband and most of his associates are staunch supporters of the Confederacy."

She turned back to the Irishman. "Your answer, Aloysius? Will you allow me to assist you?"

"Perhaps when I drive you to church on Sunday, we could take a moment to compose a letter then, madam? Private from the rest of the household. I shouldn't want Mr. Poole thinking I was reaching above my station."

The coachman's tone was tentative, but secretly he felt a rush of eagerness at the thought of writing to Seamus, a brother he hadn't seen for over five years. Or at least, that was the reason he gave himself, not daring to examine his excitement further.

"Then Sunday it shall be," Lavinia concluded.

24

Los Angeles, 2002

Julia picked up the copies of the *Los Angeles Times* lying on the doormat where they had fallen with depressing regularity. Staring at the top paper's date in disbelief, she realized Klaus had been gone for over a month.

His absence had left a void. All that remained were aural signatures, which had seeped into the brickwork, settling around the couple's movements as a tree might entwine a fencepost—ghost-trails of their lovemaking, their laughter, the cry of her name. Lying in bed, Julia had found herself expecting every passing vehicle to be Klaus's car; imagining she could hear the squeal of his brakes, the click of the engine dying, the crunch of his footsteps on the graveled pathway.

The loss of her closest friend had been as painful as the loss of her husband. Julia swung wildly between deep anger at Carla's betrayal and a desperate need to talk to her, when she would find herself dialing her phone number. And so she lay there, for nights on end, her loneliness circling above her in a numbing orbit, rocking herself, her arms clutched around her empty womb.

After a time, the antidepressants gave her grief a tone. Its ululation became muffled, merged with the roar of the freeway, the ocean—the imagined sound of a storm pounding against the eardrum, pushing everything out toward the horizon, a frequency that took her out of the small moments. Hues were brighter. *Life with the color turned up*—the psychiatrist had promised, as if centuries of philosophizing about perception could be reduced to one banally cheerful metaphor. Naturally Julia hadn't believed her, but on the tenth day, miraculously, the sky was bluer, the leaves greener, the roses bloodier.

A need to spend money was a more insidious side effect—an impulse fueled by the delusion that the dollars in her hand were toy money set against the greater tragedies of love and hate, abandonment and union. It was only after she'd spent three hundred dollars at the lipstick counter at Nieman Marcus that it occurred to her that her compulsive shopping might be drug-induced. The lipsticks stood in her bathroom cabinet, balanced on their ends like a platoon of forgotten toy soldiers.

Julia had no energy left to grieve for others. The two burning towers of New York, and the ensuing implosion of the national psyche, became even more personalized for Julia, as if her own internal logic had been shattered along with what she had naively believed to be untouchable America. Nevertheless, she found herself sobbing at news images: a child-soldier leaning against an army tank; a pool of burning oil in some distant sea; the bewildered face of a juvenile gorilla trapped behind bamboo bars.

It became difficult for her to listen to music with lyrics. Most songs, she realized, were about loss or impending loss—an incessant chorus of victimhood that divided humanity into two categories: the leavers and the left. In her darkest moments, she wondered about which synapses the antidepressants had fired and which they were repressing, but the end result was the same: her depression continued. It was a hidden iceberg, shifting and splintering; great subterranean ruptures that tore through the glittering shell of the drug, spiking in inappropriate moments of elation.

Duty of care, mouthing the words like a curse into the gathering evening shadows, Klaus and Carla had failed in their *duty of care*, for surely both friendship and marriage have an unspoken contract, Julia would argue with herself, trying to make logic out of the irrational.

Night became an escape from the world. Sometimes she'd sleep until 11 a.m., her limbs stretched over to the side of the bed that Klaus used to occupy. Waking, she would conjure up the fragrance of his skin, a rich mix of sweat and oils, the crook of his neck, the hollow of his thighs. She couldn't imagine experiencing desire with anyone else. The idea of revealing her history all over again to a new man appalled her; even contemplation of the idea felt like an obscene infidelity. It was impossible to believe she would ever share the same humor, wit, and sensibility. Klaus was meant to be her final relationship, and she clung to the conviction that he would return.

❧

Desperate for a sense of family, of continuity, Julia had placed a photograph of her grandfather, Aidan Huntington, next to the bed.

He was still a boy in the image, standing posed on the docks in front of the hull of an ocean steamer, his long pale face staring bleakly into the lens. The words *"Oona May* Cork—Chicago" were painted on the side of the ship, and streamers twisted and snaked through the air. Passengers crowded on the decks and at the portholes, punctuating the photo with fuzzy activity. An American flag fluttered in one corner, the stars trailing points in a lazy breeze. A blurred figure—probably a porter, Julia thought, was pushing a trolley past the boy.

The young Aidan looked about twelve, his curly hair was

carefully oiled and combed behind his ears, he was dressed in a jacket and knickerbockers that reached just below his knees. There was pathos in his taut, serious thin face as he attempted to appear a man. A small suitcase sat on the ground beside him while a parcel of books, belted around with leather, dangled from his hand. The motherless child, Julia thought, and wondered about Lavinia Huntington and the demise of her marriage. Colonel James Huntington had been quite a famous scientist in his own right, so Julia remembered her father telling her, but he had never spoken about his grandfather's death or the trial of his young wife. Some years after Julia's own mother had died, he had told her he'd always been convinced of his grandmother's innocence.

Switching on the lamp, Julia pulled the photo into the light. Her grandfather had died before she was born, and stories about him had always fascinated her. She remembered them vividly. Apparently, Aidan had resembled his mother, Lavinia, in coloring alone; Julia assumed the broad nose and strong chin were inherited from his father. In the photograph, his facial features were slightly blurred, as if he had moved during the long camera exposure, but his eyes were sharp. A direct stare that traveled through history and connected unswervingly with the gaze of the viewer—the child had inherited his mother's confrontational gaze. It made Julia think about her own Aidan, the son that might have been.

⊱❦⊰

As Klaus had promised, the divorce papers soon arrived, making it apparent that he must have been planning his departure for months. The revelation horrified Julia. Staring down at the documents, she found it difficult to recognize the husband she had lived with for twelve years. He must have been compartmentalizing the whole time, she concluded.

Without being allowed to communicate with him, she found herself mythologizing their life together. Holidays, birthdays, celebrations, conversations that had inspired her all came flooding back, filling her nights with crisp heightened images—everything they had experienced together amplified to legendary happiness. She had considered herself content; she had assumed Klaus was content, except for his work situation—a situation Julia knew Carla had the power to change. Was that it? Was Klaus that mercenary? Or was it that Julia had been so self-absorbed she'd been blind to his real needs? Obsessively she began to dismantle the marriage, to look for indications, torturing herself by analyzing their last few months together over and over.

25

Julia could see a reflection of herself thrown down onto the pavement she was flying over. Even in the twilight she recognized the buildings along Sunset Boulevard: the Viper Room, the House of Blues, Sunset Five, the Chateau Marmont. It wasn't an unpleasant sensation, floating on this thick viscous sea, a buoyant soft wind carrying her.

To the west she could see the incandescent strip of blue-gray that was the horizon of the Pacific Ocean. The sky itself was the dark cobalt of just before dawn; streaks of salmon-pink had begun to bleed up from the horizon, freckling the sky. In her dreaming mind, she judged it to be about five in the morning. A minute later she was passing over the emerald and russet breasts of the Hollywood hills, sweeping up from the streaming band of car lights that was Sunset Boulevard. Below, each valley cradled residential blocks that lay across the green like embroidered handkerchiefs, each with a rectangle of glistening blue—the swimming pools— that threw back a framed reflection of the firmament. The canyons wound into the hills like hieroglyphs on a raised parchment.

Mi ciudad Hermosa: the words were whispered puffs of smoke that kept her buoyant. It was only then Julia became aware of the warm weight she held beneath her; Aidan, her lost son.

As they flew, Julia realized that she was entirely unencumbered by her waking grief, and that flying like this, united with the panorama that sweltered and muttered and glinted thousands of other stories, she was finally at peace. Aiden smiled up at her and, without thinking, Julia opened her arms. The child hovered, and for an instant they flew as one, the boy a miniature shadow of his mother, across the tiled roofs until he left her side.

⤳❦⤳

"Now, you might not have voted for Proposition 49 in the past, and you might have had strong reasons not to, but you cannot tell me, Mr. and Mrs. Dumont . . ." The Candidate's voice was interrupted by the automated insertion of Klaus's and Julia's names, a robotic rendering that destroyed the attempt at a personal tone. Julia, her head buried under the covers, her nightdress wrapped around her eyes in a desperate attempt to block out the early summer light streaming in through the cane blinds, clicked the phone off and pushed it under her pillow.

"Christ," she groaned aloud. Could she get up, did she want to? It was a month since her miscarriage, two weeks since she'd received the divorce papers. The day lay cavernous before her, frighteningly empty.

She curled around her pillow, wishing she wasn't such a coward. A breeze rattled the cane blinds and jolted her back to the dream. The aerial view of Los Angeles had been so accurate she could have described the landscape to a pilot, and then there was the image of her son. Black eyes like his father; his narrow face a combination of her cheekbones and Klaus's pointed chin.

She wrapped her hands around the pillow and almost slipped back into sleep. The alarm clock startled her awake again.

She sat up and stretched then reached for a tape recorder she kept in the bedside cabinet. A psychologist she'd spoken to at the hospital had suggested it might be therapeutic to record messages to Klaus—messages he would never get to hear. She switched on the tape recorder and waited in silence. It felt like she was whispering to a ghost. The tape ran a full three minutes before she had the courage to begin.

". . . I keep finding myself laying the table for two. Sometimes, when I'm reading or watching television, I forget and think I hear your footsteps in another part of the house and call your name. It makes me feel so goddamn stupid. You live inside someone's skin for over a decade and then find you didn't know them at all. Did you ever think about the consequences of your actions? You must have. You must have analyzed every outcome meticulously. If I can't live without you, how am I to live?"

❧

Julia drove without thinking about where she was going; a hazy geographical comprehension guiding her through the maze of L.A.'s suburbs. Her cell rang; she ignored it. She knew it would be Naomi, who had developed the habit of ringing her twice a day to check that she was safe. Her friend's vigilance irritated Julia. Reaching down she switched the phone off.

She turned into a narrow street where small neat lawns encircled white bungalows, jasmine climbed over trellises at the front doors, and the obligatory SUV sat in each driveway. Klaus had originally wanted to buy in the beachside area, but they hadn't been able to afford it. Houses that were built in the Californian post Second World War industrial boom when aircraft construction usurped oranges. Julia's stomach clenched as she recognized where her instinct had brought her.

Lavender Street, Number Twelve; how many times had she visited this house? How many times?

Pulling into the curb, she carefully hid the car behind a large van. The gate hadn't changed; an old pumpkin with a grinning ghoul-face carved into its peel still sat by the fencepost—a relic from a past Halloween night.

The house was quiet; there was a light dimly visible through one of the front windows. The office, Julia thought. At least, that's what Carla called it. It was a converted laundry, barely more than a cupboard. The house itself was an original piece of German-influenced modernist architecture, a construction of planes that translated into a spacious geometric structure designed so the sun traveled around the house, flooding each room in turn with light. It's a sunhouse, Carla would say, I live in a sunhouse not a greenhouse. Just remembering her saying it made Julia nostalgic.

She recalled how she'd rushed here once at 2 a.m., convinced that Klaus was having an affair. He was away sailing and she hadn't been able to get through on his cell. The image of him making love to another woman had thrashed through her head. She knew she had to talk out her fear and had immediately driven to Carla's. Tousled, but unfazed, her friend had let her in. They'd spent the rest of the night getting drunk together on some obscenely sweet liqueur Carla had brought back from a film shoot in Krakow, regaling each other with anecdotes about the worst lovers they'd ever had. Two hours later Julia reached Klaus on his phone; he'd told her she was paranoid but he loved her anyway.

There were two narratives in Julia's head: the ongoing dialogue with the woman she had loved, an imagined conversation in which she told Carla her latest news, asked her advice, provided the unconditional empathy women offered each other; and the second, a monologue so vitriolic that Julia could barely form words to fit her anger.

Hate is an interesting emotion. Because of its epic nature, the awkward, ugly shape it makes in these rational post-modern times, it is unfashionably polarized, terrifyingly illogical, Julia thought as she crouched in her car. But hate was what she felt. Carla's betrayal was as unfathomable to her as her husband's departure, and both obsessed her—like an equation she needed to solve.

People fall in love, Julia, and they have no control over their choices. Klaus's words hung in her mind like a ghostly afterimage. Julia did not believe them. "Marriage is a negotiation of temptation," she said aloud, suddenly furious at finding herself reduced to a voyeur of a life she felt was, by rights, her own. "I could kill him for having reduced me to this," she added softly, her breath misting up the window.

The streetlights came on and clouds of gnats shifted direction like shoals of fish under the bluish glow. Julia continued watching, fascinated by the silhouettes passing across the house's drawn blinds. The gleaming hull of Carla's BMW in the driveway taunted her as she fought the impulse to get out and walk directly up to the front door.

Suddenly, it swung open and Carla and Klaus emerged. Carla adjusted Klaus's tie, then kissed him; his fingers slid down her back. Julia watched, horrified as Klaus caressed Carla's face. The gesture was so familiar it resonated in Julia's muscles, as if it were her face. She could feel the imprint of his fingers, smell the faint aroma of aftershave, soap, and oil; the imagined heat of his skin infusing her own. The memory of touch—it will con us every time. It will deceive us until death steals all sensation. This is the nature of lovemaking, she decided, watching the scene play itself out like a film sequence. Lovemaking stamps us with ownership, infuses us with the illusion of permanency, and in the very same moment dispels mortality like a cheap theatrical trick.

"You are still mine," she whispered into the drifting evening.

26

Klaus rolled off Carla, the cool sheets sticking across his sweaty back, his brain pleasantly emptied, his erection subsiding in slow enjoyable throbs.

"We have been so brave, so brave," Carla whispered. The statement, laced with tentative poignancy, dragged Klaus straight back into the bedroom. Why do women always get philosophical after sex, he pondered, trying not to resent the interruption of what had promised to be a painless slide into sleep—something he desperately needed.

"I guess so," he answered, cautiously. "But you'll be surprised, it'll only take six months before people start to forget I was married to Julia at all. Especially in this town—the most mercenary metropolis in the world."

Carla peered through the darkness, trying to read Klaus's profile. The new legitimacy of their relationship still filled her with astonishment—that he could sleep openly in *her* bed, sit at *her* table. The crushing guilt of deception she'd carried for over four months had finally lifted. She sat up and reached for a cigarette.

As the flame flared in the darkness, Klaus fought the urge to blow it out. "Honey, do you have to?"

"Yes." She inhaled deeply then exhaled the smoke away from him.

"I know it's difficult for Julia, but she'll survive. You don't get to where she is professionally without a certain ruthlessness. I think it all comes down to basic elements: ego, id, a kind of inherent ability to dominate. Julia fills her own life, and the lives of others, without even realizing it."

Irritated that, yet again, his ex-wife had crept into the bed of his new lover, he buried his face in the mattress. Reaching across, Carla tentatively laid a hand on his back.

"I just think it's important to get these things clear. And, for the record, I wouldn't have got involved with you if I'd known you were trying for a baby."

"We weren't trying! At least, not to my knowledge. Do you think this is easy for me? I lost a child, too. Do you think I don't feel guilty? You don't just stop loving someone, but it changes." He turned to her. "Do you know how long I've wanted you? How long I fought the intuition that to be with you was right and to stay with her was increasingly wrong? My only regret is that I didn't leave her sooner. Julia's not a bad woman—"

"Julia's a great woman. She may be a better human being than you or me . . ."

"It's just that her psychology, the way she's wired, is inherently oppressive. We had twelve years together, ten of which were great, but now I'm with you. So can we cut the psychobabble?"

"You're right, we have each other now and that's extraordinary. I love you—at the cost of everything else."

Distracted now, Klaus rolled onto his back, his eyelids snapping open. "We are two individuals. Sometimes with Julia, it was like I was nothing more than an appendage."

For a moment Carla wondered why Klaus hadn't been able to negotiate his own territory, but, frightened of appearing disloyal and of what she might discover, she stayed silent.

Klaus stared at the ceiling, the possibility of sleep now having fled entirely. "Okay, from now on I intend to communicate with her only by fax. That way we can track everything she says and does."

"Isn't that a little extreme?"

"I want it to be a clean break. I need that so we can come into this untainted. A brand new start—for all three of us." His hand trailed the curve of her hip.

Just then, headlights swung an arc through the darkened

bedroom as, outside, a car made a U-turn. The vehicle pulled into the curb, brakes squealing.

"Christ, not again," Klaus said, sitting up.

Carla remained curled into a ball of refusal. Julia will not ruin this moment, she will not destroy our time, she thought as the white comet of the headlights streaked her closed eyelids.

Klaus leaped to his feet. Pulling the curtains aside, he peered out into the street. "I can't believe it!" Livid, he began pacing. "That's it! I am going to slap a restraining order on her, I swear to God!"

Carla slipped out of bed, semen running down the inside of her thighs. Julia's Lexus was clearly visible under the street lamp. Carla could see the light reflecting off Julia's long black hair, the hollows of her face as she stared across at the house. Their eyes met; terrified, Carla dropped the curtain.

"She saw me. But it didn't look like Julia; she's changed," she whispered.

Klaus pulled her into his arms. "She *has* changed. We've all changed."

"You don't understand—she told me about something that happened in Afghanistan . . ." Somewhere in the distance a car alarm went off. Carla shivered. "There was an ambush and Julia killed a man."

"You can't be serious?"

"She claimed it was self-defense."

"Julia killed a man? Don't be ridiculous. She's not capable of such a thing."

"I'm only repeating what she told me: the convoy was ambushed, her escort was killed, she was pulled out of the car and there was a struggle, and she stabbed the guy."

"She would have told me. Maybe she's exaggerating— there was probably some kind of tussle, maybe someone got killed."

"Julia doesn't exaggerate. I only know because she had to tell someone here—to make it real, she said."

"But I saw her straight after the trip, at the airport. She didn't seem traumatized."

"That's the whole point—she wasn't. Klaus, are we safe? Really safe from her?"

He stared at her. "Carla, this is Julia. Naturally, she's upset; naturally, she wants to see me, even you—but she'll calm down, I promise you. In a year this will all be history."

❧

The phone was ringing. Throwing the house keys down, Julia rushed to answer it.

Silence. The crackling of somebody waiting on the other end of the line.

"Klaus?"

The caller hung up. Frantically, she punched in star 69: the number came up as unlisted. Intuitively, she knew it wasn't her husband.

She switched on the answering service. Klaus's voice sounded out into the room: *Hi, we're not in at the moment. If you'd like to leave a message, please do so after this ridiculous bleep.* Julia tried to remember when he'd recorded it; at least twelve months before. She hadn't bothered rerecording the message, as if by erasing his voice she would exorcise any possibility of his return.

Julia collapsed on the sofa and stared out at the magnolia tree now in full blossom. Whether she sat there for ten minutes or thirty she couldn't tell. Carla's startled face stared back at her from between the branches. Fear, that's what Julia had seen in her eyes. It had only been a moment, a catching of the faint pale shadow of nudity beyond the curtains of Carla's bedroom. But Julia would never forgive those eyes, the momentary expression of furtiveness. She rewound the message. Five repeats later she pulled the phone out of the wall socket.

27

Mayfair, 1861

Lavinia, the Colonel, Lady Morgan, and Hamish Campbell drove very slowly and flagrantly along St. James's in the opulent splendor of a landau, the Huntington lozenge visible on its doors. With Aloysius at its helm, and four attendants in silk knee breeches and livery, the coach proceeded down Piccadilly past the great mansions ablaze with light, powdered footmen at their doors.

Lavinia, her stays pinching at the waist, the steel undercarriage of her dress settled precariously around her, sat in a scented cloud of jasmine and orange blossom, strands of both woven into her elaborate hairstyle. The dress's décolletage displayed her flawless breasts to advantage (much to Lady Morgan's disapproval and envy) and a necklace of gold and pearl—a courtship gift from the Colonel.

The coach had been designed in an era when women's gowns were far less voluminous, and the lack of space had squeezed the two men into opposite corners.

"This new fashion makes us part-machine," Lady Morgan commented.

"Indeed." Lavinia pulled her gaze away from the spectators that had stopped in the street to gawk at the promenade of wealth. "I suspect Charles Worth had the hot-air balloon in mind when he designed the crinoline. Certainly there have been days when I feared I might be swept up by the wind and set afloat."

"There was that dreadful story about a woman who was

swept cleanly off the cliff at Eastbourne. One can only pray that she reached Calais," Lady Morgan said with relish.

"And yet you both subscribe to the fad," the Colonel pointed out.

"Would you rather we abandoned the fashion?"

"Not at all. There is steel in the crinoline; the fashion has no doubt made a direct contribution to the current affluence in Sheffield. And as I now hold shares in the industry, I can only approve." The Colonel turned to Lavinia. "You, my dear, are carrying the future of British manufacturing about your hips."

Before they could debate further, the carriage pulled up behind the other vehicles parked in a line outside the mansion on Berkeley Square.

The attendants leapt off the footboards and helped their patrons down to the boardwalk that ran from the curb to the grand entrance of the house.

The ballroom was vast, with a gallery of paintings each in an ornate frame. The white and gold doorway was topped by a heavy gilded carving. The walls were hung with shimmering patterned yellow damask and the sprung polished wooden floor had been suitably waxed for the dancing. Huge candelabra blazed with light, reflected a hundredfold in the mirrored panels of the blinds that were pulled down over the windows. Massive crystal vases filled with lilies, yellow roses, and branches of white lilac had been placed around the edges of the room, and their scent mixed with the floor wax and the perfumed candles burning in the French crystal chandeliers that hung from the ceiling.

An archway led out to a glassed-in balcony where a long table was laden with refreshments. Lavinia, craning her neck, could just see the array of ices, wafers, cakes, and bonbons stacked on silver trays. Uniformed maids, waiting to serve, stood beside the tables.

At the far end of the hall, screened by ornamental shrubbery, sat a small orchestra consisting of a piano, a cornet, a violin, and a cello.

"Come, we should claim our places," Lady Morgan murmured behind her fan as she led the others across the room to a gathering of unoccupied sofas.

About two dozen couples were already spinning around the parquet dance floor, while a flock of women—girls as young as sixteen, their mothers, maiden aunts, a few widows dripping with diamonds, and other manifestations of the moneyed female—perched on cushioned seats and ottomans around the walls. Furiously fanning themselves, the women exchanged snippets of information amid a cacophony of shrieks, mutterings, and whispered conspiracies. They resembled a reclining tribe of primates, Lavinia concluded, particularly fascinated by the contrived theatrics of the young debutantes as they endeavored to draw male attention.

On the other side of the room, resolutely grouped around a huge fireplace, a distant ancestor of Baron Wenlock's staring down at them censoriously, stood the men: the dandies, the barons and lords, the captains and their aspiring lieutenants, the landed gentry and, finally, that comparatively new breed, the capitalists—city men who had made their own wealth, either from manufacturing in the north or by exploiting the riches of the Far East and India.

Lady Morgan pulled Lavinia to one side. "Look around you—this is a circus, an extravaganza designed entirely for the exchange of trade, whether it be stock tips or the courting of an heir or heiress. You can be sure this occasion is about one thing and one thing only: who has money and who hasn't."

Discreetly tapping her fan on the side of Lavinia's hand, Lady Morgan indicated a tall, thin man in his middle fifties with a pock-marked face and a prominent, bulbous nose. In stark contrast to his ruined face his figure was expensively clad: diamond studs glistened at his cuffs, another gem sparkled at his breast, and a yellow gold silk cravat sprang from the neck of his black evening coat. He was holding court to a gaggle of elderly men, who consumed his every word with a chorus of nods, reminding Lavinia of Aidan's wooden puppets.

"That, my dear girl, is Hans Skippenmann. There are only two men in this room who can match his wealth. They say his grandfather was an Armenian. Skippenmann himself is of dubious nationality, although he claims to be of the Viennese aristocracy. He made his fortune in the Far East, supplying the medicinal needs of the Commonwealth."

Confused, Lavinia lifted one eyebrow.

"Opium, my young friend, the new gold," Lady Morgan replied in a theatrical whisper, glancing again at the magnate who was now in intense conversation with a younger gentleman of thirty, flamboyantly dressed in a velvet suit with a waistcoat made from Eastern silk.

"The gentleman beside him is Lord Merrywither. He made his money in India, but keeps a very nice house in Mayfair as well as a palace in Bombay. Each is as corrupt as the other. Lord Merrywither is a confirmed bachelor, and I do mean *confirmed*, but Skippenmann has an unmarried daughter—his only heir."

Lady Morgan flicked open her fan and shook it in the direction of the seated women to indicate a grandiose matron squeezed into a gown more befitting a woman half her size. Sweat dripped from her forehead, causing streaks in the thick layer of powder and rouge that covered her wrinkled visage. An elegant young man of twenty or so, immaculately dressed in the uniform of the dragoons, threw himself down beside her. "Lady Fairweather and her son Horatio. She plans to hook the Skippenmann girl for the young blade. Indeed, rumor has him marked for a victory. His title for her money: it is a fair trade."

A tall young woman, her elegant face several inches too long to be beautiful, her brunette hair swept up into a bouffant topped with a spray of ostrich feathers, descended upon them. "Lady Morgan! And you must be Mrs. Lavinia Huntington?"

"I am indeed," Lavinia replied.

"Be careful; Lady Bilbury collects friends as she collects dresses each season—both abandoned by Christmas. Your currency is that you are new and unknown, therefore mysterious," Lady Morgan whispered behind her fan.

"Delighted to meet you, Lady Bilbury." Lavinia curtsied politely.

"Oh, you're Irish, *très enchanté*. We have land in Ballymore, but our family seat is in Shropshire—my mother is as English as the Queen. I think she must spend no more than three weeks of the year at Ballymore."

"Ballymore Castle?"

"Do you know it? We were almost ruined by that confounded famine a number of years ago. Our peasants quite abandoned us, I'm afraid."

"Loyalty is a challenge when your children are dying of starvation, do you not think?" Lavinia retorted.

Her smile fraying at the edges, Lady Bilbury turned to Lady Morgan. "*Votre amie est un peu sérieuse, n'est-ce pas?* (Your friend is a trifle serious, no?)"

"*Mais il y a du charme dans la passion, ne croyez-vous pas?* (But there's charm in passion, don't you think?)" Lady Morgan replied in perfect French.

"*C'est vrai que je suis irlandaise, mais je parle le français couramment quand même* (I may be Irish, but I do speak fluent French)," Lavinia interjected as lightly as she could.

"Oh, there goes the Lord Chancellor. I do have an urgent matter to discuss with him, if you will excuse me." And off Lady Bilbury rushed, leaving a feather floating after her.

Lady Morgan gave Lavinia a stern look. "My dear, if you wish to make friends, you must surrender your politics. Unless you mean to go into Parliament, but, alas, until women have the vote I'm afraid you are banished to the politics of the dining table. Mrs. Huntington, none of these ladies and gentlemen is the slightest bit interested in the fate of a few Irish serfs. Our world consists of different dilemmas, in their own way just as important. After all, one's reputation *is* one's life, don't you think?"

Lady Morgan was interrupted by the Colonel and Hamish Campbell, each holding a glass of negus for the women. The Colonel handed the crystal goblet to Lavinia. "I see you have begun to make friends?" He had noted Lady Bilbury's hasty departure.

"Lady Morgan has already made some introductions," Lavinia replied through gritted teeth, suddenly painfully aware of the inadequacy of both her deportment and diction. The women sweeping past seemed to avoid looking at her, instead studiously gazing to one side or turning to their companion a little too gaily.

Hamish Campbell, sensing Lavinia's anxiety, stepped forward. "Colonel, may I request your wife's company for the next dance? Unless, of course, her card is full?"

"My card is woefully empty," Lavinia laughed.

"I give you my word, sir, I won't make love to her," Campbell added, an ironic smile playing across his lips.

"Is she not worthy?" Huntington played along.

"Indeed she is, but I had taken you for an uxorious man."

The Colonel leaned toward the young man, dangerously close, as if about to challenge him to a duel. "The waltzes have begun. You may have her for just one dance," he growled in mock anger.

Bowing, Hamish Campbell led Lavinia to the dance floor.

❧

"You have a distinct air of discontentment, my friend. At least feign happiness, James." Genuinely concerned, Lady Morgan placed her hand on the Colonel's arm. Since his marriage, she had observed a new sobriety, a dull gravity, about him.

"Lately, I have concluded that although I am capable of the

pursuit of intimacy, I am incapable of sustaining the emotion once I have secured the object of my desire. I am, alas, fatally addicted to the chase," the Colonel replied. He removed his snuffbox from his waistcoat, placed a large pinch in the crook of his hand, and inhaled deeply. "I thought I had tired of such behavior and could dispense with my old habits. But I fear I cannot, and it is a painful realization."

He pulled out a handkerchief and sneezed, leaving an orangey-red stain in the center of the white cotton. Lady Morgan, mistaking the watering of his eyes due to the hotness of the snuff for tears, pressed her hand to his chest.

"My friend, you chastise yourself too much. You are a good husband and she is mistress of one of the more enviable households in Mayfair. And you are a loving father."

"Perhaps, but I have discovered a flaw within my physique. When I was studying phrenology, I read my own skull and found that the area for affection and friendship was overdeveloped to a degree of depravity, whereas the instinct of reproduction—located in the cerebellum—was practically nonexistent. I decided then that I would not be victim to my own physiology, under any circumstance."

Lady Morgan laughed, then realized the Colonel was serious.

"Absolute poppycock," she replied. "No wonder the Austrian Emperor banned that charlatan Franz Gall. There is nothing I hate more than the notion that anything—particularly personality—is determined. I thought you had begun to have your own doubts about the legitimacy of such a science?"

"I waver; there are moments when I find the logic of it convincing, and then in the next moment I no longer know my own mind. I think it of no use as a measure of intelligence, but as a diagnostic tool I still believe it to have some value."

Eyes fixed on the dancers, the Colonel continued: "I have certain penchants—some I have acted upon, others I have not. I thought marriage might be transforming, and for a few months it was."

He watched his wife twirling on the dance floor and marveled at how this middle-class creature had adapted to the challenges and rigidities of the milieu he had placed her in.

"I love my son, Frances, more than I could have possibly imagined."

Lady Morgan studied the man before her; it had been a twenty-year friendship, an odyssey that had taken them through several marriages (all hers), several deaths, and, at one time, genuine affection. Suddenly she experienced a terrible epiphany that the Colonel's self-diagnosis was probably correct; whether the science was sound or not, as long as he believed it, it *was* so. Not wanting to reveal her profound dismay, she studiously examined the diamond tiara of a young duchess holding court a few yards away. "James," she said, still not daring to look at him, "you must not condemn yourself for what you are. We all must make good within the limitations and constraints society places upon us; people look to us as an example."

Each fell into a brief contemplation of their emotional follies, past and present.

⁕

Hamish and Lavinia completed their third rotation, the young man steering her around the crowded dance floor with a firm palm against the small of her back. As they waltzed he kept up a commentary on the social standing of the spectators, their faces a blur as they passed.

"I am a great admirer of your husband's work," he said, taking advantage of a lull in the music.

"You and I both, Mr. Campbell. Which particular area are you interested in?"

"The application of craniology to the Amazonian savages."

"Savages? My husband would not agree with the use of

that word; he has found great thinkers and artists amongst the Amazonian Indians and has the utmost respect for their rituals."

"So I have read. I have a huge respect for a man who has the independent means to explore his own interests, yet uses those interests to enhance scientific knowledge."

"And what are your professional intentions?"

As they passed the Colonel and Lady Morgan, Lavinia noticed the sadness upon her husband's face, but the sight was quickly replaced by others as her body moved in the dance's hypnotic patterns guided by the young man's hands.

"I wish to become an anthropologist, but, unlike Colonel Huntington, I do not have independent means and my father will only finance my studies if I agree to join him later in his business. Lady Morgan is my current patron; she has generously provided the funds for my first paper—a study of primitive Celtic rituals. If Colonal Huntington would only endorse it . . . I have also expressed a desire to see his collection of Amazonian artifacts, but I still await a response."

"My husband is a very private man."

"A natural trait in a genius, Mrs. Huntington. I believe him to be one of the most original thinkers in the field. Perhaps you could persuade him?"

His candor made it impossible for Lavinia to refuse him. She laughed. "I shall try, but I must warn you I have little influence."

He swung her around for another rotation, his face breaking into a boyish grin that instantly dissolved the studied sophistication he affected.

❧

The Huntingtons collapsed across the bed cover. Lavinia, still in her ball gown, her petticoats flung in all directions, looked like some airborne vessel that had been shot to the ground. Still tipsy with exhilaration and punch, she was beyond sleep. Her feet ached; already she could feel the prickling of blisters. Forcing herself to stand, she freed the fastenings at her waist and stepped out of the crinoline and bloomers, leaving just her corset that flattened her breasts.

The Colonel, speechless with exhaustion, had flung his jacket across the dresser in the corner. His collar and cravat were pulled open, and he lay there with one hand across his burning eyes, pondering whether he should get straight back up again and drive over to the Albemarle Hotel where a breakfast of deviled kidneys, bacon, and sweetmeats would provide the perfect cure for a surfeit of wine and brandy.

Lavinia threw herself back down beside him.

"You should sleep and I should go," he murmured, and flung a hand in his wife's direction to console what he assumed was a mutual malaise born of excess. To his dismay she drew the hand up to her lips and kissed it.

"Stay," she whispered.

The words *Caress me,* drummed against the inside of Lavinia's skin, a strange continuation of the pulsating waltz rhythm still echoing in her head. She wondered whether she should move towards him. The waiting was more torturous than the fear of rejection. James had not moved a single limb, yet there was hope in his passivity; surely this was acquiescence, Lavinia argued to herself.

Deciding she could no longer bear the suspense, she rolled toward him, pushing him onto his back as she moved.

James turned his face away and looked instead at Lavinia's silhouette thrown by candlelight against the far wall. With her breasts flattened and her hair up, she looked like a slender youth as she mounted him. With his wife now transformed into a stranger, James found this pinning down of his body, this sudden swing into submission, arousing. He hardened and she felt the thickness of him against her. She stared into his face. It was tilted to one side, his eyes now closed, his cheeks flushed.

"Open your eyes."

He obeyed her command, his gaze directed somewhere

beyond her searching look. Wrenching his arms over his head, she held him down by his wrists. I am towering over him, I am taking him, she thought as he entered her. Gasping, she stared into his eyes, refusing him this escape, this turning from her. All her sensuality was focused on one point of contact, the apex of their sex, and the friction grew and spread like a burning as both careered toward climax.

Despite their locked gazes, James was not with her. He had transported himself into a scenario that was entirely of his own construction; one in which he was making love to a completely different individual. But one who, disturbingly, was beginning to resemble someone he knew. Closing his eyes, he tried to dismiss the image that he had superimposed upon Lavinia's body. He hauled himself back into the reality of the moment. Here was his wife, her hair wild, each nipple a hard bud, her lips hovering close to his—nothing touching except his sex inside her and her hands burning circles around each of his wrists. She was taking him, seducing him like a man, and he couldn't deny that it was pleasuring him a great deal.

The months of frustration swelled up in Lavinia as she rode him, legs spread, her flesh stretching and softening in response to his hard organ. Her body stilled in anticipation before wave after wave of contracting ecstasy gripped her.

James, in the embrace of an incubus of his own making, reached his own orgasm, then buried his burning face against the coverlet.

28

Los Angeles, 2002

Julia hated being out of control. Hated it. "I believe in free will," she whispered in a desperate mantra as she picked up the scissors. Mania was a sinister trait; not a dramatic hijacking of the psyche, but an insidious intrusion.

Pieces of photographic paper lay in a large spiral around her, like the gatherings of an exotic bowerbird. Julia sat in its center, two thick photo albums beside her. She was carefully cutting Klaus's head out of all the images. The current photograph was of a picnic they'd had while on a holiday in Taos, New Mexico, three years before. Klaus was tanned, grinning as he glanced across at Julia, who sat bare shouldered in a summer frock. It was a disconnected moment of exhilaration—no indication of impermanency, no sign that he did not love her, would leave her.

Julia tried to remember who had taken the photo. She concluded that it must have been an anonymous tourist. The thin blades of the scissors traced Klaus's neckline, not one millimeter over. She was as careful as a head-hunter.

As she cut, she was reminded of a necklace of dead parrots she'd seen at the Pitt Rivers Museum in Oxford several years before, collected from an Amazonian tribe. This bizarre marriage of death and beauty had mesmerized her. Despite the fact that the parrots were corpses hung on string, heads lolling, their feathers were as bright and shiny as they must have been in life. Oddly macabre, it was also a wonderfully decorative piece of jewelry.

There had been a glass case full of shrunken human heads

in the museum, too. The cephalic trinkets resembled over-sized walnuts and Julia was shocked when she realized what she was actually staring at. Each mouth was sewn shut with twine, the tiny eyelids squeezed closed against terrible horror.

She remembered a father and son standing in front of the exhibit transfixed, the eight-year-old English boy describing the process of head-shrinking as patiently and dispassion-ately as if reciting a recipe for muffins. All the while, the blackened wrinkled heads gazed blindly out with an air of aggrieved perplexity, as if wondering how they had ended up mummified in a Victorian glass museum case.

Julia could hear the boy's crisp consonants even now. *So, Daddy, you pull out the skull so there's just the skin left with the hair still sticking out. Then you stuff the head with stones so that it keeps its shape, then you boil it and it shrinks right down. It takes hours. They did it for power, you know. They believed that all the power of their enemies was kept in their heads, so if you kept the head you got the power for yourself.*

Was that what she was trying to do now? Trying to get back the power Klaus had taken from her? Trying to reclaim their history so she could magically construct her own ver-sion of a future? She paused, the blade of the scissors neatly turning around one ear, ignoring the fly that buzzed around her own ear, which had flown in through the open window. She didn't dare speculate. Whatever her motives, she sensed that they were buried deeper than conscious thought.

She finished cutting, careful to keep the rest of the image intact, then placed the head at the end of the spiral, next to its thirty companions. Thirty incarnations of Klaus—some smiling, some deadpan, some squinting in the light of the flash of the camera, some defiant, some sober, but all neatly severed at the chin.

As Julia slammed her hand against the fly, killing it in-stantly, she wondered whether Klaus had felt her scissors.

PART TWO

THE SERPENT

29

Los Angeles, 2002

Naomi, clutching half a buttered croissant, stood in Julia's kitchen, attempting to make coffee with her free hand.

"Think positively: now you get to sample every dysfunctional divorcé this side of Kansas."

"What am I—the Wicked Witch of the West?" Julia said.

"No really, now you don't have to put up with all those disgusting habits husbands force you to accommodate—like baseball and breaking wind under the covers."

"Klaus is European, he hates baseball."

"Whatever. He's still a total mother-fucker. God, when are you going to start hating? I so wish you would; anything's better than this victim shit. Remember what Nietzsche said—anger is an energy."

"Naomi, you're showing your age. That wasn't Nietzsche; that was John Lydon of the Sex Pistols." Julia handed the ground coffee to Naomi, whose chin was adorned with a cascade of crumbs. "I just wish I could stop trying to analyze what went wrong. We had great intellectual compatibility, the sex was good, we shared humor, fun . . ."

"Well, for a start, this Alpha female, Beta male shit doesn't work. Support a guy and he'll end up resenting you. And as for being blatantly more successful professionally, forget it. I don't care how much lip service a guy pays to Simone de Beauvoir, Susan Sontag, or Gertrude Stein, be more successful and it cuts their balls off. I swear, they will shoot you down. More than that, they will enjoy every goddamn minute of your screaming freefall."

"Klaus isn't like that."

"Sure, he's Mister Born-Again Humanitarian and Enlightened Male."

Naomi shoved the remaining croissant into Julia's hand, then slammed a mug of black coffee in front of her. "Eat. You look like some abandoned anorexic forty-year-old extrophy wife they've just found wandering through Bel Air."

Julia took a tentative bite then realized she was ravenous.

Naomi perched on the bench, her ample curves spilling out of her brightly colored capri pants and tight T-shirt. "Let me guess, in your heart of hearts you're hoping Klaus is going through some temporary midlife madness, and one day he'll wake up, look across and think what am I doing in bed with my wife's best friend? And then he's going to come running back, screaming 'I was wrong, I love you, I've always loved you' or some such total crap, right?"

Julia looked at her croissant. "He is at that age . . ." she ventured.

"God! Julia! You're an award-winning scientist! Women like me look at women like you and we think, Yes! It is possible! We can transcend our emotional destinies, we can be rationalists, we can beat them at their own fucking game."

"Naomi, it is not a gender war out there! You are talking about individuals, complex creatures that are all different from each other, regardless of their sex."

"Right, whatever. Reality check number one: guess who I bumped into at the Latons' place?"

Fear snapped Julia's appetite in half. Gillian Laton was an older academic who had mentored Julia when she first arrived in L.A. from San Francisco. Dick, Gillian's husband, was a powerful television producer at the apex of his career. Originally Julia's friends, they had also grown close to Klaus.

"Don't . . ."

"You've got to pull your head out of the sand, girl. Personally I couldn't believe their fucking chutzpah, but then I never liked Carla. I'm telling you, the industry fucks with their heads, and after a while any semblance of ethics, humanity, or empathy evaporates and what you're left with is one smoking skeleton of white-hot ambition. That's all Carla is—a glorified development girl who got lucky. Bitch."

"They weren't . . ."

"As bold as friggin' brass. All over each other—and I can tell you, Klaus didn't look remorseful in the slightest. The guy's not having some midlife crisis; he's just as emotionally shallow as a kiddies' blow-up paddling pool. But boy, was that bitch working poor Dick. They're up to something together, I swear it. Probably some dumb TV series about abandoned wives."

"Enough!" Julia put down her cup, her hand shaking, then took a deep breath. "They are both persona non grata," she said softly.

"But is that healthy? Denial isn't closure."

"Don't let Mom fob you off with that psychological bullshit."

Julia looked up at the unfamiliar voice. A lithe adolescent was lounging against the kitchen door frame. His shoulder-length black hair was swept back in a ponytail incongruously fastened with a girl's plastic bauble, and ridiculously skinny wrists poked out from a very loose long-sleeved T-shirt printed with Che Guevara's face and the words "Freedom does not lie in martyrdom" in Spanish. The crotch of his baggy jeans appeared to hang less than a foot from the ground and on his feet he wore state-of-the-art Adidas sneakers—constructions of gold latex and red suede that resembled miniature racing cars.

"Please excuse my son." Naomi put her hand on Gabriel's shoulder. "His emotional development is AWOL thanks to his father's influence. I knew it was a mistake to let him go live with José."

"Mom! I've told you before, don't talk about me in the third person. I am here." He shrugged her hand off.

"Gabriel?" Julia stared at the youth, who was over six foot and quite possibly shaved. The last time she saw him, he'd been an ethereal-looking fourteen-year-old who hid behind large glasses and mouth braces.

"Yeah, I know. Hormones happen. Like the fucking weather—predictable, but difficult to pinpoint exactly when," he replied nonchalantly, then looked at Naomi. "Have you asked her yet?" His voice dipped suddenly into a childlike appeal, opening a chink in his aggressive persona.

"Baby, can't you see we're having a female-to-female moment?"

"No, all I see is your usual polarization of a situation that is causing Julia some distress." He turned to Julia. "Forgive Naomi, she thinks the world is one giant PlayStation: abandoned women against callous men."

"I see you've moved on from Dr. Seuss."

"Yeah, and my balls have dropped, too."

"I brought Gabriel here with an ulterior motive," Naomi said to Julia. "He's in his first year at Cal-Tech."

"That's right, you got the Xandox company fellowship. Congratulations."

"Yeah, I'm one of the multi-corporation's greatest assets, they just don't know it yet," he retorted cynically. Again, he dropped his eyes and shuffled his feet, but this time Julia could see that he was quite shy beneath the bravado.

"The course is okay," he went on, "but limited in the area of functional genetics, which is what I really want to major in."

"And he's looking for a summer placement in a lab," Naomi finished.

Julia looked down at her hands; her wedding ring, now loose from weight loss, seemed to wink up at her like a bad joke. A small cut on her index finger had started bleeding and she hadn't even noticed. The last thing she needed right now was to look after some precocious college student.

"Naomi, I'm right in the middle of a horrible separation, the lawyers are on my back, and the most ambitious piece of research I've ever taken on has to be completed in the next six months . . ."

Namoi lost her temper. "Whatever! You've always placed your career before your friends, so why on earth I thought you might change now I really don't know!"

She grabbed Gabriel and began hauling him toward the front door. Pulling himself free, Gabriel stood squarely in front of Julia.

"I topped biology, math, physics, and science this year. I speak and write fluent Spanish. I want to get into bio-tech. That's the future—brain chemistry, stem cells, the genome. I've read all your papers, including the infamous one you presented at The Violence Initiative."

"And what did you think?"

"Simplistic in the socio-economics area, but solid for its era."

Naomi pulled at his T-shirt. "Gabriel, you're wasting your time."

"I've read Rosalind Franklin's work, I've also plowed through Barbara McClintock, Linus Pauling, and Watson's *The Double Helix*—like twice. I dare you to mentor me, it'll make you famous." He delivered the speech as a rap, mimicking a rapper's shuffle and hand gestures.

"I don't know, the commission is huge," Julia said. "I have a couple of people working for me in Washington State and the midwest but in total I have to interview and test five hundred twins."

"Let me guess—that old chestnut, violence and genetics?"

"It's not an 'old chestnut'; it's a very important and potentially contentious part of the future of genetics."

"Cool, I'm into contentious."

Julia glanced down at Gabriel's large hands; they seemed adult before the rest of him, his skinny wrists a vulnerable contrast.

"You know the hours are long and the pay is lousy?"

"I don't care. I'll work for free if I have to. I'm ambitious. Cal-Tech is kindergarten in comparison."

"Please, Julia." Naomi, regretful for losing her temper, put her hand on Julia's shoulder, as if touch might sway her.

"You'll be up against several doctorate students at the top of their field, and you'd have to keep up with me."

"Hey, I didn't get my scholarship for nothing."

Julia turned to Naomi. "It just so happens there is a vacancy, but he'd have to start almost immediately."

"I'm free after June the first, and that's like next week," Gabriel answered before his mother had a chance. Naomi's eyebrows shot up; she'd never seen her son volunteer for anything so enthusiastically before.

"Okay," Julia finally replied, "but your mother will have to drive you to the lab and pick you up afterwards."

"Hey, I'm nineteen. I drive," Gabriel growled, but grinned anyway.

"Thanks." Naomi hugged Julia. "And don't worry about Klaus and Carla—I'm sure it is only a temporary hormonal relapse. He'll come to his senses." She seemed to have conveniently forgotten her original argument.

As the front door closed, Julia's loneliness sucked her back like a vacuum.

30

Mayfair, 1861

Lavinia had inherited a parlor of her own from the Viscountess; a small room tucked away at the back of the house, it was located on the ground floor and had French doors that opened directly onto the garden. Lavinia suspected it might have once functioned as a storage room of some sort, and that the Viscountess had had it furnished for herself almost as a secret folly. Situated away from the kitchen and servants quarters, it was a refuge in the mornings when most of the servants were occupied in other parts of the mansion.

Against one wall stood an oak bookcase full of books Lavinia had brought from Ireland; amongst them novels by Victor Hugo, George Sand, and Thackeray, plus a slender volume entitled *Prison hours: a diary of Marie Lafarge wrongfully imprisoned for the murder of her husband*. It was the autobiography of a young French woman who claimed she had been erroneously accused of her husband's murder. A celebrated *crime de passion*, the case had gripped the imagination of Lavinia's father and the British and French public. It had provoked moral outrage, dividing those who supported the wife (she had suffered great physical abuse) from those who condemned her as a heinous criminal, viewing murder of one's husband as an effrontery to the very stability of society. The Reverend Kane, appalled that the French should waive the death penalty, had written a letter to *The Times*. Years later, however, when the adolescent Lavinia secretly read the diary, she had greatly admired Madame Lafarge's pursuit of idealistic love and her desperate attempt to free herself of an abusive husband forty years her senior.

Lavinia now sat at a desk positioned below the bookcase, her head bent over the whispering box.

Dear Mama, it has been a good three months since I arrived in Mayfair. At first the lack of female companionship and social engagement depressed me greatly. But now, since James asked me to assist him in the composition of his book, my days are filled with the most extraordinary intrigue as I walk beside him through the jungles of South Amazon, and experience his exhilaration and awe at the discovery of some exotic creature or primitive man. It has given us a new intimacy and I plan to reintroduce such sentiment to the bedroom, where my husband has, alas, been most absent of late . . .

The rattle of pebbles against the French doors disturbed her. She looked up from the whispering box and opened one of the shutters. Aloysius stood on the other side, glancing around nervously. Lavinia indicated that he should wait. After wrapping the whispering box carefully in a silk kerchief and hiding it in a drawer, she went to the parlor door. She checked that none of the servants were lingering in the corridor outside, then locked the door and quickly opened the French doors to let the coachman in.

"You were not seen?" she asked.

"I believe not, madam."

"Good. I fear I am the subject of unnecessary malice amongst the servants; is it not so, Aloysius?"

"They cannot place you, madam, and that always makes downstairs nervous."

"I thank you for your plain and honest speaking," Lavinia said, and pulled a blank sheet of paper from her writing desk. "So, we are to compose a letter to your brother." She dipped her pen into the inkpot. "I trust you have a correspondence prepared?"

Every part of the coachman radiated agitation, as if the gaunt unwieldiness of his body belonged only in Nature. In this room, with its dainty furniture, delicate china, and carved objects, he felt fettered and clumsy, fearful he could accidentally smash an ornament with an ill-judged stretch of his arm. Taking a deep breath, he began dictating.

"My dear Seamus, I am content to hear that you are safe and well. Five years is a long time not to hear from a brother." Lavinia's nib squeaked against the paper as she raced to keep up. "I write to wish you good luck and courage in your soldiering, but also to tell you that our grandfather is now with the angels. He passed last spring and it were—"

"*Was*, Aloysius; *was* is the correct tense."

"I will say it how I speak. Then he will know it is from me," he replied defiantly.

Lavinia couldn't help but smile. His vernacular brought

Ireland right into her parlor. "In that case *were* shall stay. Pray continue." And, dipping her pen into the inkwell, she waited, nib poised.

Aloysius paused, relishing the moment: the sight of a gentlewoman waiting for his command a furtive but satisfying pleasure.

"And it was a grim and tortured struggle," he resumed. "In short I were happy to see him finally at peace. I have a good position here in London as head coachman. You always said I would get ahead. And I strive to send coin back to Ireland for our poor sister Maureen and her child, Peter. Now that you have an address, please write as often as you wish. Stay safe and may God's protection be over you, Your brother Aloysius."

The pen continued to scratch into the silence.

Aloysius, suddenly lost for the appropriate protocol, turned to leave.

Such awkwardness in men always reminded Lavinia of bears, the likes of which she had once seen goaded into ridiculous antics at a visiting Russian circus in Dublin. She had felt for the animal then, his dignity destroyed as a short man in scarlet pantaloons danced around him shouting orders, the bear swaying in outraged bewilderment.

"Oh, for the Lord's sake, sit down. The chair will not bite."

And so the coachman sat, a little intimidated. Lavinia finished writing, then carefully secured the letter with a blob of sealing wax.

"I have written the address on the outside; the postmaster should be able to deliver it," she said.

"Many thanks, Mrs. Huntington."

"My name is Lavinia."

Amazed, Aloysius stood up again, his large hands dangling uselessly. Lavinia, mortified at her audacity, could only conclude that she had been prompted by acute loneliness; as if she needed to hear her name spoken in the accent of her girlhood.

"My apologies for my lapse of manners, and if I have made you uncomfortable."

She went to the French doors and stared up at the skyline of chimneys leaking their inky spirals into the darkening sky.

"Sometimes it is difficult to breathe in London." Lavinia stretched her hand out and touched the glass for a moment then turned back. "The air is so foul and thick with industry. I miss Ireland and my father. I fear I might have taken his affection for granted in the past."

"Madam, my Ireland has been a grave for a good ten years and I'm thankful to be out of it. I am practical; I don't long for memories that never were. I live only for now."

"A wise sentiment, but do you not also think of the future?"

"Plans are for the rich," he replied bluntly, then regretted his harshness; was her birthright her fault?

He is like a sealed box, Lavinia thought, watching him shifting restlessly in his knee-high riding boots. Did she trust him because he was from the same country, or was it because his obstinacy revealed a shared loathing of artifice?

"There must be something you miss," she ventured.

"I miss my horse; the salt on the night breeze when there's a storm out at sea; and a small finch I had trained as a pet. The rest can go to Hell."

Lavinia held out the letter.

"One day perhaps we will both go back."

"To Hell or to Ireland?" he replied with a bitter smile.

❧

No matter how old or how young a person, the full flowering of spring, with its daffodils and crocuses, creates a renewal of sensuality, however icy the preceding winter.

And so Lavinia found herself basking in a newfound optimism as she and James drove along Rotten Row, for it seemed as if the whole of Hyde Park was illuminated by a golden light that caught at the unfurling buds and tendrils.

The notorious avenue, where reputations were both cemented and destroyed, was crowded with society's elite: some on horseback; some in open carriages; some walking with nursemaids, children, lovers. This was the time for acquaintances to mend their rifts, for the desirer to "accidentally" encounter the desired, for commercially minded men to exchange stock suggestions and the odd racing tips, and all the while advertising their most precious asset—their marriageable daughters. Some of the most important mergers of the powerful dynasties of the Empire had been initiated here under the seemingly innocent guise of a casual introduction. But nothing was casual in the choreography of this weekly pageant. Many were the mothers who encouraged their daughters in their horsemanship, knowing an upright spine, a well-fitting riding habit, and a good seat to be as seductive as any beautifully performed Mozart sonata.

Aloysius, dressed in his smartest livery, sat in front of the Huntingtons' phaeton, guiding the two prancing geldings along the graveled road. The Colonel, sitting next to Lavinia, who had Aidan on her lap, kept his eyes trained straight ahead, a tactic that enabled him to avoid acknowledging all but his oldest acquaintances or those worthy of introduction.

"Colonel Huntington!" Hamish Campbell rode up beside the phaeton and tipped his riding hat politely at the couple.

"Colonel, I have taken the liberty of writing to the Anthropological Society of Paris and, after reading more of your work, I'm afraid I must canvass you again regarding the endorsement of my essay and the perusal of your Bakairi artifacts."

"You really are most persistent," the Colonel responded dryly.

"I am also a man who is not used to being refused, nor do I intend to make rejection a bedfellow," the young man replied, his arrogance offset by his charming delivery. "Would Sunday at three suit you?"

"We will expect you on the hour," the Colonel replied, puzzled at how he had been manipulated into agreeing.

"Until then, good afternoon, Mrs. Huntington, Colonel." Tipping his hat again, Hamish Campbell trotted off.

"A persistent young man, but elegantly persuasive. I suppose I shall have to tolerate him," the Colonel said, flicking away a buzzing bee.

"He will be part of the next generation of anthropologists and useful in the promotion of your reputation," Lavinia replied, placating him. She placed her hand on his knee.

31

Camp Pendleton, 2002

"Frankly, I think it can happen to anyone, Professor Huntington."

"Call me Julia." Sensing that the soldier was close to confiding in her, Julia let the tape recorder roll on.

"Yes, ma'am." He grinned, the smile of a child. There was a radiance about him, an innocence, and Julia couldn't help but feel charmed.

"Something or someone has morally wronged you—well, there is nothing more lethal than a wronged man. Now, I don't know if this kind of thing has happened to you, ma'am. First time it happened to me, it was my wife. She betrayed me. It's there in my file. I was married two years and I nearly killed the man I found her with. Luckily, he didn't press charges."

Winston Ramirez didn't look as if he could even grow a beard, yet he'd served six years in the marines, and been involved in countless operations and one full-blown war. His file also noted that he'd been a straight A student at high school.

The youngest SEAL on record, Winston had exceeded his commander's expectations by volunteering for four operations back to back with the barest minimum of leave. The twenty-nine-year-old appeared to thrive on conflict, the bloodier the better.

Half African–American and half Latino, Winston had been adopted by a middle-class African–American couple and had grown up in Ladera Heights, California. His identical twin had been adopted by a blue-collar couple who lived on the other side of America, in Atlanta. Interestingly, both men had ended up in the military; Winston's brother, Michael, was an airborne ranger. They had never met.

Winston's case had come to her attention because, unlike some of the others in the database, he didn't have a history of abuse or any social or economic deprivation. His adoptive parents were stable, law-abiding, and, by all accounts good nurturers.

His identical twin Michael, by contrast, had grown up in an abusive household, and as a child had displayed a broad, though fortunately mild, range of antisocial behaviors. Michael had joined the army at eighteen, younger than Winston, but had attracted similar attention as his twin, and had been selected for ranger training. He had earned his wings in one of the elite airborne divisions, and had excelled under fire in frontline combat. Like Winston, he had displayed no signs of post-traumatic stress disorder. The twins showed very similar readings in their brain scans when viewing images of combat, and almost identical readings for associated heart rate and blood pressure. It was a clear example of genetic inheritance dominating over environmental nurturing.

Wrapping the tourniquet around the marine's upper arm, Julia searched for a suitable vein.

"What about your adoptive mother and father, Winston?"

"Well, ma'am, they're nice, God-fearing citizens who go to church and pay their taxes. My mom's a primary school teacher, my dad's an academic. They were active pacifists, funnily enough. They campaigned against the Gulf War in '91, anti-nuclear. You know the type—well-meaning Democrats.

To my way of thinking, maybe a little naive. Anyway, it nearly killed my father when I joined up. We talk now, though—just not about the army."

"You know your twin brother is an airborne ranger?"

"So I've heard."

She slipped the needle into his vein. He inhaled sharply, then smiled crookedly. "I'm not real good with needles."

"Almost done. I was asking about your brother . . ."

"We've e-mailed but we haven't met yet."

The syringe was a quarter full, the entire matrix of Winston Ramirez's lineage concealed in that small amount of blood.

"He's taken a posting in Afghanistan, too," Winston went on. "He's going to arrive a day after me. Between me and you, ma'am, it's weird—like, we ask each other the same questions at the same time."

"But you must be excited about meeting him?"

"I am. But also I'm a little scared—maybe we won't get on . . ."

"Twin brothers, similar hobbies, similar ambitions—you'll like him."

"Maybe, maybe not."

Julia pulled the needle out and pressed a cotton ball against the welling puncture, then taped a plaster strip over it.

Winston pulled on his shirt, then bent over and clicked the tape cassette off.

"This is off the record, but ma'am, have you ever wondered why the department's suddenly got someone like you on the case?"

Sensing a slight threat under the question, Julia didn't answer.

Winston continued, "I guess it's because of what happened in Brazil last year. A lot of taxpayers' dollars went up in that operation—a few guys at the top probably did some heavy-duty soul-searching afterwards."

"What operation in Brazil?"

He buttoned up his shirt and grinned a teasing half-smile.

"If you don't know, I ain't telling."

~❧~

Julia sat in a Starbucks at the edge of one of the gated communities south of the border. The gridwork of mock-Mediterranean mansions with recently planted bougainvillea tacked against their stucco walls was visible from the freeway, the fecund irrigated landscape a vivid emerald—the artifice of the great Californian dream. Outside the fence, the native scrubland was a burnt brown.

Sipping her coffee, Julia studied the marine's file. The twins' biological parents both had criminal records, with the father showing characteristics of extreme violence, suggesting a genetic basis to the twins' violent disposition. She needed to locate the parents, take blood samples and brain scans, and find out about their own parents—the twins' grandparents. Julia was excited by the notion of tracing the lineage of the trait until she noticed a footnote at the bottom of the page: *Parents deceased*. It was like coasting down a road only to discover it was a dead end.

The thought led her to her own ancestry, to a memory of sitting on her father's lap and questioning him about Lavinia Huntington and the awkward expression that traversed his face as he evaded some of her questions. What had really gone wrong with her great-grandmother's marriage, she wondered now.

Her coffee was cold. Julia stared out at the Mexican gardener fastidiously blowing leaves from one side of the path to the other. It was one of those timeless sunny days that transformed everything—the sky, the freeways, the malls—into oblongs of color: salmon-red, beige, pale indigo. Looking around, she realized she was in a landscape of consumerism, with all the recognizable totems found in any corner of the country: McDonald's, Dunkin' Donuts, In-N-Out Burger,

Riteway, Borders—a two-dimensional environment that felt unanchored and impermanent, as if it could all float away at any moment. Is everything expedient, Julia wondered—marriages, houses, cars, identity?

Crushing her polystyrene cup, she attempted to dismiss the sudden image of Klaus clowning for her in the mall car park. As recollection jabbed her sharply between the temples, she understood exactly what Winston Ramirez had meant by the phrase "morally wronged"; she knew his anger.

32

Mayfair, 1861

Colonel Huntington stood in the center of his study, holding aloft a skull whose cranium was carefully marked into divisions with red ink, like the topography of a recently discovered planet. Behind him, the glass doors of the display bureau housing his collection of skulls and artifacts stood open.

Hamish Campbell, dressed in a striped sack suit, sat near the Colonel, writing neatly into a leather-bound notebook. Lavinia sat by the fireplace.

"As you know," the Colonel said, "I am an associate member of the Anthropological Society of Paris, but despite my friendship with Monsieur Paul Broca, I disagree with his notion of measuring intelligence by the size of the brain. I side with Broca's rival, Louis Pierre Gratiolet, who believes that brain size bears no relationship to intelligence."

Surprised, the young man looked up. "Surely you don't also believe there is equal intelligence between men and women, even between races?"

"Is that so preposterous?"

"Preposterous? It's ridiculous. You just have to observe the behaviors of savages or of women. For example, have you ever seen a man lose his logic and engage in a fit of hysteria?"

"Have you ever observed a boxing match, my good fellow?"

"Regularly, sir. And I'll have you know, I regard pugilism as a highly sophisticated and controlled ritual that requires considerable manifestation of intelligence."

"Perhaps," conceded the Colonel, "but, unlike Gratiolet, who still believes the intellectual inferiority of women and natives can be measured by earlier closure of the skull sutures, I suspect our capacity to measure intelligence is too narrow. There has been far too much emphasis on the importance of craniology in anthropology; I myself have been guilty of this. However, I do not entirely dismiss the importance of phrenology, particularly in the diagnosis of pathology—but I digress."

"But, with respect, sir, you cannot afford to doubt your own research. That would make you a heretic within the movement," Campbell blurted, distressed by the Colonel's argument.

"Indeed. It should be noted that Gratiolet is a self-declared Royalist, whereas I regard myself as a follower of Gladstone. Is our destiny to be shaped solely by the size of our brain, our race or our sex? I find myself wondering whether nurture has rather more to do with shaping us. Of course, whether such a utopia will ever exist where such a hypothesis could be tested remains to be seen. Somehow I suspect that such a notion is beyond the vision of most *Homo sapiens*."

Intrigued, Hamish walked over to the bureau bookcase, where he picked up a small stone axe, its flint tied to the roughly hewn handle with reeds.

"Sir, you do realize that if your ideas were proved correct, over one hundred years of study would be rendered irrelevant, perhaps even vilified as hocus-pocus?" He swung the axe as if to emphasize his point.

"Of course he does!" Lavinia sprang up and took her

husband's arm. The Colonel, bemused by Hamish's irate tone, calmed her then turned back to the young man.

"Believe me, I have not come to these conclusions lightly. My close observation of the Bakairi led me not down the path of racial superiority; to the contrary: of course there was poverty, of course there was ignorance, but there were other intelligences operating of which we have little or no understanding. Not inferior, not necessarily superior, simply profoundly different."

The Colonel walked over to the bureau bookcase. "I usually keep this locked for I am ashamed of its contents. I have not collected a skull for a good ten years."

Flushed and confused, Hamish pointed out a small skull with jutting frontal development. "You cannot believe that a prognathous skull with a small cranium can possibly house the same intelligence as, say, a Napoleon?"

"I repeat, sir, I am not entirely convinced one can measure intelligence by brain size alone. In fact I shall go one step further and suggest the possibility that intelligence may not be confined to the brain but exist in other parts of the body, both visible and invisible, including the soul."

"What? Now you are a mystic as well as an idealist?"

The Colonel laughed at the expression of indignation upon the student's face. "At the moment, I am content with the role of Doubting Thomas. Please don't look so distressed, Campbell. I hope I haven't thoroughly disillusioned my one fervent admirer?"

"To the contrary, you have merely fueled both his curiosity and his imagination. The time with the Bakairi tribe must have been most formative."

"Indeed, I am collating my notes into a book, with the help of my wife, whose intelligence *I* have never questioned."

Hamish turned to Lavinia. "I beg your pardon, Mrs. Huntington, I didn't mean to slight the weaker sex."

"I shall assume it was a comment made in ignorance not malice, Mr. Campbell."

"So I am forgiven?"

"You are tolerated but not absolved of your presumption."

The Colonel broke into a low chuckle as he closed the bureau, locking it with a small brass key.

"My wife learned her scientific skills at the side of her father, the eminent naturalist Reverend Augustus Kane. Now, I believe it is time for the gentlemen to retire to the library, where a good claret and a cigar may lead to more frivolous discourse." Sensing an unspoken tension between the two younger people, Colonel Huntington hurried them out of the study.

❧

Hamish exhaled, sending a thin stream of cigar smoke through the bluish atmosphere. Sitting opposite the Colonel, his feet comfortably perched on an ottoman, he contemplated the room. It was the perfect literary gentleman's retreat: a circular space lined with bookcases from ceiling to floor, all carefully ordered according to subject, which was exactly how Hamish would organize his library, when he had the fortune to afford one. The books themselves reflected the Colonel's diverse interests: Plato, Socrates, Epicurus, as well as more contemporary titles such as Macaulay's *History of England*, Darwin's *Beagle Diary, Uncle Tom's Cabin*, Lady Montagu's *Letters from the East*, and many others beside. To the young student, the collection was an exhilarating insight into the mind of his mentor.

He glanced furtively at Huntington, who was stretched back in his chair, the quintessence of a man at his intellectual pinnacle, courageous in his opinions, resolute in his pursuit of originality. Would Hamish ever achieve such ease in his own skin? Would he ever *belong* so unselfconsciously?

One of the Colonel's trouser legs had ridden up; the vulnerability of this strip of flesh suddenly seemed so seductively within his reach that it took all Hamish's resolve not to lean across and caress it. Instead, he glanced over at the leopard skin covering the parquet floor and found himself wondering how Huntington might look naked upon it.

Trying to exorcise the salacious image, he glanced up to the mantelpiece. A sculpture of a female figure squatted there. Looking at her pointed breasts, swollen belly, and rather pronounced vulva, he assumed she must be a fertility goddess, a trophy from some exotic expedition—the Pacific Islands perhaps?

There were several other artifacts around the room: a mummified head with wisps of hair trailing behind its shrunken ears; a totem pole embellished with several bearlike creatures; a bow made from bone and hide—each contributing to the ambience of the library as a place of learning and bizarre ritual. The most spectacular was a canoe strung from the rafters above their heads, a hollowed-out log etched with sticklike animals and figures, and smelling faintly of charcoal.

The Colonel followed Hamish's gaze. "A burial canoe, they would place their dead in it and send it burning down the Amazon. I commissioned that one for myself. The shaman insisted. He told me that now I had eaten and shat with them, I would have to bury two souls: my black one and my weak white ghost brother."

The two men laughed. Again, Hamish felt the excitement of approval, of belonging.

"Interesting how the Celts, too, sent their dead across the water," he said.

"It is one of the eternal elements, water. We float in the womb, and at our death they send us floating back out into that great lake."

"Colonel . . ."

"James, call me James. I think we can dispense with formalities."

"James, I am seeking a position to further my studies. The subject I have chosen for my doctorate is fairly contentious and I need to prove I have both the support and the tuition of a respected professional."

"What do you want from me exactly?"

"An endorsement for my first published leaflet." He placed the manuscript that had been sitting on his lap onto the ottoman. "And I would like to volunteer myself as your assistant for a period—say, a year—before I go up to Oxford. If you were to agree, I would consider it a great honor."

"Does it not concern you that we are of differing opinions when it comes to craniology?"

Hamish tapped his cigar into the ashtray and studied the underbelly of the canoe. His father was a timber merchant who had made a modest fortune through supplying artisans with the best and most seasoned woods. Hamish thought of him now, how he would be fascinated by the exotic nature of the wood hanging above. A man born and bred in Lancashire, the merchant had been determined to ensure that his only child would become a gentleman. He had succeeded to the point that father and son had become estranged. Hamish recalled now with shame his pomposity and his mortification at his father's dialect and rustic manners. To his secret regret, he knew he would be embarrassed to introduce his father to Colonel Huntington.

The wood merchant had made enough money to send his son to Eton, but not enough to guarantee a stipend that would allow Hamish the trappings of a city gentleman all his life. Thus Hamish had made his way by capitalizing on his charm, his good looks, and intellect. He had ingratiated himself with the wealthiest boys at school, engineered weekend invitations to their country estates, charmed their mothers—many of them young and beautiful—in the thousand ways a handsome young gentleman could. In short, Hamish Campbell was gifted with all the attributes ambition required; something Huntington had recognized in his first encounter with the young man and of which he had initially been most suspicious.

Now Hamish needed a new patron. The relationship with Lady Morgan had suddenly become complicated, and he was running out of strategies to avoid a physical liaison. It was a dilemma; Lady Morgan was besotted, and Hamish was genuinely enamored of her wit and ironic social commentary. Yet here before him was a benefactor who could also function as his mentor—an entirely different proposition, and one that was infinitely more exciting. But could Hamish afford to ally himself with someone whose controversial views might prejudice his own future publications?

He glanced at the painting that hung above the walnut desk and immediately recognized in Icarus the young James Huntington. It must have been painted when Huntington was not much older than himself. The splendor of the youth was undeniable: his pale skin shone like Carrara marble; the fine dusting of dark hair that led down to his sex was rendered with such painstaking detail as to suggest each individual hair prickling along the skin. Hamish marveled at the delicacy of the brushstrokes. He could almost smell the sweet sweat of the young man as he contemplated the great expanse of crisp morning air, the shafts of the rising sun transforming the valley spread before him into a tantalizing patchwork of emerald hills, towers and citadels set against a distant sea. No wonder Icarus jumped, thought Hamish, and he was filled with a great exhilaration at the wealth of opportunities now spread at his own feet.

Lavinia walked down the stairs after checking on her sleeping son. Through the half-open door of the library she could hear the two men in intense discussion. Tantalizingly, the conversation was not fully audible.

Lavinia glanced around to see whether any of the servants were visible; the corridors were empty. Silently, she moved closer.

"Well, is it such a dilemma that you cannot answer?" The Colonel's rumbling baritone rolled across the gentle hiss of the fireplace. An ember crackled.

"I am prepared to embrace your findings if I am able to

arrive at them through my own observation," Hamish said, "as your assistant."

"How very noble of you," Huntington replied, astounded by the impudence of the young man. "And what do you imagine your tasks may be?"

"I would be your personal secretary."

Outside in the corridor, infuriated, Lavinia gripped the doorknob. Surely James can see through the young student's obsequious manner, she thought, fighting the impulse to interrupt.

"Are you sufficiently advanced in your field that you believe you can offer a contribution to a scientist whose experience spans decades?" the Colonel continued.

"Forgive my audacity, sir, but I have been told by my professors that I have an original eye."

The Colonel stood up and poked the fire. As he did so, he caught the reflection of the doorway in the mirror over the fireplace. He could just make out the pale phantom of his wife's dress in the sliver of shadow between door and frame.

"Lavinia, would you care to join us?" he asked without turning.

Lavinia entered the library sneezing at the thick cigar smoke. She placed herself in front of Hamish Campbell, who immediately rose to his feet.

"My husband has an assistant. He has no need of another." She could not contain the tremor in her voice.

"My wife has extraordinary hearing. I am thinking of offering her services to Scotland Yard."

Hamish repressed a smile as Lavinia glowered at her husband.

"Oh, do sit down." The Colonel strolled to a large globe in the corner and began to spin it in an attempt to dispel his irritation. "In truth, Lavinia, it would benefit me to have an assistant with formal training, as well as someone who will be able to help me present my lectures."

"But I can do that."

"My dear, it is essential that my work is respected, especially given its controversial nature. I cannot possibly expect my fellow anthropologists, particularly the less enlightened ones, to take me seriously if I employ my wife as my assistant." He turned to Hamish. "You understand my quandary?"

"Indeed." Hamish hoped his reply was sufficiently diplomatic.

"What remuneration would you expect for your efforts?" the Colonel continued, ignoring Lavinia's evident anger.

"Merely the cost of my transport from Islington, sir, and enough to cover my inks and pencils. Luncheon, I expect, would be provided, and any other additional expenses would be negotiable," Hamish answered tentatively, glancing at the furious wife.

"Then it is agreed: you may start on Monday."

"But what about my work on your book, the months I have labored?" Lavinia demanded.

"You are now free to dedicate yourself to the many delightful pursuits of a society wife. I am surprised you are not more enthusiastic about the arrangement," the Colonel concluded, smiling.

"I cannot believe you would insult my intellect this way!" Furious, Lavinia made for the door. "I take my leave, Mr. Campbell. No doubt I shall have the pleasure of your company thrust upon me regardless."

Hamish, being of a modern sensibility, did not take offense.

33

Los Angeles, 2002

There were fifty cases pinned up: twenty-five sets of twins. Under each army-file photo was pasted a synopsis of the soldier's active duty; his family history including any evidence of violence or abuse; medical history (paraphrased into a neat page emphasizing genetic illness or malformations); a photographic printout of his DNA blood analysis, tracking circulating hormones and mood-controlling neuropeptides like serotonin, endorphins, adrenaline, and noradrenaline; and brain scans and EEG responses to violent visual imagery.

By a systematic survey of total gene activity profiles and computer analysis, Julia hoped to locate one gene—or possibly a network of genes—that was repeated in all the interviewees, linking their specific behavior pattern to a genetic origin and thus proving it was a heritable trait.

The pinboard was the first thing you noticed when you entered the room. The collection of charts looked like some sort of bizarre topographical map, Julia thought. Some of the subjects were smiling; some appeared entirely vacant behind the eyes; and some of them seemed barely grown men. As Julia searched their faces she was surprised to find herself flooded with a sense of protectiveness. She paused, mortified.

As a scientist, she had learned to objectify the people involved in her research; it was a necessity as any emotional involvement could influence the outcome. Have I been too detached in the past? she asked herself. Does my enthusiasm blind me to the needs of others? Was that why Klaus left?

Pushing her doubts to the back of her mind, she returned to her work. But her anxieties stayed with her. She couldn't look at these soldiers anymore and see them merely as vessels for chemical codes for form and behavior; they'd become victims of genetic predeterminism. What made an individual capable of killing without remorse, she pondered.

A tentative knock on the door interrupted her.

◆◆◆

"The Human Genome Project's principal objective is to determine the sequence of the three billion nucleotide base pairs that make up the human DNA, identify the 20–25,000 human genes embedded in this sequence, and to store this information in databases for further research and for the betterment of mankind—"

" 'Advancement' might be a stronger word than 'betterment.' "

"I like betterment, better, even better than betterment."

"Stop being cute. You were doing great up until then."

They were sitting at a small Formica table in the corner of Julia's office. Gabriel had his notebooks spread out, his beaten-up laptop open and running; he was reading aloud from a term paper on the debate around the ethics of genetic selection. His cell phone stuck out of his shirt pocket and his jeans were slung dangerously low.

He scratched his head, fighting a desire for a cigarette, then took the opportunity to surreptitiously examine Julia as she leaned back in her chair. She looked sadder than before, if that was possible. It was as if someone had stolen her energy, the very element that defined her.

Gabriel thought about the travesty that had been his parents' marriage; was this the kind of misery he had to look forward to?

Perversely, he noted that this air of defenselessness suited Julia; it softened the edges of the dispassionate professionalism she usually emanated. Her long slim legs were stretched out before her; her black hair hung to her shoulders and was slightly messy, as if she'd run a comb once through it that morning and not touched it since. She was handsome as opposed to beautiful, he decided; the structure of her face was too strong to be called pretty; only her wide mouth and sea-green eyes saved her from a certain masculinity. She had a face full of stories, he marveled, stories that begged to be caressed into being. The sensual note continued as his eyes wandered across the breadth of her shoulders and he found himself calculating that she must be almost exactly his height—how would that be in bed?

Stop, she's your mentor, he cautioned himself; nevertheless, it was her intelligence that he found most exciting— the unique combination of scientific rigor and imagination. Secretly he was terrified he lacked that extra component— the ability to break away from preconceived ideas and look at a problem laterally. Was it fearlessness, or simply a question of practice? Whatever the answer, he hoped to absorb a little of her alchemy and use it to his advantage.

He glanced at the information board. A navigation of genetic disturbance was what Julia had called it; Gabriel hadn't been sure whether she was being cynical. Sometimes he found it difficult to tell. The men stared back at him defiantly. Some of Julia's subjects weren't much older than him, and some of them looked Latino, too. Remorseless killers or heroes?

Either way, they all had the look of the outsider, the ostracized. No matter what Julia thought, Gabriel was convinced that nurture was the bigger villain.

He shifted his gaze to the window; in the distance he could just see the top of the quadrangle and the fountain. It was one of those warm summer days when you could almost smell the faint scent of eucalyptus on the breeze, the air shimmering with a vibrant buoyancy. The warm curve of sunlight falling across his face made him restless.

Julia's jacket hung over a chair where she'd thrown it that morning. He liked the way it looked: it made him think of the woman he remembered from childhood: intense, a little reckless, but always focused. Julia had always shown a passion Naomi's other friends lacked. Gabriel regarded most of them as resigned old hippies. Julia had been different. She was renowned in the way he wanted to be, eccentric in her thinking—and she worked in an industry that would affect future generations for decades to come. There was no ambiguity about the fact that he found her intensity erotic.

"So you think I'm cute?"

"It doesn't matter what I think."

"Don't say that; it's a negation of the Self, and I mean that in a Buddhist way, nothing to do with Nietzsche."

"You are precocious."

"Apparently. Okay, I'll change 'betterment' to 'the advancement of mankind.' Or should I go 'human species'?"

"'Mankind's' kind of sexist. How about Homo sapiens?"

"Yeah, I like that, that's very *Planet of the Apes*. What do you think about the rest of the paper?"

"I think it's good, but a little unsophisticated. The structure of DNA is more complex than that, as is the sequencing of the genes on the chromosome. We may be able to identify which gene or genetic mutation makes someone susceptible to schizophrenia, but we don't yet know the trigger that causes the gene to come into play. To make things even more complicated, the very same gene might have a positive function in another human being—say, to fight off a particular disease. Therefore, to talk about isolating genetic disorder and breeding it out is not a viable future scenario."

"Then why spend so much money on the Genome Project? Why open the box if you're not going to play with the toys?"

"Because it helps us understand disease, so we can streamline medicine, and also evolution. In a way, I think it unites us . . ."

"How?"

"Well, for a start it proves we really do spring from one mother."

He grinned, thinking about his own mother and how he loved her and would fight to the death to protect her, but couldn't stand living with her.

"The mother of all mothers. Mind if I smoke?" Without waiting for her reply Gabriel produced a cigarette and a lighter.

"I guess I'm confused. On the one hand, I can see the advantages; on the other hand, I can foresee a world where every potential parent will have to go through a screening process before being allowed to procreate, or maybe even get relocated to an area where their unborn baby's skills will be more in demand. I mean, I have a grandfather who committed suicide, a cousin with obsessive compulsive disorder, and my dad's seriously word blind—where does that put me as a potential gene donor?"

"I think the word you're looking for is 'father.'"

"Whatever. I mean, how do you feel? You've got to have some family skeletons in the cupboard, right?"

"Naturally, but because I know the genetic probability of that propensity, I can change my lifestyle to factor that in. Knowing allows me to make an informed choice. Genes interact with environment; it's not one or the other."

"And what about those guys?" Gabriel pointed to the pinboard. "Why would a gene that allows someone to detach emotionally during violent conflict be successful in an evolutionary sense?"

"The answer to that is obvious. Somewhere in history, evolution favored an early *Homo sapiens* who defended his tribe, perhaps even colonized another tribe, ruthlessly. Sometimes I think of genes as a letter that gets handed down the generations, but the letters get scrambled slightly with each delivery, altering the meaning. Okay, back to real work," she said, indicating the pinboard. "The first things we have to rule out are the obvious candidate genes that have already been associated with antisocial behavior, violence, etc., like MAOA and any other possible hormonal links."

"I've labeled and filed the DNA samples we have so far. Do you want me to run them over the microray as we go?"

"That would be great. Mine for MAOA and any other heightened expression that shows up."

Gabriel threw his cigarette butt out the window. Then, without turning, he asked the question he'd been wanting to ever since he'd walked into the room. "So what happened between you and Klaus? I remember meeting him as a kid and he seemed a really nice guy."

He swung back to her and watched her tidying her desk, her cheeks burning.

"C'mon, try me. I am wise beyond my years when it comes to matters of women and men. Believe me, if you'd sat in Naomi's kitchen for as long as I have listening to my mom and every other jilted woman from here to Haight-Ashbury, you'd be wise, too."

She put down her files. "Okay, so what's your advice then?"

"Become a lesbian. Men aren't worth it."

He threw the comment out and waited, his long angular face set in a morose tightness that he knew she would not be able to read.

"But you're a man."

"Yeah, and if you had as much testosterone pounding through your body as I currently do, you'd be a horny, confused bastard, too. He left you, right? No warning, no signs."

Julia folded her arms resolutely. "I don't want to talk about it."

"Maybe there were clues, but you were just too terrified to go there—you know, fear of abandonment and all that crap."

"I said I don't want to talk about it."

There was a silence. Outside, a plane climbed its way up out of the afternoon's smog.

Gabriel, staring at the pinboard, thought about his parents' divorce. José, his father, had left Naomi when she'd reached the age of thirty-eight, but the indications had been there before. There were so many differences between them. His father was first-generation American and wrestled with the traditional expectations of the Latino women he'd grown up around. Expectations that Naomi—a secular Jew who came from a lineage of domineering women—had found quaint at first, then repressive. Then, when José's career as a painter took off and Naomi found herself at home alone with a young baby, she began to blame José for her own lack of artistic success. By the time José introduced his new dealer to the family—a dynamic Latino woman ten years his junior—Gabriel, even as a seven-year-old, had recognized the demise of the marriage.

"It suits Naomi to think of my father as pathological." The earnest tone in his voice surprised even himself. "But she's wrong. If she'd read the signs, she could have saved the marriage. I believe that, I really do."

"Sometimes things happen that you can't explain," Julia countered gently. "Sometimes people just aren't honest, good, or courageous. Even the ones we think we know really well."

"Does that mean you believe in the concept of amorality?"

She looked at him. It was a genuine question; a leap into the abstract that had taken her by surprise. She thought about the soldiers she was interviewing, about war, holocausts, and all the other morally careless and culpable acts human beings had committed against one another, and in that moment, looking at this boy-man sitting awkwardly astride a chair, the afternoon coming in the open window behind him, she realized that she did. She did believe in amorality.

"Does a genetic disposition to kill without emotional regret absolve the killer?" Gabriel persisted.

"It's never that simple. External events, a combination of genetic factors—all come into play to trigger an action—"

"—or reaction." Gabriel finished her sentence.

34

Mayfair, 1861

Well, Mama, you would not believe the crusade I have been forced to undertake by my husband and his co-conspirator to establish myself in this uppity village of Mayfair. I am to host an At Home—a high tea of cucumber and watercress sandwiches for a select group of eminent guests. Surely there can be nothing more dreary, and all of the persons I wished to invite have been dismissed by Lady Morgan as too "bohemian" or not of "our" class. Naturally, doctors and lawyers are not to be allowed entry. Any single man has to be a baronet, a peer, or at least a commissioned officer. Lady Morgan is partial to the dragoons, and, as the Charge of the Light Brigade and the current misfortunes of the Russian Empire are still of interest, she assures me she will do her utmost to secure an actual eyewitness. Frontline raconteurs, she calls them, and tells me such gentlemen are invariably handsome and penniless but essential for ambience.

I have sent over forty cards to all manner of mansions and city palaces—an exhausting and demoralizing experience. Lady Morgan is convinced that the majority of the invited will attend, if only to gape at the exotic Irish renegade. It is a travesty: she has decided I must have an impeccable lineage and has commissioned a family tree from a draughtsman who specializes in such forgeries. It is an impressive piece of foppery, with a family coat of arms of a mermaid seated upon a unicorn, and an ancestry going back to the King of Connacht himself. Papa would die of embarrassment if he should hear of it. Lady Morgan has insisted I hang it in the parlor, where the high tea is to take place. I just pray no one will ask me about my illustrious forebears.

Even more mortifying is the rumor Lady Morgan has deliberately planted suggesting James is on the brink of publishing a book as scandalous and as controversial as Charles Darwin's. Suddenly everyone wants to meet the young wife of the man who may be the next candidate to take the scientific world by storm. If only it were true, and if only James had let me continue as his assistant. The ennui of piano lessons, sewing, and endless trivia about who is about to marry whom shall yet be the death of me.

My husband has banned me from both library and study and I now have only dear Aidan to entertain me. I should not complain; the child is a delight. But I miss the hours of industry by James's side more than I could have possibly imagined.

Our marriage is much changed, and not for the better. I do not trust this young man James has taken into his circle, and I fear we grow further apart by the day—

"Mama!" Aidan's exclamation brought her back to the room. Playing at her feet, he held up a toy rabbit. "Kiss!" he demanded.

Reaching down, she embraced the toy, then softly closed the lid of the whispering box.

It was late and most of the household had retired. James had not returned from his club and Lavinia, in nightdress and dressing gown, unable to sleep, found herself pacing the corridor. Before she realized it, she was standing outside the door of James's study. The door, a portal most recently locked from her, now stood tantalizingly ajar. The faint scent of cigars and other masculine odors—leather, boot polish, and lemon-scented cologne the Colonel was fond of wearing—drifted out of the room, drawing Lavinia into the sphere she so missed. The glowing embers of a recent fire still shone from the hearth and she could see the scattered papers of his work abandoned on the desk. She paused, breathing in the scent, then stepped quietly into the study, locking the door after her.

It was as if her husband had just left the room. Running her hand along the leather of the armchair, she imagined that she could still feel the heat of his skin, the weight of his body still impressed upon the cushion. She wanted him then, wanted his arms around her, his lips on her mouth, her neck, her breasts. She sank into the seat, her thin silk nightdress riding up between her legs. Lit just by the dying fire and the street lamp shining in from outside, the Colonel's primitive artifacts looked like beautiful, libidinous onlookers, consensual in their own erotic writhing.

Lavinia's hand wandered down, caressing her thighs. She imagined her hand was James's hand and that he was taking her there—in the most sacrosanct of all his territories. She was wet, lost in the fantasy, pleasuring herself. She opened her eyes, her gaze falling upon a smooth ebony figurine of a man, his polished head glistening in flicking light. She reached across and picked it up from the low table before her, then spread her legs wide, one over each arm of the chair. She ran the head of the figurine up her thigh and across her sex. The satiny touch of the polished ebony became her husband's yard, the thickness and weight of it familiar against her skin. Then, imagining his urgency, his measured strokes, she pushed the head into her, faster and faster until exploding, she felt herself contracting around the smooth wood.

Afterwards, she wiped it with her nightgown and placed it carefully back onto the table where she had found it.

The day of the At Home had arrived and Lavinia, stiff from sitting upright for three hours and profoundly bored by the chatter that dominated her parlor, felt the irresistible desire to jolt the two young heiresses sitting opposite out of their conceited self-righteousness. A pair of smugly rotund eighteen-year-old twins aptly named Celeste and Clementine, they were the daughters of an immensely wealthy merchant. Lord spare me such ignorant women, Lavinia thought. Have they no interests beyond securing a husband? Her mind turned to her husband and Hamish Campbell ensconced in James's study—how she longed to be there rather than enduring this parody.

She leaned forward. "All aristocracy has blood on its hands. There is not one family south of the Scottish border that does not have some history of enslavement. The French understood this. And now America, whose own Declaration of Independence took its cue from the French Revolution, is in the throes of a bloody civil war. Mr. Lincoln is a brave man indeed."

At which Clementine dabbed a few tears from her eyes. Her sister, however—a more corpulent version of Clementine— puffed up her skirts in readiness to defend her father's reputation as the owner of several cotton plantations in America's South as well as one on the island of Jamaica.

"Papa is a good man," she announced sanctimoniously. "Why, he gave all of the slaves a picnic for last Easter Sunday, and we had raised the pork ourselves."

"I have seen men dying of starvation, and you talk of the seating arrangements at the Derby Day banquet as if it were a matter of life or death." The compulsion to shake the sisters out of their twittering complacency threw Lavinia into a further rant.

"Which proves my hypothesis correct," Lady Morgan interrupted, with an eye to the sisters' chaperone, a dowager of great social influence who, at that moment, was fortunately having trouble locating her ear trumpet, "that an Englishman, unlike an Irishman, would die of embarrassment long before he died of starvation."

There was an awkward pause during which Lavinia silently vowed never to trust a woman who regarded human suffering as appropriate material for a witticism. Deciding to ignore the comment, she turned back to the sisters. "Tell me, how *has* your dear papa educated you?"

The twins exchanged flustered glances: the Irishwoman

confused them; she was so unpredictable in her conversation. Clementine finally spoke up.

"Well, Celeste has a wonderful soprano, and Mama is forever boasting of my needlepoint."

"But what of intellectual matters—books, the classics, the pursuit of science, the arts . . . Are you really devoid of all curiosity?"

"Papa does not approve of books, oh no, not at all, he is always reminding us that a bookish woman will drive a husband away. He has educated us for marriage."

"My father educated me as if I were a boy. I am fluent in Latin and have a good understanding of mathematics, biology, and the physical sciences. I can only imagine how you must view the world without the benefit of such faculties?" Lavinia's voice was full of mock sympathy.

While Celeste tried to work out what the word "faculty" meant, Clementine glanced at Lady Morgan. "But surely that would be most unusual, even for an Irish Lord—"

Lady Morgan, determined to avoid further social chagrin, interjected before Lavinia had the opportunity to answer. "Mrs. Huntington's illustrious father was the most delightful eccentric who did so want a male heir."

~❦~

"Their name means 'Sons of the Sun' and their goddess is Evaki. They consider her the guardian of both the day and the night. At night, she keeps the sun hidden in her cooking pot; in the morning, she releases it, thus creating the day. If we agree on the connectivity of all of these gods, who in other mythologies would be Evaki's match?"

In the silence of the study, Colonel Huntington and Hamish Campbell were examining the tribal groupings and icons of the Bakairi.

"The Egyptian goddess Bast, the Irish Aimend, and Sul," Hamish answered, proud of his knowledge.

"Exactly. You see, under the skin humanity's dreams are

identical. We all dream the same symbols—of the god we would like to become, of the monster we fear we might really be."

Secretly enthralled by the notion of encountering his mentor's inner demons, Hamish looked down at the notebook, hoping to conceal his sudden distraction. "Mrs. Huntington has done an extensive job on the first few chapters," he said. "I hope I can continue the task in such a professional manner."

"You are generous. Her writing style has a theatrical flair it is true, but it is exact observation I require, not dramatic ornamentation. Confidentially, your work is superior."

Exhilarated by the praise but not wanting to show it, Hamish carefully studied the various artifacts on the table, paying particular attention to two huge Yakwigado masks made from tree bark and daubed in white, red, and black. Next to them sat a small figurine of a man. Made from ebony, the polished phallic head held a certain fascination and Hamish couldn't help but extend a finger to stroke the smooth satiny surface.

The Colonel watched him. The symmetry of the youth's face was a source of endless fascination. He observed how the light caught at the blond down that ran across the upper planes of the boy's face; the hair became coarser as it dipped into the hollow between cheek and jaw, then flared out with an erotic violence across his lips and mouth. The azure of his eyes was so deep it did not look to be natural, and his dark brow served to illuminate the gold of his hair. There was something perturbing about extreme beauty in either sex, the Colonel philosophized. It was like a third presence, an independent entity separate from the observer and the observed.

"I have read about your experience with the Bakairi," Hamish said, breaking the extended silence. "You consumed a local hallucinogen?"

"It is called ayahuasca, made from the vine *Banisteriopsis caapi*, a powerful narcotic. The experience taught me that our perception of the known universe is defined by our cultural understanding of it, and that alone."

Hamish Campbell showed a certain inquisitiveness that the Colonel recognized as being one of his own most powerful characteristics as a youth: an enthusiasm for the mystical.

"But to have experienced such intense transportation . . ." Campbell began, then faltered as he met the Colonel's gaze.

For a moment, the two men looked at each other, each fighting the compulsion to touch the other. The tension was broken by a bell ringing elsewhere in the mansion.

"I believe we are called to dinner. I insist you stay and eat with us," the Colonel said, distracted by the sculptural quality of the young man's well-formed hands.

"But I am not dressed . . ."

"I have a dress coat of dark broadcloth which you may borrow." The Colonel placed a hand on the youth's shoulder in a gesture he hoped would be seen as paternal, despite the tremor that ran through his body.

"I am not sure your wife would find my presence at your table desirable."

"Poppycock! Besides, it is *my* table."

The table was set formally, and all eight candles in the walnut and silver Dutch chandelier that hung over the long mahogany table were blazing. Set defiantly in the center of the jacquard tablecloth was a heavy, flamboyantly molded silver epergne, its stand supported by two Rubens-like female figures. A pair of candelabra stood either side of the epergne, their light setting the five or six crystal decanters and the silver serving dishes aglitter.

The dining room itself was a square room, heavily paneled and draped with thick blue velvet curtains. Consoles and side tables crowded the walls, some covered with family memorabilia and others with silver serving dishes. A painted firescreen stood before the huge hearth, to shield the diners nearest to it from the heat.

The immensity of the table was emphasized by the fact that only three places were set for dinner, each with fine crystal glasses, and heavy silver forks, spoons, and knives on either side of the green Wedgwood plates.

Lavinia, in a low-cut, short-sleeved muslin dress, a simple choker of jade around her neck, sat to the right of her husband, picking at her plate of oysters. Hamish Campbell watched her, wondering at the strained awkwardness between husband and wife.

"Your kitchen boasts a good cook," he complimented Lavinia, and picked up the handwritten menu Mrs. Beetle had prepared. "Oysters Katharine, cream of celery soup, fillet of sole with Gruyère, pheasant Mandarin with carrots Vichy, followed by gooseberry fool and a savory—you indulge your guest."

"Lady Morgan has been talking to our cook," Lavinia replied dryly. "Lady Morgan has begun to dictate much of what happens in this household; she has even insisted that I subscribe to the *Englishwoman's Domestic Magazine*. It is full of information—from recipes for ginger beer through to a hundred uses for an old muslin dress. A talented individual, she has even managed to establish a salon of voyeurs, all of whom are breathlessly awaiting my husband's forthcoming publication. We only pray that you are a speedy and proficient midwife, Mr. Campbell."

Hamish laughed politely, but noted that the Colonel remained silent.

Lavinia, deliberately ignoring her husband's discomfort, continued. "Indeed, I myself have been reconstituted, grammatically parfait, and am to be served up with the appropriate amount of relish. I just wonder how long society will remain intrigued by this enigma Lady Morgan has so successfully constructed."

It was hard to keep the anger out of her voice. How could James imagine she would be content to pursue such banality? How could he reject her contribution to his work so easily?

I must play his game, she thought, then find a way back to his study.

The Colonel, choking on a crust of bread, coughed into his napkin.

"From the number of times the doorbell chimed, I assume the At Home was a successful undertaking?" he inquired, now concerned about Lavinia's manner.

"In that all forty guests appeared, yes. However, three left prematurely due to an impromptu lecture on the evils of the Confederacy."

"Given by yourself no doubt. The departed have my sympathy. Lavinia, you really must learn to separate the political from the personal."

"There was little of the personal about today's gathering, and Lady Morgan's efforts on my behalf have been entirely political."

For a moment there was only the clinking of glass and the noise of the diners eating. A footman, whose sole duty was the pouring of the wine, filled Lavinia's goblet then moved on to the gentlemen.

"So, Mr. Campbell, what new and extraordinary things did you learn today in my husband's study?" Lavinia returned to the fray.

Unused to the tumult of matrimony but an expert on the nuances of charm, Hamish mustered both his courage and his wit. "I learned about the Bakairi and a ritual called Lemaquely, where a Spirit will advise a woman on how she is to behave within the community—and list her personal shortcomings. Any scolding from the Spirit is regarded as an honor. So you see, even the Bakairi have a Lady Morgan spirit."

All three laughed, and the Colonel took Lavinia's hand.

"There, my dear, you can take comfort from the fact that the Bakairi have their social codes, just as we have ours in Mayfair."

The play of her husband's fingers across her wrist caused Lavinia a small flutter of arousal; he had not touched her

since their lovemaking after the ball. What did Hamish
Campbell promise her husband that she couldn't offer? Intellectual companionship? The possibility of reliving his youth
through the younger man?

"It seems to me that women are freed from their responsibilities only when they are merry widows or eccentric old
spinsters," she concluded. "The rest of us have to make do."
She turned to the student. "Sir, I would exchange the drawing
room for the study any day."

35

After the men had again disappeared into the study, Lavinia
sat down to read. The crackling of the fire, the incessant
ticking of the clock, the rustle of footsteps outside, and the
faint, distant cry of a rat catcher all contributed to a certain
restlessness—even the words on the page seemed to flutter
like moths. Glancing up from the page she decided she could
not stay a moment longer in this mausoleum, deprived of
conversation and company, while in the room above the two
men navigated the wilds of the Amazon.

Jumping to her feet, Lavinia pulled on a long hooded cloak
and made her way to the stables, careful to avoid the seemingly omnipresent housekeeper, Mrs. Beetle.

Lavinia sat in the enclosed carriage, her face concealed by
her hood. Outside, from Curzon Street all the way up to the
notorious Shepherd's Market, groups of prostitutes lingered
around doorways and shopfronts, their outrageously painted
faces tinted yellow by the gaslights as they paraded hopefully for passing trade. Staring out, Lavinia searched for one
particular girl whose visage was engraved upon her memory.

In the driver's seat, Aloysius was surly with disapproval. "No good will come of this, madam, I'm telling yer. 'Tis a man's world and best left that way," he shouted down to her, as, to his disgust, an ancient whore winked up at him, her copious cleavage mottled and wrinkled.

But Lavinia, fascinated by the vulgar gaiety of the women and the manner by which they marked their territory, sometimes spitting and shooing off competitors, was enchanted. These women appeared to enjoy a freedom that intrigued her. It was a pageant, she decided, and there were many characters she recognized: the ingénue with her virginal white gown; the duchess with her fleshy jowls and paste; the bohemian with her loose hair and floating robe under which her naked shoulders shifted provocatively.

"Lady, you shopping for someone or are you here for yourself?" A pockmarked face loomed out of the mist.

Lavinia, startled, shrank back. "I am looking for someone in particular."

"Someone's particular or someone's peculiar?" the prostitute chuckled, revealing a broken tooth within the deep crimson mouth.

Aloysius shook his whip at her. "Away with you!"

Laughing, the whore vanished into the night. The coachman shivered; it was getting colder. "Madam, we should be leaving. The master will be wondering where you are!" he called.

At that moment, a tall slim figure emerged from a doorway and slipped between the mingling streetwalkers, her face illuminated for an instant by the gaslight. Lavinia, forgetting herself, stepped down from the carriage and ran toward the woman, her skirts becoming soiled in the puddles of mud and horse manure.

Catching her by the shoulder, Lavinia peered into the woman's face. It was the girl she had seen walking with James outside the bookshop, but close up her features were heavier, her skin coarser, than Lavinia had imagined.

"May I help you?"

The well-spoken alto voice disorientated Lavinia.

"Will you talk to me?" she asked. "Just for a few moments?"

The girl hesitated as she assessed Lavinia's expensive dress, the fur-trimmed cloak.

"I will pay you well," Lavinia pleaded.

"As you wish, but I have an appointment later."

Inside the coach, the girl appeared even taller and more awkward. She lifted her black net veil embellished with sequins and sat back against the leather as if she were accustomed to such luxury, her long gloved arms draped elegantly across the back of the seat, her limbs arranged with a self-conscious air. Her perfume was a strong musk laced with lilac; it filled the carriage and seemed an extension of the dramatic face paint and clothing. There was something about the severe angles of her face that reminded Lavinia of her husband's Amazonian masks. Was this what James had been attracted to, these unabashedly sensual planes? Watching the whore, Lavinia tried to imagine her husband making love to such a being. It was all too easy.

"I want you to tell me what my husband likes," Lavinia said, hoping the whore would not be able to read her expression in the half-light. The girl laughed, taking care to cover her flawed teeth with her hand.

"My brave friend, I know many husbands. Which is yours?"

Again, Lavinia had the uncomfortable impression that the girl, who appeared no older than herself, was superior in both experience and years.

"Colonel Huntington. I saw you both together several weeks ago."

"Ahh, so the Colonel has finally married, and one so young and pretty."

"You have known him for a long time then?"

"Indeed, several years. He is a good and kind patron. But you look unhappy—really, there is no need."

"Surely a philandering husband is a source of unhappiness."

"Ah, so this is why you have sought me out. To discover why he makes love to me and not you?"

Lavinia, unable to speak, nodded. The young woman smiled enigmatically and then, without a word, pulled her wig off. It was then that the masculine angularity of her countenance was explained. Amazed, Lavinia cried out.

"Do not distress yourself, my dear. I am sure he cares for you in his way. Besides, I have not seen him for a good month. No doubt he has become one of those 'reformed' gentlemen."

The transvestite pulled out an elegant pocket watch attached to his waist by a gold chain. As he opened it to read the time, Lavinia noticed it was engraved with the initials *AC*.

"Now that your question has been answered, I will have to leave you. But first I have a question for you."

"What could that possibly be? Unless you wish to question my intelligence?" Lavinia replied angrily.

Smiling gently, the youth placed his hand over Lavinia's, as concerned as any gentlewoman might be in the circumstances. "You mistake me. I do not pass judgment; I merely wish to make an inquiry of my own. Do you have an older sister, or an aunt perhaps? You bear a remarkable resemblance to an old employer of mine, also an Irishwoman."

"I have neither sister nor aunt."

"Your mother?"

"My mother died when I was two."

The youth pocketed the five guineas Lavinia gave him, then peered closer at her face, searching her features. He sighed. "Remarkable."

Replacing his wig, he opened the carriage door and climbed down. "You may remember me to the Colonel. I am known as Polly Kirkshore." Then, smiling whimsically, he slipped away into the night's embrace.

36

Los Angeles, 2002

A butterfly hovered and skipped over the surface of the swimming pool, incongruous against the background of telegraph poles reaching up beyond the wire fencing, its multi-hued wings catching the sunlight, the long tips of its wings trailing behind—a winged messenger of the natural world.

Julia sat marooned in a cane reclining chair, the blood sample she'd come for safely stored in the briefcase at her feet. Lieutenant Colonel Axel Jensen, a bulky sixty-year-old whose leathery tanned stomach fell in gentle ripples over his loose swimming trunks, sat beside her, ice clinking in his glass. He smiled, revealing immaculately capped teeth. Julia knew they were capped because the day before she'd met his identical twin, whose teeth were comparatively decayed.

The house, located in a quiet street in Van Nuys, was a collision of painted steel and stucco. The concrete and grass patio curved around the pool, and sliding glass doors revealed an open plan kitchen with a sunken seating area furnished with leather sofas. There was even a bar with a bamboo canopy. It was the ultimate playboy's den circa 1972, and, judging by the peeling paint and chipped pool tiles, it had not been renovated since then. Axel Jensen, the personification of old-world masculinity, appeared a natural extension of his environment.

After glancing down to check that the tape recorder was working, Julia peered into his mirrored sunglasses. "So, tell me about what happened in the Gulf."

"Well, I was in command of an airborne ranger unit,

professor. People like us—soldiers who are sent in behind enemy lines to locate and eliminate the brains of the beast—we're the elite. We're there because we want to be. We're trained hunters."

"All the other survivors from your unit developed PTSD, except you."

"They also developed Gulf War syndrome, a third testicle, and all kinds of other shit. Don't get me wrong, I'm not saying it doesn't exist; I'm just saying there's a psychology that's better suited to this job."

A jet roared overhead, followed by the screeching departure of a coterie of crows that had been perched on the telephone wires.

"I guess I'm a rare kind of creature," Jensen went on. "Every time I was in combat, something would go click in my head and I just carried out my missions as efficiently as possible and as ruthlessly as necessary. You've interviewed my twin, Lance—Lance the accountant, I call him. You want to know why I think we are similar? We both hate mess, Professor Huntington. Lance hates messy numbers, and I hate messy situations. He likes correcting the sums; I kill to save lives. That's war. I have a gift, but I've used it for the common good. Another margarita, ma'am?"

He held up his empty tumbler, the slice of lime on the edge of the glass like a defiant balancing act. Julia smiled. "No, thanks."

"Then you won't mind if I do. And you can switch that damned thing off." She clicked off the tape recorder.

He stood up lazily, muscles bunching in the varicose-vein-laced calves, and sauntered to the wet bar. Reaching for the plastic flask of tequila with one hand, he pulled open the bar fridge door with the other.

"This report of yours . . ." He poured the tequila, then the margarita mix, into the glass with the practiced gestures of the habitual drinker. A bowl of limes sat on the counter, already sliced and waiting. ". . . are you keeping the names of the soldiers involved out of it?" He swung around, a new drink miraculously in hand.

"Absolutely. All information remains confidential."

"Pity. I like the idea of immortality. My name immortalized in the pursuit of science. The only damn way this name is going to be remembered."

She felt him watching her, like a predator sniffing out vulnerability in its prey—yet she sensed he liked her. Glancing around at the neglected, inherently masculine surroundings, she wondered whether it wasn't simply because she was female; her maroon summer dress a seam of color that blasted through the washed-out concrete, the bleached cane chairs, the desiccated cactus leaning against the stucco. Suddenly claustrophobic, Julia checked her watch and stood. "I should be going. Be good to avoid the afternoon pile-up on the freeway. Thanks for cooperating. I'll ring you later with a time to come into the laboratory, Lieutenant Colonel."

"Sure. They can say what they like about Axel Jensen, but they can't say I'm unpatriotic."

She held out her hand and he shook it. He radiated a mix of cheap cologne and dried chlorine cut with the faint smell of coconut. The familiar aroma reminded Julia of a certain generation of men—her father's generation—and she found that she had warmed to the soldier, regardless of his politics.

Sensing the change in her attitude, he held on to her hand a moment longer than necessary. Julia pulled it free.

"One last thing," she ventured. "There was an incident in Brazil last year . . ."

The lieutenant colonel's body language altered instantly; the first time that afternoon he appeared off guard.

"They briefed you on that?"

Julia hesitated and in that split second he read the lie. Taking her by the elbow he started to lead her to the front gate.

"I'm retired now. I'm way out of the loop, just an old dog

waiting to die. It pays to play dumb, Professor Huntington, that's one thing I've learned. Don't be the branch they want to chop off—because they will do it. I guarantee it."

❦

Julia drove down the freeway analyzing the two interviews. Lance, the accountant, sitting in his immaculate office, where even the paperclips looked as if they'd been filed, appeared almost autistic in his lack of social interaction. But he had identical mannerisms to his soldier brother, even down to a twitch under the left eyelid. Both men had married at the same age to similar-looking women; both had musical abilities; both professed to a faith—for Lance Jensen it was evangelism; for Axel Jensen, nihilism. Lance had left the army before he experienced any action, but was it possible that, in an extreme circumstance, he would be able to kill without experiencing remorse afterwards? Or if the mutant gene function existed, might it be lessened in the identical twin— only triggered by an extraordinary situation?

The thought led Julia to her own family. If her great-grandmother murdered her husband, what did that mean in terms of her own genetic inheritance?

I'm slipping into paranoia, Julia told herself. If there is such a mutant gene function, the chances that I've inherited it are slight—almost negligible.

As she parked the car, the image of the lieutenant colonel's face when she asked him about the Brazil incident—the way it hardened, the sudden detachment that infused his gaze— came back to her, and lingered all afternoon.

37

The hum of the incubators was comforting. Julia loved this sensation of being in the kernel of activity; the laboratory was a sanctuary, a quiet place of study where she could escape and exist entirely within her work.

Having stained the chromosomes in selected cell samples from her subjects, she was now carefully manipulating the dish under the lens of the microscope. A small screen next to it displayed the magnification process, allowing her to focus her attention on the chromosomes' arrangement and juxtaposition as she looked for any irregularities or distinguishing features.

After recording her microscope and DNA analysis in her workbook, Julia stood in the middle of the laboratory and stretched out her arms. The sudden inrush of the outside world terrified her—knowing she had to keep busy before the insidious sense of loss that haunted her crept back in, she packed away her notes and went to her office. She booted up her laptop, then Googled five words: *Brazil, 2001, U.S. Special Forces*. The only result was a concise description of a small squadron stationed outside of São Paulo. No mention of any "incident."

Julia was tempted to phone Colonel Smith-Royston, her contact at the Defense Department, but Axel Jensen's words troubled her. It would be foolish to assume she could trust the Defense department official entirely.

Logging off, she leaned back in her chair and realized that for the first time in two months she had nothing to do. It would take forty-eight hours before the next phase of her experiments could proceed, and the thought of driving back to an empty house on a Sunday was unbearably depressing.

◈

As Julia walked up the hill to the observatory, she wondered whether she was the only single person in the whole of Griffith Park. Large Latino families wound their way out of the crowded car park, their dark-eyed children trailing behind, some chewing on twists of sugared churros; others clutching huge batons of ice cream that dripped white streaks down their T-shirts. Couples of every nationality were clustered on park benches staring down at the view, or promenading along hand in hand; the young men jaunty with self-importance, the girls in their Sunday finery. Some hobbled along in tight jeans and high shoes. Others looked as if they had come straight from church, with neat freshly ironed blouses and pleated skirts, their hair corn-braided, as if after the worship of God came the worship of Nature.

Julia started along her favorite track. It snaked through the hills in lazy bends and sharp corners, passing small ravines and twisted trees set low in the natural scrubland. As she climbed higher, the groups of strolling families disappeared and soon only the dedicated walkers and joggers accompanied her. The air grew cooler and the sound of the city fell away. Breathing hard, she paused, resting her hands on her knees. Below stretched downtown Los Angeles, the last of the afternoon sun bouncing off the skyscrapers like a running seam of quicksilver, an afternoon mist beginning to taint the air with a soft green.

The mechanical croaking of frogs radiated from a pond beneath a wooden bridge. Julia squatted and stared at the miniature ecosystem. It was little more than a glorified puddle, the brown water tangled with weeds, a Coke can half buried to one side, forming an exotic jetty. A microcosm that seemed entirely separate from the world above. Watching the progress of a tiny emerald beetle that was balanced precariously on the can, Julia lost herself. Then, as she stood, she remembered this was the very place she'd stopped to catch her breath six months earlier with Klaus.

They'd paused to look out over the city; the endless panorama had seemed like an optimistic metaphor for their future. She'd leaned against his chest feeling profoundly content, the scent of him faint against the smell of eucalyptus. The distant car hoots and city rumble drifted up like forgotten smoke.

"Enjoy the view, darling. Life's about to get very busy," she'd said, referring to her looming trip to the Middle East and Klaus's latest writing commission. But Klaus had remained silent, and when she looked at him she'd seen that he was absolutely distanced from her, his gaze searching the view below. In that moment, she'd had the uncomfortable impression that he was looking for all the possibilities that had eluded him—romantic or otherwise.

Now she realized his behavior was probably an indication of discontent, one of the signs Gabriel had mentioned.

Winston Ramirez's voice sounded in her mind, as if bubbling up from the mud, from the noise her walking shoes made as they hit the ground: one foot, two foot, three. *What you've got to understand is the ease of killing if you have that extra capability to put things in a box. This is my killing box. This is my love box, my hate box, my family box. A good soldier doesn't confuse them. Ever. It's impersonal. But you know what: If someone wronged me, really wronged me, and it did get personal, I could kill, then walk away. It's that extra capability. You can't fake that. You've either got it or you ain't.*

Julia knew how that kind of killing felt. She'd experienced it in Afghanistan, and she could understand the motivation that might make a person kill again.

~≈~

After pulling into the driveway, Julia rested her head on the steering wheel, dreading entering the empty house. Crickets and the faint drone of somebody's lawnmower faded up from the silence. Suddenly there came the slam of a door from somewhere inside the house. Jolting upright, she reached into the glove box and pulled out the wrench she kept there, then climbed out of the car, gripping it tight against her chest.

As she moved tentatively toward the front door, Klaus emerged, holding a cardboard box. He stopped and stared at her.

"What are you doing here?" Julia demanded; it had been two and a half months since he had left and she was shocked to see him now.

"I left a box of tools here, sorry. Anyhow, I still own half the house, remember? That investment remains unresolved."

Julia stepped toward him. "Klaus, we had a good marriage."

"Don't."

"I still love you."

"Please don't make this any harder." He didn't look at her, but focused somewhere around her forehead, as if he were gazing into the distance. "We can't talk about this now. Not like this."

"Then when? You refuse to see me. How can you just annihilate ten years of marriage? Our future, all that we planned for?"

He picked a snail off the garden wall and threw it over to the neighbor's side. An automatic habit from when they were living together. He's still territorial, he still cares, Julia thought, grasping at any hope.

"Everything that needs to be said has been said." He still wouldn't look at her. "You needed me to be someone I just wasn't, Julia, and I went along. I've spent more than half my life pleasing women and denying myself."

Stunned, Julia sat down on the car hood, her hand still clasped around the wrench. She didn't recognize her husband now as he slowly turned purple with rage, all traces of intelligence dissolving from his face. Now he looked at her, jabbing a finger at her accusingly.

"And you know what else? The only mistake I made was in being too weak to leave you earlier!"

Screaming, Julia lifted the car wrench and lunged toward him, her fury filling her with an extraordinary strength. Klaus's face immediately stretched into a caricature of fear.

"You're fucking crazy!" He pushed her back down onto a small shrub, the branches scratching and cutting into her back. Kicking him away she swung wildly with the wrench as he ducked, narrowly missing the swinging iron.

"I'm fucking crazy?" she yelled. "Do you know what you've done?!"

Suddenly arms grabbed her from behind. "Whoa!" Gerry, the neighbor, pulled the wrench from Julia's hand. "I was wondering where this got to. You guys borrowed it about five years ago and never gave it back."

Nobody laughed. A police helicopter circled overhead as it always did at about 6 p.m. The noise of Klaus and Julia gasping for breath merged with the beat of the rotating blades.

Gerry dropped his hands and laughed nervously. "Wow! Well, I'm impressed. You guys do great argument."

Julia, her whole body shaking with grief and rage, lunged for Klaus again. He stumbled back.

"Enough, Julia, enough!" Gerry grabbed her.

Ignoring him, she continued trying to reach Klaus. "What's in the box? What are you taking away now?!"

She wheeled around, Gerry still trying to hold her; their struggle resembled a bizarre ballet, except its violence made the choreography frighteningly unpredictable.

"If you don't stop, someone is going to call the police," Gerry hissed in her ear.

Klaus stooped to pick up the carton. "These are mine, Julia—photos from before we were married, before I knew you. That's all I want, the rest is yours. I can do without the memories."

He walked toward his car. Julia twisted in Gerry's arms. "Don't go! We can talk! Klaus!"

He turned. "Get some help, Julia."

She broke away from Gerry and ran full pelt toward Klaus. Weeping now, she clutched at his arm. He pushed her to the pavement. As his car sped away, the trees, the street and the sky seemed to come crashing down upon her.

38

Mayfair, 1861

The photograph was of the Colonel, with tribal elders standing either side of him clad in painted wooden masks large enough to conceal their heads and shoulders. Long strands of dried grass were attached to the masks and ran down to the ground, completely hiding their bodies and any other indication that they were human. The painted faces of the mythological creatures—dark forehead, a streak of white from brow to chin, a simple oval symbolizing a mouth, circles or curved streaks for the cheeks—stared back at the viewer, sinister, not of this world.

Hamish gazed at the Colonel's figure dwarfing the tribesmen, his eyes blazing as he stared beyond the camera lens, beyond the known world. The young student, soporific from dinner, imagined how the ritual might have been—the gyrating natives, the masks swaying mesmerically in the flickering fire.

"The day before, we had all fasted to purify our bodies to prepare them for the Spirits," Huntington explained. "Gilo, my guide, who also worked as my translator, sat with me in a clearing they had made especially on a riverbank. The shaman was a man of about forty years, which is old indeed for the Bakairi. He stood only four foot eleven inches in height but had a ferocious nature. He was a true statesman. He promised me that I would see my Spirit, the gods of my people. At the beginning of the ceremony, we all performed a dance to cleanse the air of evil and to entice the spirits to come up from the river and enter the masks that the twenty-one shamans wore. Campbell, you should have seen how the young boys' dancing swept up the red dust, stirring up a cloud in which shadow became spirit became man became shadow again. It was extraordinary. Then, after the drumming stopped and all the jungle birds filled the clearing with their shrill screeches, the chief shaman stepped forward. 'I am the embodiment of Evaki, I am her page!' he chanted. 'You, white ghost! I will dance your past, I will dance your future!' "

The Colonel paused, the memory transforming his expression. Outside, a coach and horses rattled past, creating an avalanche of hoof-falls that hung for a moment then faded.

"And did he?" Hamish leaned forward eagerly.

The Colonel hesitated; whenever he had related this experience before, he had always censored it. Why did he now feel the need to confess to this youth? Was it the desire to be unburdened? To admit to an epiphany that he, a self-declared atheist, regarded as spiritual? Perhaps he was looking for absolution . . . but to be absolved by an apprentice, a novice half his age?

Could he really trust him? He studied the youth; the look in Hamish Campbell's eyes, the open enthusiasm that played across his features again reminded him of his younger self. The Colonel decided to continue without expurgation.

"In a manner, I think I experienced both my future and my death there. As the shaman began to mimic my walk, my slightly hunched shoulders, the perplexed knot of my forehead, the swing of my traveling stick clearing the foliage, I could see myself: prejudiced, burdened by all the preconceived notions I had carried into the jungle six months before.

Then, suddenly, I saw myself at ten, alone, fearful; then at sixteen, bursting with all the arrogance of youth; and then, like ripples across one's reflection in water, I saw my own death mask. I tried to flee but I was fastened to the ground as firmly as an insect to a specimen glass. I could not tell you whether I stood there for hours or days, but I can tell you I saw their goddess of death, Calounger, with her skull head and burning eyes. I saw their gods, Campbell, I swear it. This scientific rationalist witnessed the very fabric of another culture's belief. I tell you, there is not one truth but many."

There was a beat. The Colonel, embarrassed at having sounded so youthfully impassioned, set the mask down and waited. He must believe I have lost my sanity, he thought. What an idiot I have been to endanger my reputation. Finally the student spoke up.

"What I'd give for such an experience—to throw off the shackles of the conventional world, to see into another sensibility!"

Relief flooded the Colonel's body. He felt intoxicated, inspired by his companion's obvious enthrallment.

"What would you give?" It was a rhetorical question. The Colonel had sensed already what Campbell would offer.

Hamish glanced at Huntington. The man's tone was brazen, and yet it was a delicate moment: to presume wrongly would be certain social suicide.

"I think that as an anthropologist it must be considered an essential part of one's training. To experience such a profound insight through a single ritual—"

"And a little ayahuasca," the Colonel interjected, smiling slightly.

"—and under the guiding hand of a mentor, to understand that the known world can be so easily usurped—for something far more exhilarating and dangerous . . ."

"Indeed."

The two men laughed, a deliberate ploy to break the suddenly charged atmosphere. Each felt a nervousness not unpleasantly laced with elation and erotic desire. As the Colonel leaned forward, his knee brushed Campbell's flanneled leg, an almost imperceptible contact that both were excruciatingly aware of.

"I can make it happen," he said softly and quickly, before he had time to regret the words.

"And that could only be a source of both pleasure and delight," Hamish replied unflinchingly.

⟡

The carriage pulled in behind the mews. It was past midnight but Lavinia could see lights still burning in the windows of James's study. Aloysius helped her out of the coach. She stood for a moment in the moon-drenched courtyard, the cold air suspending all reflection. She looked as if the wind might flatten her like a paper doll, the coachman marveled. He wondered at the conversation that had passed between the curious boy-whore and his mistress. Then, anxious she might catch a chill, he stepped forward.

"Madam?"

Dragging her eyes back from some distant place, Lavinia looked at him, and it was as if she was looking at him for the first time as an equal, in every way.

"Aloysius, I have been naive." Her voice trailed away until only the steaming breath of the horses and the creaking of the wind through the branches could be heard.

Aloysius stood there, his arms turned to stone not able to take her as he wanted, but frozen like some huge clumsy giant, silently cursing this land and its people for the injustice and unnaturalness of it all. Then, to his great amazement, Lavinia stepped forward and rested her head against the front of his greatcoat. His heart fluttered like the wings of a trapped bird until she turned and walked into the mansion, leaving him standing in a maelstrom of his own bewildered emotions.

39

Los Angeles, 2002

The radiologist carefully manipulated the probe while watching the ultrasound screen. Julia, looking up at the ceiling, tried to pretend she was somewhere far away, not with her heels hoisted up in stirrups and a mechanical device inside her vagina.

"Of course, at your age a late miscarriage is always a risk," Dr. Weinstein, the gynecologist, said.

"Doctor?" The radiologist, an earnest Chinese–American woman, rested the probe against Julia's left side. A faint throb began to punch back at the apparatus. The gynecologist peered at the screen. A small whitish mark blocked the faint scan of a long serpentlike trail: Julia's fallopian tube and ovary.

"How long since the miscarriage?"

"Three months, doctor," the radiologist replied before Julia had a chance to.

"Hmmm, can we look closer at the other side?"

Again the probe circled—like a horrible mechanical pig hunting for truffles, Julia thought bleakly.

"Are you still with us?" Dr. Weinstein, an amicable man in his fifties with a string of qualifications after his name and a reputation as one of the best at Cedars Sinai, touched her shoulder. He smiled but the concern slipped through his eyes anyhow.

"I believe so."

"Good. Get dressed and see me in my surgery in ten minutes."

❦

The ceiling to floor windows in Dr. Weinstein's consulting room showed a panoramic view that stretched toward Miracle Mile and the poorer suburbs that made up East Los Angeles. He frowned at Julia.

"Julia, you should have come in sooner, when you first felt pain."

"Sorry, I've been in such a mess that I don't even think I realized I was in physical pain. How bad is it?"

Dr. Weinstein sighed. He'd been her gynecologist for over fifteen years and behaved more like a surrogate father than a doctor.

"I'm not going to lie to you—your womb has sustained some damage that we didn't initially pick up. The good news is that we can fix the infection with antibiotics. The bad news is that it has left scarring on both tubes."

"I won't be able to have another pregnancy, right?"

Dr. Weinstein looked down at his desk then absentmindedly said, "Given your age and the damage the miscarriage has caused, pregnancy is no longer an option. I'm sorry, Julia."

It was what she had suspected. But hearing the actual words in Dr. Weinstein's precise tone was far more distressing than she'd imagined. She focused on a photograph on the desk of the doctor at his son's bar mitzvah. I mustn't lose control, I mustn't break down in public, she told herself. In the midst of her rising grief, she noticed absurdly that the doctor and his son had the same ears. A sharp pain shot through her vertically, but she knew it was emotional. What was left? Her career. Was that enough? It didn't feel like it; not now. A great rage began its bitter wave through her body.

"Listen, you've had a big shock," the gynecologist elaborated. "But things will get better. They will. I know it's a cliché, but time is a great healer."

You bet it's a cliché, Julia thought, hating him in that moment for his glibness and the conceit of a man who had a family.

Sensing her distress, he took her hand. "Julia, have you ever thought about turning to some kind of spirituality? Faith can be a great comfort, especially at times like these."

"You know me—the last atheist in southern California," she joked, her cracking voice betraying her.

Outside, in the narrow corridor between the reception and the surgery, finally alone, Julia collapsed against the wall, holding her sorrow against her as privately as a lover.

40

London, 1861

The Colonel smoothed out the sheet of paper and stared down at its blank expanse. Then he dipped his pen in the ink and, pensively, almost shyly, wrote across the top: *Advice from an old father to a young son.*

Dearest boy, he continued, *I am writing this as you lie asleep in your cot in the nursery, a mere babe, but I am imagining you to have grown into a fine young man. Some instinct—the premonition of an old soldier, if you will— instructs me to immortalize my authority in case I am no longer of this world by the time you are of age.*

Follow my advice, my son: always live according to your true nature, whatever the cost to the loved ones around you. To do otherwise is to live a lie, and I have discovered this to be untenable and unethical.

Exercise both your curiosity and your imagination, for

there are no greater gifts; and no greater wisdom than the breadth of experience—learn not by example but by following the courage of your convictions.

I do not know what you will think of me. I know I have been weak and fallible, but I have never lacked valor, either on the battlefield or in other arenas of human affairs. When you look upon my writings and my portrait, do not make a myth of me, but see me as a man. And, like all men, I have been made vulnerable by my humanity . . .

He heard the slam of the front door in the distance, footsteps ascending and then filling the hallway outside. Lavinia, returning from the park with the nursemaid and Aidan. Quietly, the Colonel closed his writing desk.

❈

Where things decayed and loved ones lost
In dreamy shadows rise,

And, freed from all that's earthly vile,
Seem hallowed, pure, and bright,
Like scenes in some enchanted isle,
All bathed in liquid light.

As dusky mountains please the eye,
When twilight chases day;
As bugle-notes that, passing by,
In distance die away;

As leaving some grand waterfall,
We, lingering, list its roar—
So memory will hallow all
We've known, but know no more.

The bookseller was right: Abraham Lincoln was a better statesman than poet, Lavinia conceded as she sat reading on the window seat. Gazing at the journal, she was reminded again of her encounter with Polly Kirkshore. Why had the whore asked if Lavinia had a sister, or even a mother? Could it be that her mother *was* living, perhaps even here in London?

She replaced the book on the shelf and perused its companions. Pressed up next to George Combe's definitive text on phrenology, *The Constitution of Man,* was a book whose spine read: *Flowers, herbs and cacti of delirium: the New World flora of a tantalizing and dangerous nature.* The feathery head of a flower protruded from its pages.

Intrigued, Lavinia pulled the book down. Settling back into the sun-filled warmth of the window seat, she turned to the inventive bookmark. The page showed an illustration of the ayahuasca vine, *Banisteriopsis caapi.*

Lavinia read on.

> In the northeast of Brazil, the natives worship a goddess called Jubbu-jang-sange. To conjure her, the shaman will brew a magical potion made from the root bark of Mimosa hostilis mixed with the ayahuasca vine. Although not poisonous, fatality has resulted when the potion is taken with other hallucinogens, such as opium or peyote.

She paused, wondering at the properties of a goddess who promised her worshippers the ability to see with the eyes of God and who also held the hidden danger of death. Was this part of her seduction; to walk at the edge of one's human existence and stare Death fully in the face? To taste immortality just for a few hours? Was Death female to these people? The idea fascinated Lavinia.

41

⟨❧⟩

They had agreed to meet at Trafalgar Square. It was not covert so much as convenient: they were to drive to the Royal Academy together. As Lady Morgan sat waiting in her carriage, she stared up at the Nelson Column. A monstrous act of pomposity, she thought to herself, remembering the square as it had been twenty years before. Her late husband had been an associate of the architect Charles Barry, who had complained bitterly about Nelson's plinth being imposed upon his design. In the end, celebrity had triumphed over art and the column had been erected, to loom over Barry's design forever.

What narcissism, Lady Morgan observed, thinking about the egocentricity of the great sea admiral. Admittedly Nelson had saved England from the clutches of Napoleon, and perhaps from the dismantling of the British aristocracy (here Lady Morgan shivered and crossed herself; several of her husband's cousins had lost their heads in the French Revolution). But sometimes, in secret, very unpatriotic moments, Lady Morgan found herself wondering what would have happened if Napoleon *had* invaded. Certainly both fashion and food would have improved, and there was a certain philosophical intensity and moral laxity about the French that Lady Morgan secretly admired. The English vilified the Corsican, but really he was far more than just a malevolent dictator, she concluded. Perhaps this was how history was shaped—accidentally; a whirling ballerina pirouetting from one battle to another, collapsing into the arms of whomever won. Was fate really so arbitrary?

Lady Morgan glanced across the square. It was crowded

with the usual throng of carts drawn by heavy draft horses, plumes of their steaming breath cutting into the air as they strained under their various loads of coal, wood, and vegetables. Several flower girls stood on the street calling out their wares, wearing cheap straw hats with poppies woven through the straw. Street peddlers ran between the city gentlemen in their tails and top hats. The ubiquitous clerks scurried alongside, arms full of papers. A chimney sweep and his climbing boy loitered nearby, the sweep flirting with a barrow girl who stood over a brazier of roasting chestnuts. A matchstick girl, tray hanging in front of her, shouted sporadically, while a muffin man, ringing his bell furiously, added to the pandemonium.

Hordes of urchins darted amongst the pedestrians, sooty-faced, bare-footed, their torn trousers held up by string. They whistled, cheered, and generally caused havoc.

A peeler kept vigil, his horse prancing nervously as the carriages rattled past. A cartload of night soil trundled by, sending a wave of noxious air toward the open window of the carriage. Lady Morgan lifted her perfumed handkerchief to her face. Just then she spotted a crossing sweeper running before a well-dressed young gentleman whose good looks and groomed appearance set him apart from the crowd. His back bent obsequiously, the sweeper cleared aside the horse droppings and debris that covered the pavement ahead of the man.

They reached the carriage and the crossing sweeper put out his mitten-covered hand for a tip. By the time the man had paid him, there was an urchin offering to open the carriage door for him. Hamish Campbell angrily dismissed him with a wave. Hoisting himself into the brougham, he took a seat opposite Lady Morgan, slightly breathless from his brisk walk.

"Why, we have become quite clandestine," he remarked as Lady Morgan offered him her lips. He kissed her on the cheek instead and, flicking the tails of his plaid frock coat clear of the seat, leaned back against the cushioned upholstery.

"Clandestine? It is only married individuals or unchaperoned virgins who need be clandestine," Lady Morgan retaliated. "No, I'm afraid we have become quite estranged. And that, my elusive friend, isn't nearly as exciting."

Hamish pulled off his cream kid gloves and rubbed his hands together in a vain attempt to alleviate the cold that had cramped his fingers. He had been avoiding this encounter for as long as he could; it was only when Lady Morgan's manservant visited with a second request that he had acquiesced.

"Are you feeling neglected, Frances?"

"Feeling neglected? Why, I *am* neglected. I've had no escort for the past two operas, and I've had to resort to becoming that tedious child bride's unofficial social secretary. And, as we both know, the husband is far more fascinating. *N'est-ce pas?*"

Sensing a trap, Hamish remained silent. The confessions people threw carelessly into such lapses of conversation had always astounded him and he knew Lady Morgan hated silence almost as much as she hated being ignored. He stared out of the window, painfully aware of her gaze, then felt her hand on his knee.

"You do understand?" she murmured softly.

Hamish noticed a small boy feeding the pigeons, accompanied by his uniformed nursemaid, and thought of more innocent times.

"Frances, we have never been lovers."

Floored by his directness, Lady Morgan blushed, something she couldn't remember doing for years.

"No, but I thought . . . it was implied . . ."

"There was nothing implied."

She watched his face closing against her and decided upon another tactic.

"My dear boy, you cannot imagine what joy it gives me just to have you sitting here by my side. And we have enjoyed such extraordinary conversations; I had hoped it would lead to greater intimacy . . ."

Hamish was intensely aware of the social repercussions of incurring her wrath, and decided it would be wise to allow her hand to linger on his thigh. He received a small but not insignificant stipend from Lady Morgan, not to mention the advantageous introductions she facilitated. However, she was renowned for her possessiveness—a trait Hamish had known about when he embarked upon his original campaign. But some events in life could not be controlled or circumvented, even by the most ambitious of men.

"I am Colonel Huntington's assistant. The job is demanding."

"Indeed. So demanding that you cannot see me in the evenings, nor even visit Highfield Manor."

"I will hunt with you, if that's what you wish."

"You know what I wish. But I understand. As I know well, James is *très amusant*."

Hamish winced, a small tic appearing under one eye.

"I want you back in my salon," Lady Morgan said bluntly. "As I've said many a time, I am an understanding woman, probably one of the most forgiving in Mayfair. God forgive me my guilelessness."

"Indeed, Frances, you are known for your good grace."

Hamish couldn't keep the sarcasm from his voice. She decided to ignore the remark.

"But, my dear," she gave his knee a playful squeeze, "I think the real question is whether the young wife would be so understanding. After all, she is one of those tiresome women who is foolish enough to believe she is in love with her husband."

Hamish placed her hand back onto her own lap. "Madame, are you attempting to blackmail me?"

His voice, deceptively friendly, was in complete contrast to his query; a technique he had observed in his benefactress when she intended to disorient her enemies. Recognizing the mimicry, Lady Morgan threw back her head and laughed. The boy was quick and could really play the game, she acknowledged, realizing that it was this very trait that had attracted her to him in the first place. Now she desired him more than ever.

"Would I be that gauche? But I should warn you, there are some men who are like light white wine; delicious as you drink, but, alas, soon evaporate from the palate. Then there are those rare individuals who resemble a regal claret: complex, full-bodied, perhaps difficult at first but completely seductive in a way that can haunt one an entire lifetime. Be careful, my friend."

She caressed his cheek lightly, then opened the carriage door. The day and its trivialities rushed in, a welcome reprieve for Hamish, who now only wished to be somewhere else.

❦

"I believe there is a time in one's life when one becomes profoundly aware of one's own mortality, and it is at this juncture that one may enter a state of such moral dissolution that one is capable of doing anything or becoming anyone merely for the experience of sensation. In my case, the premature death of my mother ignited a desire for experience—to toy with death, to lose myself in pure sensation. And, my friend, I did. It was simply good fortune that I retained enough wit to record my experiences for posterity. My adventures became my study and then my profession. However, at the age of forty-five, a great sadness paralyzed me, the most extraordinary sense of futility pervading every action. I decided I needed an heir, someone who would carry my lineage through future generations. I had tired of short-term pleasures, of affairs, of *masculine* encounters . . ."

Here the Colonel faltered, causing Hamish to glance up from the oars.

They had hired a boat to row on the Serpentine—an innocent pastime for two friends on a breezy Saturday afternoon.

There was little one could do, out there in the open, surrounded by grassed parkland that had begun to crackle with the approaching season. It had been the Colonel's intention to talk about very uninnocent things in an innocuous landscape, the landscape of his adolescence.

"It was at that point that I decided to get married," he went on. "Lavinia's youth attracted me. I suppose I expected a rejuvenation of my own spirit, an infection of enthusiasm."

"And did you?"

Hamish, watching a man on the bank tossing bread to a swan, held back his own nervousness. Such restraint, he thought; if only he knew how restrained I am.

"Initially, there was an excitement. She reminded me why I had sought meaning in human behavior and cultures. But perhaps it is a futile exercise to categorize, to impose a logic upon the primal instincts of Man."

"Phrenology is a genuine science, James. It is researched, substantiated, as is anthropology."

"Or are they colored by Man's insidious need to define everything and everyone? We are changelings, my sweet friend; evolving entities, not fixed by Nature."

The Colonel paused again, the shadow of a weeping willow crossing his face as they floated past the bank. Hamish thought he spied a pensiveness that softened the determined jaw. Then, quietly, the action hidden within the confines of the rowboat, the Colonel reached across and took the younger man's hand between his own.

"I have tried to be responsible," he said.

The landscape seemed to exhale before they spoke; the weight of their words brushing against lips, the incrimination of implicit desire thickening the air. Hamish squeezed the Colonel's hand, the slightest of movements.

"You cannot be what you are not."

"Ahh, but who am I?" The Colonel's whispered reply was a question that required no answer.

42

Los Angeles, 2002

The diner was popular with the Sunday crowd—fashionable young couples who lived at the foot of the Hollywood hills. Dating from the 1930s, the restaurant was decorated with signed photographs of the various celebrities who had eaten there. The waitresses, wearing aprons trimmed with white frills, hovered around the glass-topped tables edged with silver chrome. Charlie Parker played out of an old-fashioned coin-operated record booth in the corner, the robotic arm swinging over the vinyl to land in the shining black groove and releasing a voice from over forty years before. Some tables had strollers parked next to them, the bewildered babies marooned in them gazing wide-eyed at other children perched on their parents' laps, many screaming for attention. Filled with the scent of frying bacon undercut by the aroma of maple syrup, the whole restaurant was alive with conversation and laughter.

Julia sat alone in a corner booth, reviewing her research notes. She'd gone to the diner after her customary trek through Griffith Park. The diner was a place she used to frequent with Klaus and one she'd only just plucked up enough courage to return to, determined to reclaim some of her territory. A boy of about three, dressed in denim overalls and oversized sneakers, wandered up to the table; his eyes wide with solemnness, he offered Julia a sugar container. This could have been my son, she thought, blinking back sudden tears.

The boy watched her with a fascinated perplexity, wondering at the shifting expression on this strange woman's face.

Before Julia had a chance to take the sugar container, the child was swept off his feet and carried away by his disapproving mother.

"Julia?"

Recognizing the voice, she looked up. Carla stood in front of her table, looking almost as shocked as Julia.

"I was just sitting over there . . ."

Julia froze, too anxious to look behind her in case Klaus was at the same table.

". . . with my father," Carla explained, sensing her apprehension. "I was on my way to the restroom when I saw you."

"What do you want, Carla?"

Carla, shifting nervously, put out her hand. It hung in the air, unspeakably small against the immensity of the gesture.

"I heard about the miscarriage. Julia, I am so sorry."

Julia was speechless. She glanced at the exit; she could walk out, but she was still waiting for her breakfast, and as the restaurant was crowded it would be impossible to leave quickly with any dignity.

"How dare you? Do you have any idea what you've done?" Julia's angry tone attracted the attention of the people at the next table.

"Julia, I swear if it could have been any other way—"

"You expect me to believe that? You have no notion about love or friendship. Now get out of my sight."

Carla walked away. A moment later, Julia saw her leave with her father.

"One serve of crispy bacon, two eggs sunny side up, hash browns with one side of pancakes." The waitress, indifferent to the lingering tension in the air, in pigtails, bright pink lipstick, her teeth covered by metal braces, noisily plonked the plate down in front of Julia. "Enjoy."

❦

As she ate, Julia tried to lose herself in her research notes but found her mind wandering to Lavinia Huntington. How had that young woman survived standing in the dock, listening to the accusation of murder? Had she loved her husband? Was it possible that James Huntington could have driven her to murder? Suddenly furious with her own circumstances, Julia put down her fork, and after leaving money on the table, left the diner.

❧

The magnetoencephalography equipment covered the shorn heads of the nonidentical twins like bizarre space helmets. Wires ran down the back of their necks and into two computers that sat side by side in the laboratory. The two men were watching a large screen showing footage of one soldier killing another with a bayonet. They were separated by a partition so they could not be influenced by each other's reactions.

Julia and Gabriel studied two monitors, one for each man, showing a magnetic mapping of the regions of the brain that were firing synapses in response to the visual stimuli.

An area lit up on the left monitor. Gabriel leaned closer. "Subject B."

"His name's Ronald—Ronald Mack. His brother is Sammy," Julia said.

"Yeah, whatever. Ronald's amygdala just got all excited, suggesting he might be experiencing an increase in fear and anxiety."

"Nothing's registering in Sammy's."

"Sammy's the ace commando, Ronald's behind the desk, right?"

Julia nodded. She pulled out the printouts of the brothers' gene activity profiles; the specific gene she had isolated was circled in red pen. Sure enough, Sammy's DNA showed high activity of a previously uncharacterized gene she was beginning to suspect was the gene function she was searching for. The same gene showed a different activity profile on Ronald's chart—a clear indication that their individual reaction to violence was genetically wired.

"Check this out—there's no variation in the MAOA expressed, which means . . . ?"

"It's definitely a mutant gene function."

"Exactly. And I've decided to christen it: ANG–1. ANG standing for anger."

"So now we have a name for the Minotaur in the labyrinth but we still haven't actually caught sight of it."

"That, my friend, may take months."

"I still suspect there's another factor involved, one we're not testing for yet."

Julia glanced at Gabriel, surprised by his confidence but sensing he might be right. Perhaps she had underestimated him; he had the same focus she'd had at his age—the right kind of meticulous curiosity and tenacity needed to make a good scientist. To her annoyance she suddenly saw him as a man, and an attractive man, at that.

"Ah, but here's the paradox: are we hunting the Minotaur or is it hunting us?" he asked, the intensity in his voice intriguing her further.

43

"I know I may seem an unlikely candidate for scientific progress unless it's in the area of robotics . . ."

The audience—a mixture of business delegates, scientists, and various industry representatives—laughed uproariously. The Candidate, famous for playing an android in a blockbuster action film in the late twentieth century, laughed with them, his squared jaw wide, teeth glinting unnaturally.

"Oh please," Julia murmured sarcastically to Andrew, who looked particularly resplendent in a Gucci suit he'd obviously purchased for the occasion.

"Give the guy some respect, he's a demi-god." Applauding enthusiastically, Andrew's gaze never left the stage.

Isolated in her cynicism, Julia glanced back at the Candidate, thoroughly unamused by the sycophantic display of hero worship. The conference hall was festooned with banners advertising Xandox's company logo—a double helix composed of glittery silver arrows—and posters of the Candidate. The giant pharmaceutical company had staged the event in an attempt to seduce the government into passing legislation that allowed contentious research, such as stem-cell and genetic manipulation, under the guise of promoting working relationships between commerce, politics, and science.

"I believe that with sensible and faith-sensitive legislation, we can see this state leading the world in this revolutionary and exciting field. Science is big business! I am big business!"

The crowd erupted again, swept up by the Candidate's rhetoric. Even Julia had to admit he had a gift for infecting everyone with his celebrity, as if by supporting him one was instantly elevated from the banality of everyday life and propelled into a parallel glamorous universe—fame by proximity.

"So I want you guys . . ."

You guys—there it was again, she thought, the insidious suggestion of the personal.

". . . to loosen your ties, drink as many margaritas as you can—after all, Xandox is paying . . ." (Another big laugh here.) ". . . talk business to each other, make deals—let's put California on the map again!"

The Candidate waved, then was swiftly escorted from the podium by four squat, muscular bodyguards.

The two geneticists pushed their way through the crowd to a waiter. Grabbing two margaritas, Julia handed one to Andrew.

"What the hell is faith-sensitive legislation?" she asked.

"Stem-cell research, sweetie, it's the next ticking clock.

The President wants the industry to use adult stem cells only, or embryonic stem cells that are already in storage."

"There are problems with that."

"Sure, but the guy's got the pro-lifers breathing down his neck. Hey, as we know, the path of progress is littered with bioethical potholes."

Andrew scanned the crowd, looking for the right industry representative to lobby. Unlike Julia, he was good at working the room. Watching his face alight with enthusiasm made her feel guilty. Julia knew she should be doing the same. Events like these were invaluable opportunities to canvass for more funding; she couldn't remember ever witnessing this many power brokers together in the same room.

"Jesus Christ, is that Professor Bedelmayer over there?" Andrew whistled in awe.

A towering figure in his early eighties, Bedelmayer was universally feared. President and co-owner of Xandox, he'd studied alongside Crick and Watson at Cambridge in the 1950s, and held an MBS (Harvard) and a PhD (MIT). He was one of the few men in the States who had the influence to completely bury a research venture or kick-start it with full funding. In short, he was considered a deity.

Julia swung around and tried not to stare. She had only seen the man once before—on the front cover of *Forbes* magazine.

Andrew took a big swig of his margarita. "Okay, so he's at the top of my dance card, followed by . . ." He shamelessly rotated 360 degrees, then reversed 30. "Sony over there—they have a division I want to get sponsorship from. I have an idea about nanotechnology being able to speed up detection processes. What about you? Girl, you have to get out there and mingle. Besides, you're the only one here with legs."

Reluctantly, Julia surveyed the small clusters of businessmen, then noticed a short man striding toward her.

"Damn, I've been spotted."

"Who?"

"Starboard. Some rep from Xandox, I owe him a call. Cover me while I lose him."

Andrew glanced at the man who was now about twenty yards away. "He is rather attractive in a bearish kind of way."

"Please, Andrew."

"Just remember, you owe me, big time. Now vanish."

Andrew moved in front of her and smiled in an overtly sexual manner at the representative, who, confounded, stopped in his tracks. Julia disappeared into the crowd, weaving her way to the other side of the hall, glass in hand. Someone grabbed her arm.

"Professor Julia Huntington? I've been looking for you."

A bullish man in chinos and an expensive Ralph Lauren suede jacket cornered her.

"Jonathan Jenkins," Julia said. "A dubious pleasure."

Jenkins was the head of the claims division of an insurance company for whom Julia had once written a report on DNA and its uses in insurance claims—something she'd regretted ever since.

"I can live with that," Jenkins said. "I hear you've landed a very interesting commission for the Defense Department."

"You insure the army now?" Julia replied deadpan. Jenkins broke into unconvincing laughter.

Cornered, Julia scanned the crowd—and thought she sighted an escape route. A man in his mid-thirties, sun-tanned, standing by himself near a drinks table, smiled at her. Julia automatically smiled back, even though she didn't recognize him.

"I need to circulate," she said. "You know how it is at these events."

As she stepped away, Jonathan Jenkins grabbed her arm—tightly. "Don't be such a party pooper," he hissed.

"Hey, Julia, we have a conference call at nine," the sun-tanned man called out as he strode toward them. He was well built, his casual clothes hiding a body that looked threateningly muscular, and there was a vigor about his movements that suggested to Julia he could possibly be military. Now closer, Julia could see that the attractive symmetry of his face was muted by a nose that looked as if it might have been broken once.

He glanced at his watch. "That would be right about now." He put his hand firmly on Jenkins's shoulder. "Now, if you would just let go of the lady."

Reluctantly, the insurance representative released Julia. "Sure, can't keep business waiting," he said, and turned to face Julia, the threat transparent in his countenance. "We'll be tracking your progress, Professor."

Julia watched him vanish behind the suits.

"I'd thank you," she said, "except I don't know you. Or do I?"

"Not yet, but relax, I'm on your side."

There was an air of quiet intensity about him, a feeling of self-containment. Julia gleaned he wasn't entirely comfortable in crowds.

"And it's an honor, Professor Huntington, to have rescued you from some B-grade gorilla in a cheap suit. I'm assuming he wasn't the boyfriend, right?" In that same moment he noticed her wedding ring. "Oops, sorry, you must think I'm a compulsive flirter. I didn't see the ring."

"I'm separated . . . recently."

"My condolences."

"Accepted."

He smiled, his blue eyes crinkling up against the tan, and Julia realized, to her intense irritation, that she found him attractive. She walked away and took refuge behind a huge fern. He followed.

"Can we talk about your research? I believe I have some information that could prove very useful."

"Which particular research? My laboratory covers a lot of areas."

His relaxed attitude disappeared in an instant. He took her arm. "Hey, I'm risking my neck just talking to you, and I haven't got much time, so if you cut the bullshit, I'll cut the bullshit. This report for the DOD—it's going to affect a lot of people. A lot of people I care about. Can't we at least sit down and trade information?"

"Who are you? Military?"

"Kind of."

"How do I even know you're U.S. military?"

He pulled out a card and held it up. She read it quickly before he slipped it back into his pocket.

"Okay, so you're Delta, but that ID is obsolete."

"You know your protocol."

"I have to."

"I was court-martialed at the end of last year, for my involvement in Brazil."

"You know about the incident in Brazil?"

As two men wandered past, Julia's companion broke into a Bronx accent. "That's a really brilliant way of mapping gene clusters—maybe I can incorporate that into my own work . . ."

The men disappeared through the exit door. Julia turned back to her mysterious cohort.

"You really have read my work."

"Yeah, and I know my alphabet too. It's vital we talk."

"How do I know whether I can trust you?"

"You don't."

"Do you have a phone number?"

"Don't worry, I'll find you."

On the other side of the hall, Gabriel stepped tentatively into the auditorium. He was dressed in a brand new Hugo Boss suit. He'd bought it on credit; it was the first suit he'd ever owned and the formality of the outfit made him feel self-conscious—gauche even. Horribly aware of being the youngest there, Gabriel touched the invitation in his suit pocket to reassure himself. Xandox was his college sponsor.

A female rep hanging around the entrance scanned his

name tag. She spoke briefly into a cell phone then approached him.

"Gabriel Mendalos? Welcome. The head of the Californian division is very keen to meet you."

"He is? I didn't think he even knew of my existence."

"Of course I do." A long-haired friendly-looking man in his late twenties, wearing a T-shirt printed with a cartoon of feuding microbes, put out his hand. "We track all our prodigies; after all, you are our future. Matt Leman."

Gabriel shook his hand, embarrassed at being overdressed.

Taking his arm, Matt Leman led him to the bar and, without asking his age, handed him a margarita. Gabriel, sipping the drink, gazed around: some of the faces he recognized from science magazines and pharmaceutical brochures.

"Congratulations on the new laboratory position by the way." Leman slapped him on the back.

"You know about that?"

"Like I said, we like to track our investments. Professor Huntington is the top in her field. You'll have access to the best research going."

"I know, that's why I pursued the position."

"She got lucky, you're going to be the best, too, soon."

"I'm only in my first year."

"Vision, Gabriel. You've got genius; you just need the discipline and vision to take you there."

"Really?" Gabriel's eyes narrowed; no one had ever called him a genius before. He knew he had ambition but he was aware that he lacked the flare of original thinking extraordinary research required—the kind of original thinking Julia was famous for. "Yeah, that's all great hypothetically but it's a cut-throat arena—just look at all these guys totally stoked, all wanting to be immortalized for the next major breakthrough."

"All the more reason to keep your eyes and ears wide open. Trust me, you're in the right lab, your . . . mentor, she doesn't know what she's sitting on half the time, but a guy like you—young, hungry, with a cutting-edge commercial sensibility, I just know you'll be doing the right thing at the right time. Listen, if there's anything that's coming in—you know, results you want to brainstorm independently, ring me. I know Xandox would really appreciate the on-going report."

Half-appalled and half-intrigued Gabriel watched as Matt Leman slipped his card into his breast pocket. "Now, is there anyone here you'd really like to meet?" The executive put his arm around Gabriel's shoulders and swung him back toward the reception room. Gabriel looked around; a man in his eighties stood beside the podium, towering over the men around him with a supercilious air of power. Gabriel knew who he was immediately.

"The area I'm interested in is biology and genetics. Take greenhouse, for example—why can't we bioengineer a tree that's genetically manipulated to absorb large quantities of carbon dioxide? I'm telling you, there's money in greenhouse."

"What did you say your name was, kid?"

Julia, recognizing the first voice, looked over to the podium, where she was amazed to see Gabriel conversing with Professor Marvin Bedelmayer as casually as if he were his recruitment officer.

By the time she swung back to her companion, he had completely disappeared. Confused, she glanced around. There was no sign of him. Who was he? Obviously some disgruntled ex-Delta Force guy, but why come to her? Even if she did locate the mutant gene function, how did he think it was going to affect him and his friends?

Julia looked at the other delegates—they seemed oblivious to her encounter. For one bizarre second, she wondered whether the man had been a manifestation of her own imagination. Just then Gabriel's voice traveled across the hall again, breaking into her thoughts. Determined to prevent what she perceived as professional suicide, she marched toward the podium.

Gabriel caught sight of her. "Oh, here comes my Ph.D. advisor, Professor Huntington."

Bedelmayer wiped a thin sheen of sweat from his face with a large handkerchief. He was grossly overweight and the temperature of the room was affecting him. He peered at Gabriel, a wry grin playing over his thick lips. "You look mighty young for a Ph.D., son."

"I'm a prodigy, sir." Gabriel turned to Julia. "Professor, I was just telling Professor Bedelmayer here about how I intend to work for Xandox—after my doctorate's finished, of course."

People had begun to turn and stare. Blushing furiously, Julia faced Bedelmayer. "I'm terribly sorry, Professor Bedelmayer."

"What for? The boy's got chutzpah. Besides, he's the only one here that's had the balls to come up and talk to me. He's been telling me some interesting things. Hey, kid, when you come into Xandox for the job interview—say, in five years' time—you make sure you bring that genetically engineered tree, okay?"

The onlookers broke into laughter. Gabriel, suddenly humiliated, struggled with his embarrassment.

"I'll do that, sir."

Julia placed her hand on Gabriel's shoulder. "Gabriel, I'll see you outside."

"But—"

"Now!"

Gabriel disappeared toward the door. Julia turned back to Bedelmayer.

"Julia—"

"Huntington. I know. Interesting area—genetics and violence."

He watched her, one thumb in a pocket, his arm rested

across his huge stomach. Beneath the benign appearance shimmered absolute power. Julia felt herself suddenly trembling.

"Excuse me, sir. I should go find my precocious assistant."

44

Gabriel was standing outside the building, eating an orange from one of those packing-box stalls constructed by an innovative Mexican; a hopeful outpost beside a traffic light. Julia had never bought anything from those stands in her life. Trying not to show her disapproval, she strode over to Gabriel. The stallholder, a diminutive man of about fifty, his face a map of sun and poverty, his clothes still dusty from the drive across the border, sat on an upside-down milk crate, a small portable radio filling the air around him with tinny Mexican pop serenades, voices from a whole other world.

The vendor looked critically at Julia then back at Gabriel. *"Tu novia esta bonita, pero es muy vieja, hombre.* (Your girlfriend's pretty, but she's old, man.)"

Gabriel grinned, knowing that Julia didn't understand a word.

"Si! Pero como yo lo veo las mujeres son como el vino, entre más viejo mejor (Yeah, but good women are like a good wine, they both get better with age)," he replied.

Both men broke into laughter, which infuriated Julia as she sensed the joke was about her.

"Gabriel, you had no right turning up at an event like that. How did you get in anyway?"

"Actually, I was invited. I was sponsored by Xandox, remember?" He plucked another orange from the stall and threw it to her. "Here, have an orange. What's the big drama? Bedelmayer liked me, plus it just might inspire him to throw some more money your way." He looked down at his trousers thoughtfully. "Did I overdress?"

He lifted one trouser leg and Julia saw that he was wearing lime-green socks. He grinned.

"I figured I'd never get in in my jeans," he went on. "I heard a rumor Bill Gates might be there. Maybe if we go back in, I could find him and tell him about my computer modeling idea?"

"No! Now, do you need a ride home?"

"Maybe."

"Is that a yes or a no?"

"Well, yes in that I'm not really into the one and a half hour ride back on the bus; and no as in do I really want to sit next to a pissy woman for an hour? Admit it, you're angry."

"Furious. But don't despair, with that kind of audacity I'll probably be knocking on your door in about ten years' time asking you for a job."

"Probably," he replied straight-faced as they reached her car.

Julia clicked the doors open. "Get in, brat!"

"Only if you promise to stop off for a drink with me in this really cool Latino bar I know."

"Absolutely not."

A Mexican flag was draped above the bar, framed by photographs of famous footballers—Oscar Perez, Rafael Garcia, and Manuel Vidrio. At the apex of this rainbow of athletic celebrity hung a garish painting of Jesus Christ with the traditional bleeding heart and crown of thorns; beneath him the Gaudalupe Madonna hovered in crimson and blue, faintly reminiscent of the reproductive organs of some bizarre fruit.

A small TV to the left played a football game, the commentary in Spanish, while on the other side of the bar, surrounded by tables and chairs, a guitarist was busy setting up for the night on a tiny stage which was really a glorified corner.

"He's the best," Gabriel said, "you should hear him. Angels speak from his fingers."

"I hadn't figured you for a poet."

"Yeah well, babe, I'm full of surprises. What would you like?"

"Listen, I'm buying okay? I figure the chances of being arrested will be considerably less that way."

"In that case I'll have a vodka martini, no olives and as dry as the desert."

Julia ordered the drinks. Behind them the guitarist started to play—an exquisite flamenco that spun in cool flurries around the snatches of Spanish he murmured into the microphone.

The bar, about the size of an average lounge room, began to fill with patrons: a group of laborers, boots still dusty; afternoon office workers in suits; a couple of art students. There was even a firefighter, still in uniform, who sat quietly down, placing his helmet below the small glass-topped table. Most of the crowd were Latino.

"How do you know about this place?" Julia said.

"My father brought me here once. He taught me the art of listening, whereas Mom taught me the art of not listening."

She laughed, trying not to react to how handsome he looked in the half-light. He nodded to a pretty young barmaid who smiled back seductively. Noticing the flirtation, Julia wondered how much experience he'd actually had with women.

"Naomi does talk a lot," she said.

"Most of it rubbish. I love my mother but I don't think she's the most emotionally evolved creature."

"That's harsh. How is José?"

"You remember him?"

"Sure. I knew your parents when they were first married. He was real fiery back then. Actually he was a little scary."

"He just believes in principles. He's had to fight for everything he has. Everything. That generation had to. It's different now. Now it's cool to be Latino. Mom hates him. She thinks he sold her out; did the usual male thing, traded up for a younger woman."

"And didn't he?"

"Mom let herself go. She gave up on herself and the marriage long before José left her. Anyhow, if that's true, how come younger men like older women?"

"They do? That's news to me."

"I do."

Julia laughed, then wondered if he was flirting with her.

"Gabriel, you're nineteen. A twenty-two-year-old would be an older woman to you."

Again, he felt his fingers itching for a cigarette. He glanced away. She really had no idea how condescending she was, or who he was. He decided to take a risk.

"Age is irrelevant," he said. "What's important is the intensity with which we experience life. So many of my older friends have switched off that intensity. It's like their expectations of their environment, their relationships, their jobs, even the way they see, has begun to limit their actual experience of those things. They stop seeing, stop becoming excited. So they stop learning. Does this make them more adult than me? Look at Einstein—he was as curious and as excited as a child until he died."

Julia searched his face thoughtfully, wondering if the intensity he was talking about was youth or an imaginative zest for knowledge that, in most people, got blunted by caution. Did it matter? Just hearing him made her nostalgic for her younger self.

"Sometimes things happen that make you lose your faith."

"Is that what happened to you?"

"Hey, I'm still excited by my work—more than excited, profoundly inspired—but I'm a realist now. And that's a much harder thing to be. It means you're responsible for everything—luck, hope, belief."

Gabriel stared at Julia, noticing for the first time that her lower lip was fuller than the upper. If it hadn't been for the watching barmaid—an ex-girlfriend—he would have kissed her. Instead, he slipped his hand across the table and touched her, a tentative curl of his finger against her skin.

"You have to leave a little room for spontaneity."

Startled by the undeniable trickle of desire that had started to creep across her palm, Julia pulled her hand away.

"I should get you home."

They stepped out onto the pavement. Dusk had settled over Silver Lake. They had a view down a canyon populated by a forest of dwellings, all idiosyncratic in their design—1920s mansions, California bungalows, 1970s apartment blocks. At times like this, Los Angeles reminded Julia bizarrely of the hills of Tuscany.

Gabriel slipped his hand around her waist, an awkward movement that left her momentarily unguarded, then pulled her into an embrace, his mouth searching for her lips. There was no ambiguity now as she found herself enveloped by his soft hair falling over her face, the tequila thumping in her head. And, to her amazement and shock, she opened for him, felt that instinctive rush of longing, his lust powerful enough to trigger her own. His erection hard against his trousers, insistent as he pressed himself against her; his hands everywhere, in her hair, under her blouse, reaching for her breasts; the beauty of him, his tongue, lips, his skin ridiculously soft, a wondrous contrast to the muscularity of his torso.

Julia's body was thrown violently into memory, this sweetness of lust, of being wanted, of wanting. But as she ran her fingers down his body, she found his hips absurdly slight beneath her hands, his skin too smooth. She closed her eyes and tried to lose herself. But couldn't. This was not her husband, the familiarity of his bulk, of his scent. There was a desperate edge of nervousness to Gabriel's embrace that was all wrong. She pushed him away.

"We can't."

"Why not?"

"It would be exploitative."

Lost for an answer he tried to kiss her again, but she turned her face away and he missed, his mouth awkwardly clashing against her cheekbone.

"Julia, I'm not a child and you couldn't corrupt me if you tried."

But she was already walking toward the car.

45

Mayfair, 1861

The church filled with the pealing of bells. Kneeling, Lavinia looked up at the crucifix and wondered at the lives of the saints: did they experience corporeal passions? She remembered the trials of Saint Anthony in the desert, and Jesus's temptations in the wilderness, but what of the female saints? A large silk bonnet suddenly blocked her view.

"Are there sparks crackling behind me?" Lady Frances Morgan whispered theatrically. "For I am sure I am about to be struck down."

"Lady Morgan?" Lavinia glanced around; the priest was speaking to a parishioner on the far side of the church.

The dowager clattered her way along the pew to sit next to Lavinia. The priest—young, recently appointed, and well formed—hurried past. Lady Morgan arched her neck as her gaze followed his progress.

"I am so pleased the Protestants don't demand that their clerics practice celibacy. It seems such an unnatural restriction upon a man, even a holy one." She turned to Lavinia. "I should imagine it is to do with the notion of dedication. One sacrifices all for the worship of God. Sacrifice is a terrible thing. I don't believe in it, nor in martyrdom. We only live once, my dear. There is no redemption in suffering. Now, I believe a stroll down Regent Street is required. There is nothing like the purchase of something frivolous to counteract an attack of religious fervor."

"I have my man with me."

"He can follow with the phaeton. The wind has blown the stench of the river away from the city and I, for one, need to oust the cobwebs from my bones."

They stepped outside, where Aloysius was waiting beside the carriage, his cap tipped back, his eyes closed as he turned to the sun before another cloud obscured it, his countenance luminescent in its pale beauty.

Lavinia coughed politely. But Lady Morgan had already observed a subtle shift in the young woman's poise. Taking Lavinia's arm, she propelled her gently down the street. "We really must find you an occupation—charity work perhaps?" she announced, glancing back at the coachman who was now swinging himself up to the carriage. "And quickly," she concluded.

Lavinia was perplexed. What had the aristocrat observed that she, herself, was unconscious of?

"Trust me, my dear," Lady Morgan continued, "there is nothing more joyful than being exempt from the marrying game, the race to land a rich husband. Because, my dear friend, as the weaker sex, that is what we are all driven to: to seek the shelter and support of the male. And what a feckless sex we are. Economics drives the world, not the ridiculous notions of passionate love the novelists and poets peddle to us. I was indeed blessed by the benevolence of my late husband, for his premature passing allowed me to discover my vocation."

"Your vocation, Lady Morgan?" Lavinia ventured, wondering what that might be, other than to act as catalyst for the scandals of Mayfair.

"It is men and the study of them, to put it bluntly. And I have not regretted a second of it, no matter what that lewd scandal sheet *Punch* might insinuate. For, you see, widows have a moral duty to enjoy all the pleasures long-suffering wives are denied."

Lavinia glanced back at Aloysius driving alongside them, sitting up on the phaeton seat and oblivious to their conversation. Lady Morgan's carriage followed behind, flamboyantly embellished with her late husband's family crest and a pattern of fleurs-de-lis.

"Is that how you perceive me—as a long-suffering wife, Lady Morgan?"

"My dear, you are the very archetype. And that is precisely why I am telling you that we women must not allow the peccadilloes of our husbands to oppress us."

Taking care to hide the distress that suddenly gripped her, Lavinia turned away to admire a milliner's window display.

"The Colonel was, arguably, the most accomplished of my salon. He is an extraordinary individual, Lavinia."

The young woman started, for it was the first time Lady Morgan had used her Christian name. It led her to believe the aristocrat was, for once, speaking entirely without irony.

"And extraordinary individuals have extraordinary infatuations," Lady Morgan went on, "as I have recently experienced myself. I am losing someone very dear to me, just as you are. Mr. Hamish Campbell is my touchstone of youth; he was to be my last indulgence. But I find now, to my great chagrin, that I cannot do without him." She took Lavinia's arm. "So now you know: even the most cynical of us have our follies."

The phaeton pulled away from Hanover Square and made for St. James's Square. Although there was still a faint chill in the breeze, it was evident to Lavinia that summer had arrived. The streets were full of couples walking arm in arm. Lavinia enviously watched a man and his wife promenading: the synchronicity of their stride indicated a seasoned knowledge of each other, the ease of trust, she thought. The husband was portly in tails and a top hat, his brocade and satin waistcoat gleaming like the breast of a punchy cockerel, his wife fluttering beside him.

A few yards on, a young clerk skipped around a couple of girls, both skittish in striped damask. The young man's antics drove the girls to laughter, and they fled their pursuer, their ringlets bouncing. A watching rat catcher, his traps hanging from his belt, lounged against a lamppost, pipe in hand, while his terrier snapped at the passing girls.

Courtship was everywhere; even the pigeons nesting precariously on the ledges of the soot-blackened buildings seemed to be either engaged in the act of fornication or in contemplation of it.

And what of my marriage, Lavinia wondered, is it just a pretense? A sham union? What right did her husband have to banish her from his study and his bed?

Was Lady Morgan insinuating that James and Hamish Campbell were lovers? Horrified, Lavinia contemplated the possibility. She had hoped the encounter with Polly Kirkshore was an abnormality, a weakness for the exotic in which her husband indulged occasionally, an indulgence that would not destroy their marriage. The notion was barely tolerable, but she had found a logic within herself to accept such behavior. But if James's friendship with Hamish Campbell was that of an intimate nature—she remembered how Hamish Campbell had looked when the Colonel complimented him. She knew that sensation, that excitement at having won a rare tribute. Was James really capable of such a betrayal?

The breeze lifted a mass of dead leaves, discarded newspapers, chicken feathers, and an abandoned child's bonnet blackened with horse manure; the medley whisked down the cobblestoned road like a whirling dervish. Watching, Lavinia could only think of this spinning confusion as herself.

Prospero's face, lit by the gas footlights, was instantly transformed into a wizard's head of shadow as he lurched toward Caliban to grasp a handful of the half-man, half-beast's matted hair.

>"*Abhorred slave,*" the actor's voice rumbled across the
>   stage.
>"*Which any print of goodness wilt not take,*
>*Being capable of all ill! I pitied thee,*
>*Took pains to make thee speak, taught thee each hour*
>*One thing or other: when thou didst not, savage,*
>*Know thine own meaning, but wouldst gabble like*
>*A thing most brutish, I endow'd thy purposes*
>*With words that made them known. But thy vile race,*
>*Though thou didst learn, had that in't which good natures*
>*Could not abide to be with; therefore wast thou*
>*Deservedly confined into this rock,*
>*Who hadst deserved more than a prison.*"

Caliban reeled blindly under Prospero's hand, and for a moment Lavinia felt a great rush of empathy for the ragged creature, here depicted as a primitive man, a manifestation of primal emotions unfettered and unchecked. Caliban cannot help himself, she suddenly realized, he is the victim of his mother's polluted seed. It was an epiphany that depressed her greatly.

Caliban, a great mane of hair hanging down his naked torso, whirled violently, like a Minotaur cornered in a labyrinth of his own making, yet he could not reach Prospero.

> *"You taught me language; and my profit on't*
> *Is, I know how to curse. The red plague rid you,*
> *For learning me your language!"*

Was this what was meant by "the noble savage"? Lavinia wondered, thinking on the Bakairi and what complexity her husband might have inadvertently brought to their pristine world.

Lavinia was distracted by a rustling from the box next to them, which had been empty at the beginning of the play—conspicuously so, as this was the opening night at the Strand Theatre and the famous thespian Charles Kean was playing Caliban. Peering into the semi-darkness, Lavinia recognized the box's recent arrival as Lord Arthur Clinton—Hamish Campbell had pointed him out to her at the ball so many weeks before. But who was the young woman sitting on his far side? She wore a dark blue velvet gown with an elaborate collar of diamonds and pearls, one languid hand draped over the edge of the balcony. As the woman leaned forward to gain a better view of Kean, Lavinia recognized her: Polly Kirkshore.

Lavinia glanced sideways at her husband watching the performance through opera glasses.

"Don't you know her?" she whispered, indicating the couple.

A startled expression crossed the Colonel's face for a moment, before he collected himself.

"Don't be absurd. I barely know Lord Clinton."

Lifting the opera glasses, he turned back to the stage.

The foyer was crowded. Its walls were hung with red velvet and large gold chandeliers dripped candle wax onto the milling spectators below. The Huntingtons stood pressed against the gilded banister, the Colonel searching the faces for the possibility of advantageous commercial encounters.

Staring down into the throng, Lavinia caught sight of Polly Kirkshore as he pushed his way toward the ladies' parlor. His coiffure and shoulders stood out among the surrounding women. Lavinia observed that the transvestite's great deceit lay in the confidence with which he moved, completely at ease in the social milieu. He looked like any wealthy debutante, perhaps a little tall, perhaps slightly ungainly in the feet and hands, but if one had any doubts they would surely be dismissed by the natural arrogance of his carriage.

"I must reacquaint myself with a friend," Lavinia told her husband.

"Be quick." The Colonel turned back to the crowd.

The ladies' parlor was a large low-ceilinged chamber, its walls lined with mirrors. Uniformed maids stood beside a rack of steaming face towels, while a seamstress, kneeling, mended a tear in a woman's skirt. Several women reclined on chaises longues, fanning themselves furiously. Polly Kirkshore sat at a dressing table, fastidiously reapplying rouge to his cheeks and lips. The youthfulness of his skin and his impeccable grooming made him a personification of feminine beauty—something many of those present, all ignorant of his true sex, aspired to.

Lavinia sat on a stool behind him and caught his eye in the mirror.

"I suspected it was you in the next box. How is the Colonel?" Polly Kirkshore lowered his rouge.

"He doesn't know you."

A very slight vulnerability ran across the transvestite's face.

"They never do. I suppose he will not know me in the foyer either."

"Do you think my husband could love me or any of my sex as a man should love a woman?" Lavinia's voice was barely a whisper.

"I believe we are not fixed beings but creatures whose affections lie beyond the dictates of Society. Besides, my friend, there are many loves, therefore he must love you in his own particular manner. But you haven't sought me out for this question alone?"

He applied paint to a beauty mole just below his eye. His green irises and painted eyelids reminded Lavinia of an Egyptian goddess, his beauty amplified by the studied ruse.

"You asked me whether I had an elder sister or a mother in London," she replied softly.

"It was nothing, merely a remarkable resemblance."

"But if I did . . . have a mother . . ."

"If you did, I am not convinced you would want to claim this woman."

Lavinia leaned closer to avoid being overheard. Some intuition told her to trust the youth. "I have a whispering box—a simple ornament they gave me after they told me she had died. For years I have spoken into this box, to a mother I imagined would embody all of the qualities one would want in a parent. Now I have discovered that I have lived my life in imagined projections. I no longer wish to be so credulous."

Without turning from the mirror, Polly Kirkshore reached into his jeweled purse and pulled out a small pencil. Turning his theater program over, he scribbled down a name and an address.

"I know her only as Meredith. She would be about forty years of age. I believe she was originally from Anascaul."

Polly, watching her amazed face through the looking glass, slipped the paper scrap into Lavinia's hand.

The bell rang for the next act. With no more to say, the two rose.

46

Aloysius opened the carriage door. As he helped Lavinia down, he held her gloved hand longer than necessary.

"Pardon the impudence, madam, but another letter has arrived from my brother and I was wondering whether you had the time . . ." His voice trailed off as his courage failed him.

Lavinia, distracted by the events of the evening, had entirely forgotten his presence.

"Of course, come to my study once you have seen to the horses. No one will be about at this time."

She smiled sadly, leaving the coachman wondering about her happiness.

"The tenth of May, in the year of our Lord eighteen sixty-one.

It was a week ago, brother, that the bugle call took us into battle, the first real engagement in over two months. The Union was to storm Camp Jackson, outside of the Confederate city of St. Louis, and there was much civil disorder. I had not slept the night before, knowing that the infantry would be the first to face the muskets and bayonets of the enemy. We Irish had armed ourselves with prayer, hardtack, and some good whiskey a rogue foraged from the other side, but there was not a man amongst us who did not feel fear in that terrible silence as we waited for the order.

As for the fighting itself, Aloysius, I am beginning to believe there are fellow soldiers who feel a horrible excitement at killing. I have seen them slaughter the enemy as if he were less than a hog. I am not one of them. It is only the loss of a comrade that can madden me enough to treat the dead like wood and the living like animals. There is no joy in bayoneting another man, be he Confederate or otherwise. It was terrible. A quarter of our platoon was slaughtered by musket fire, and many will die later under the sawbone's knife, but we have secured the camp.

Now there is rioting in St. Louis itself. The Union is the invader here, not the liberator, and I see the hatred in the faces of both men and children. Ireland is as distant as the night stars.

I am glad to hear of your employment and that you have not gone the way of many a young Irishman in a city not renowned for its hospitality. I trust that you have remained a good Catholic and ask you to remember me in your prayers.

In great affection, your brother Seamus."

Lavinia folded the letter and pushed it across the desk toward Aloysius, who stood with his back to the fireplace, his hessian shirt tucked into his riding trousers. Picking the paper up awkwardly, he hid it in a pocket.

"Thank you, madam. I would have asked Mr. Poole to read it, except I have no desire to confirm his prejudices about the uneducated Irish."

"Indeed, he is a withered stick of a man who worships nothing but the starch in my husband's collars."

"As for the housekeeper . . ."

"Pray have no inhibitions for my sake."

"Well, they say she has the second sight, which speaks through her gout-ridden knee. If I were you, madam, I'd be careful."

They laughed, the constraints between them vanishing momentarily. Lavinia rose and walked toward an octagonal cellaret; opening the lid, she took out a decanter of sherry and two glasses.

"Not for me, madam. I should get back to the stables."

She poured two glasses anyway.

"I'm sure the horses can wait."

Handing the crystal glass to Aloysius, she took a sip herself, thankful for the spreading warmth that briefly suspended any outside concerns.

Aloysius, amazed at the delicacy of the glass, held it up to the candle.

"It is for drinking, not for gazing at," Lavinia said, amused.

The coachman, determined not to be considered vulgar through any haste to taste its contents, placed the glass on the desk and, covering his embarrassment, picked up the stereograph sitting there. Turning it sideways, he tried to see how it worked.

Lavinia slipped a stereoscopic card into the gadget, then held it up to his face, enveloping him in her perfume. Its scent disoriented him further.

"It is a stereograph, Aloysius; the images are made more vivid through the two photographs."

"A wonder. I can see a small bird suspended above the soldiers, its wings beating the air."

"The series is on the Crimea War. The Colonel keeps them as a memento—the point of which escapes me, as every night he dreams he is back there and wishes it were otherwise."

Aloysius stared through the two lenses. It was as if he could smell the rotting flesh of the dead cart horse that lay just beyond the trench, could feel the mud caking on his skin as it had on the young soldiers. A terrible shame came over him as he realized that the two infantrymen had quite likely been killed and he was looking upon the faces of the dead. He did not care for the sensation. Placing the machine firmly back onto the table, he took a large gulp of the sherry only to break into a coughing fit.

"Tell me about the friendships of men, Aloysius."

Startled by the question, he carefully placed the glass down again.

"I shall try, madam, but I am not a social creature myself. In truth, I prefer horses to men."

Lavinia smiled despite her growing apprehension. "You drive my husband some nights, do you not?"

Aloysius, now seeing the stratagem she had embarked upon, deliberately emptied his face of any judgment.

"Aye, madam."

"Is he often with Mr. Campbell?"

"They visit the clubs and sometimes other houses."

"What manner of houses?"

"I am not at liberty to say, but you should take comfort in that they are the same houses frequented by most of Mayfair's married men."

"Cold comfort. I have lost him, I fear." At which her whole demeanor collapsed. Near tears, she looked down, painfully aware of her trembling hands.

Aloysius, flabbergasted at her sudden loss of composure, spontaneously reached across to take her hands. Then he remembered his place and instead leaned over her with a clumsy grace.

"*Ná bídh ag caoineadh anois, ná bídh ag caoineadh* (Don't cry, please don't cry)," he whispered in Gaelic, not knowing whether she would understand him or not. To his amazement, she looked up at him and replied in the same tongue.

"*Nach mé an t-óinseach cáillte.* (What a fool I've been.)"

"The man still loves you," he replied, as directly as if she had been a weeping serving girl and he her brother.

"You think?"

"I am sure," he answered, as unconvinced as the young woman before him.

❧

Mama, I no longer know if you are alive or dead, but my imaginings have made a habit of you, rendering you as substantial as the walls of this bedroom, sitting there listening to me patiently, and now this habit has become an addiction. Ridiculous, really, to be comforted by whispering into a plain wooden box, but perhaps that is the very nature of faith.

It is almost day, and I have had the most fearful night. James quite abandoned me after the theater, claiming he was to join a game of commerce at his club. He has not returned. The whole night I have tortured myself by imagining him engaged in all manner of debauchery. Now my anger has become resignation. I still love him, but I do not want to live in a marriage without affection. Can I win him back? Could I ever forgive him? I know I cannot live without him—without his love or approval. Tell me, Mama, what does a wife do in such circumstances?

Lavinia crouched at the window, the whispering box open on the sill. Every one of her muscles had become gnarled wood; exhaustion gripped her as the house seemed to inhale and exhale with the growing dawn.

The sound of approaching wheels on the street below brought her to her feet. A hansom cab pulled up to the curb and a coachman leapt down and opened the door. The Colonel stepped out. Even from this height, Lavinia could see his face looked worn and haggard, as if he had not slept.

Stamping the ground, the coachman turned his back on the cab, hugging himself in an effort to keep the cold from his bones. There was something deliberate about his movement that caught Lavinia's attention.

Hamish Campbell emerged from the coach, coatless, his shirt rumpled, his collar collapsed, his color as high as if he were intoxicated—a dishevelment that gave him a reckless beauty. Grabbing the Colonel's lapels with both hands, he pulled the older man toward him. At first, Lavinia thought Campbell might strike him, so rough and fast was the gesture. But instead he embraced him, full and passionately.

Lavinia watched transfixed, her face a small white oval in the high window. Her husband responded, his hand resting for a moment on the younger man's waist before pulling away. Without any further exchange, Campbell climbed back into the hansom cab as the Colonel slipped a coin into the waiting coachman's hand before disappearing under the portico.

"You waited up, I warned you not to." James stood at the door, shoes in hand. His eyes were bloodshot, his speech slurred. A sweetish smell emanated from his clothes. Lavinia recognized it as the odor she had noticed before in his study—opium.

"Sleep would have been more constructive." She turned away from him, distress hollowing her face.

James sat heavily, resting his head in his hands. She walked over to him.

"You had affection for me once," she said.

He lifted his face to kiss her, but she could not respond.

"And I still have!"

Outside, a church bell began to peal plaintively.

"Where have you been?"

"I told you—at a card game, at the Carlton. Mr. Campbell and myself were challenged by Lord Ealing and some young squire. I won. Ealing's a fool—he wagered some hunting lodge north of Carlisle and lost it. I suppose one shouldn't expect too much from the offspring of first cousins."

"Was the card game the only event of the night?" she asked, trying to hide her anger.

"Don't question me, Lavinia. I am weary to the bone."

Suddenly losing control, Lavinia began pounding him with her fists—short blows that rained down on his head and shoulders.

Only once had such blind emotion overtaken her: when, as a child, she had stabbed the peat-cutter boy. The expression of surprise on the boy's face came back to her now as she railed at her husband; she wanted nothing in that moment but to destroy him.

Astonished, the Colonel leapt to his feet and wrestled her down to the bed. He stared down at her through the film of veins that snaked through his eyes, his puffy red face inches from her own. "Have you entirely lost your mind?"

He slapped her across the face, knocking her back to the mattress. Then, standing, he touched the bruises now blossoming on his neck and face.

"You are suffering from hysteria. Of this I am now certain."

Lavinia curled up and buried her face in the coverlet. The Colonel took a small vial from a drawer beside the bed. Pulling open her lips, he squeezed several drops of laudanum between her gritted teeth.

"Now go to your room."

Lavinia fled, clenching her face in an effort not to weep.

The Colonel walked up to the nursery, profound weariness resounding in every step. Pushing the door open, he was thankful for the anonymity of the shaded twilight beyond.

Aidan lay folded tightly into his bedding, one hand pressed against a cheek. The Colonel, careful not to wake him, crept over to the cot. The expression on Lavinia's face as she had attacked him; a twisted detachment he'd never seen before except on the faces of some soldiers in the throes of war, stayed with him. She cannot be allowed to carry such potential within her, he thought. I must find a cure for this derangement.

He brushed a lock of hair away from his sleeping son's eyes, then silently lowered himself into an armchair and watched Aidan sleep until the first sunlight slid under the room's heavy drapes.

the window.

...

47

Los Angeles, 2002

The steam spiraled up toward the pale orange ceiling. A plastic submarine, propeller spinning, circled Julia's knees with
endearing intent. The scented candles in a row along the
edge of the bath were unlit. It had been one of Julia and
Klaus's rituals: a prelude to lovemaking in the bath. The
thought of lighting them now made her ill.

The bathroom was at the back of the house, on the ground
level. Klaus had planted gardenia and roses around the window that ran the length of the bath, so that in the summer
they could open it and let in the scent of the garden. The window was slightly ajar now, and in the distance Los Feliz
Boulevard rumbled faintly like a faraway sea.

The water was as hot as it could be without scalding her.
Julia wanted to draw all pain to the surface so that she would
feel nothing, be nothing. The skin on her fingers was wrinkled and her feet felt like sand. She rocked herself backwards
and forwards, backwards and forwards; the movement was
comforting, as if the axis of the world was tilting with her.
Her face was swollen from weeping, her burning eyes puffy
sponges under her fingertips. She knew that if she stopped
rocking, Klaus's face screaming with anger would loom up
from the milky surface of the bath water, followed by Carla
standing in the diner, staring at her blankly.

There was a rustle outside the window, audible even un-
derwater. Julia sat up, water streaming off her body. Coy-
otes? Skunks? Opossums?

The rustling grew louder. Now frightened, she reached

across and grabbed a towel. Just then Gabriel appeared at the window. Julia screamed and he dropped back down.

"Sorry." His muffled voice came from somewhere beneath the window.

Laughing out of sheer relief, the towel wrapped around her dripping body, she opened the window completely. He lay on his back clutching a large bottle of tequila, which appeared to be half drunk.

"It was meant to be a romantic surprise but I guess I messed up. Also, in case you think I'm some kind of sexual pervert, I had no idea that this was your bathroom."

He stayed lying, the patch of grass beyond the flowerbed was surprisingly comfortable and he calculated that it might be sensible to appear vulnerable until he gauged her emotional reaction.

"Gabriel, it's been a rough day and an even rougher evening. I really need my solitude."

Julia started to close the window, but before she had a chance to pull it shut he'd stretched his long leg out and jammed his left sneaker into the gap.

"Julia, I stole my best friend's car to drive here, Mom has no idea where I am, and I'm missing my favorite band. You've got to let me in."

"Promise you won't jump me?"

"On Einstein's grave and the whiskers of Schroedinger's cat."

Julia looked down: Gabriel resembled a cross between a fallen Renaissance prince—his shoulder-length black hair spread across the surrounding leaves—and a toppled circus clown, one foot still caught in the window. He grinned back, one of those eternally youthful smiles that split the world into optimists and pessimists; the smile of a beginner.

"Besides, if I continue to lie here I'll catch pneumonia, or maybe rabies from an angry squirrel, and you'll have an incredible amount of explaining to do to my mother."

Julia's head disappeared. A minute later he heard the back door being unlocked.

"Yes!" he whispered, punching the air.

She threw on an old jumper of her father's, which had been knitted for him by her grandmother—one of those early 1960s-style knits with a wide neck and loose cables that rippled down to her knees. Julia had had it since she was a child, having rescued it from the opportunity shop when her mother had given up darning it. Whenever she wore the jumper she'd imagined she could detect the faint aroma of tobacco and shaving soap on the neck—a scent that had instantly placed her back in his arms.

Wearing it now, she thought somewhere in the recesses of her mind how absurd it was to wear a ratty old article of clothing that was over thirty years old, however comforting. Unchaining the door, she peered into the darkness. Beyond the yard, the valleys and hills of Silver Lake were peppered with small oases of light and activity—other people's lives. The view used to inspire her.

Gabriel appeared, shaking the leaves from his hair. Julia pushed open the fly screen and he stepped in.

"Your eyes are all swollen."

"Today is Klaus's birthday. I tried to ring him but . . ."

"I'm sorry."

"It was stupid really—it's been a week of accidental confrontations. I ran into Carla, someone I once thought of as my closest friend. Everything feels as if it's unraveling and I can't seem to exorcise a terrible fight I had with Klaus. If only I hadn't lost the baby things might have worked out differently."

Julia turned away, hiding her face as it folded up in grief again. Pretending not to notice, Gabriel pulled two glasses from the cupboard, then orange juice from the fridge.

"What are you making?"

"Tequila sunrises—Mom taught me. It's the only legal remedy to post-separation trauma I know."

He handed her the drink, the blood-red orange juice settling to the bottom of the glass like honey.

"Fighting is part of life. I used to hit Mom all the time."

"You did?"

"Sure, and she hit me back. The classic was when I was about eleven and my parents were arguing about something— school fees, I think. Dad hit Mom, then I hit Dad for hitting Mom, then Mom hit me for hitting Dad."

"Gabriel! That's terrible."

"No, that's family. We live in this fucked-up politically correct world that suppresses nature," he said grandly, trying not to be distracted by the length of naked thigh that had crept out from under the pullover she was wearing.

"It's called civilization."

"Whatever."

Julia shivered despite the warmth of the kitchen. He touched her hand.

"Are you okay?"

"You don't understand. It was terrifying, I really wanted to kill him. It wasn't so much that I'd lost control as much as something else had got control of me. It's happened before, with far more devastating consequences."

Gabriel moved closer; he'd never wanted someone this much, nor been so calculating about it. With every other girl it had been spontaneous, instant lust, instant gratification, but with her it was different, adult. Fascinated by the soft down on her forearms, he was finding it hard to concentrate. Dragging his eyes away he spoke up.

"Anyway, terror is good, isn't it? I experience it all the time. Like the other night outside the bar—you were terrified but you were enjoying yourself. Admit it."

His persona suddenly slipped into the bravado of the adolescent—so patently insecure yet ridiculously audacious. Julia couldn't help smiling.

"Gabriel, you weren't scary."

"I wasn't?"

Deflated, he wondered why the idea was emasculating. He'd hoped she had been a little frightened—of the consequences of them actually making love.

"Neither were you," he lied, trying to navigate the excruciating anticipation he felt about making a pass. When was the right time? It had always seemed to him that such events opened up magically: the man simply moved toward the woman and it happened miraculously, without any clumsy banging of noses, clashing of teeth, misdirected tongues; without the woman pushing the man away in horror.

How do you read women, he'd asked his father once. All José had said was that it was like the weather: you look for a moment between the clouds. When the shifting, impenetrable emotions of the woman momentarily cleared, then you pounced. Gabriel had listened doubtfully. His father was an old-fashioned Latino who inherently believed that a woman wanted to be taken, whatever she might think consciously. Naomi's friends had taught Gabriel otherwise. And then there was Julia: complex, distraught, and intriguingly intelligent. Whatever his head might think, his body and its pounding hormones were propelling him toward one action and one action only.

"You know it was wrong, don't you?" Julia finished her drink. It had been strong, the tequila a slow burn momentarily erasing her sorrows. "You know that as your employer and elder, I have responsibilities, an emotional understanding of events that gives me an edge over you."

"Right, like that's really apparent."

"And . . . it should be special . . . you know . . . with a girl your own age."

Christ, she thinks I'm a virgin. Gabriel almost burst out laughing. He would have, but Julia looked so solemn sitting there, her face scrubbed clean, her skin a red and cream patchwork.

And suddenly, there was the break in the clouds. He saw it just as his father had described: an infinitesimal shift in her features. Fearing that any hesitation might lead to a lost opportunity, Gabriel reached across and lifted her hand. Turning the palm up, he kissed it. Then, standing, he pulled her toward him, threading his fingers through the loose knit of her pullover, touching her skin, reaching for her breasts, taking her mouth into his.

This time Julia didn't want to hesitate; she craved the release, to know she was desirable, that he desired her. And the loveliness of him was wondrous. Marveling, she cupped his head with her hands, engulfed by the sweet, clean smell of his hair. His shoulders, on the brink of bursting into their full breadth, reminded her that he wasn't quite a man, but she was beyond caring. She forgot herself, who she was and who she was with, as his lips caught at her. Teasing out that cord of sex, the edgy precipice between lust and desire. Amazed at the fierce trembling that had started somewhere below her belly, she stared down as he pulled the jumper up to her breasts. Then, her buttocks resting against the edge of the stool, his mouth traveled down her body, biting gently along the way until he reached her and spread her, his lips and tongue greedy for her clit. Gasping, she leaned back against the bench, her elbow almost knocking over the half-finished glass of tequila.

Gabriel looked up from her pubic hair, along the whole terrain of her body as it rose above him. He thought she looked magnificent, her features softening as her ecstasy came in mounting ripples he could read beneath his fingers, against his lips. He wanted to make her scream, make her take him seriously, to see him as an equal.

As she drew close, she pulled him up by his hair then kissed him deeply, his face and mouth smelling of her. Without a word, he slipped out of his pants and pushed inside her, his cock rigid against his slight hips, his soft pubic hair. The shape of him was so profoundly different that she struggled, her body adjusting to the new parameters, fighting part of her that clung to the illusion that by making love she was breaking a spell, severing a visceral cord that still existed between her and Klaus. Irrational. Animal knowledge.

Enjoy this. Relax, she argued with herself.

But before she had a chance to protest, Gabriel had hoisted her onto his hips. Her legs wrapped around his waist, her arms around his neck. The fragrance of mouthwash, gum, and, strangely, chocolate rising up as he walked her, trousers still caught around his shins, in a half-shuffle into the lounge room.

They reached the couch; slowly he lowered her down while trying to stay inside her. He succeeded. They lay there for a moment, Julia's legs wrapped around him, his cock still hard in her, her breasts pushed up against his face.

"Okay, so I suspect you're not a virgin."

And they both broke into laughter, the shape of him vibrating within her. Then, as he took her breasts into his hands, she rode him until all was burnt away.

Afterwards, they lay there together, Gabriel curved around her back, Julia staring out into the room, its familiar corners now alien.

"I would have killed him," she whispered into the creeping darkness, to no one in particular.

"I know." He softly kissed her neck.

PART THREE

THE FALL

48

Mayfair, 1861

"No, James, I will not allow it!"

"It has to be done. The examination will not be thorough otherwise!"

"But you don't even entirely believe in the science."

"As a tool for diagnosis, I believe phrenology to have merit. You are ill, Lavinia, with an ague of both spirit and mind."

Lavinia sat on a chair in front of the fireplace, her hair loosened around her, her maid hovering nervously with a pair of scissors in hand.

"But my hair, James! The indignity of it! And how, pray, am I to present myself in public?"

"We shall purchase a wig, a beautiful wig. Please, my dear, I shall tolerate no argument."

Lavinia, a bruise still visible under hastily applied pearl dust, touched the ends of her long mane. Could she endure the humiliation? And would she be able to conceal such an outrage?

The Colonel gestured to the maid, who moved forward and tentatively lifted a lock of hair. She paused, scissors open. "But madam has such beautiful hair."

"Oh, for pity's sake!"

The Colonel grabbed the scissors from the maid and began

hacking at the great length of his wife's hair. Mute with horror, Lavinia watched the locks fall and curl about her feet like the abandoned fur of some extinct animal.

Minutes later, Colonel Huntington stepped back from his handiwork. Lavinia, shorn, had the appearance of a beautiful youth: her large eyes, incandescent with rage; the wide cheekbones, exaggerated by the lack of framing; her small lips disappearing into the pallor of her face. Without cosmetics, the only hint of femininity was the delicate cast to her features, but this too suggested a youthful masculinity. To his great and secret shame, the Colonel found the transformation to be of sensual fascination.

"Mama!"

Both the Colonel and Lavinia swung around to the door. The nursemaid holding Aidan in her arms stood shocked by the fragility of the young woman's face. The boy stared at his mother, then burst into loud sobbing, hiding his face in the nursemaid's shoulder.

"Come now, come, it is still your dear mama." Lavinia held out her arms.

The nursemaid, avoiding the Colonel's disapproving gaze, carried the child over and placed him in his mother's embrace, where, after some coaxing, he fell into an awed silence as he reached up to touch the shorn head in wonder.

Later that day, well concealed under a wig that her husband had promptly purchased, and over that a large straw bonnet, Lavinia climbed into the carriage.

Aloysius, assisting her, took the opportunity to glance into her face. There was no doubt the young woman had been struck. For one insane moment the waiting coachman considered confronting his employer, but then reminded himself that what was between husband and wife should remain there, whether they be royalty or beggars. Let their quarrel stay their quarrel, he warned himself, but his fists tightened under his riding gloves nevertheless.

The Huntingtons sat before a large, heavy-legged Jacobean oak desk that was covered in piles of documents. Dr. Jefferies was an unprepossessing individual of five foot or so, with copious amounts of hair springing from both his nostrils and ears, and two thick black eyebrows that bristled like outraged caterpillars above small deep-set eyes, all contrasting with a smooth low brow and bald pate.

The physician's head was disproportionately large and wobbled atop a thin scrawny neck from which hung flaps of wrinkled skin. He resembled a turkey, Lavinia thought; one of those absurd, childlike observations that occurred in moments of great distress. A short benevolent turkey. It was a strangely comforting notion: a short benevolent turkey could not condemn her as insane, surely? Petrified as she was, he might indeed discover an inherent trait she had no control over.

The dimensions of Dr. Jefferies's head were particularly conspicuous when set against the gallery that lined the wall behind him. The room was crammed with models of heads—some, plaster casts of living beings; others, bone-white craniums. At least a dozen, each mapped with the different areas common to emotional organs, stood about the room. Here, one labeled *The Negro*; there, another labeled *The Jew, The Slav, The Indian*.

Lavinia couldn't help but be mesmerized. A large skull with deep-set eye sockets that appeared to stare at one had the title *Aryan* (*Germanic*) written beneath its pronounced jawbone. Beside it sat a smaller skull marked *The Anglo Saxon*. A whole row rested below these: *The Schizophrenic, The Megalomaniac, The Melancholic*, and *The Nymphomaniac*. Suddenly horrified, Lavinia wondered what she would be labeled: *The Celtic Madwoman*? Did these categories really exist or were they just prototypes?

To distract herself from her growing dread, Lavinia concentrated on the phrenologist. Had he been drawn to the science by the gigantism of his own brain? Wouldn't such an ambition be described as a form of narcissism? The laudanum, which she had been taking since the night before last, had leaded her mind but had also infused her imagination with an eccentric logic.

A small coal fire glowed in an oversized hearth, a bamboo screen discreetly masked one corner of the room, and three of the bookshelves covering the walls spilled forth all manner of tomes and documents. The fourth wall was hung with a plethora of charts: phrenological graphs, acupuncture charts, and ancient anatomical diagrams inscribed in Sanskrit.

Dr. Jefferies stood up and came around from behind his desk, revealing the rest of his worn green velvet topcoat, tweed trousers, and a pair of purple Turkish slippers upon his large feet.

"Open your eyes wide, please," he requested in the manner of a friendly family physician.

Lavinia obeyed, and he bent to look into her dilated pupils, enveloping her in a miasma of unwashed clothes and stale tobacco laced with a faint trace of old beef stew.

"Laudanum, Colonel Huntington?" he asked.

The Colonel was seated beside his wife, and had not bothered to remove his Macfarlane overcoat, which still glistened with that afternoon's rain. "I had no choice. She has developed hysteria, Dr. Jefferies."

"Quite!" An exclamation that left the Colonel wondering whether the good doctor approved of such medication or not.

The physician straightened and walked vigorously over to the window to pull the thick faded velvet drapes closed. The room immediately took on a covert atmosphere. With surprising gentleness, Dr. Jefferies took Lavinia's hand and stroked it paternally.

"And now, my dear, could you please remove your bonnet and wig . . . behind the screen."

After a nod from the Colonel, Lavinia stepped behind the bamboo screen. On the other side were a rococo mirror and a mannequin's head—the kind you might find in a hat shop—on a small console. She untied the ribbons of her hat and slipped it off, followed by the wig, which she placed on the mannequin's head. She glanced into the oval mirror. It was the first time she had looked at herself since James had cut her hair. The face that stared back from the glass appeared startlingly young. In a moment of bewilderment, Lavinia looked behind her, not recognizing herself. Then she touched the glass.

What have I become, she wondered. Is this some creature who has lived under my skin all these years only to emerge now? Where is the young Irish girl who stood at the mirror in her father's house all those months ago thrilling at the adventure before her? Where is my happiness? My spirit? All that had defined me?

Eyes gleaming, the phrenologist ran his fingers across the bumps and slight indentations that made up the landscape of Lavinia's skull. Revolted by his touch, Lavinia clutched the arms of her chair to stop herself bolting from the surgery.

"Fascinating." His breath was a noxious wind that forced Lavinia to hold her own.

Taking a pair of callipers that hung on a hook on the wall above the desk, he measured both the length and width of her skull as delicately as if he were handling an ostrich egg, then scribbled a few figures into a small notebook.

Reaching back to the desk, Dr. Jefferies picked up a soft wax crayon, which he used to mark and divide areas on Lavinia's skull as dispassionately as a surveyor might draw up a plan for a railway. It was a curious sensation. She felt like an anatomical display, a novelty.

She glanced over at James. His expression disturbed her; she had never seen him look at her so coldly.

"As you know, the human brain is divided into twenty-seven organs, nineteen of which are shared by both beast and man." The phrenologist pointed to a section at the top of the head. "One, the reproductive instinct; two, the love of one's offspring; three, the ability to be affectionate, to have friends. Four, self-defense, courage, and aggression. Five, the tendency to murder—in animals this would be the carnivorous instinct. Six, guile; seven, covetousness, the tendency to steal; eight, arrogance, a love of authority, pride. Nine, vainglory—"

"Quite, quite, Dr. Jefferies," the Colonel interjected. "But you forget that I myself have been a student of phrenology. With respect, we are here for a diagnosis not a lecture."

"In that case, I shall curb my loquaciousness, Colonel Huntington, and continue my examination."

The crayon circled a bump on the left side of Lavinia's head. Dr. Jefferies tsked in disapproval, then sent his pen scratching even more vigorously across the notebook.

"That protuberance is the result of an injury as a small child," Lavinia said. "I remember it vividly."

"There is no such thing as accident when it comes to the skull. Each indentation or bump is a clear indication, a clear pathway to an emotion. Therefore, I would appreciate it if the subject refrained from expressing an opinion during the examination."

He continued his inspection, making a two-dimensional map of Lavinia's cranium until a whole topography was spread out before him, with small labels and arrows describing each characteristic. Finally, he looked meaningfully at the Colonel, who, taking the hint, turned to his wife.

"My dear, I think it more fitting if you now adjourned to the waiting room while we discuss the diagnosis."

"But it is my skull, therefore I believe it is my right to hear the diagnosis also."

"To the waiting room, please. There will be no argument."

Reluctantly, Lavinia slipped on her wig and bonnet then left the room.

Dr. Jefferies flicked up his coat tails ceremoniously before sitting. After placing his thick spectacles upon the pinched bridge of his nose, he indicated that the Colonel should join him.

The Colonel peered across the desk at the sketch of his wife's skull. His practiced eye immediately discerned areas of character development; observations he could not argue with.

"As you can see for yourself, your wife's skull is small, suggesting a limited intelligence. She has a definite leaning toward hysteria, seen here in the distinctive dent in the organ of moral sense or sensitivity."

The Colonel winced, a facial tic Dr. Jefferies noted immediately.

"I assume, as one man of science to another, I can speak frankly?"

"It has to be done. But I'm afraid I don't subscribe to the notion that a small skull indicates limited intelligence. If anything, I suspect my wife suffers from a surfeit of intelligence, which sits uncomfortably with her gender. However, I have noticed that since the birth of our son, and particularly in the last few months, she has become increasingly distraught."

"Precisely. Any hormonal disturbance in the womb will contribute to this type of hysteria." Dr. Jefferies pointed to another shaded area on the sketch. "Do you know anything about your wife's mother, her history? Often these abnormalities run in families."

"Lavinia's mother died when she was a baby. The Reverend Kane did not like to speak of her, except to say she was high-spirited and of extremely attractive appearance."

"I see. Ah, the dangers of marrying below one's class." Here the phrenologist sighed most ominously. "This structural irregularity is developed to the point where she may tend toward irrational outbursts that manifest physically. Has this been the case?"

"Only a few times."

"There is also negative development in the guile organ located just above the ear. Is her menstrual cycle regular?"

"I believe so."

"But she suffers from emotional polarity, irritability, skin rashes?"

"On occasion."

"This would be the heat radiating from the guile organ. Other noticeable irregularities are the organ of the memory of facts—this appears to be misshapen, suggesting a tendency to distort facts and all remembered events; her sense of spatial sensibility is malformed, and there is a considerable indentation on the organ of the connectiveness between numbers." He looked up from his notes. "She is no mathematician."

"What woman is?" the Colonel retorted, increasingly dismayed.

"More positively, she has a very well-developed organ related to poetic talent, and also for religion—shown here in this particular protrusion. Both of which could serve to rein in her other traits."

"Overall?"

"Overall, I would say we are dealing with a hysteric who suffers delusions of an imaginative kind. This particular hysteria is almost always inherited from the mother. Of whom we apparently know nothing?"

He looked up from his notes and fixed the Colonel with a skeptical stare.

"I have told you what I know. But her father is a close associate. Although somewhat poetic and a romantic by nature, he is a rationalist of the staunchest kind. He will be most upset to hear about his daughter's condition."

"It would be prudent not to tell him, Colonel Huntington. Rest assured, I do not believe your wife is of any danger to either yourself or your child. However, there was a case I read about in *The Phrenological Journal*. I believe the year was 1843 . . ."

Dr. Jefferies reached into his desk to pull out a yellowed

leaflet. He opened it to an article illustrated by a diagram of a woman's head.

"Mary McDougal, convicted of murder in 1842." Excited, Dr. Jefferies looked up. "Dr. Combe had the good fortune to purchase her skull after execution. It showed some similarities with that of your dear wife—except, of course, in the organs of poetry and religion."

The good doctor smiled, exposing a row of stained and blackened teeth. Colonel Huntington detected an element of Schadenfreude, and decided there and then that he disliked the man regardless of his accuracy.

"But we are agreed that she is merely a hysteric?"

"We are." With a hint of regret, Dr. Jefferies closed the leaflet.

"And what would you prescribe to contain such a condition?"

"Difficult to say, Colonel, given that these are innate traits that will only increase as the subject matures. Stimulation will only encourage them. More laudanum, perhaps. Music is a wonderful tonic, but play her only the more frivolous composers—Mozart, Vivaldi and the like. Avoid Beethoven and Bach to prevent over-encouragement of the nervous system."

"Lavinia has a hungry intellect. In this she is more like a man."

"My dear fellow, do not make the fatal error of mistaking pathologically unnatural appetites for genuine need. To encourage her in this will only worsen her condition."

"I understand."

The phrenologist, now humming triumphantly, rolled up a copy of Lavinia's chart and pressed it into the Colonel's reluctant hands.

Lavinia gazed out of the barred side window that looked out over Harley Street. The reception hall, with a stained glass window set above the front door, was little more than a converted hallway. A tall sallow-skinned nurse, her starched uniform folded like cardboard upon her bony chest, glanced over contemptuously.

I could leave now, Lavinia thought, escape into the anonymity of the working classes. She remembered a scandal that had swept the parlors of Dublin some two years before, when eighteen-year-old Lady Milhurst had eloped with a valet. When news of the notorious couple had emerged a year later, the valet was found languishing in the debtors' prison, while the young aristocrat was incarcerated in the Bedlam madhouse, deranged. It was a sobering morality tale.

What skills do I have to survive, Lavinia asked herself. Could she become a governess, a companion? She would have to escape to the continent. Calculating all possibilities, she opened the purse that hung at her belt. It was empty. Lavinia was completely dependent on her husband for both shelter and food. Panicked, she glanced down at her dress. If she pawned it, it would only bring in enough funds to live frugally for a month. The gold earrings she wore perhaps another month, and then where would she go? She knew that her father would not welcome her penniless and scandalous return. Not only would it compromise his friendship with James, it would be the end of his parish and his social standing in the community.

And what of her son? She would not dare to take him from his father. Despite all, James was a loving and attentive parent. What right did she have to deprive him of his child?

Outside a lame beggar woman, no older than thirty years, hobbled past the window pushing a barrow filled with all her earthly possessions. An ancient terrier rode atop the pile like a king, with a Union Jack tied around his neck. Everyone feared the workhouse, Lavinia thought; even the rich.

Nevertheless, that night, in the privacy of her own bedroom, before the lassitude of the laudanum hijacked her senses, she began to compose a letter to the Reverend Kane.

My dearest Papa,

I am writing to you out of desperation for I fear my marriage is no longer a safe haven for either myself or my child. I respect the long and intimate acquaintance you have enjoyed over the years with my husband, but I have found him not to be the man I thought he was. He is possessed of a dissolute and decadent nature, which he cannot help.

Father, please allow me and my child to return to Anascaul. Without your support, I am penniless and entirely dependent on the shelter of my husband's house. I know the implications of my request, but if you are a true Christian you will grant me this.

In hope,

Your loving daughter.

49

Los Angeles, 2002

"From what you describe, it sounds like Tom Donohue. He was Delta Force—one of the best until last year. Then he went AWOL suddenly after a special op."

"Was there any particular reason?" Clutching the phone, Julia stood at the back door and stared out at the yard. Gabriel had left half an hour before and it was still early morning in California—afternoon in Washington. Colonel Smith-Royston sounded like he was in the middle of his day, while exhaustion and the previous night's tussles permeated Julia's whole body. Leaning against the doorframe, she decided not to dwell on the morality of her actions.

"I cannot release that information," the colonel said, his voice dropping into a sudden formality, "my job would be on the line."

"Now I'm really interested."

"Don't be. This guy is bad news. Do you want me to post some security outside the lab?"

"No, he didn't strike me as dangerous."

"He is, just like any zealot on a mission is. If he appears again, you're to ring me immediately, Professor Huntington. You got that?"

"Yes, sir, cross my heart and hope to die."

"Julia, you're to take this guy seriously, you understand?"

There was a distant click on the phone line as Smith-Royston hung up, and Julia had the uncanny sensation that someone else had been listening in.

Sipping her coffee, she sat down on the doorstep and, watching a blackbird wrestle a worm out from the lawn, wondered how the search for one mutant gene had suddenly become so interesting for so many people.

❦

Julia waited a moment before entering the laboratory, feeling anxious about how to relate to Gabriel since their lovemaking the night before. She smoothed down her skirt and pulled at her shirt cuffs. She was determined to maintain the equilibrium in the laboratory at all costs. I must retain my authority, she resolved before opening the door.

The four assistants were in the dry laboratory, clustered around Dr. Jennifer Bostock's computer. Leaning over Jennifer's shoulder, staring at the screen, Gabriel whistled in disbelief.

"The guy must have had a pass. Night security is wicked."

"Has there been a break-in?" Julia said.

"About three this morning."

"Why didn't you ring me earlier?" Julia pushed her way through to the desk.

"We thought you might like to sleep in," Gabriel said with a straight face before winking at her. Julia blushed and glanced at the other students. They appeared oblivious to the flirtation.

"Check this out. Emmanuel, the security guy, gave it to me." Jennifer Bostock hit a key and the grainy interior of the wet lab came up on screen, the image angled down from a high point.

They all leaned closer to the screen as a figure, barely visible in the dim light of the footage, his face masked, entered. His torch sent a ghostly streak through the black and gray recording as its beam bounced along the darkened shelves and cluttered benches. For a moment the footage blanked white as the arc of light swung across the hidden camera eye.

"Is anything missing?" Julia asked.

"No, that's what's so strange."

On screen, the figure moved cautiously, poised like a dancer.

"This guy's professional."

"Yeah, freaky, eh?"

"Wait, the best part's coming up."

The intruder pulled a small digital camera from his back pocket and began photographing. Julia stood back, horrified. "So do we know what he got?"

Jennifer hit the pause button and the image froze. "Not much, really. I don't believe he knew what to look for. I mean, he took shots of Oona's wheat grass, for Christ's sake!" She snorted derisively. "Could have been one of those mad animal liberationists again. I don't know why we don't just put a sign up for the guys—you know, something like 'There are no live animals, small children, or white supremacists kept on the premises.'"

"What about the Defense Department project?"

The assistants glanced at each other sheepishly. Finally, Gabriel spoke up.

"Yeah, he took shots of the DNA results. But unless he

had access to the research notes, it wouldn't make any sense at all."

Julia sat at her desk wondering who would go to such extremes. Valco? Her work might be of interest to the insurance company if a genetic propensity was proven to directly affect people's ability to work, but such information was at least a decade away. Could it be the ex-Delta soldier, Donohue? Could he have lied to her? Was it possible he was working for another government?

There was a tentative knock on the door. Gabriel hovered in the doorway, unsure about whether he should come in. Julia smiled at him and he walked over to the desk.

"Gabriel, about last night—"

He held his hand up. "Please don't make the mistake of underestimating my intelligence. Besides, I seduced you, so in case you're having doubts you're morally redeemed."

"Just promise me you won't tell your mother."

"Sorry, company policy—never sign a contract you can't keep."

He opened the file he was carrying to reveal a series of developed images of DNA: they resembled blurred bar codes. Julia pulled the lamp across, spilling light over the photographs.

"We mined for ANG–1," he said, and placed five of the images beside five traced graphs, each with a name written above it—the source of the DNA. "Jack Lewis, Mathew Catherton, Kurt Moony, Clive O'Hare, Carlos Santos—some of them representing an identical twin, some fraternal. All of them top combat soldiers with extensive frontline experience—high risk-takers, adrenaline junkies—none of them suffering from posttraumatic stress disorder. All showing the same genetic profile for the genes tested."

Julia scanned the results, trying to contain her growing excitement, then leapt up and went over to her filing cabinet. She quickly flicked through the hanging personnel files and pulled out the individual folders of the twin of each of the named men. She placed these against the files already laid out.

"Benito Lewis—identical twin—and yes, same genetic profile . . ." She glanced down at the notes. "Same behavioral traits, saw service in Srebrenica, Afghanistan . . . no post-trauma . . ." She glanced at another set of files. "George Catherton, nonidentical twin, different ANG–1 sequence to his brother Mathew—he has ANG–1B—requested transfer from platoon after frontline encounter in Kuwait and has suffered post-trauma. Looking good, looking good . . ."

"Julia, I still don't believe this can be the only factor."

"Relax, nothing's proven until we have the results in on all five hundred. But I want you to narrow the testing down to this specific ANG–1 sequence difference, and I'll tell the out-of-state researchers to do the same."

"There's something else you need to know—a matter of great scientific import."

She looked up at him, worried he might have made a miscalculation.

"I shall probably attempt to seduce you again."

She couldn't help but smile.

"At your own peril. Just remember, there's no way this is *ever* going to be a relationship."

"Who said I was after a relationship?" Grinning, he left.

Julia looked back at the different sets of research results. Something played at the edge of her mind, tantalizingly out of reach. She sensed Gabriel was right: there was a missing factor she hadn't added into the equation; but the more she concentrated, the more it eluded her.

50

The Vicarage Anascaul, County Kerry
June the 10th
In the Year of Our Lord 1861

My dearest daughter,

I was most troubled by your letter. I cannot believe an individual as upstanding, as intelligent and as dedicated a father as Colonel Huntington could be the cause of any marital or domestic distress. You have in the past been given to flights of the imagination (a trait you inherited from your dear unfortunate mother) and so I am inclined to think that your correspondence was written in haste during an attack of negative fancy. I urge you to remain in your marriage and to fulfill your wifely duties to their utmost. You have had the extraordinary good fortune to marry into an established family of impeccable breeding, and into a manner of living I could never have provided for you.

Obviously there will be sacrifices, especially when there is such an age difference between husband and wife, but it is one's duty to tolerate a degree of incompatibility within matrimony (indeed, I have often lectured from the pulpit on this very same subject). Out of respect for my good friend and son-in-law, but also with the understanding of the implications for my grandson, I cannot agree to taking you in.

Turning to happier matters, we are in the full flight of summer here and the lavender in the garden is most . . .

Lavinia sat in a yellow satin armchair, her father's letter, half-read, resting on her lap. The Colonel moved toward her and Lavinia turned the letter over, hiding its contents.

"Dr. Jefferies believes you to be a hysteric," he said. "A trait inherited from the maternal line. Lavinia, do you know anything about your mother?"

Colonel Huntington knelt and took one of his wife's hands into his own. Her fingers were freezing, he noted. Since the visit to the phrenologist, now over a month ago, they had barely spoken. Lavinia had escaped to the nursery while he, ashamed and uncertain over his own behavior, had retreated to the safe haven of his club.

Lavinia stared at the fire, the flames now twisting into the shape of Polly Kirkshore's hair, his mouth. If my mother is living, she can only belong to that world of criminals and prostitutes, she thought.

"I believe my mother to be dead." She did not look up, fearing he would see the doubt in her eyes.

"Are you so unhappy?"

Wondering at the honesty of his concern, Lavinia did not take her eyes from the fire.

"The night I was at the window waiting for you," she said. "I saw Mr. Campbell and yourself . . ."

A coal rolled out of the grate onto the stone hearth. Neither kicked it back. The Colonel forced a short bark of a laugh. His wife's insinuation—if proven—was a criminal offense. She was unpredictable in her emotions and mental equilibrium, yet if she were to go to a magistrate . . . Such a possibility terrified him.

"Campbell is an enthusiastic youth, idealistic in his beliefs," he answered carefully, his tone deliberately neutral. "He seems to have conceived of a kind of hero worship for me, which can become quite tiresome. Perhaps it is this which has driven your wondrous imagination to all sorts of wild inventions."

"I wish I could believe you, but you two have an intimacy that is exclusive of everyone."

He caressed her hand, trying not to reveal his fear through his trembling fingers.

"Believe me, Lavinia. You must."

All of his past and the possibility of any future seemed to hang upon this conversation. If Lavinia were to betray him, the Colonel knew there would be a trial, public humiliation; he would lose his good name, his son, all possibility of an ongoing professional reputation. He would be imprisoned; his life would be over.

"I cannot help but conclude your hysteria is the result of a good intellect gone to waste. Your mind needs occupation." He stared up at the painting above the fireplace, wildly searching for a strategy. "I have been asked to compose a pamphlet for the Royal Society on the botanical specimens I collected in the Amazon. Are you interested in writing this?"

Having dangled the bait, the Colonel waited, his future suddenly as fragile as the Chinese porcelain flower resting on the mantelpiece before him.

Finally, Lavinia looked at him, her face devoid of emotion. "Is the pamphlet to include the plants that are used in the religious ceremonies you told me about?"

"Indeed. I intend to execute one of these rituals in a couple of months."

"You will take the ayahuasca brew? You will summon the goddess of the Bakairi?"

For the first time in over a month, Lavinia appeared animated. The Colonel smiled, encouraged by her enthusiasm.

"I will try. If you wish, you could observe and take notes."

"You would not employ Mr. Campbell for such a task?"

"From now on, the two of you shall work side by side."

"Will he agree to such an arrangement?"

"He will have no choice."

"Then I think I should welcome the distraction. Thank you."

The Colonel smiled again more warmly. "Enough of that."

Trying to conceal his immense relief he moved toward her then drew her to her feet and led her into the master bedroom. Pulling at the buttons of her blouse, he began to undress her.

The laudanum made Lavinia a somnambulist, hovering above James's caresses—until he touched her sex. Then she pulled his mouth to hers, hands, arms, fingers clawing desperately to reclaim the lovemaking they had lost themselves in so many months before.

James, overwhelmed by the familiar yet estranged body under his hands, could not repress the images that flared over his wife's breasts, her hips, her mouth. A young man—his neck, the touch of his hands, his mouth. James pushed against her while secretly craving the hardness of the youth's body beneath his own.

I can find myself again; I can, and I must, he told himself over and over, while Lavinia, burying her face against his neck, allowed his lovemaking to eclipse all but the faintest sense of betrayal.

51

The days drifted through summer. Lavinia had rejected most of the social invitations that Lady Morgan had organized for her. She wanted to believe her husband's reassurances that he no longer socialized with Hamish Campbell outside of his research.

Before breakfast, Aloysius would drive Lavinia to Ladies' Mile. At the same time, Colonel Huntington took a brisk ride down the tree-lined Avenue of Rotten Row. After breakfast, Lavinia would retire to her study to pay the household bills, with Mrs. Beetle supervising, while the Colonel continued with his anthropological work, accompanied by Hamish Campbell.

After lunch, Lavinia would join the two men at their labor. The atmosphere in the study was most uncomfortable. Hamish Campbell worked on one side of the huge center table, his notes and drawings spread before him. Lavinia sat on the other side, the herbs and dried fungi in their jars and on specimen plates creating a barrier between her and the youth.

The two barely conversed, except to exchange the minimal courtesies. If the Colonel happened to be in the room, they both attempted to monopolize his conversation in the most competitive manner.

Gradually James became more attentive, insisting on weekly sojourns to the duck pond at Hyde Park with Lavinia and Aidan, and calling Lavinia to his bed—evidence he had foregone his previous ways and was giving himself solely to her.

Lavinia, for her part, had examined her situation from many angles and concluded that she still loved him and could not leave him. With each day spent by he husband's side, she felt her anger and resentment dissolving. Determined to be an attentive wife, she vowed to ignore Lady Morgan's warnings.

Some weeks later, the Huntingtons and Hamish Campbell found themselves together in the members' stand at Hurlingham to view a polo match between the Horse Guards and a Monmouthshire team.

Shouting encouragement to a cousin who rode with the Horse Guards, the Colonel appeared indifferent to Lavinia's and Hamish's discomfort. The two sat stiffly beside each other while the riders thudded past, polo sticks swinging, pushing their mounts through the cruel twists of the sport.

The Horse Guards had the advantage until a particularly

skillful player darted between his opponents, his stick whirling like a baton, monopolized the ball and whacked it between the poles to secure a win.

"Damnation! I have just lost twenty guineas!" The Colonel collapsed back onto his seat.

A woman several rows away turned at his voice. "Ahh! The elusive Colonel James Huntington!" Before any of them had time to respond, Lady Morgan was busy weaving her way through the chairs and picnic baskets.

Once before them, she studied the party with an aggrieved air. "All three of you have been the most absent of friends." She turned to Lavinia. "I'm afraid your presentation to the Queen is now quite out of the question. As you did not respond to my note about the date I had proposed, I'm afraid I was forced to cancel it."

"I apologize, Lady Morgan. I have been much occupied of late."

Lady Morgan peered under Lavinia's straw bonnet.

"Indeed, Mrs. Huntington, I do hope it was not due to illness? You appear to be wearing a wig."

Lavinia turned a beetroot red and the Colonel stepped forward protectively.

"Lady Morgan, what a fortuitous coincidence. You must forgive us, we have all been busy with my current academic pursuits. You see, I have now recruited *two* assistants."

"How extraordinary, to have *two* handmaidens to your genius," Lady Morgan remarked, relishing both Hamish's and Lavinia's uneasiness.

Behind them, the riders trotted back to the stables and the onlookers moved gaily onto the grass. Soon the playing field was speckled with brightly colored bonnets and sober gray and black silk top hats as spectators diligently pressed the upturned grass back into place, pushing at the clods delicately with the tip of a pointed shoe or the toe of a riding boot.

Lady Morgan led their small group determinedly toward

the crowd, propelled as much by the possibility of an advantageous encounter as obligation. The others followed somewhat reluctantly.

"You do both of us a disservice; we are more than handmaidens," Hamish said as he sidestepped a pile of horse manure.

"Indeed? James, are you to foist another tome onto the innocent public?"

"Several, my dear—one on the rituals of the Amazonian Indians, another on the jungle's flora."

"Such dedication from all three of you. The Colonel's study must be a veritable hothouse."

The Colonel knocked a grassy sod with his walking stick; it went flying. Ignoring his evident irritation, Lady Morgan continued merrily.

"Whatever your roles, you do make a *très jolie ménage à trois*."

Outraged, Hamish took her arm and marched her away from the others.

"You have overstepped the mark, Lady Morgan. Surely I am the true cause of all this peevishness?"

Opening her parasol, Lady Morgan tilted her dismayed face away from him. Staring down at the torn grass—so carefully cultivated, so easily destroyed by a game—she realized with a jolt that the last remnants of affection between them, and all possibility of seduction, had evaporated. Feeling very old indeed, Lady Morgan looked around at the crowd, the young women vying for the attention of the handsome polo players. So much of her identity had been invested in this notion of eternal beauty: a masquerade she had maintained her whole life. For two decades she had used her lovers like an elixir, their youth inspiring her wit, their presence generating an allure to dress up an aging façade.

Those who wavered she won over with gifts or the tantalizing promise of social promotion. For those who were offspring of the merchant class, Lady Morgan offered an invaluable introduction into an elite circle that offered not just prestige but extraordinary professional opportunities.

"Morgan's Finishing School" was the satirical moniker by which the young blades referred to the wealthy widow. An affair with her was an almost obligatory rite of passage, and most certainly an entry into the season and its ever-important business contacts. They may have ridiculed her in the clubs, but many of her former lovers still carried a secret appreciation for her passion, her ability to enrich their notion of culture—both the getting and cultivation of it, and, finally, for the core of sentimentality buried under her famous irony.

Oh, ingrates, all of them! Furious, and profoundly saddened, Lady Morgan forced herself to wave at a passing acquaintance. How wrong I was to advise Lavinia Huntington to ignore her husband's indulgences, she concluded, her fixed smile aching as she strove not to appear in the slightest part dejected.

"Did you hear me?" Hamish insisted, frustrated by her aloofness. "I will not have my good friend and his wife insulted."

Embarrassed at being confronted in a public place surrounded by her peers, many of whom would relish her discomfort, Lady Morgan hoped that her flushed face might pass as a reaction to the summer heat.

"Mr. Campbell, I will not tolerate such intimidation. Does the wife know about the true nature of your friendship with the Colonel?"

"And I will not tolerate your attempts to manipulate me into an affection I do not feel. Good afternoon, Lady Morgan." He tipped his hat to her and walked away.

On the other side of the field, Lady Gillingham lowered her binoculars.

"It appears that dear Lady Morgan has lost the last of her flock," the stately dowager remarked to her younger companion, the recently widowed Lady Dove.

"I have always thought it prudent to keep one's paramours within the aristocracy," Lady Dove replied.

"Indeed. One may expect a greater degree of discretion in the right circles. Not to mention cleanliness."

Squinting again through the binoculars, Lady Gillingham noted a minute breach in Lady Morgan's composure, a slump of her shoulders that suggested an unexpected vulnerability. In the next instant, she was as before, gaily laughing and entirely ignoring Hamish Campbell and his companions. However, the fatal observation had been made.

"It *does* seem that, finally, poor Frances has faltered," Lady Gillingham concluded with satisfaction.

❧

Lavinia immersed herself in a novel by George Sand as a distraction from the discomfort of the bumpy highway. The Huntingtons were returning from the polo match and had offered Hamish Campbell a place in their carriage. The three sat in absolute silence. Lavinia imagined herself as one of the author's misunderstood heroines, noble in her pursuit of love over conventional expectation to marry for position and security. Surely there can be nothing more laudable, she concluded, looking across at the Colonel.

The countryside rolled past in a series of tableaux. Lavinia, drawn from her book by her thoughts, stared out of the window. A farmer plowed a muddy field; a group of men were busy raking straw into a stack, the dried grass thrown up like snow in a storm; a young girl herded a flock of pigs down a country lane, a terrier snapping at the creatures' muddy trotters. Lavinia thought how Aidan would have enjoyed seeing the snorting animals.

As they entered a village, the rutted lane became a cobblestoned road and Lavinia could hear the horses' hooves clattering on the hard surface. They passed a Tudor inn that had probably stood there for the past four hundred years, the rim of its thatched roof almost buried in the wildflowers that grew in clusters around the building. Beside it stood the town hall, built of Georgian gray stone; next to that, two tenement-style houses of garish red brick, newly built, the scaffolding still jutting out like an awkward skeleton.

A recently constructed railway station came next, and Lavinia guessed the tenement houses must be accommodation for the railway workers. Many of the villages on the outskirts of London were expanding, boosted by the influx of workers now able to commute on the new railway system.

A duck flapped lazily across the glassy surface of the pond in a small green at the center of the village. Soon, even this quintessentially English landmark might disappear, Lavinia observed.

The landau pulled up at a railway crossing, where a sign proclaimed HALT in gleaming red paint. A moment later, the cry of a train whistle pierced the air and the locomotive steamed past, a silver-steel centaur that puffed and bellowed as it stretched recentlessly into the future.

Lavinia watched the train passing, saw the children's faces pressed against the glass, the heads of other passengers turning like pages in a book—an elderly matron, grief bowing her head beneath its black veil; four young soldiers grinning drunkenly; a lone adolescent boy dressed in a school uniform. Lavinia had wanted to travel to the polo match by steam train, she had wanted to feel the roar of this industrial revolution beneath her, but the Colonel considered such travel vulgar. The machine screeched again as it streamed away from them and their lives. Somehow, Lavinia felt less emancipated with its vanishing.

Turning back to the carriage, she saw that Hamish Campbell's foot was pressed against that of her husband. James was feigning sleep, his face resting against the leather upholstery. In that moment, catching Campbell's glance at the older man, Lavinia's worst fears about the nature of their friendship were confirmed.

52

Los Angeles, 2002

Julia sat in the car mesmerized by the traffic light. Lost in intense thought, the engine purring under her skin as she waited, the red traffic light as hypnotizing as an errant sun.

Years ago she'd learnt that the best way to trigger inspiration was never to search for it directly, but to look sideways. She'd tried daydreaming, running until all conscious thought had been burnt out of her head, writing the quandary down and leaving it by the side of the bed as she slept—anything to trick the mind into taking a lateral leap.

As a child, Julia had done much of her musing in the back seat of her mother's '68 Mercedes. Every so often her mother would drive south from San Francisco, down the coastline of Big Sur, to escape the tedium of her job. She would bundle her daughter into the back of the car, along with a tent, an eiderdown, a flask of instant coffee, a portable TV (which they never ended up using), and a box of oranges picked from the tree in their yard. They would always start out late and it would be dusk before they hit the coastal road. This was the one part of the trip Julia really loved—leaning back, her face upside down as she watched the evening sky descend through the rear window, the stars and the moon streaming away almost as fast as they appeared; the cosmos, the infinite unknown, each galaxy embodying a million possibilities. Out there in the great unknown, she could be anyone, do anything. Aged seven, she'd seen the immense velvet night as a metaphor for her own future, which streaked forward as inevitably as the white stripe of freeway that disappeared, beat after beat, under the speeding car.

A couple crossed the road at the lights. The man was tall with thick brown-blond hair and was wearing the same comfortable sporty clothes Klaus might have chosen. He had his arm around the woman. She looked a couple of years younger than Julia, her long legs encased in tight black pants, expensive sneakers on her feet, a loose duffle coat trimmed with fur around her shoulders. As they passed in front of the car, Julia could see that the woman was pregnant, well into her third trimester—the stage Julia would be at now if she hadn't lost the baby.

Absurdly it then occurred to her that a single freak event had sent her life into chaos—like an aberrant collision of particles. That would have been my life if it hadn't been for that one day, she concluded. Fascinated, Julia couldn't pull her eyes away from the woman. Only when the car behind hooted impatiently did she realize the lights had changed.

She accelerated out onto the freeway. The road ahead widened into a clear panorama broken only by telephone poles sprouting rhythmically across the terrain. Long dash, short dash, long dash—a Morse code of wooden posts. They jolted her back to the image of the stained DNA barcodes. What did her case studies all have in common? Dyslexia? Insomnia? Low levels of serotonin? Learning disabilities as children? She remembered some of the men had displayed problems with speech and math as children, but what did that prove? Some had bad skin, and many were tall, but how were all three linked? There must be one other factor she could search for that would be the clincher, the final piece in the puzzle.

An eighteen-wheeler truck roared past in the next lane. A bumper sticker on the back, *Forget the Bull Ride the Cowboy*, sat next to an old election sticker that read *Eat Dick and Lick Bush*. As Julia accelerated past the truck, she caught sight of the driver in her rear-vision mirror: a huge muscular tattooed character sporting a gray ponytail—the ultimate male. Ultimate male. The phrase repeated in Julia's head. Men with Jacob syndrome—an extra Y chromosome, XYY—were usually tall, and often developed acne. Could it be possible that the extra Y chromosome was the missing factor? She picked up her cell phone.

"Gabriel, you know that missing factor you mentioned? I want you to test for Jacob syndrome."

❧

The retired sergeant yanked the metal tag on the beer can, poured himself a glass, then filled one for Julia. He flicked away a fly and sat back in his plastic chair. The desert sun had shrunk his face into a bronzed mask of fine lines, and the gray stubble on his head was still shaved into an army buzz cut. They were sitting in his yard—at least, that was how Dwayne Cariton had described it. *Drive out and we'll have iced tea in my yard. Best backyard this side of the Mojave.* It was a square of obsessively groomed lawn fenced in by wire. Beyond stretched the Mojave itself, miles and miles of red-brown scrub, behind which the blue hills of the desert loomed.

Two planes stood in a small airfield just over the back fence: a Douglas A–1E and a Cessna L–19 Birddog, standard Vietnam issue. Their wheels disappearing into an iridescent strip of heat, they reminded Julia of tremulous dragonflies about to take off. A control tower—a glorified water tank—was situated to one side of the runway. *Cariton's Flying School* was painted on the side in green and orange letters, now peeling and rusty. Cariton had established the school after his discharge from the army, shortly after the My Lai massacre.

The sergeant scratched at the plastic strip taped across the vein where Julia had taken her blood sample. "Jesus, that needle hurt. Mother! Where's those beer nuts?!" he yelled at the top of his lungs, seemingly to no one in particular.

For a moment, Julia wondered about his sanity and her safety—his file had indicated that he lived alone. But a minute later a Filipino woman, somewhere between thirty and fifty, appeared, silently placed a bowl of nuts next to the quietly whirring tape recorder sitting on the Formica table in front of them, then disappeared into the back of the house, which Julia now noticed was on wheels. Dwayne followed her gaze.

"Yep, it was one of those ready-made houses they deliver to your vacant lot. Hell, when they rolled up with that thing, I thought, what the heck, I'll keep it on the trailer base; then I can disappear quickly. That was back in '72. I needed to disappear back then."

He picked up a beer nut and threw it at a puppy dozing behind an empty chair. "Some of the men in the platoon couldn't get through the day without being totally bombed out of their brains. Others, they just loved the frontline adrenaline. Then there were those who didn't know who they were until they were actually fighting. Yeah, maybe that's it. You just don't know until you're there, swept up in the smell of it. Man steps out of his rational mind in those times."

"And you had no nightmares, no episodes, flashbacks, psychosis, afterwards?"

"Never. I sleep like a baby—did before, do now. People are just too fucking sensitive nowadays, living is a dirty business, dying is dirtier."

"Most soldiers who went through what you did were pretty roughed up, emotionally and mentally. So that makes you unusual."

"Well, them's refreshing words to someone who's been regarded as a freak most of his life. The way I see it, there's guys out there who are built for battle. They're not crazy, they're not psychopaths, they're just warriors—warriors who crave the noble war. And you know what else, Professor Huntington, now, right now in these fucked-up times, our nation needs these men more than anything."

He threw another nut at the puppy.

"I had a visitor the other day—son of an old friend of mine. Angry young gun, one of the D guys. Sniffing around like a dog looking for a bitch in heat, asking all kinds of questions—just like you, Professor. One thing's for sure—if you do find this mutant gene thing, I reckon it's gonna be dynamite. Don't fancy standing in your shoes, girl."

❧

Gabriel stared down at the file; he had begun to see a correlation between some of the readings, it was just the whisper of an instinct but already he could feel the rattling excitement of discovery. It would be the flip side of the mutant gene, a positive way of utilizing it. If he was correct, he imagined the commercial potential to be enormous, far more extensive than merely genetically profiling potential combat soldiers.

Sitting there, at the desk, Gabriel envisaged surprising Julia with a whole proven hypothesis, executed independently of her; in secret, parallel to their primary research. How satisfying would that be? If his hunch was right, he could prove that he was her equal, that, despite their age difference he was able to match her—even challenge her intellect. She would have to take him seriously as a lover then. Now if only he had someone he could test his theory on, someone who believed in him.

Remembering his conversation with Matt Leman a couple of months back at the conference, Gabriel booted up his computer and began to compose an e-mail to the head of Xandox Pharmaceuticals' Californian division.

53

By the time Julia got the blood sample back to the laboratory it was after hours, the night porter was on duty and the staff had gone home. The place was eerily empty.

Placing Dwayne Cariton's sample in the freezer, she closed the fridge. A noise in her office made her swing around—the light was still off but the door was now ajar. Looking around wildly, she picked up a scalpel then, feeling faintly ridiculous, tiptoed to the office.

"I'm sorry if I scared you." The voice, somehow familiar, was a deep whisper in the dark. Trying to swallow her terror, Julia switched the light on. The office chair swiveled around.

"Tom Donohue," the terror sounded out in her own voice.

Still clutching the scalpel, she stared at the handsome tanned face. He smiled, the disarming smile of a sincere man—she didn't lower the blade.

"You've been briefed, I see."

"I have, and apparently you're dangerous."

He reached into his jacket and pulled out a hand gun, which he placed on the desk between them. "So are you. I read the Afghanistan report."

"That was meant to be confidential."

"The military's a promiscuous world. If you weren't a scientist, they'd probably be trying to recruit you." He indicated the scalpel. "You planning to trim my toenails?"

She lowered the blade. "It was you, wasn't it, who broke in last night?"

In lieu of an answer, he stood and walked over to the pinboard, ran his finger along its rim. "Kurt Moony, Winston

Ramirez, Jack Lewis. I know some of these guys. Some of them I actually care about. How about you?"

"What do you want?"

He sat on the desk and began tapping it with his fingers: a rapid little drum roll. He turned back to the pinboard. "Psychopaths, cold killing machines, or simply men lacking a piece of heart?"

"You've got three minutes to convince me not to ring Smith-Royston," Julia said.

"Nice guy; pity about the politics." He pulled out a cigarette packet. "What did they tell you about me? That I'd fallen out of the tree? Gone AWOL? Lost the grand design?"

"Something like that. You can't smoke in here."

He ignored her and lit up.

"Well, I guess from their perspective it's all true. Frankly, I've never felt more lucid."

"Okay, now it's down to two minutes. Surprise me." She edged closer to the phone.

He glanced at her, and for a moment he appeared fallible.

"About a year ago, one of our junior diplomats went missing in São Paulo. Kidnapping is rife in that part of the world. Last year was particularly bad due to the national election. President Cardoso had problems—problems he called upon the U.S. to help with. There was a village, a small Bakairi Indian outpost on the banks of the Parantinga River—we were led to believe a local drug lord had taken refuge there and was using it as a front for his operations. The junior diplomat who went missing—well, he'd been a little outspoken about this particular drug lord. Seems he'd had a kid brother who died of crack cocaine. So we got the intel he was there and worked up an extraction plan. Normally I craved those black ops—the more dangerous the better—but this one was different."

"Who's 'we'?"

"A ten-man Delta squad; top of the evolutionary tree, Professor Huntington, the very best. I was in command. We were dropped by a bird upriver then traveled down by canoe in the middle of the night. The settlement was located in the center of thick jungle and we were told there were hidden gunposts protecting it. We arrived at 3 a.m., suited up in camouflage with our NODs hanging around our necks. We crept up through the foliage to the central cleared area of the village. We didn't see the gunposts but we'd deliberately avoided their marked locations. The village itself wasn't what we'd expected. There were these spherical huts made of reeds—about twenty of them clustered around. It was like stepping back a hundred years. I mean, there was nothing—except one antenna coming out of one hut—to tell you what century we were in. I remember that antenna because it was what I clung to in the moment. Tom, I remember telling myself, it's a front, the activity's all underground, some buried bunker where the hostage will be right now, chained, his head covered by a sack that smells of shit, fear hacking away at his religion. We'd been briefed to expect guards, but as we circled the huts we found none. And it was so quiet. I'm telling you, when we reached the center of the group of huts, with no sound at all but the crackle of the jungle, it spooked even me. Then there was a movement, a quick darting, and this terrible face came out of the dark—screaming mouth, huge eyes. Patrick—he was the youngest—he jumped on it, knife ready. It was an old man—some mad tribal elder wearing this crazy wooden mask. It took us all by surprise—we'd been briefed to expect machine-gun-wielding pimps in flak jackets. There was something so out there about this man's fury, his fucking mad blind courage. I suspected he was on something, some kind of local hallucinogen. He struggled like a wildcat, but Patrick finally took him down as silently as he could. Not silently enough though—suddenly, all hell broke loose. Villagers started running out from the huts— men, women, boys, even old men armed with machetes, knives, sticks. Well, my boys panicked and started firing. When the screaming stopped, there was only the wail of a baby and those whispering trees, those horrible whispering trees. I gave the order to search the huts for the entrance to the bunker. In the fourth hut we found a trapdoor leading down to a small dug-out, but all it contained was a couple of rusty AK–47s, a few tribal masks and a stack of leaflets in Portuguese ranting about land rights and some local mining company. No cocaine baron, no kidnapped American diplomat. It had been a setup. The villagers were armed because they were defending their land, and it turned out the Brazilian official who'd given us the intel coordinates had some powerful mining friends who wanted them moved. We cleaned up as much as we could, left the appropriate clues to make it look like a local raid. Shot the two remaining witnesses because they'd heard our voices, knew we were American. The Brazilians found the body of the diplomat a week later, dumped in some trash can in a São Paulo slum. Don't get me wrong, Professor, I'm a pragmatist, wouldn't have had my job if I hadn't been. But this time we had our own casualties—not on the day, but within a few months. Of my ten-man squad, three went AWOL: one shot his wife on leave, two committed suicide. Four developed psychotic episodes: three of them resigned voluntarily; the fourth was committed to an institution. The eighth man took up heroin full-time. Only two of us developed no symptoms whatsoever. One went straight onto covert operations in the Middle East, and the other filed the report. He also asked for an inquiry, but was warned he'd be facing a court martial, not an inquiry, if he didn't shut up."

"That was you?"

Donohue didn't answer. Instead, he stood and pulled out a photo pass for her laboratory and placed it on the desk.

"The Department hired you six months later. You see, people like me represent a huge financial investment—money the Department can't afford to lose. You'll find your mutant gene function—that I don't doubt. And it would be very nice to be able to prevent the kind of misery those eight guys in my squad endured. But I suspect it'll turn out like the Hydra—there won't be just one propensity attached to your gene function, and some will be good, some bad." He sat down on the desk again and held Julia's gaze. "I don't know what I'm defending anymore. You see, when I did, it was easy; now life's got complicated, my job's got complicated. I know this much: I might lack the ability to feel remorse, but that doesn't mean I haven't the intellectual capacity to develop compassion. But I'm one of the lucky ones. There'll be hundreds of thousands out there, for generations, who won't be so lucky; a sub-set of men targeted for one thing and one thing only, who will blindly follow orders, never fall out of the tree, and never find their compassion."

"You want me to stop my research," Julia said.

"I'm asking you to consider the human consequences of releasing that information. There, now you know the truth. Tom Donohue is a dangerous idealist, so strike me down."

He stood and started for the door.

"If you don't know who to trust, keep the gun. It wasn't me who broke into the lab last night."

After he'd left, Julia opened the chamber of the Magnum and spun it. There were no bullets.

54

London, 1861

The lecture hall at the British Association for the Advancement of Science was a large auditorium that had been built to commemorate the coronation of Queen Victoria herself. It contained at least four hundred wooden seats trimmed with green leather cushions, lined up in neat rows that ran from wall to wall with a central aisle cutting through from the double entrance doors to the podium. The side walls were decorated with wooden plaques upon which, immortalized in gold lettering, were listed the members of the society as far back as 1670.

Above the stage was a large stained-glass window consisting of a quartet of panels, each depicting famous explorers. The first was a scene of Christopher Columbus arriving in the Americas. The Spaniard (in pantaloons and feathered hat) stood on the shores of the New World holding out what appeared to be a string of beads to an awestruck native. The next panel was of Captain Cook at Port Jackson, about to be speared by an Australian Aborigine; the third (a more recent addition) was of Dr. Livingstone at Lake Victoria; and the fourth panel showed Marco Polo standing on the Great Wall of China.

The podium below held a piano (used for the occasional social gathering, and this evening pushed to one side) and a long table in the middle, upon which, at this moment, stood a large decanter of the best port the society had to offer, a glass in front of each panellist, and a jug of water. The air was thick with cigar and pipe smoke; a cloud of which had one of the speakers, the Reverend Gilbert Rorison, struggling for breath.

"I cannot believe that this creature," he coughed, pointing to the pelt of a large male gorilla, which his co-speaker and fellow anti-evolutionist, gorilla hunter Paul Du Chaillu, had displayed in a rather gory fashion, hung from a steel stand to mimic the living creature's erect position, "that this creature is my direct ancestor. My learned colleague Paul Du Chaillu will confirm the reasons for my convictions, having hunted and observed the creature at close quarters—"

At this point, half the audience—the charterists and workers to the left of the hall, who equated the plight of the gorilla (a creature they had embraced as their long-lost primate brother) with conflict over slavery in America—booed heartily.

The chairman, the eminent Professor Horatio Thorn, president of the society and famous for his 1830 essay entitled *The Breeding Rituals and Gestation of the Egyptian Dung Beetle*, hit the table with a wooden hammer. "Can we please have order in the hall! Order!"

At which the audience, after a few shouts of "Murderer!", relishing the volatility of the debate, settled into good humor.

"As I was saying," the Scottish Episcopalian minister continued, undaunted, "I have wondered publicly in my article on genesis whether Professor Owen—an associate of the good Professor Huxley here—believes that Man was produced by Creative Law, and in that manner supernaturally through the womb of the ape?"

Professor Huxley, a man in his late forties, one of the Society's more youthful members, sprang to his feet.

"Semantics! Divine intervention is not the issue; the issue is evolution. As an anthropologist, I can assure you that however uncomfortable the notion might be, we are descended from apes. Transmutation is a reality, my friends."

Du Chaillu rose to speak. "I have observed these heartless and ruthless beasts at considerable length, and I can reassure you that no ancestor of mine ever bore any relation to this demonic creature."

Again, the crowd roared in indignation. Colonel Huntington, sitting four rows from the front, glanced nervously at the side door. His student was late. Wondering at the capriciousness of the younger man, the Colonel realized how much he had invested in Mr. Hamish Campbell and how vulnerable that made him. And now what? He did not know if he could go on repressing his great, secret desire without falling into an abyss of despair—with which he was not unfamiliar. If he were to pursue it, he risked everything: his standing as an anthropologist and both their careers and reputations. Yet he found it impossible to keep away. He had to see him, to know that he was close. It was a compulsion; a fatal affection.

A movement at the periphery of his vision caught his attention. Dressed in a summer suit with a canary yellow silk waistcoat, Hamish Campbell appeared the embodiment of youthful confidence. But as he drew near, the Colonel could see dark shadows under his eyes and exhaustion in his face.

Hamish took the empty seat the Colonel had kept for him and turned his face to the front. The men barely acknowledged each other.

"You got my message?" the Colonel said eventually.

"Evidently."

The Colonel's eyes slid sideways, furtively searching the boy's face.

"Are you well?"

"As well as can be expected. I am in arrears with my rent and my servant complains he has nothing with which to keep the creditors at bay."

"My secretary will take care of it."

Hamish pressed the carved ivory head of his walking cane against the Colonel's knee; it was the head of a horse, a gift. It was a tiny movement, barely visible to those around them, but to the two men it was momentous.

"I cannot erase my affection for you, as dangerous as it might be to pursue it. But I would rather not continue working by your side. It is too great a torture," Campbell murmured, audible to the Colonel alone.

Just then, the audience, following the heated debate on stage—which now had the Reverend Rorison holding the Bible high in his right hand and Darwin's *On the Origin of Species* in his left, demanding they should decide between Man or God—rose to its feet in outrage. The two men were left seated, an island in a sea of legs.

"Do you think it easy for me? I am trying to protect both our welfares." The Colonel, taking advantage of the distraction, turned to face Campbell, the distance between them now physically painful.

"James, I don't want protection, I want to live. Do you understand?" Hamish fought the desire to caress the older man with every inch of his body. "I need an answer. I cannot feign indifference for much longer."

55

The two coachmen sat on hay bales, their game of All-Fours barely illuminated by the tallow candle burning in its tin pan. Samuel, his jacket loosened around the neck, his teeth stained brown from chewing tobacco, slapped his hand down triumphantly.

"That is a high trump for the Yankee!"

"Bejesus, I'm glad it's only glass marbles we're playing for."

As Samuel swept up the cards, his sleeve rose above his wrist and Aloysius noticed a small circle with a cross within, branded into his dark skin. He grabbed the wrist and held it to the light.

"The mark of a slave, my friend, so my master knows whose property I am."

"You can be owned by no one, Samuel, not you, not your soul."

"But I am, and no matter how many liberties my master might afford me, in the end this speaks."

He rolled his sleeve down. In the distance church bells rang eleven o'clock.

"Boss'll only be reaching his port and cheese," Samuel said, looking out toward the yard. "Lucky for you I've only got an hour before I have to be back on that coach." He swept the three marbles into the leather pouch he had pinned between his knees. "So how is it, my friend? Has she got you reading and writing yet?"

"No, but I have sent two letters back to Seamus, with her assistance."

"She sweet on you?"

Aloysius cuffed his friend about the head. "You keep your wicked thoughts to yourself, Samuel, and pray you won't go to Hell."

"She's a woman, ain't she? With all them same sweet parts any woman has."

"She is Mrs. Huntington and my mistress. I'll not think of her in any other way."

Samuel whistled disbelievingly.

"All I knows is that a stallion and mare don't concern themselves with who's master and who's mistress."

"If men were horses, we'd both be rich."

As if in reply, one of the geldings whinnied. Both men looked up as footsteps sounded outside. Indicating that Samuel should keep silent, Aloysius crept to the barn door.

Peering into the night, he could just see a slight hooded figure making its way across the cobblestoned courtyard to the back gate. Recognizing Lavinia's profile, Aloysius watched as she lifted the latch of the gate and disappeared into the mews lane beyond, leaving him wondering where and whom she was visiting so late in the evening.

The hansom cab driver glanced over his shoulder at his passenger, perplexed by the address she had given him. She appeared respectable enough: the dress coat she wore was velvet, and he had seen her step out of one of those expensive mansions. A governess perhaps, fallen on hard times? Burton Street was not a place where the cab driver cared to transport anyone, lined as it was with the less salubrious brothels.

He peered closer at her face; she was young and appeared refined, authoritative, in her manner. Could she be one of those notorious women who "collected" maidens? He had heard about such women offering to mind young girls at railway stations for their parents, then disappearing with the girls never to be seen again. A gentleman could pay as little as three pounds for the pleasure of deflowering an eleven-year-old virgin, and there were many who were happy to sell their children. His wastrel brother had been one, and the driver had a secret horror of accidentally encountering his niece, her face painted, skirts tucked up, whoring under the gaslights of Burton Street.

As the hansom cab approached the East End, the streets narrowed and became more squalid. Open sewers ran alongside the gutters, and the stench of the river rose with the night fog. Some streets lacked gaslights and the driver was forced to navigate solely by the cab lantern and the candles barely illuminating the grimy windows of the passing terraces.

Lavinia hadn't seen such hovels since the time she'd visited the shanty towns with her father during the Great Famine. She could see children sleeping beneath parked carts, atop piles of horse manure, under bridges, curled against each other in small groups, the filthy soles of their naked feet turned against the world.

As the carriage approached the docklands, the stench got worse. Holding a handkerchief to her nose, Lavinia felt nauseated. She was terrified about what she might come upon. What kind of debauchery did Meredith Murphy live in? Was it possible the woman could be her mother—a creature so profoundly different from the imagined companion who had been her solace all these years?

Finally the coach pulled into a long street filled with terrace houses end to end. Unlike the rest of the sleeping city, however, the houses here were blazing with light. Over each door hung the sign of a brothel. The hansom cab driver gruffly informed her that this was the correct address, and then, after the tip of a florin, reluctantly promised to wait for her.

Determined not to show her growing apprehension, Lavinia stepped down, skirts held high to avoid the thin stream of raw sewage that floated past. Ignoring the wolf whistles from the street workers who clustered under the gaslights calling out for gin or rent money, Lavinia pushed open the wrought-iron gate and climbed the steps to the door, which was painted a lurid green. A brass knocker cast in the shape of a lascivious mermaid hung in the center beneath a brass plaque, scratched and defaced, which read: *Meredith Murphy's School for Wayward Young Ladies. We cater for the discerning gentleman.* Underneath was nailed a piece of board with *Ready Gilt. Tick Being No Go* scrawled upon it.

Before Lavinia had a chance to use the brass knocker, the door swung open. A young boy of ten years or so, dressed incongruously in an oversized sailor's tunic and trousers rolled to the knees to fit, squinted at her suspiciously then looked down at her expensive and now dung-splattered boots.

"Our souls don't need saving. Mrs. Murphy reckons we're all living in 'eaven here anyways," he declared before slamming the door shut.

Undaunted, Lavinia lifted the brass knocker and banged it against the heavy wood. A second later the boy opened the door again.

"I am no evangelist, young man. I am here to see Mrs. Meredith Murphy. I assume she still lives here?"

"Lives 'ere? She owns the bleedin' joint."

Lavinia followed the boy into the hallway. Some of the doors along it were ajar, and a couple of prostitutes, flushed and with tousled hair, peered out to see the cause of the commotion. A well-dressed portly man in his sixties, sitting in a chair against a wall, immediately hid his embarrassed face behind a ha'penny rag upon seeing Lavinia.

Whistling, the boy escorted her to the foot of a narrow staircase that ascended steeply into darkness.

"Mrs. Murphy," he squawked, "you got a visitor! Well-heeled and all posh at the mouth!"

Behind Lavinia, one of the girls, no older than fifteen, half-naked, her blonde hair a frizzy disheveled cloud, her eyes two black smudges above rouged cheeks, broke into a hacking cough. The low murmuring of a man's voice responded. Shrugging with resignation, the prostitute turned back into the room.

The boy swung around. "Tuesday ain't a good day for Mrs. Murphy. Ghost day, she calls it—takes a lot of gin to exorcise them spirits, she reckons. Speakin' of which, madam, would you care for a dram? We always offer our gentlemen customers one."

Lavinia shook her head and again the boy shouted up the stairs. Finally, there came the slam of a distant door and the creaking of floorboards. A melodious voice sounded out from the dark. "A visitor, you say?"

Lavinia's heart leapt; the accent was unmistakable.

"Well, if he ain't paying and he doesn't want one of my girls, I don't care how posh he might be, he can feck off back to Gleann Cholm Cille for all I care!"

"I am not here for any business, Mrs. Murphy, but I think you will want to meet with me," Lavinia called up, cautioning the boy with one gloved hand.

A walking cane emerged from the shadows, followed by the nebulous outline of a woman. A pile of hennaed hair swept up in a bouffant crowned a face whose past attractions appeared ravaged by drink and misery. The nose, once aquiline, now showed the bulbous tip of the alcoholic; the large dark blue eyes were besieged by wrinkles and the mouth hung slack. The woman appeared to be in her late forties, although Lavinia suspected she might be younger. Leaning heavily on the walking stick, the proprietress descended the stairs. Catching sight of Lavinia, she paused, staring hard.

"Sweet Jesus."

She dropped her walking cane, which clattered noisily down the stairs before her like an omen portending bad news. The boy rushed to hand it back, bowing obsequiously.

"Mother?" Lavinia murmured, looking into the eyes she recognized as her own. Feeling faint, she steadied herself against the wall.

"Bartholomew!" Meredith Murphy barked at the boy. "Unlock the front parlor and bring me a bottle of gin!" Swinging back to Lavinia, she turned the corners of her mouth up into the semblance of a smile, revealing several missing teeth. "I believe we have an occasion."

The parlor was a dingy, stuffy room holding a small velvet chaise longue that had seen better days and two armchairs. Bartholomew had stoked the fire until it was roaring. Lavinia, mindful of fleas, sat on the edge of her chair, an untouched grimy glass of gin sitting before her on an upturned traveling trunk (still marked Rosshare, Ireland) that served as a table.

"'Tis a miracle—I look at you and I see myself. I wasn't much younger than you when I gave birth." Sighing, Meredith Murphy lifted her second glass of gin and drained it.

"If you're imagining an apology or some such sentimental whimsy, you can forget it," a sudden cough broke the gravelly alto of her voice. "I left Anascaul and that sanctimonious misanthrope who begot you because I wanted to, and I have never felt the slightest regret. Oh, do not misunderstand me, I loved him—the cockeyed affection of a muddle-headed girl, but it were love. Then after you were born, the fighting began. The bloodiest fisticuffs that ever happened behind drawn curtains. Your father grew too ashamed even to give the Sunday sermon. Oh, it was a terrible time."

"I cannot believe my father struck you."

Meredith Murphy burst into a fit of growling laughter that threw her back against the ancient cushions. Wiping the tears from her eyes, she straightened herself. "It weren't him, darlin', it were me! Temper of a banshee. I had to leave. There were times I believed I might have even harmed you, poor wee bairn that you were. You know that scar your father has, on his left cheek?"

Horrified, Lavinia nodded.

"That were a pair of curling tongs I threw at him. The poor man was right to kill me off and bury me. He did you a favor."

Meredith Murphy leaned forward, breathing a stench of gin, stale perfume, and rotting teeth over Lavinia. "My own flesh and blood, so beautiful. You've done well to get where you are. I shan't compromise you, daughter, not over my dead body, that much I can promise you. Meredith Murphy looks after her own. But tell me, is there a child? Do I have a grandchild?"

"A boy called Aidan."

Overwhelmed, Meredith clasped Lavinia's hand to her bosom. Lavinia, revolted, pulled herself free and, murmuring her excuses, fled.

While the hansom cab jolted over the huge potholes that pitted the lanes, Lavinia considered how transformed her future was now; would she ever be able to forgive her mother for abandoning her? And could she ever abandon her own child, even if it meant surrendering him to a better life?

Once secure in the sanctuary of her own bedroom, Lavinia lifted the whispering box from the mantelpiece. She placed it on the stone of the hearth and stood for a moment with the heel of her shoe poised, ready to shatter it into pieces. Then, changing her mind, she hid it in a drawer.

56

"Free will is a nineteenth-century liberal mythology—we learnt that in first-year philosophy. It's the legacy of Rousseau and all those other deluded utopians, so are you going to seduce *me* now?" Gabriel raised one eyebrow provocatively, his face a streaked montage of light and shade.

Julia rolled over onto her front, pulling the duvet with her, and looked at him. The sun fell across his torso and face, highlighting the fine hairs that swept down his chest to his pubic hair. He had one hand behind the back of his head, his face tilted toward her. Running her fingers along the sweep of his nose, she noticed how his mixed ancestry showed in his face: the Semitic nose, the sharp Latino cheekbones, the hooded green eyes, the olive skin. He will probably never be quite as beautiful as he is now, she marveled, pushing her own age and the implications of their relationship to the back of her mind.

"You're outrageously precocious," she said, "however, you know as well as I, that while we might be genetically predisposed toward an action, that doesn't mean—given social conditions, intellectual discipline, cultural contexts—we actually carry out that action."

"You don't really believe that, do you, or you wouldn't be doing the research you do."

In the ensuing silence, Julia wondered about her true motives. An image of Tom Donohue, and then a masked Amazonian Indian fighting for his life suddenly seemed to loom up from the patterned bedcover; was she being disingenuous? Was she placing ambition over ethics?

Gabriel rolled onto his back and watched a daddy longlegs pick its way delicately across the ceiling.

"We have another hour before I'm due home," he said, and nudged his hard penis against her thigh.

She smiled; she'd forgotten that other wondrous thing about younger men: the fourth erection. He pulled her across and she fell onto his chest, his thick soft lips searching for her tongue, sucking at it, tugging a path of ecstasy that shot right through her center. Her vagina, swollen from so much lovemaking, felt as if it had been transformed into a new organ, a deliciously burning extension that made her hum with pleasure. He buried his face between her breasts.

"I can't believe how gorgeous you are." His voice was muffled as he pressed her flesh against his cheeks.

"Not too old?"

He gazed up at her. "You must be joking, you're perfect. Besides I told you before, I prefer older women."

"I thought I was your first."

"Exactly." He began pushing her high above him until she was forced to steady herself against the wall, her hips held over him, his face buried in her, her buttocks cradled in each of his hands. Naively, she'd imagined she would have to teach him the intricacies of the female body. Instead she'd found him reminding her of the enthusiasm of first lust, the sexual imagination that always colored the beginning of a liaison.

She closed her eyes. She'd always been better at giving sensually than receiving. Klaus had this in common with her; they'd even joked about it. Klaus. Her memory stuttered like a faulty fluorescent. She opened her eyes; for a second, the curve of Gabriel's chest turned into Klaus's; his mouth, her husband's.

Determined to exorcise the vision in sensation, she lowered

herself onto Gabriel, the smell of her a sweet smudge across his face. Pinning his arms above his head, she caught the tip of him between her labia. Closing her legs, she rode him like a man.

His huge eyes stared up at her as he tried not to orgasm, summing up a thousand irrelevancies as distractions—the names of protein molecules, the number of Bob Dylan hits between 1968 and 1978, the Dodgers' highest score for that season; until he knew from a sudden tightening that she had started her orgasm, and a huge jolt buckled his own body.

Julia lay in the crook of his arm, her limbs lolling in total relaxation, echoes of her climax still ricocheting through her.

"I would love to give you a baby," Gabriel's voice broke into her reverie, a rare moment of no thought, a respite immediately lost as recent history rushed in.

"Thank you, but that's an absurd idea."

Belittling me again, he thought, staring up at her beamed ceiling, wondering how long the age difference was going to linger between them. She can't help herself, he decided. It would be immature of him to be offended, but he was anyway.

Julia turned away; her back was an arch of freckles and tanned skin Gabriel longed to touch. Curling around her, he was amazed by how imposing she looked but how small she was to hold.

"Is it?" he ventured.

Her whole body tightened against him and for a moment he was terrified he'd lost her. They lay there in silence, the smell of sex sharpening the air.

"It's strange," Julia said eventually, "I keep thinking I'm going to drop back into that one minute and then my marriage will continue uninterrupted, as it did before. It seems so completely against nature, the idea that Klaus is happy with someone else and his life has moved on, whereas mine's still in suspension."

"But this is life. I am life."

He made her turn toward him. She looked through him in a way that made him shudder.

"No, you're not," she replied softly.

❦

Julia sat at one of the lab computers, studying a set of graphs. The incubator hummed behind her. Gabriel had run the tests for Jacob syndrome but none of the subjects had proved to have the extra Y chromosome. She'd been forced to discount it as a factor.

She pulled up ten files: half were identical twins, the other half non-identical. A file lay open on the desk: a report on one set of identical twins, the Taylors. Horace Taylor, a corporal, had been court-martialed in 1991 for breaking the Geneva Convention on Treatment of Prisoners of War during the first Gulf War. Acquitted due to lack of evidence, he had again faced charges during the Kosovo crisis while stationed there with UN forces, accused of using unnecessary force during a raid on a Serbian gunpost.

Julia scanned down the page: there was a small mention of his twin, Jack, but as he had spent less than one year in the military before resigning, there was very little data about him. She googled his name. Up came three links: one was about a retired baseball player from the 1950s—same name, different guy. The other two were articles from the *Los Angeles Times* and the *San Diego Times*: *Actuary slays family in rage* ran one of the headlines. She read on:

> *Actuary Jack Taylor, thirty-eight, was arrested yesterday for the murders of his wife, Joan, and their two young sons. Taylor, described as a quiet, fastidiously neat man and a chess fanatic, came home from work early on Wednesday to discover that his sons had accidentally knocked over a chess game he was halfway through. Furious, he went to his garage, collected a*

rifle and shot all three members of his family dead. He then changed his bloodstained clothes, walked to the nearest police station, and made a full confession.

Julia checked the date: two years after his brother had stood trial for the Gulf War incident. Jack Taylor must have experienced an impulse toward the same uncontrollable violent outbursts.

Would it have been possible for Jack Taylor to have controlled himself if he had known about his genetic susceptibility, she wondered. Could he have sought help to circumnavigate situations that could trigger violent reaction? Could he have stopped himself from murdering?

57

Mayfair, 1861

The painted tin soldiers were divided into two lines. On one side of the toy brick barrier crouched the Russians, their rifles aimed at the platoon of mounted British cavalry on the other side. The horsemen held tiny steel swords raised above their heads. Miniature green plaster hedges and trees—stolen from another game—formed an incongruous no-man's-land between the trenches.

The Colonel moved the leading horseman forward, pushing the tiny tin man and his horse through a hedge, knocking it sideways. Aidan, sitting on a blanket beside his father, watched appreciatively while the nanny, knitting in a corner, looked on.

"You see, it was like this," the Colonel told his son, "blind hubris, the collision of old warfare with new weaponry. We did not stand a chance, my boy."

He knocked the cavalry piece down. Suddenly, Stanley's face flashed before him and he was there, back in the trench, clutching at the torso of his dead friend.

"Papa."

The sound of Aidan's voice brought him back to the moment. He knelt against the ottoman, his hands trembling. He'd noticed these lapses had started to intensify recently, the nightmares becoming more frequent. I cannot continue like this, the Colonel thought. I cannot escape my nature.

He glanced down at the fallen cavalryman. The roaring sound of a thousand galloping hooves swept through him like a wave as he sat pinned, trying to control his dread. Aidan leaned forward and with one flailing arm knocked over the whole platoon. Immediately, the Colonel was back there on the battlefield, clutching the neck of his panicked horse.

"No!"

Terrified, he struck the child, who broke into loud wailing.

The nanny sprang to her feet and snatched the crying child away. The Colonel, coming to his senses, went to comfort his son but the child pulled away from him, flinching.

"It's all right, my lad. Papa was just having a nightmare, that's all."

The Colonel kissed his son's wrinkled, screaming face then, ashamed, left the nursery. Outside, he paused, resting against the banisters, trying to stop the shaking that racked his entire body. He knew that only one man's touch could drive out the terror. I must see him, he decided.

58

I don't know who I'm whispering to anymore, but you are my creation, and the solace I take from these confessions compels me to continue.

It is late July. My hair has grown back to my shoulders and I have fashioned it into ringlets. Unknown to James, I have stopped my dosage of laudanum and that dreadful time seems almost behind me. I am close to completion of James's pamphlet and am most proud of my handiwork.

I had assumed us happy again, but three weeks ago his nightmares of war worsened again. He has become a haunted man. On one occasion he terrified the housemaids by barking orders at invisible soldiers. He neglects his scientific duties and returns from his club later and later. My queries are met with a sullen aggression, as if he is intent on enclosing himself in a citadel of private grief. Even his companion, Hamish Campbell, has stopped visiting the house.

I am at my wits' end. James has been gone for three days and nights now, with no message. I have sent a man to the Carlton but even they have not seen him. I cannot just sit and wait for his return. I find I do not wish for him to disappear from my life.

Lavinia closed the whispering box and caressed the carved wooden top. Then, throwing on a shawl, she stepped swiftly out of the bedroom.

Drawing the door bolt, Lavinia entered the kitchen. The glow from her candle skipped across the silent utensils hanging like gleaming stalactites from the ceiling rack. She slipped past the vast pantry and the wooden icebox, beyond the coal chute that led into the cellar, and stepped out of the back door into the yard beyond.

The warm pungent atmosphere of the stables enclosed her. The sleeping horses filled the low building with a strange tranquillity, the serenity of a world that transcended the indulgences of men.

Several luminous black eyes opened and blinked slowly. One mare snorted nervously. Lavinia whispered, hoping to calm her. The foot of the attic ladder was visible in the far corner of the stables. Stepping carefully to avoid the soiled straw, she made her way to it and began to climb.

"Who goes there?" The cry sounded out from above her head.

"Your mistress!"

There was a rustling, then the grumbling voice of a boy—one of the stable lads, Lavinia assumed, remembering that all of the stable staff shared the loft. The thump of footsteps traveled overhead, then the trapdoor was thrown open.

"Has there been a death, madam?" The coachman rubbed his eyes blearily. He had hastily pulled his breeches over his nightshirt and flung on his riding jacket. There had been an illegal cock fight in Chauncery Lane that night and all the stable, bar two boys, had attended. It was a pastime Aloysius did not discourage, believing it innocuous entertainment that assuaged his lads' high spirits.

"No death." Lavinia fought a sudden sense of foolishness. "I need you to take me to the master."

"I don't think that would be wise, madam." Somewhere in the darkness behind him, a boy whimpered in his sleep—the youngest stable boy struggling with a dream, Aloysius thought, and, not wanting to wake him, he stepped down and closed the trapdoor. "The master has ordered me not to disturb him under any circumstances."

"But you know where he is?"

"Naturally."

"Is he alone?"

"I cannot answer that, madam."

"Is he with Mr. Hamish Campbell?"

"I will not endanger my employment, Mrs. Huntington, you know that."

A night wind rattled the shutters of the barn door and Lavinia, bare-shouldered, shivered. She was still wearing the evening dress she had put on for a lonely supper attended only by servants. She steadied herself against the wooden railing.

"You realize I could have you dismissed?"

"You could, but it is not for a servant to go against the word of his master. I'm sorry." Aloysius averted his gaze, ashamed of his cowardice.

Lavinia looked at the horsehair button at the top of his nightshirt. His black chest hair curled over the top; the sight rendered him human.

"Please, Aloysius, it has been three days without word from him. I am at my wits' end. I fear for his life." She clutched at his hand. "For the sake of our friendship, please."

The coachman hesitated, calculating the consequences if he should acquiesce. He looked down at her; she was thinner, the bones of her face pushing up under a new anxiety.

"If I take you there, will you promise to insure my position?"

"I swear."

The coachman glanced at her evening gown. "As a lady, you will not be allowed entrance."

"In that case I shall dress as a youth. They cannot refuse a boy."

"They can and they might."

"I am prepared to take the risk. Now, lend me the stable boy's clothes."

❦

He drove her to Mincing Lane in the City. In the dawn sky, the moon had faded to a cadaverous phantom that glared censoriously down. The street was empty except for the market stall owners who had begun to drift in like mute specters. Their labor was a mechanized dance: arms swinging as the wooden carts became transformed with all manner of goods—fruit, cloth, cabbages, pots and pans. Donkeys and ponies stood patiently alongside, snorting into the chilly air.

The carriage pulled up suddenly, the road blocked by a herd of cows, stamping and defecating in startled panic. Four herdsmen, their boots and breeches stained with mud and manure, swished willow sticks above their heads, whistling and shouting into the sleepy silence as they moved their animals toward the slaughterhouse, indifferent to the coachman's frustration.

Lavinia opened the carriage window. Immediately, the stench of the street flooded in—the odor of fear radiating from the cows, the acrid smell of coal smoke, the stink of a nearby gutter running thick with sewage. Floating over the top of it all was the incongruous musk of joss sticks, trailing smoke from a smoldering bouquet strapped to the side of a Chinese peddler's cart.

One of the cowhands whistled, wondering what an ill-dressed lad was doing driving in a coach and not on top with the coachman. "Cheeky stable boy, you got there!" he yelled to the watchman. "Thinks he's king of the muck heap!"

Aloysius pulled at the reins, steadying the horses, which were infected by the cattle's nervousness.

"Just move your animals, we've a gentleman to collect!" he called down.

"Some gentleman to be around here this time of the morning!" the cowhand yelled back, much to the amusement of his companions. In a minute, they and the swaying cattle were swallowed by the fog.

The coach halted beside a coffee house. Its sign— *Garraway's Coffee-house. Established 1645, for the pleasure of gentlemen*—swung above a door painted in gold and scarlet. Next door was an antique shop displaying all kinds of exotic objects in the window: Chinese rugs, porcelain vases, small statues of Chinese deities, jewelry, and other antiquities. The words *Feng's Oriental Palladium* were painted across the glass window. In the center of the display stood an opium pipe mounted on a small red velvet cushion, a sign below reading: *For the sophisticated gentleman of leisure*.

Stepping out of the coach, Lavinia pressed her face against the glass window. Through the smoked pane she could just discern some tables and chairs. The shop appeared empty except for a single candle burning deep in its recesses.

"Madam, it is dangerous to dally." Aloysius took her arm. "Come."

"But where?" Lavinia looked around; there was no sign of any establishment that appeared open for business. Apart from the stalls, which were now piled with wares, the street was silent.

In lieu of an answer, Aloysius led her to a door where he knocked four times, a distinctive tattoo. After a minute or so, an extremely rotund youth of Oriental appearance opened the door, his face a series of voluptuous curves that converged at his nose—evidently split in two by a knifing. A long scar ran from his cheek to beneath his rippled chin. Squeezed into breeches with a silk tunic over the top, he had long plaited hair that fell behind him to below his waist, and a woven silk hat on his head. His body was bent in an attitude of deep suspicion, and his hand slipped down to his hip pocket, where Lavinia was convinced a blade was concealed. He nodded at Aloysius then peered mistrustfully at Lavinia.

"Who's this? Your boy?" He spoke in a broken English heavily tainted with an East End accent.

"Yes, and he is loyal and discreet," Aloysius replied, placing a hand on Lavinia's shoulder.

Lavinia, fearing her countenance would betray her, looked down at her shoes only to realize that she was still wearing her pumps. Hoping the Chinaman might dismiss this as an eccentric English custom, she attempted to conceal one foot with the other.

Finally satisfied, the Oriental turned to the coachman. "You early, he want you?"

Aloysius, acutely aware that he was risking his position, hesitated for a moment. Then he said firmly, "This was the time my master arranged."

Coughing violently, the Oriental spat a scarlet thread into the gutter. Then, after glancing up and down the street for the police officer who often patrolled the borough, he opened the door wide.

The faint aroma of coffee drifted lazily through the air and, once her eyes had adjusted to the darkness, Lavinia noticed that the tables were still piled high with dirty plates from the night before, and used clay pipes flung like broken fingers into bowls of ash.

Beyond the tables was a counter covered with brass cups and glass jars packed with herbs and curios. Behind the counter stood an iron stove, for brewing; above it, shelves of jars of coffee, their brand and nationality painted on the side. A curious silk tapestry hung beneath the shelves.

The Chinaman led them to the hanging, then lifted the fabric to reveal a door. He tapped gently and a peephole appeared, the shiny orb of someone's eye behind it.

"*Ni an quan ma?* (You are safe?)"

"*An quan. Wo he peng you yi qi lai de.* (Yes. I come with friends.)"

The heavy wooden door was pushed open; beyond lay a parlor. The walls were hung with silks and in the corner an old Chinese man plucked at a xianzi, the wooden drum of the stringed instrument clasped between his naked feet, the mournful notes hanging in the air like thin silver threads. Against the walls were low sofas upon which the customers lay or lounged in various states of torpor. They were a motley group—English, Chinese, Indian, men from all walks of life.

In one corner lay a turbanned merchant, an obese man in his sixties whose naked stomach rolled over his pantaloons.

Next to him was a woman of about thirty wearing a stained day dress of lilac silk, its sleeves dirty and torn. She scratched madly at her arms, which were covered in scabs.

Crouching beside each customer was a Chinese boy who meticulously cleaned the stem of the opium pipe with a bamboo reed, then, after rolling the black resin into a soft ball, packed the bowl swiftly—an execution that ensured the customer was continuously smoking.

A long moan of elation or pain—Lavinia found it hard to distinguish—came from the shadows near her feet. Propped up against the wall was a young English girl, her eyelids drooped, her face a waxen mask, dried vomit down her torn dress. Her hand scrabbled at the thin cotton.

"Where is he?" Lavinia whispered, wondering if the lounging addicts were even aware of their presence. Aloysius indicated the far corner of the room.

The two men lay together on a low divan, a smoking candle barely illuminating them. Huntington, naked under a loose silk shirt, his beard grown and unkempt, was almost unrecognizable. Campbell, his arms and legs curled around the older man, mumbled to himself, smiling inanely. Lifting a heavy hand, the Colonel reached for the pipe his boy offered. Resting his elbows on the small child's shoulders, he inhaled, the embers of the drug glowing as he sucked greedily. Hamish, lolling drunkenly, continued to cling to him.

Carefully picking her way through the supine smokers, Lavinia reached her husband and knocked the smoking apparatus out of his hand. Completely ignoring her, he scrambled around on his knees desperately looking for the smoldering pipe that had fallen between the cushions.

"You are to come with me," Lavinia said.

"Pretty boy," he slurred, reaching for her face.

Hoping to shock some sense into him, she shook him violently. "James, it is I, Lavinia."

He pushed the cap from her head and her hair fell to her ears.

"So it is. Hamish, meet my wife. Such a pretty boy she makes." He languidly threaded his fingers through Lavinia's ringlets.

Suddenly, his demeanor altered. Grabbing her hair, he pulled Lavinia down toward him, his breath an acrid concoction of indigestion, opium, and stale wine.

"You have no right to be here, do you hear me? No right!"

"You must come home. It is your duty."

Pushing her aside, he reached for the silver pipe that was being offered to Hamish and, inhaling, collapsed back onto the cushions.

"Aloysius, help me!" Lavinia commanded.

The coachman reluctantly stepped out of the shadows and hoisted the Colonel up under his arms. He dragged the lolling body out of the opium den, through the silken wall hanging and into the coffee shop, the Colonel's inert feet banging against the tables.

59

Lavinia sat at the foot of the bed and watched her husband sleep. She had kept vigil for over six hours, watching him toss and turn, a fine film of perspiration covering his face, his hands curled up in childish rage. She wondered how many men were folded within him like the Russian doll stored in her trousseau: father, scientist, husband, visionary, addict?

She closed her eyes; the trip back from Mincing Lane had been harrowing. The Colonel had collapsed in the carriage, his face ashen, his limbs twitching as the rising sun progressively illuminated every mark of pain on his waxen skin. He looked like a man already murdered by his own unhappiness.

He stirred in his slumber, a lock of hair falling across his heavy brow. Very lightly, before she could stop herself, she caressed his cheek. His skin was hot to the touch.

"Water," he croaked.

Lavinia poured him a glass from a jug on the side table, then helped him to sit. He tried to grasp the glass, but his hands shook furiously; water spilled onto the coverlet.

Taking the glass, Lavinia held it to his lips. As James drank thirstily, his bloodshot eyes fixed upon her. Finally, he pushed the glass away. Lavinia, dreading the moment he would speak, got up and pulled the curtains open.

A sparrow shot across the window: a feathered meteorite against the city skyline with its turrets, spirals, and redbrick rooftops. Lavinia pondered the simplicity of the bird's life, and for a moment wished she were outside, unburdened by all that lay within.

In that same instant, the Colonel found himself blinking at the sunlight he hadn't seen for over a week. He looked down at his scratched hands, the wasted muscles of his arms.

"I refuse to live as a hypocrite, Lavinia."

"You cannot love him."

He answered by his silence. A terrible silence into which Lavinia's whole future seemed to collapse.

"Arrangements can be made," he said eventually. "As far as the outside world is concerned, we will continue to live as man and wife."

She sat there, barely hearing him.

Clambering out of bed, the Colonel stumbled for a moment on weakened legs, his ankles bony below the hem of his nightshirt. He looked across at the photographic portrait they had sat for: husband, wife, and son. They were the archetypal Victorian couple: his propriety and wealth indicated by his silk waistcoat, his fine pocket watch, his whiskers groomed and waxed; Lavinia, handsome in dark damask, held the sprawling baby on her knee, dressed in bonnet and smock. They could be one of a hundred society families, he

suddenly thought; it was a mendacious image, the very artifice of respectability. Then the thought of losing Aidan shot
through him like a deep and sudden bereavement. A child
needed his mother above all else. God help the foundation
upon which this society is built, he concluded, his knees
feeble from hunger and illness.

Lavinia's gaze followed his. "I will not allow it. You have
an obligation to your son, to myself!" she cried.

Fearing the servants would overhear, he gripped her
wrists, pressing her arms against her body.

"You have no choice!" he hissed, his face inches from
hers.

She kicked at his ankles, forcing him to drop his hold.
"But I have. I can denounce you."

Furious, he swung at her without thinking. His fist caught
the edge of her cheek with a sickening thud. Lavinia fell to
the ground and cowered there, her hands over her head. The
Colonel steadied himself against the wall, then, gathering his
strength, pulled her up and wrenched her toward the door.

"Do so, my dear, and I shall take the child and see you in
the workhouse within the year."

He pushed her out into the corridor, surprising both Mrs.
Beetle and Mr. Poole who were bent over at the keyhole. The
servants stepped aside as the Colonel, still clutching Lavinia
by the shoulder, propelled her toward the stairs.

"Now, out of my sight!" He returned to his room and
slammed the door.

Lavinia, stumbling from her husband's final push, tottered
for a second. Then, with a heavy thump, she fell down the
first flight of stairs, her skirts flying as she bounced across
the wooden steps to land heavily against the banister.

She lay there like a tossed rag doll, her neck crunched
against the wall. Then, as consciousness returned to her limbs,
a dull throbbing started above her temples and beat its way
down to her left shoulder. She opened her eyes, her cheek
already a puckered mauve swelling, blood from her nose

streaming onto the patterned carpet. Transfixed, the servants watched from above. Upon seeing that she could move unassisted, they slunk away to their tasks.

Slowly, Lavinia picked herself up, feeling for broken bones. Holding a handful of her skirt up to her bleeding nose, she hobbled down to the ground floor. Through her undamaged eye she saw the housemaids pause in horror, then turn away, embarrassed.

Limping, Lavinia arrived at the door of the kitchen, where the cook, busy preparing a goose, paused with a handful of stuffing in one hand. Her mouth dropped open in shock.

"Oh, you poor young thing!" She rushed to press a napkin to Lavinia's face. "Should I call for a doctor?" she whispered, feeling the violent trembling of the young wife's body in her arms.

"That will not be necessary." Mrs. Beetle, lips pursed in disapproval, stood at the door. "Madam can attend to herself, Mrs. Jobling. Now, if you could continue with the preparations for this evening's supper."

Shoulders rigid with anger, the cook pressed the napkin into Lavinia's hand then returned to the bench. Lavinia swung around to face the housekeeper.

"Where is Daisy, my maid?"

"It is her evening off."

"You are a callous woman, Mrs. Beetle."

Affronted, the housekeeper straightened her shoulders, a parody of outraged authority.

"I shall wait upon the master's instructions and his instructions only. Until then, Mrs. Huntington, I believe you will be able to attend to yourself."

Outside, the autumnal air cooled Lavinia's swelling cheek. Aloysius was standing with his back to her, brushing down one of the horses. His sleeves were rolled to his elbows and his arms were muscled and thickly veined, the limbs of a working man. The horse's black coat glistened and it stood patiently, eyes half-shut in bliss, until it sensed the Irish-woman's presence. Its nostrils flaring as it smelled her blood and fear, it whinnied, tossing its head. Aloysius turned.

"Bejesus, I'll kill him."

It was only then, as her composure fragmented, that Lavinia broke into sobbing.

❦

He sat her down atop a rickety wooden stool and sponged the blood away from her eye as gently as he could, but the cut was deep and he feared her nose was broken. A pool of pink-ish stained water lay in the enamel bowl perched on a bag of oats.

"You must leave him," he said.

"And go where? My father will not have me, I have already written . . ."

Her high lace collar was sprayed with blood, and some of her hair had been pulled away from her scalp.

"I have no inheritance of my own," she went on. "Besides, my father could not suffer the disgrace. There is one place I could go, but it would be little better than the workhouse."

The smell of hay seeped up through the floorboards and light filtered in from the attic window, which Aloysius had propped open with a piece of wood. There were four iron beds in the room, lined up in military fashion. A handmade rack along one wall held the coachmen's riding coats. Nearby, a small poppet made from rags peeped out from under a horsehair blanket; it belonged to the youngest stable boy who was only nine.

"If he were not a gentleman and my employer, I would kill him, God help my sinful thoughts."

He stood before her, the desire to stroke her hair, to pull her toward him and protect her, paralyzing him. He did not trust himself even to take the stained cloth from her hands.

She held it out to him, and as he reached for it their hands touched. The wanting shot through both of them, the knowing of it bolting their bodies to the floor. Lavinia caressed his thumb, his forefinger, his index finger—the wonder of his rough and calloused skin catching in her throat.

They stood like that for a good while, framed by the barn window, all the lovemaking that was possible contained in just the touch of their fingers, tip to tip.

Colonel Huntington, washed and dressed in his morning coat, his hair swept back off his brow, stepped out into the cobbled yard. Sobered, he was full of remorse.

He glanced at the stable, then blinked, squinting at the blurred silhouette there. Upon recognizing the outline of his wife and the coachman, he turned away and stared up at the sun, warming his blanched face. He had come to apologize, and possibly to call a doctor to the house, a discreet and loyal friend. But now he questioned his own sudden jealousy as he looked on.

60

Los Angeles, 2002

"This island's mine, by Sycorax my mother,
Which thou takest from me. When thou camest first,
Thous strokedst me, and madest much of me, wouldst
*   give me*
Water with berries in't, and teach me how
To name the bigger light, and how the less,
That burn by day and night: and then I loved thee
And show'd thee all the qualities o' th' isle,
The fresh springs, brine-pits, barren place and fertile:

Cursed be I that did so! All the charms
Of Sycorax, toads, beetles, bats, light on you!
For I am all the subjects that you have,
Which first was mine own king: and here you sty me
In this hard rock, whiles you do keep from me
The rest o' th' island."

Caliban, dressed in a feathered loincloth and painted with tribal markings, lurched toward Prospero and the front of the stage. Julia, sitting in the front row, flanked by Gabriel and Naomi, flinched. Gabriel had insisted Julia accompany him to the student production, set on a Spice Island in the seventeenth century, and, at the last minute, Naomi had invited herself along, too. Although Julia was sure her friend knew nothing of their affair, she couldn't help feeling unpleasantly furtive.

On the stage, Caliban was stilled magically by Prospero, dressed as a Dutch spice merchant. Dumbfounded, the ogre staggered drunkenly, his eyes wide with childlike surprise. Julia was transfixed: here was a man fated by his genes, unable to wrestle a way out of his inherent monstrosity. It was heart-wrenching. Julia could barely watch; she recognized the expression of horror on Caliban's face, that moment of realizing one was fatally imprisoned by one's own nature. Images of the knife sinking into the side of the young Afghani, a startled goat, the falling shepherd, swam before her.

Suddenly claustrophobic, she stood and, despite the disapproval of the audience around her, pushed her way toward the exit sign and out into the cool forgiving night.

She stood on the basketball court that ran alongside the campus building. The air tasted faintly of barbecues, the day's heat still radiating off the concrete. A silver balloon floated across the tarmac, trailing its string forlornly. The stadium lights suddenly flicked on, flooding the court with neon. Julia leaned against the wall and breathed in deeply, trying to stem a growing sense of panic.

Gabriel stepped out of the auditorium, the sound of the play instantly flooding the court, the theatrical declarations incongruous in the still night.

"Personally I've always thought Caliban should never have trusted Prospero in the first place," he said.

"He'd never met a civilized man before. He didn't know not to trust."

"Come here." He wrapped his arms around her and pulled her into an embrace.

"Gabriel, someone will see us." Nevertheless Julia rested her head on his chest.

"I don't care."

After a moment, she pushed him away. "I would like to surrender to you, but I can't."

"Why not just enjoy the moment; away from the rest of the world we're great together. That's all that matters."

Looking at him standing there, his face so open and hopeful, made her want to believe, want to give into the illusion.

"Apart from the obvious difficulties . . ." she said, then faltered, not wanting to bring up the age difference for fear of hurting him. "There just isn't enough left of me to become involved with someone else. Surely you can see that."

He looked away and she knew she had hurt him nevertheless. Picking up a pebble, he threw it across the court and into the green, then swung back toward her. "Not everything needs defining, Julia."

He stepped back into the theater, leaving her staring at the Santa Monica skyline and the rising moon.

"Have you noticed that Gabriel's changed?" Naomi asked.

Julia reached for a bowl of peanuts and stuffed a handful into her mouth nervously. "I think he's in love," Naomi continued. "But you'd know all about that."

Coughing in panic, Julia spat peanut pieces all over the front of Naomi's smock, but her friend didn't seem to notice. "Well, I guess that's only natural for someone his age," she said, then wiped the front of Naomi's dress with a paper serviette.

Naomi leaned forward, swaying slightly. "And you know what else? I know who it is." She looked at Julia knowingly, who felt a slow burn of panic rise from beneath her collar.

"Naomi, I can explain—"

"She's very beautiful, don't you think?" Naomi continued, much to Julia's confusion.

"She is?"

"India—the girl playing Miranda. I mean, it has to be her, right? Gabriel's never shown an interest in the theater before, then suddenly he has to see this particular production. It's why I insisted on coming—I had to see her close up. She is gorgeous." Bleary-eyed, she peered into Julia's face. "Did he say anything to you? You guys seem really close—I'm almost jealous. I mean, it was me who used to have all these fantasies about my son being my best friend. He was until he turned thirteen. Now we lead entirely separate lives. I wasn't even sure he was straight until now."

"Naomi, you're raving."

"I'm not raving, I'm stoned. Parental nerves. I was so excited about meeting his first girlfriend, I had a joint in the car before the play. I hate this 'responsible parent' shit."

Gabriel appeared, holding a tray with three plastic champagne glasses balanced precariously on it. Naomi immediately grabbed one.

"Just in time." She knocked back the champagne. "We were just discussing your sex life."

"You were?" Gabriel looked at Julia, surprised, while, behind Naomi's back, Julia gestured wildly at him.

"Absolutely—your sex life with India." Naomi pinched her son's bottom. "She's so gorgeous."

"She is?"

"Oh, please, Gabriel, now I know why you've been so distracted. You should have told me."

Concerned that her facial expression might betray her,

Julia moved toward the exit. Gabriel followed with Naomi stumbling behind.

"Mom thinks I have a girlfriend. Don't you think that's hilarious, Julia?"

Naomi looked at her son, then at her friend, utterly perplexed. Panicked, Julia broke away.

"I have to go, I have an early start tomorrow." She turned to Gabriel. "See you at the lab on Monday."

Surprised, Naomi and Gabriel watched her push her way through the thronging parents.

❖

Gabriel stood facing the pinboard. He didn't want to turn around; he was too angry.

"You do understand?" Julia said. "I've transgressed. By sleeping with you, I've broken the unspoken code between lecturer and student—"

"You're not my professor, you're my employer. Besides, I seduced you, remember?"

Ignoring him, Julia paced the room. "Not to mention the trust Naomi has in me. How dare you place me in that situation!"

He swung around. "I'm a grown man, I can get involved with who I like."

Outside, Jennifer Bostock, seeing the arguing couple through the glass panel of Julia's office door, paused, her hand still clutching a test tube.

"Gabriel, I'm in the middle of a separation. I'm not ready for anything except a breakdown!"

"Speaking of which, I do think you should get some help. You know, maybe a psychologist or something—"

"Don't tell me what I need!"

Gabriel, glancing over Julia's shoulder, caught sight of Jennifer Bostock outside the door.

"Julia, you're shouting and people are noticing."

Spinning around, Julia looked through the glass panel of the door, then flung it open.

"Just a difference of opinion about methodology," she said sharply.

Jennifer retreated and Julia slammed the door behind her. Suddenly exhausted, she collapsed onto the edge of the desk.

"I am so tired of trying to control everything."

Gabriel caressed the back of her neck. "Then don't."

She leaned against him. "You don't understand, I have to."

61

Mayfair, 1861

Lavinia had been summoned to the conservatory; a large domed structure that jutted out from the side of the main building. Filled with palms and succulents, with jasmine curling around the white iron trellis that formed the glasshouse's internal skeleton, it was a place where Colonel Huntington had attempted to recreate the tropical rainforest he had experienced in his travels. A macaw named Horatio sat on a perch in the corner, a chain wrapped around its ankle. Around the parrot, reaching up toward the roof in multicolored fronds, stood a mass of exotic orchids. It was the latest fashion in London, and Colonel Huntington was famous for the variety and obscurity of his own Paphiopedilum collection, which included wild orchids as well as the miniature orchids of the Amazon.

Positioned in the center of the conservatory was a cane table and chairs. A maid served out tea and scones as the Colonel sat reading, his face buried in a copy of *Punch* magazine.

Lavinia, a sticking plaster across her bruised face, limped past the ferns and quietly took a chair opposite her husband. It was difficult to be near him.

The Colonel laughed out loud, startling her. "The cartoonists are parodying the endless debate between the Anglicans and the Darwinists yet again," he said, "and this hunter, Du Chaillu, continues to provide amusing fodder with his extraordinary tales of gorillas kidnapping female missionaries and the like. All complete poppycock."

In the ensuing silence, Lavinia heard an orchid blossom fall to the ground. Finally, the Colonel lowered his paper. Unable to help herself, Lavinia flinched again. Noticing, he dismissed the maid, then settled back into his chair and examined his wife.

"I am full of repentance, Lavinia." He took her limp hand.

Unable to meet his gaze, she stared at an orchid, the beauty of the flower mocking her misery.

"I had no wish to injure you. But you will not accept that I must be true to myself."

"You have a child, a career." Angry, she pulled her hand away.

Shrugging, the Colonel reached into his waistcoat pocket and pulled out his snuffbox. Pouring a large pinch into the crook of his hand, he inhaled deeply.

"From what I observed this afternoon in the stable, you have no right to speak of a duty of care, Lavinia." He sneezed a fine mist of powder.

"You spied on me?"

"I was not spying. I had come to make amends."

"The relationship between Mr. O'Malley and myself is entirely innocent. He is a friend—as much as a servant can be a friend. He was the only one to comfort me."

"Perhaps, but I saw another emotion at play."

She could not reply; he was right. But even though the two of them had stood there, their hands interlocked for a length of time that was indeed scandalous, they had not spoken. The knowledge that any declaration would be disastrous to them both had prevented any conversation. Instead, Lavinia, finally pulling her hands free, had collected the soaking poultice of herbs the coachman had prepared for her injuries and left without a word.

In the corner of the conservatory, the macaw cracked a hazelnut, scattering pieces of shell.

"There will be no separation," the Colonel said. "My social standing will not permit it. My duties as a husband—other than economic—will cease from this point. I will not allow you, nor any other, to dictate how or with whom I choose to spend my time. You are a child in these matters. I have strived, in my own way, to protect you from certain aspects of my character. But you have been obstinate and naive to insist on fidelity. Man is simply not constructed to live in such a fashion. For the sake of propriety, we shall continue to attend the remaining events of the season as man and wife. Meanwhile, you will respect your vows and perform the role of loving mother and dutiful wife."

"And what of my needs?"

"You have food and lodging, the dress and accoutrements of a lady of society, and the good name of a gentlemen—that is more than most. Be thankful, Lavinia." He reached for a scone. "But there will be no betrayal under my roof."

She stared at him. There was a detachment about him she'd never seen before. The Colonel picked up the copy of *Punch* again, signaling the interview over.

To disappear to France or Germany, would that be possible? Such a flight would mean a life of poverty and social ostracism. And what of Aidan? What right did she have to condemn their child to ignominy?

She lifted her hand to her throbbing cheek. Noticing, the Colonel sighed guiltily.

"I will ring for my doctor. He is an old family friend and

extremely discreet. But if he should ask, you have fallen from a horse, do you understand?"

Lavinia nodded silently.

⁂

Aloysius pulled the coach into the curb and steadied the horses before loosening the reins. He hadn't been able to speak to Lavinia since the day of the quarrel. He was determined not to lose his board and living over a woman he could not have, but the persistent sense of belonging with her filled his days with doubt and his nights with temptation.

Then another letter from his brother arrived: impenetrable black letters dancing upon a piece of paper that appeared bloodstained in one corner. Placing it under his horsehair pallet, Aloysius had slept on it for a week, hoping the meaning might seep up in his dreams; but instead, a fear that it contained news of his brother's death started to whisper poisonously in his ear.

The coachman wove the reins between the iron railings and, after checking the note was still concealed in his sleeve, went to open the carriage door. The Colonel climbed out first, trying to prevent his spats becoming mud-splattered. Under the shelter of an umbrella held up by Mr. Poole, he ran for the steps of the mansion. As Lavinia stepped down, Aloysius slipped the letter into the sleeve of her fur coat.

"Midnight, the wine cellar," he whispered.

The coachman waited, a shawl crossed over his chest and tucked into his belt. A lantern lit the rows of dusty bottles stacked sideways in their racks. The air was musky, cold, and damp, reminding him of the marshy ditches he sometimes hid in as a child. Handwritten labels in French were pinned above each wine bottle. A wooden cask of brandy sat squatly against the other wall, an old saber hanging incongruously above it. Hearing the swish of Lavinia's skirts, Aloysius's heart leapt high in his throat.

Lavinia came down the narrow steps. She stood for a moment, holding her candle aloft, peering into the darkness, then, finding the pale moon of his face, she smiled, reassuring him. "I have read the letter."

"And is my brother still with us?" he interrupted, unable to contain himself.

"He is injured, but I believe he will recover."

The coachman dusted off the top of a cask with the end of his shawl. Sitting, Lavinia pulled out the letter from her pocket and read it aloud.

> *"May in West Virginia, the year of our Lord 1861*
>
> *Brother, today I have seen many fight and die bravely, fellow Irishmen fighting for the freedom of other men, so they will never have to suffer the serfdom we ourselves have suffered for so long. Aloysius, I have received a bullet to the leg. As I write, the injured and the dying lie all around me in a tent below the battlefield. This will be a united nation, even if it be over my dead body, brother, and there is more opportunity for the Irishman here than you could possibly dream of. Join me, Aloysius, and write so I have a voice to encourage me in my recovery.*
>
> *Yours, Seamus Kildary O'Malley"*

Aloysius was silent as he absorbed his brother's words, Lavinia's crisp enunciation of the Irish rhythms making a curious music. Through its cracks he could see his brother lying in the hospital tent, bent over the page, his fingers curled around a pen, the dried blood caking his saturated bandage, surrounded by an encroaching sea of death and groaning that he pushed away with each pen stroke. *My dear brother . . .*

"You should go," Lavinia said. "There is nought for the Irishman here except prejudice and ridicule."

He returned his attention to her, dragging himself away from a distant drum roll that he imagined would both inspire and terrify. Her proximity was stupefying; there was nowhere he could picture himself so entranced—not even on the deck of a ship approaching a fabled harbor that promised freedom for all men. But he could never tell her that.

"Maybe I will go, maybe I won't. But what does emigration do to a man with his homeland burned into him like stigmata? Now Ireland may be a miserable windy corner of the world, but it's what I'm made of and in the end it'll drag me back, kicking and screaming, whether I like it or not."

"But to reinvent oneself, to escape all one's mistakes and others' judgments. Wouldn't that be grand?"

He edged closer to her. He could smell her perfume: an aroma of lily of the valley and the slightly oily musk of her hair. He saw the faint scar above her lip that her husband had given her.

"Is that what you want?" It was almost a whisper, dangerous in its intimacy.

Marveling at the green of his eyes, she wondered at the constrictions that kept her sitting there and him pinned to the floor. Her mouth dried as she stared at his naked throat, the feathery curls of his chest hair. To keep looking would be to touch.

"Aloysius, I have a child to think of. I am well looked after—many would envy my social position. I have tried to forgive my husband. Instead, I find myself possessed by a great anger."

He held his hands tightly by his sides. Otherwise, he feared they would lift of their own accord and betray him.

"But even the practical cannot live without affection."

And it was then that she slipped from the barrel and fell into him, catching at his clothes, his mouth, the hot shock of his tongue. She taking him, because in that first touch Aloysius heard nothing but the roar of his heart like a bagged cat under his flannel shirt. He struggled with the enormity of their actions until the heat of her breath burst all that he knew that was wrong and he forgot who he was and who she belonged to and catching at the thousands of buttons of her dress that popped under his clumsy fingertips like roasting chestnuts and her breasts, white as marble angels, falling clear so he could take them between his lips, and sweet Jesus there was no way he could stop now until his fingers found her and played her until she was wet and sweet for him, her hands at his neck, pulling his mouth down until he was buried beneath her petticoats, and the tent his brother was lying in and the tent of her skirts became one huge kaleidoscope, the lawny scent of her clawing at the back of his throat, his cock as huge as he'd ever known it, a great rod with which he could smite with just one thrust all of the indignities, all of the humiliations she had suffered. Her thighs quivering against his palms until, standing, he pulled her up onto his hips, steadying himself with one hand pressed against the dusty wall, her ankles locked behind his back.

And the tightness, her wanting, that parted for him as she lifted herself and rode him. Her small breasts pressed against his face, the wine bottles rattling in their racks faster and faster until she cried out, her cheeks as scarlet as the field of poppies he'd once lain upon, her skin a mottled battlefield of bite-marks and desperate handfuls. Only then, watching her half-open eyelids luxuriant with orgasm, her mouth swollen and bitten, the sapphire streak of her blue eyes as she tilted her face to the candlelight, did he reach his own climax and, to his great chagrin, found himself sobbing.

Back in her bedroom, Lavinia stripped off her stained dress and washed out the coal dust herself, then hid her torn camisole at the back of a drawer.

Half naked, she sat on the edge of her bed and examined her neck in a hand mirror. She touched the row of bruises he had left with his mouth in wonder, the tattoo of his caresses still echoing.

Then, trying not to think of her husband at his card game five streets away, she threw open the traveling bag she had brought from Ireland and packed a day dress, a shawl, and two pairs of boots.

Walking over to the dressing table, she opened the drawer and took out the gold and pearl earrings, three necklaces—one pearl, two diamond—that she had inherited from the Viscountess, and wrapped them carefully in her undergarments.

Finally, she went to the nursery.

62

Reluctantly, Aloysius hauled the bag up the steps of the old terrace. They were grimed with centuries of soot and grass widened the cracks between the stone slabs.

"'Tis no place for a child nor a lady," he muttered, eyeing the prostitutes, who, sensing the gravity of the situation and awed by the luxury of the brougham, hung back in silence. Lavinia, clutching Aidan, reached the top step and rang the bell.

"I could have driven you to a better boardinghouse," he said. He wanted to put his arms around her to stop her shivering, but it was impossible to shake the suspicion that such an embrace would be a terrible transgression.

"And how am I to pay? I have some jewelery to pawn, but I intend to use the money for a passage to France."

"You are to France?" Trying hard to disguise his emotion, he cursed himself for his naivety—he had imagined they would have a future together.

"I will find a position as a governess. And if you were with me, you could find a position also."

"I don't speak a word of French." Aloysius was gruff in defense.

"I will teach you."

Gloriously relieved, he kissed her, ignoring the wolf whistles from the watching prostitutes. Suddenly, a torrent of filthy water cascaded from a window above. Aloysius looked up at the torn and faded velvet curtains as the now empty pail disappeared.

"Still, I would rather you found a better lodging."

"Aloysius, it's my mother's house and it will only be a temporary measure," Lavinia replied tersely, the immensity of her actions already prickling at her scalp, feeling uncomfortably like fear.

"Your mother's?"

Before she had a chance to explain, the front door swung open. Meredith Murphy stood in the hallway, her dress tidy and the stray wisps of hair tucked neatly back into her coiffure. Finally, Lavinia could see remnants of the beauty her father had spoken of.

"Come in, child," the woman said, "before the babe catches a fever. Your servant—that'll be the one with the cheeky tongue—can wait outside."

"He is not my servant and he will come with me," Lavinia replied firmly, thankful that Meredith Murphy appeared sober.

The bedroom at the top of the boardinghouse was a loft with two windows that looked up to the sky. A china washstand stood in the corner of the room; there was a reasonably sized fireplace (at which knelt Bartholomew, the young boy Lavinia had met on her previous visit, puffing a pair of bellows into the flames), and a large bed, covered in a bedspread embroidered with the Brian Boru harp, was pushed against the wall.

Aidan, wrapped in blankets, lay sleeping in the middle of the lumpy horsehair mattress, his face softly oblivious to the mayhem that surrounded him, his bent arms raised to his ears, his fists clenched in his customary manner.

"He might be a good man, but you cannot afford to love him, Lavinia. Have you ever stopped to think what this will do to his livelihood? You will be disgraced, but that coachman will, quite likely, never work again in this town. And he is naught but a boy."

"We will find a way."

The two women sat in armchairs by the fire, Meredith smoking a clay pipe. Lavinia, made drowsy by the flickering flames, was dazed by the speed with which her circumstances had changed.

A portrait hung above the mantelpiece: her parents some twenty years earlier. Her father, dressed in his clerical robes, looked rawly earnest in his youthfulness, while Meredith was almost unrecognizable—there was an optimism in her wide catlike face (no longer visible in the older woman) and her dark blue eyes danced with wry humor. She sat in half-profile, looking up at her husband, the Reverend's hand on her shoulder. Fascinated, Lavinia tried to fathom the sentiment that had made her mother keep the portrait all these years.

Emptying her pipe into the fire, Meredith coughed then spat to clear her lungs.

"What of my grandson then—what can you offer him instead of his father's fortune? Think I don't know what it's like to part with a child, to place its happiness before your own?"

"But I am his mother," Lavinia replied faintly.

"And I was one, too. It is not a woman's world, Lavinia; all marriages end up a prison and most husbands are rakes, whether it be in their dreams or on their travels. Your father would call your husband's behavior a sin, but in my profession I've learned there are all manner of men and quirks and it is not for us to judge. You were blessed. Your prison was a palace. You should have stayed there."

Reaching into the purse hanging off her belt, Lavinia pressed a one pound Bank of England note into her mother's hand.

"We'll be leaving as soon as I've booked a passage to Marseilles."

"Save your money." Meredith handed back the note. Standing heavily on her walking stick, she limped to the door.

"Lock yourself in tonight. I shouldn't want any clients stumbling in. Sleep well, daughter."

"But where will you sleep?"

"Sleep?" She broke into a cackle that finished with a wheeze. "Morpheus and I have not had words for years."

Lavinia bolted the door and, after blowing the candles out, lay down on the bed. A moment later a loud thud somewhere below, followed by the sound of a man groaning in pleasure, made her sit up. She wrapped the lumpy old pillow around her ears then broke into a sneezing fit because of the dust. Another loud cry from the room beneath woke her ten minutes later; it seemed as if the rickety terrace was literally shaking with the spooning that was occurring between its thin walls. Somewhere below, someone started to play reedy-thin but beautiful violin music. Lavinia wondered what manner of musician would play in a brothel. Suddenly, she was scratching furiously; after locating the culprit, she crushed the bedbug between her fingernails.

She lifted Aidan into her arms, his sleepy head lolling against her bosom, and stared up at the night sky while the music of the violin filled the bedroom like writhing snakes.

❧

"I will have you dismissed without a character reference. You will be utterly without employment. I promise you, you will see the inside of Mount Street workhouse within the month."

The Colonel stood in front of the huge marble fireplace, his voice barely containing his rage.

"That might be, sir, but I cannot help you for I've no idea where Mrs. Huntington is."

The Colonel's cane smashed down onto a console, cracking the marble top and narrowly missing the coachman. Aloysius did not flinch.

"Damn you! This is my wife and child!"

His narrow shoulders hunched, his eyes downcast, Aloysius tried to think only of the notion of a new life awaiting him across the Channel.

"I am sorry, I cannot help you, Colonel."

Staring at the gaunt young Irishman, whose truculence transformed him into a graceless block of wood, the Colonel wondered what Lavinia had seen in the youth.

"You are dismissed. Pack your bags and collect your papers. I expect you out of the house by tonight."

Strangely relieved, Aloysius walked to the door. "Even if you do find her, she will never be yours," he said before turning to leave. It was the first time he hadn't bowed to his employer.

Lavinia's bedroom was a jumble of upturned drawers and opened cupboards, her clothes and papers scattered across the carpet and bed. The Colonel looked around wildly; he'd searched everywhere without finding a single clue. The only calling cards he'd found belonged to associates he had imposed upon her. It appeared his wife had established no intimates of her own.

Thinking on where he would hide something himself, he again ran his eye over the room. The photographic portrait of their family sat on top of a commode, the drawers of which were pulled open, undergarments spilling out. He lifted the framed picture and opened the back, then removed the thin layer of card that kept the photograph in place. A slip of paper fell out. To his absolute amazement, the address scribbled upon it was that of Polly Kirkshore.

As Lavinia and Bartholomew picked their way through the filth and refuse, the boy shooed away the hordes of child beggars that descended like locusts. Many were crippled, but it was the small girls who were missing jawbones and fingers that horrified Lavinia the most.

"Surely they weren't all born that way?" she asked.

Bartholomew laughed. "Born like that? You are green. They're phos girls, from the Victorian Match factory. The phosphorus has begun to eat their bones like, some of them are lucky to 'ave any fingers left at all. Nothing they can do like that, can't even whore."

He led her through a back alley. Lines of washing hung above them stretching from window to window; the ever-present stream of sewage ran down the center of the tiny lane, while a group of stray dogs barked at a tethered pig outside the canvas shack that served as an entrance to a hovel.

As Lavinia hurried to keep up with the boy, the money she had received from the pawnbroker, now secured inside her blouse, bounced against her skin. The pawnbroker had given her twenty guineas for the earrings and one of her diamond necklaces. Lavinia calculated the money would be enough to buy three passages and board for a month in France; after that they would have to find work. A great excitement had begun to bubble up in her chest, usurping her fears. For the first time, she was in control of her own fortune.

They turned the corner and arrived suddenly in Burton Street. A coach stood in front of her mother's house. Lavinia recognized the Huntington crest and saw Mrs. Beetle waiting beside it. At that moment the Colonel emerged from the brothel carrying Aidan, who was kicking and screaming. Meredith Murphy stood in the doorway, arms crossed, her face as dark as a thundercloud. Breaking into a run, Lavinia shouted her son's name.

Handing the child to Mrs. Beetle, the Colonel swung around to meet his wife.

"You can't take him!" Lavinia tried to reach Aidan, but Mrs. Beetle quickly lifted the child into the coach as the Colonel grabbed Lavinia to pull her away.

"I can and I will, and you will come with us!"

Struggling, she tried to break his hold. "I will not!"

"Is this what you want? To stay here in this hovel with your degenerate mother?" he hissed. "Dr. Jefferies warned me of this."

"I am my own person!"

"Understand this, wife, if you do not step into this carriage I shall have you in the Bedlam asylum before sunset, and I promise you will never see your son again."

63

Los Angeles, 2002

"He's going to win, it's just too seductive, too damn Hollywood—people love that shit. Celebrity is America's aristocracy—it's been said before, but it's so surreal to actually see it happening before your eyes, the way people are sucked in."

Andrew lifted his Cosmopolitan and mournfully contemplated the pink-tinged liquid. They were sitting at a bar on La Brea. It was 6 p.m., the cocktail hour, and the two geneticists were engaged in a political debate.

"It's not that simplistic. He embodies masculine leadership, an I-ain't-gonna-take-this-shit attitude," Julia said. "Love him or hate him, the current senator doesn't embody that in any shape or form. It's a reaction to the World Trade Center nightmare—everyone's scared."

Julia checked her watch. She'd left the lab an hour ago and was waiting for Gabriel to call in with some results.

"So goodbye gay rights, goodbye abortion rights, goodbye stem cell research, hello twenty-first-century puritanism. Oh boy, I need another drink."

As Andrew, flirting with the barman, ordered another round, Julia watched the aquarium that doubled as a wall. A large silver carp, its tiny fins rippling like overpowered propellers, gaped directly at her, its lugubrious expression bearing an uncanny resemblance to her colleague's.

"So, how *is* the research going?" Andrew asked in a deceptively casual manner.

"Okay," Julia answered carefully, knowing full well that if she shared any of her discoveries, he would incorporate them into his own research the next morning. Competition between scientists was ruthless, particularly in an area where new findings meant celebrity, publication, and funding that was crucial to survival. All Julia's staff signed confidentiality forms.

"They're an imaginative mob at Defense," Andrew went on. "I mean, they're prepared to throw money at the wackiest research but only on condition they get to do whatever they like with it at the end. Intriguing."

There was a pause while Andrew waited for Julia to volunteer more information. Instead, she studied the carp, which was still gazing at her, and wondered about a Darwinian aspect to competition—did it really push people toward flashes of insight or would cooperation be a more successful strategy? As if in answer, a smaller fish swam past and bit the unsuspecting carp on the tail.

"I mean, don't you ever have ethical qualms?" Andrew persisted.

"Sure, but why do you assume I would have one in this case?"

"C'mon, Goldilocks, genetic detection of antisocial or violent behavior, plus a myriad of other factors all aimed at creating an über soldier—who wouldn't?"

"And I thought you asked me out for a drink because you were concerned about my emotional fragility."

"Whatever it is, I think you've cracked it." He downed his cocktail, deliberately ignoring her last remark. "There's an excitement about you. Either that or you're getting laid."

Julia smiled mischievously.

"Oh my God, there is someone! Oh, thank Christ, I was afraid you were going to become one of those embittered divorcees whose vaginas mummify. Seriously though, I am *so* happy for you."

He fiddled with his watch a moment, his eyes glinting wickedly.

"So I guess it's cool about Klaus and Carla?"

Julia looked at him, confused.

"She's pregnant. Talk about moving on. The guy is ruthless . . ." His voice trailed off as he watched her face blanch. "You did know, right?"

Trying not to react, Julia grasped the edges of her barstool as the room appeared to tip on its side. She imagined the fish in the aquarium struggling upstream as the water tumbled out onto the floor.

"How pregnant is she?" The hysteria in her voice betrayed her.

"Oh shit, you didn't know. Julia, I am so sorry."

"How far?"

"Six months. I thought you knew—everyone else does."

Six months. She must have been pregnant when he left her, at least three months.

"She stole my child," Julia whispered, too faintly for Andrew to hear.

❦

Slamming the front door behind her, Julia went straight to the bedroom. After opening the cupboard door she hauled out a box that had been tucked away at the back. Sitting it on the bedroom floor, she stared down at the cardboard lid, then ripped open the tape that sealed it. The baby clothes were still in their wrappers, pristinely folded under clear plastic. She pulled one package open. The cotton smelt fresh and was impossibly soft against her skin. She unfolded the jumpsuit and spread its arms and legs out on the carpet. It lay like an abandoned starfish, the sight of the empty hood lancing her heart in a sudden intake of breath. Julia reached for a second outfit and then another and another, until the floor was covered with baby clothes, arm touching sleeve, blind foot touching toe. She sat at the very edge of this carpet of loss, then suddenly swept the clothes up in her arms.

They had used the incinerator—a wire basket full of ashes and charred wood, which was tucked behind Klaus's work shed—to burn the dead leaves from the garden. It had been Julia's task to keep the lawn raked while Klaus worked the flowerbeds. She stood over it now, the flames of the fire she'd made from twigs and newspaper crackling under her hands. Slowly she fed the baby clothes to the blaze, the blue cotton smoldering for a second before bursting into red as embers ate through the soft cloth.

This is a funeral pyre, she thought to herself. I am burning my future.

64

Mayfair, 1861

Lavinia had shut herself in the bathroom to escape the constant vigilance of the household. She sat on a cane chair beside the huge enamel bathtub. She was thinner; her birdlike wrists poked beyond the lace cuffs of her blouse. It was hard to keep her fingers steady as she opened the lid of the whispering box. Fearful her voice might be heard beyond the locked door, she spoke even more quietly than usual.

It is now September and weeks since I tried to escape. The little joy I have is in my child, my reading, and the thought that Aloysius might have finally escaped to America. Lethargy now possesses me, my silent friend: I move my mouth and limbs but melancholia has made me a sleepwalker. James now insists I take two doses of laudanum—in the morning and at night—and, although it eases my grief, the drug has made me clay. He has confiscated the money I had made from pawning my jewelery and claimed back both the necklaces and the earrings himself; an embarrassment he is fond of reminding me of daily. But there is a far worse restriction: James has employed his aunt Madeleine Huntington as my custodian. This obsequious relative is in perpetual debt to my husband, who has provided her with a meager stipend all these years. She is with me constantly and watches me like a hawk. She even insists on sleeping in my room at night. What can they be afraid of? That I shall sprout wings?

To add to my humiliation, James, to stifle any rumor of my unhappiness, has taken to public displays of affection, caressing me at the dining table, proclaiming both my wit and my physical attributes. Yet he turns away from me in the privacy of our own chambers. If he will not love me, and will not let me go, what hope have I?

At the sound of the doorknob being rattled, Lavinia shut the box and hid it behind the water closet.

～

"It was gracious of you to accept my invitation, Lavinia. I am glad we have resumed our friendship." Lady Morgan stood in the center of her elaborately furnished and now crowded parlor. "These luncheons are a wonderfully informal means by which one is able to maintain one's female acquaintances. I see you are accompanied by the Colonel's ever vigilant aunt?"

Madeleine Huntington, an unprepossessing woman in her late fifties, her mouth irredeemably twisted by a hypochondria that resembled self-pity, sat perched several feet away. Lady Morgan, taking Lavinia's silence as answer, tapped her fan discreetly in Madeleine's direction.

"Oh, she is legendary," she murmured in an undertone. "Lady Curton even hired her to guard her eldest daughter after she was found *in flagrante delicto* with a young swain. Dreadful creature, a veritable parasite who thrives on the misfortunes of others. May the good Lord save us from such a fate."

Then she spoke up. "Miss Huntington was a virtuoso on the harp when she was younger. Is that not so, Madeleine?"

The old woman's wooden dentures slipped a little as she smiled. "An exaggeration, but I did perform at a few soirées, which, I'm told, were memorable."

"Perhaps you could play for us now?"

As Madeleine Huntington took her place at the harp, the rest of the guests broke into small clusters in order to exchange the gossip that was an essential commodity—who was courting whom, which Scottish estates one had to be invited to for the hunting season, the latest mode for riding skirts and so on.

"Gwen, have you heard about the Tillings scandal?" Lady Morgan leaned in close to Lady Gillingham. "Apparently Countess Tillings finally tired of the Count's numerous liaisons. By fortuitous coincidence, the Count was a frequent user of Fowler's Solution—for aphrodisiac purposes naturally . . ."

"Naturally."

"Which, as some of the ladies here know, contains arsenic and is fatal in large quantities . . ."

Lady Gillingham's eyebrows shot up in mock horror. "She didn't?"

Lady Morgan tapped her nose with her fan. "I have it on entirely reliable authority—directly from her maid. Of course, they can't prove a thing."

"Well then, we must have a tea party to comfort the newly bereaved widow," Lady Gillingham concluded merrily as she reached for a sandwich.

"Can it not be proved he was poisoned?" Lavinia interjected, fascinated.

Lady Morgan, embarrassed by the young wife's blunt indiscretion, glanced around to see if anyone had overheard.

"Poisoned? Goodness, child, the gentleman merely met with an accident, a natural consequence of his use of the drug. Why on earth would there be an investigation? My dear, you have so much to learn."

Lady Gillingham, determined to steer the conversation into safer waters, leaned forward. "You will attend the hunt this Sunday, Lady Morgan? You were sorely missed last week."

"I would, except I have lost my companion and it really does not suit a woman of my position to be seen unaccompanied."

"Frances, dear, just cultivate a replacement. The city is full of them, and we have all learned to tolerate the mercantile class."

"No, Mr. Hamish Campbell was my final folly. I have arrived at the point in my life when I must surrender myself completely to the pursuit of charitable acts."

"There are worse fates than having a fountain dedicated to oneself."

"Indeed, a seat at the opera would be worse."

They all laughed, but Lavinia's unhappiness undermined the frivolity of the moment. She fidgeted constantly and an unnatural brightness glimmered about her eyes—a consequence of an overuse of laudanum. Although she was painfully aware that her trembling hands and propensity to interject impolitely betrayed her, Lavinia could not help herself—she was no longer in control.

"Well then, surely we can expect your company on Sunday, Mrs. Huntington?" Lady Gillingham inquired.

"I'm afraid my husband has asked the aforementioned Mr. Campbell to accompany him, so I shall take the opportunity to promenade with my dear little son through the park."

"The Colonel is seen with that young man awfully frequently these days. Why, only the other day Lord Birley remarked how Hamish Campbell is as close to Huntington as a son, 'but twice as beloved.'"

Lady Gillingham glanced at Lavinia, hoping to catch a nuance of expression that would betray a greater meaning.

Lavinia winced, then allowed the laudanum to mute her flooding anxiety.

"My husband has a penchant for nurturing aspiring young scientists," she replied, and fixed her expression into a grimace of pleasantry.

"As he should." Lady Gillingham, trailing silk, floated away to another group of women.

❧

Lavinia spent the following day in James's study. She had placed a specimen of the root bark from *Mimosa hostilis* and a section of ayahuasca vine, used by the Bakairi to make their Jurema brew, on a small stand and was sketching it studiously while Aunt Madeleine executed her needlepoint by the fireplace.

Lavinia stared at the withered bark and twisted vine, thinking on their properties. She remembered the book she had read, which described how the extracts could be lethal if mixed with opium or peyote fluid. Could it be administered in a manner that would be undetectable? And how would one mix it with opium? Was this a way she could win her freedom?

She glanced across at her custodian, the danger of her observations making her pulse race for the first time in a month. And what of the moral ramifications? Even if she did succeed, her soul would suffer eternal condemnation. I would be less than human, she reminded herself. But the thought of her life petering away in the twilight of this house while she mouthed the platitudes of an empty marriage was overwhelming.

The click of Madeleine's needle against the rim of the sewing frame intermingled with the tick of the clock and the rattling rain dashing against the windowpane. The scarlet thread ran from a bag at Aunt Madeleine's feet up through her skeletal hands, relentlessly twisting backwards and forwards. Lavinia was gripped by a desperate realization: my life will never change; this is how the years will seep away, incrementally.

James was to perform the shamanistic ritual in a week's time and she was to administer the sacramental brew. Why had he given her that power? Surely he must know how much I have begun to loathe him, she thought; is it possible that secretly he wishes for his own death? Has he unconsciously chosen me as his deliverer?

Completing the sketch, Lavinia lifted the root bark to her nose. The scent was of burnt wood and something else, something she'd smelled before but couldn't quite place.

She glanced over at the photograph of James in the Amazon. He was half-naked, his body painted with ceremonial mud, his masked face turned to the light that slanted through the jungle foliage—a changeling, half-man, half-god, a creature trying to live another man's myth. If there remained a union between them, it was here, incarnate in the ideals of James's younger self. I loved him, Lavinia told herself, despite his paradoxical character and his rejection, but now all that is left is smoldering resentment.

She replaced the root bark, then recognized the other elusive scent: ground tobacco.

The creature lay on the kitchen table, its shell a slimy leathery helmet, its flippers flailing wildly against the slippery wood, its neck extended as it snapped madly at all who approached it.

"I should never have undone the twine," the cook wailed, backing into a corner armed with a rolling pin. "It's a vicious beast. Do you see them gnashers on it?"

"Don't be ridiculous, Mrs. Jobling—turtles do not have teeth. They have beaks, like birds."

"Do they now? Next, you'll be telling me they have feathers too! In which case, the bloomin' thing might just take off and fly out the window!"

"No need to get uppity, Mrs. Jobling. But I suggest you kill it sooner rather than later. The soup takes a good four hours and we have to carve the flesh off well before then."

"I know my job, Mrs. Beetle," the cook retorted. She tentatively crept forward with the rolling pin raised. The turtle backed away, made a clucking sound with its beak, and lunged, nipping at the cook, narrowly missing her apron strings.

"For the life of me I can't do it! You take charge." And she pushed the intended murder weapon into the housekeeper's hands.

Mrs. Beetle, pulling herself up to her full height of five foot two, circled the reptile like an experienced hunter.

"Right then, you little devil." She slammed down the rolling pin.

As it descended, the animal scurried sideways and the rolling pin hit the table, denting it. The turtle tottered on the edge, then fell, its four flappers paddling wildly in midair. It landed on its back on the kitchen flags.

"What is all the commotion?" Lavinia entered, having heard the crash from the front hallway.

"Sorry, ma'am, but we're trying to kill the turtle for the soup."

The creature flipped itself upright and scuttled toward Mrs. Beetle's ankles. Screeching, she leapt onto a chair.

"Oh, for goodness sake! I'll show you how it's done!" Lavinia grabbed a meat cleaver from the bench and turned to the animal. Immediately, the turtle retracted its head, arms, and legs, becoming an impenetrable dome of checkered shell.

Cleaver held high, Lavinia crept toward it, then stood as still as a statue, waiting. Slowly, the turtle emerged, neck swaying as it peered from side to side with myopic curiosity. With chilling dexterity, Lavinia brought the cleaver down onto its neck. But the blade caught the edge of the thick shell, only partially severing the head. The creature's eyes turned up in aggrieved surprise.

A great anger roared up in Lavinia and she slammed the blade down over and over, as if she were obliterating all the obstacles in her life.

Horrified, the cook stayed her arm. "Ma'am, the animal's dead now."

Lavinia watched the convulsing reptile—sounds in the kitchen rushing back into her pounding head as she lowered the blade.

65

The Huntingtons sat in the open-topped phaeton, the Colonel resplendent in top hat and frock coat, his young wife in pale yellow satin with Aidan held securely on her lap. As they drove along the pebbled lane in Hyde Park, two men cantered up to the coach.

"Huntington! Extraordinarily good game the other evening." The older man, in his early sixties and corpulent, sat high in his saddle, his riding jacket, jodhpurs, and boots immaculate. " 'Tis a pity you had to fall so heavily."

"It was a pleasure to lose to you," the Colonel replied, tipping his hat. "May I present my wife. Mrs. Lavinia Huntington; the Marquis of Westminster."

"An honor, sir." Lavinia dipped her head.

The Marquis assessed her charms with a blatant gaze that traveled from her waist across her bosom to the top of her feathered bonnet.

"A wife, eh? Must have been out of town when you were presented." He turned to the Colonel. "My compliments, Huntington, you've done well for an old rake. By the way, I've spoken to my man about that apartment. Should be ready in a day or two."

"Thank you, sir, that's very decent of you."

"Anything for an old Etonian," the Marquis replied, and trotted off with his escort.

"You have purchased a property?" Lavinia asked as the Colonel relaxed back into his seat.

"I have taken a set of rooms to continue my study away from the house. I felt it was more conducive to my research."

"And you will be studying there with Mr. Campbell, I assume?"

"He is my assistant."

They drove on in silence. Lavinia wondered whether this would mean new freedom for herself or merely further estrangement.

"I shall, of course, continue to employ Madeleine as your chaperone." The Colonel tapped the new coachman on the shoulder. "Home, John."

The phaeton swung around, scattering a flock of pigeons that had gathered on the gravel. Just then they heard the clatter of hooves.

"Colonel Huntington! Colonel Huntington!"

It was Lady Morgan, in a curricle. With a jolt, Lavinia recognized the coachman sitting beside her. She lifted her head and Aloysius smiled. The Colonel followed her gaze.

"The confounded audacity!" Furious, refusing to acknowledge either Lady Morgan or Aloysius, he turned his head resolutely forward. "Drive faster," he instructed his driver.

The horses broke into a trot, but the curricle followed at a swifter pace. The pursuit started to draw the attention of the surrounding carriages and riders, several heads turning in amazement. Lady Morgan's curricle, having the advantage of speed, pulled alongside them.

"James, dear, I do hope you did not intend to snub me?" Lady Morgan called gaily.

The Colonel, shaking with fury, tapped his coachman on the shoulder and the phaeton slowed down. "Not at all. I simply had not seen you, Frances."

"How uncharacteristic of you. I'd always thought that one of your greatest attributes was your power of observation."

"In which case I apologize for disappointing you."

"I find disappointment increasingly commonplace these days, but I accept your apology."

"I see you have a new coachman. My congratulations," the Colonel remarked cynically.

Tight-lipped, Aloysius tipped his cap at the Huntingtons. Catching his eye for a second, Lavinia smiled slightly.

"I found him wandering the streets of Kensington and recognized him immediately." Lady Morgan leaned towards the Colonel. "He's a wonderful horseman, and even has some blacksmithing skills. Extraordinarily, he had no references on him, none whatsoever. Well, I said, a good stablehand is so very difficult to find these days. You don't mind, do you, James?"

The Colonel's face twitched as he worked hard to contain his expression.

"I don't mind at all. Doubtless you will find him more trustworthy than I did. Good day."

As they drove off, Lavinia turned to watch Aloysius's diminishing figure. Then she buried her face in her son's fragrant hair.

From her bedroom window, Lavinia watched James's carriage leave for the evening. He was going to his club, where he now spent every night. The vigilant Madeleine had retired two hours earlier on the pretense of a migraine. After pulling the curtain shut, Lavinia left her room.

The library was still cloudy with cigar smoke. James's open diary lay atop a side table beside his usual armchair. Lavinia sat down and began to read.

One morning I was called to the hut of the shaman, who wanted me to witness the execution of some local justice. A man's mother-in-law had accused him of stealing her daughter's soul through sorcery. The accused—about twenty years of age—seemed sullen and withdrawn. On closer inspection, I realized that the sullenness was in fact terror. Strangely, when the shaman questioned the man, he said nothing to defend himself.

The wife was brought to the hut on a stretcher made of woven palm leaves and wood. She seemed comatose, but

*other than that appeared completely healthy. It was, in
fact, as if he had stolen her soul. At the appearance of his
wife, the accused started to speak. From what I could
glean from my translator, it was a confession. His words
ran as follows: "We are locked together like warriors. I
acted to save my own life."*

*Despite my pleas, they executed the man by a ritual
spearing later that day. By the evening, his wife had begun
to show signs of recovery.*

A maid entered the room and started clearing away the
remains of a plate of *marrons glacés* and Turkish delight the
men had been consuming. A nearby ottoman was dusted
with icing sugar and spilled snuff. Lavinia picked up James's
silver snuffbox. It was half-empty, even though it must have
contained a good ounce. She stared at it, the ghost of an image
forming in the smoky atmosphere.

The maid, an irrepressibly cheerful eighteen-year-old,
who had been born into service and was already betrothed to
one of the valets, dampened the embers in the fireplace.

"Dolly, I must replace the master's cognac," Lavinia announced. "I see he has finished it tonight." She spoke clearly,
wanting the maid to remember her words.

"Don't concern yourself, madam. I can do that."

"No, I shall do it. My husband is particular about his
cognac."

Lavinia found small things to busy herself with until the
maid had left the room. Then she picked up the snuffbox
again, turning it thoughtfully in her hand. Walking over to
the desk, she emptied its contents onto a sheet of paper. Then
she lifted the *Mimosa hostilis* root bark from the stand she
had placed it on earlier for study, and using a laboratory
knife, shaved off a quantity. She ground it to a fine brown
powder using a pestle and mortar, then turned to James's
locked cabinet where she knew she would find a vial of
peyote fluid.

Staring down at the dampened rust-colored powder, it seemed to her that she was looking back over the last three years of her life: the sands they had walked along when James first courted her; the oak of her husband's locked bedroom door; the dried blood on her face after James had struck her; and, finally, the relentless sensation of suffocation and increasing fear. *He has stolen my soul.*

The sentence reverberated over and over in her head as she meticulously tipped the ground mixture into the silver box, then added a layer of the Colonel's own snuff. Closing the lid tightly, she shook the box vigorously. When she opened it again, the poison was undetectable.

※

"Is it wise, James?"

"Is what wise?"

The two men lay in each other's arms on the large divan the Colonel had purchased for the Westminster apartment Hamish now resided in. A velvet throw half covered them, and a fire sank low in the grate across the lavishly furnished drawing room. Its high ceiling, dating from the previous century, was covered with a plaster relief of gods and angels. Hamish sat up, his smooth white back facing the Colonel. He reached for a cigarette and placed the slim stick into an ivory holder, his fingers trembling from an excess of drink and opiate.

"To have your wife assist at the ritual when I could so easily do it."

"I have made a promise. I cannot take everything away from the poor child. Also, remember, she could destroy us with one word."

Hamish knew James was right: the need for discretion was essential. But it disturbed him to know that the young wife had so much power—he did not think her rational. He ran his fingers lightly across his lover's naked shoulders. The Colonel's body, half reclining, was a series of undulating curves—

chest, belly, thighs; the scale of him gave his corpulence a grandiose quality. He looked, Hamish decided lovingly, like a well-fed Zeus.

"In that case, why not let her have her own paramour?"

Closing his eyes, the Colonel sighed heavily.

"I have found that I am still possessive. Whether this is a kind of love, I cannot say, but I still regard her as my wife. Other than that, I cannot—*we* cannot, that is to say, you and I—afford the scandal. Lavinia is still my wife, and the mother of my son."

"James, there is great anger in her. It would not be intelligent to rely upon her during such a risky venture."

"Then you do not truly understand me. It is this very danger that is so alluring."

66

Los Angeles, 2002

The quake shook Julia out of sleep, a subterranean rumble that threaded itself through her sleeping and rattled the bed. She sat up as the brass frame trembled in unison with every piece of glass, every door and hanging picture in the house.

Her dream still lingered about her: she had been running in a labyrinth, a series of corridors whose earthlike walls sprang up like trees behind her as she ran. There had been a creature, a man, chasing her—she remembered the heavy thud of his feet, his bellowing breath that echoed down the long halls. Terrified, she had stumbled. Lying on the ground, she had looked back to find the huge eyes of a bull staring down at her, his man's chest heaving as he stood over her— the Minotaur. It was then that the earthquake woke her.

Julia waited to die. She wanted to die. There was a curious symmetry to this, she thought: here she was, childless, without husband, alone in a rattling house waiting to die; while on the other side of town, Carla, heavily pregnant, lay wrapped around Klaus, probably terrified she was about to lose everything. I have already lost, Julia concluded, strangely invincible in her indifference. The usual panic she felt during earthquakes—diving under the bed, or running to stand in a doorframe—seemed to have left her entirely.

The shaking stopped. Julia reached across and opened the bedside cupboard drawer. The gun Tom Donohue had given her lay there, on top of some old letters; somehow, the sight of it was comforting.

She was interrupted by the phone ringing. "Julia, are you okay?" Gabriel, disembodied, sounded even younger.

"I'm intact, although I think the fridge might have taken a walk."

She reached for the remote and switched on the TV at the foot of the bed. Immediately a news item came on about the earthquake: *7.5 on the Richter scale, the epicenter in the Mojave Desert, one casualty at a military base . . .* The words raced like ticker tape across the bottom of the screen, while above a smiling nubile blonde, who looked too air-brushed to have an anus, advertised hemorrhoid cream.

"I love you." Gabriel's voice was drowsy, as if he were stoned or drunk.

"No, you don't. You're in the grip of hormonally driven lust. It might feel like love, but trust me, it's not. Besides, I don't want you to be in love with me. I'm far too dangerous and irresponsible."

"You're not dangerous, you're just confused and vulnerable."

"Take my word for it, I'm dangerous."

With the phone hooked under her chin, Julia surfed the channels: an embracing couple, a shot cowboy falling into a ravine, a space shuttle blasting its way through the azure of the outer atmosphere and into deep space. Is tragedy a perspective, a narrative, something we ourselves imposed on the most ordinary of events, she wondered—a stifling marriage, an impossible love affair?

"I'll ring you tomorrow," she said, distracted by the television.

"Julia, I'm worried about you. You seem really tense and yesterday—"

"Gabriel, we've just had an earthquake, it's four in the morning."

Julia hung up. Enveloping herself in a dressing gown, she walked out into the lounge room. Settling into the leather armchair, her feet tucked up under her, Julia let her gaze wander to the portrait of her great-grandmother. In the growing light of the dawn outside, Lavinia Huntington's eyes seemed to stare back at her sympathetically. She looked so young; too young to be encumbered with a child and to be the mistress of the palatial estate just visible beyond the forest glen. Julia looked at the bow Lavinia held in her hand, in keeping with her persona as the goddess Diana. The fletch on the arrow protruding from the dead stag matched those on the arrows in the quiver slung over her shoulder. Had Lavinia Huntington murdered her husband or not?

Suddenly, Julia leapt up.

At 6 a.m. Westwood village was deserted. A cleaning van, its huge circular bristles whirling against the empty curb, crawled down the street. On the other side, an early morning worker opened the McDonald's burger bar on the corner.

When Julia arrived at the gates of the university, the night security guard, secure in his cubicle, appeared to be dozing. His head rested on an open copy of the *National Enquirer*, a cup of coffee cooled in a polystyrene cup beside him. Julia drove slowly past his booth into the parking lot, careful not to wake him.

The campus was hauntingly empty. Early morning mist

trailing across the lawns and into the quadrangle seemed to hold in its faint white tendrils the after-images of all the students who had ever studied there.

Julia's footsteps clattered across the paving. The silence all around and the unfamiliar isolation made her feel defenseless. Panicked, she broke into a run.

❧

Inside, the darkened laboratory was a familiar womb of chemical smells and electronic purrs. Julia switched on the lights. Immediately, the fluorescents splattered into life.

Unlocking the door of her office, she went to her computer and called up her work from the day before: the gene activity results showing the genetic correlation between the final four subjects she'd narrowed down to. Was she staring at the descendant of the first murderer in the history of mankind? The first *Homo sapiens* who had smashed a rock against his brother's skull? Did this gene function stretch back that far? And if so, why had it survived this long? Was there a need for it in the species—an evolutionary bloodletting?

Julia gazed down at her hand, then pulled a sterile slide from a drawer. She punctured herself in the thumb and squeezed a drop of her blood onto the slide—a thick, darkish film. She marked the slide with a number rather than her name. She didn't want Gabriel to know it was her DNA and gene activity profile he would be testing.

On the way home, Julia stopped by a gun shop and bought some bullets for the gun Tom Donohue had given her. Next door was a florist. Deliberately emptying her mind of thought, she walked in and meticulously selected a large bunch of lilies, tuber roses, and narcissi—flowers she knew to be Carla's favorites. The note read simply: *Carla, congratulations on the pregnancy. Julia.* She stood by the counter, all conscious responsibility now pushed deep down below the instinct of her actions, flowing blindly like liquid glass—relentless, unstoppable. The florist's voice breaking into her thoughts startled her as she asked if Julia wanted the bouquet sent by express delivery.

Gabriel slept again after the quake, but somewhere in his dreaming landscape the sense that he should be up and working nagged him. A bleep from his laptop, telling him he had mail, woke him completely.

He slipped off the bed and, naked, sat down, and opened the reply from Matt Leman, which contained several more questions about the characteristics of the mutant gene function.

67

Grabbing Gabriel's hair, Julia pressed her pelvis down hard, riding him vigorously, straddling him as he sat pinned to the kitchen chair. There was a violence to her lovemaking, a desperation in the way she had taken him with very little foreplay, her hand reaching for his penis as if she was determined to be the aggressor.

It had been a week since they'd argued in Julia's office and her intensity now frightened Gabriel, this frenetic seduction that bordered on a rape. What was she trying to do— obliterate all emotion in their lovemaking? Perhaps even obliterate herself?

He struggled to see her face: her hair snaked across her forehead, her eyes were squeezed shut in concentration. Wrapping his arms around her, he held her tight, as if to squeeze all the fear and rage out of her. It was a futile gesture. Gabriel had never been so aware of the limitations of his experience. Her grief was overwhelming and elemental, like the earthquake, like the few deaths he had known: inevitable, non-negotiable, and utterly daunting. He closed his eyes to block out her grimace. The chair, rocking under their weight, nudged a fruit bowl, which went crashing to the floor, spilling apples and oranges.

Julia's thighs clenched as she began to reach orgasm. Gabriel, now determined to throw himself into her excitement, clasped her buttocks, playing her. They both came shouting. A second later, the neighbor's dog started howling.

"This has got to be the last time." Her legs were still slung over him, her skirt pushed above her hips; her breasts hung freely over the top of her blouse.

"You were fantastic," Gabriel lied. Penis shriveling, pants down to his ankles, he stayed in the chair.

"Did you hear what I just said?"

Julia turned away as she adjusted her bra, feeling self-conscious about the age difference that showed in their bodies.

"Look if it's the love issue you're worried about, you can relax. I'm over it. It's not like I don't find other girls attractive."

Face hidden, Julia winced at his use of the word "girls."

"Good, because after the project's finished I don't think we should see each other for a while."

Gabriel pulled his pants up, secretly disappointed Julia hadn't reacted with jealousy.

"But I'm happy to help you get into any postgraduate course you want. Then I might go away, to a place no one can find me," Julia added.

Suspicious, he studied her as she straightened her clothes. She'd been acting strangely all morning—curiously cheerful in a way that was at odds with her usual acerbic wit. Her hands reached up to tie her hair back. The gesture, unselfconsciously innocent, was too seductive for Gabriel to resist. He stood and, caressing her face, swept the rest of her fringe behind an ear. "I could still give you a baby."

She pushed his hand away, irritated. "Gabriel, I can't conceive anymore." She was surprised to see him blush. "No need to look so shocked. I just had some problems, after the miscarriage."

Reduced to silence, he pulled on his sweatshirt, wondering about the complexities of women and whether he would be negotiating them for the rest of his life.

"Who cares, Julia? You have an incredible career and you're on the crest of another huge achievement—anyone can have children."

From the tone in his voice, she instantly knew that he'd heard about Carla's pregnancy.

Smiling crookedly, she fumbled with his trouser belt, an excuse not to look him in the eye. Instinctively, Gabriel pulled her onto his knee and began rocking her, as a parent would comfort a small child. Julia was again struck by the absurdity of life: the youth comforting the middle-aged woman as if she were a child.

"I've known for weeks about your ex having a baby, I just didn't know how to tell you. I'm so sorry, Julia."

Through his skin Gabriel felt her tremble, even though she was smiling brightly. The contrast was disturbing.

"You're right, anyone can breed."

They were interrupted by the sound of the telephone. Julia climbed off Gabriel's knee and answered it.

"Julia?" Klaus's voice sent a seismic wave through her body.

"What do you want?" Julia kept her voice flat, emotionless.

"I think we should meet—to discuss the possible sale of the house."

"I thought it was agreed I would buy you out when I had the money."

"The situation has changed now that Carla's pregnant," he replied, somewhat self-defensive in tone.

"So I hear, congratulations."

"Thanks. And thanks for the flowers—she really appreciated them. This can't be easy for you."

Gabriel watched Julia's fingers twist the phone line.

"Perhaps you should come over. We can do this in a civilized manner—over dinner maybe?"

"Are you sure? That would be great."

Klaus sounded obscenely relieved, Julia noted, her heart thumping furiously against her ribs.

"How about next Friday, at eight?"

"Eight would be fine."

As Julia replaced the receiver, Gabriel saw her hands were shaking.

68

Mayfair, 1861

"Madam, there is a servant here, sent by the ambassador of the Confederate States," the footman said, waiting by the door of the parlor.

Lavinia glanced at her custodian, who was in the window seat, knitting.

"I shall have to receive him in the morning room. Do you mind, Aunt Madeleine? I believe this may be an invitation of some importance."

"You go on. I shall still be here when you get back."

Trying not to appear too hurried, Lavinia followed the footman to the morning room.

Samuel stood in the middle of the room, awkwardly turning his cap. He dared not sit down, so walked over to an eighteenth-century statuette of a naked Venus atop a console; he thought her proportions ideal.

Lavinia entered the room, followed by the footman. Samuel immediately stood to attention.

"You may leave us," Lavinia told her servant.

Bowing, the footman closed the door behind him. As soon as he'd gone, Lavinia went to Samuel and took his hands in her own.

"Have you news? Pray God you have."

"Our friend is well and is close by."

"Tell me the address and I shall contrive a way of seeing him."

Samuel glanced at the window; upon seeing it was free of any onlookers, he leaned toward Lavinia.

"My lady, he is waiting in your cellar this very minute," he whispered, smiling.

The tallow candle sputtered and sent a faint curl of white smoke up to the ceiling. The cellar was dark and the strong musk of old wine saturated the air. To Aloysius, it seemed their lovemaking still hung in the shadows like a twisting phantom. Remembering, he closed his eyes. Never had he taken such risks; never had he thought himself capable of such ambition. Lavinia's invitation to France had opened up a myriad of possibilities above and beyond being in service and he'd been possessed ever since.

A flicker in the candlelight made him open his eyes again.

There were no words, just the hunger of their embrace, the lilac scent of Lavinia's hair and her tongue curling around his own.

"We have no time," she murmured as they clutched at each other's clothes. Catching her hands, now tracing a path from his lips to his groin, he lifted them and held them tightly in front of him.

"I want you to come with me, Lavinia. My brother has sent me money. We can sail together to America; start a new life, the three of us. There, no one cares what your past is; there, everyone begins as equals."

She stopped trying to touch him. Aloysius saw how the past weeks had marked themselves across her face in years; her pupils dilated, her eyes dulled.

"There might be a way," she whispered, more to herself than to him.

Sensing some great jeopardy, Aloysius fought the impulse to cross himself.

Sitting at his desk, the Colonel dipped his pen into the ink-pot, then paused, wondering at the sense of destiny that had consumed him since the evening before. Was it the impending ceremony, the thought of reaching a state of mind that transcended the ordinary? Or was it something far more subtle? A hidden fear perhaps? This exhilaration of the nerves reminded him of the sensation of waiting upon a great battle, and it was not entirely an unpleasant phenomenon—at least it woke the spirit. And, at that conclusion, he began to write.

> *Dearest boy,*
>
> *I hope you will read this when you are of an understanding age and will not judge me too harshly. I pray I shall still be on this earth when you have reached your adulthood and that we may enjoy the pleasures a father and son can, but please, if I am no longer with you, make your own judgments independent of your mother's opinions. Know that whatever tribulations lie between your mother and I, I have always loved you.*
>
> *Yours in loving kindness,*
> *Your father*
> *Colonel James E. Huntington*

Lavinia had dressed in a mauve evening gown, the garment she had worn the morning after their wedding night. She stepped into the Colonel's bedroom searching for a clothes brush. It was an innocent intrusion and she expected her husband to be at his dresser.

Instead, the bedroom was empty, the hearth still glowing. A pile of folded letters sat on the polished rosewood desk, tied with a ribbon. Unable to contain her curiosity, Lavinia pulled one out and read the first two lines: *Dearest boy, I cannot describe the desolation I feel when I am apart from you . . .*

Lavinia didn't need to read any further; she assumed they were her husband's correspondence with Hamish Campbell. Possessed by a furious impulse, she threw the pile into the fire, where they were quickly consumed.

❧

The Colonel knelt in front of the hearth, the firelight throwing gold and red stripes across his face. An oval mirror stood propped against the wall. His reflection stared back from the smoky glass: the jowled pallid face of a middle-aged man, eyes tentative but intrigued.

This is my other self, he thought, the wood hard under his knees, my spirit brother in a mystical world where right is left, where the laws of physics are distorted.

The study had been transformed into a mysterious cavern. The servants had lighted several dozen candles, which now shone from every shelf and alcove. The masks hanging from the ceiling formed a critical audience of celestial beings; the candlelight transformed their spiraling tassels of coconut fiber into hangman's nooses, their protruding wooden lips into screams. Painted wooden shields and spears around the walls seemed to dart between the curious shadows in the labyrinth of light created by the smoldering tapers.

The Colonel pulled off the thin cotton smock, letting it fall to the ground. My nakedness will be a metaphor; all that defines me is now stripped away. I am Adam, the first man. The corpulent white male stared back at him defiantly. Was he this being? He touched the cold mirror in genuine wonder. How had he become so old, so heavy in his flesh? He recalled his younger self, beautiful even to himself.

"The ochre." He reached out with a flourish, his movements already taking on a ceremonial gravity, his nudity giving him a vulnerable dignity.

Lavinia handed him a basin full of the sticky reddish ground earth the Colonel had brought with him from the Amazon. He smeared it across his chest and shoulders in the ceremonial pattern the shaman had taught him, slowly touching his own skin as if he were exploring an unfamiliar body.

There were questions he needed to ask, signs to look for, symbols of the unconscious, which, by the cold light of the next morning, he would draw upon to construct a useful logic. Do all men share the same gods? How does culture create perspective? He hoped to find evidence of his thesis that the dreams and fantasies of men were universal, that there was a shared language of myth.

The goddess would help him: Jubbu-jang-sange, the Virgin Madonna, Mother Earth—however she was named was unimportant. She had helped him before; on the battlefields of the Crimea, in the opium dens of Indo-China, on the beaches of the Irish Sea. I have to surrender myself, he thought, and glanced at Lavinia. She will be my deliverer or my executioner.

The last daub of ceremonial paint ran in a lurid yellow line from throat to abdomen, separating left from right, Heaven from Earth. Already, as the paint dried on his skin, he had begun the process of making magical his own image, an empowerment that would climax with the donning of the mask.

Lavinia's figure was a medley of purples and blues, the pale crescents of her breasts rising from her dress. The Colonel felt the desire to make her unquestioning again, as she was at the beginning of their courtship. He felt that he had begun to stiffen, her gaze exciting him. If Eros joins with Hecate, so be it, he thought. Ignoring his erection, he stretched out his left arm.

"It is time."

Lavinia handed him the stone ceremonial goblet with various deities carved upon its surface. The dark spiciness of the Jurema mixture wafted through the room. Holding the goblet with both hands, the Colonel drank its contents completely then handed it back to her. He knew it would be some time before the potion took effect.

Hoisting a pigskin cape painted with totemic symbols over his shoulders, he lifted one leg and one arm, mimicking the movements of a long-legged flightless bird, as he had seen the Bakairi do.

Opening a notebook, Lavinia watched. James had instructed her to write down each step of the ritual and to note the physical symptoms of the drug. The task distanced her; it was an objectification that gave her courage.

"And now?" she asked.

"Now we wait."

The Colonel closed his eyes. Lavinia slipped the snuffbox out of the purse hanging from her waist. In her hands it felt immeasurably heavy despite its small size. How much did a man's life weigh? How much was her future worth, her freedom? Silently she placed the snuffbox in front of her husband.

The Colonel took two large pinches, inhaling both deeply. His head jolted back as the powder shot up his nose like lava piercing rock. Giddy, he swayed a little. Already his hearing had sharpened to the point where he perceived the breath of the maid polishing the silver one flight below; the sound of his wife's hair slipping across her silk dress metamorphosed into wind through a forest. He knew the next sense to be affected would be his vision.

"This is happening faster than I expected," he said. "Make

a note: at six o'clock aural distortion began." His voice boomed through his body like the growl of a foghorn and the scratching of Lavinia's pen against paper was unbearable.

"Hand me my mask," he commanded. He wondered if his words were audible, for to him they sounded like gibberish. His lips felt heavy as his jawbone tightened like a jailer's screw. "And quickly," he slurred.

His speech was thickening, Lavinia observed, as she lifted the mask to his face and secured it tightly, as he had instructed, with a cord that ran behind his head.

Suddenly the Colonel's gravitational axis shifted dramatically. Through the mask's eye-slits he watched the ceiling extend, becoming the inky-black stretched membrane of a bat's wing opening to the hot heavy sky of the Amazon.

"I am back," he whispered. He looked to his other self, the naked white man whose head lolled under the weight of a carved wooden mask, and, with painful clarity, saw that he had become his spirit echo. A bluish mist streamed from the man's head, filling the room.

Convinced that he would die when the room filled completely, the Colonel clawed at the mask. "It's happening too quickly," he screamed. Doubled over in agony, his body thrashed like a landed fish.

The Colonel's spirit self gazed down at this latest indignation. Why am I not frightened? he pondered. Then, sensing another presence, he turned. A creature he did not recognize sat rigidly in a chair.

Another jolt of intense pain shot through the Colonel, pulling him back into his skin. The floor rippled and buckled beneath him like an angry sea, while the hanging masks transformed into all his childhood fears. His mother's cloying features loomed from the shadows, her lips and nose extending like fingers. The face of his father's corpse suddenly bolted across the floor like a skinned rat. A boy he had tortured at preparatory school leered at him from the mirror;

and the dead Russian soldier gazed blindly at him, his clouded eyes as beautiful as a whore's.

Where was the sense of omnipotence he had experienced before? He felt no power; only terror.

The doors to his cabinet flew open and his collection of skulls lunged at him, jaws snapping, each bite another agonizing cramp.

And who was this luminous figure that stood a hundred feet high above him? Tantalizingly she receded then reappeared. Struggling, he tried to remember who she was and why she was there. Was she his salvation? Gripped by a convulsion, his body thrashed against the wooden floor.

To Lavinia, he looked less like a man than an animal. The ochre had smeared a rainbow on the parquet floor, and excrement coated his thighs and buttocks. He will die soon, she thought, and he will be with his goddess. She could not afford to acknowledge his agony; it was as if a deeper impulse had hijacked her. Just die, she prayed, finish it now, quickly. Death, the grotesque banality of matter, of all human frailty, finally transforming into the jerking end-pantomime she'd always suspected it to be.

Clawing at the mask, the Colonel tried to stop himself from choking on his own vomit. As he stared out at the whirling world, the goddess of death, Calounger, appeared. Her eyes were fiery pits reflecting the end of all the men he'd seen die, the last of whom was himself.

And then, as a massive seizure lifted him off the ground, the image of his lover appeared, reaching out from one of the goddess's huge eyes that now filled his sight. Hamish's long muscled arms picked him up off the ground and pulled him into a sweet embrace. Finally, the pain ceased.

The stench of feces and vomit was overpowering. James's body lay twisted on the floor, his skin rapidly graying into the ashen complexion of the dead.

Lavinia, breathing heavily, leaned against a wall. Shock rapidly distanced her, taking her back to the moment before she had entered the study, wiping her involvement from her memory in a feat of self-deception and self-preservation.

I am not responsible for the man on the floor. I do not know him. These white arms that extend out so innocently from mauve satin sleeves, these hands stained with the rusty powder of death, are not mine.

Trembling, she sank to the ground while the reconstruction of events flew about her like a flock of whirling ravens. When she was sure of her story, she pulled the servant's bell.

69

Los Angeles, 2002

Gabriel stared through the lens of the microscope at the sample Julia had given him. It indicated heightened activity for ANG–1, but there was something odd about the sample itself, something he couldn't quite place.

Remembering a reference in a file that might help him, he went into Julia's office and started rummaging around in the filing cabinet set against the wall behind her desk. As he flicked through the files at the back of the cabinet his eye fell on a large envelope marked *Defense Department. Strictly Confidential* hidden in the Z section. He held it for a moment, hesitating, then, convincing himself it was his moral duty to read the document, carefully pulled the envelope out in a manner that would enable him to return it to the correct place without detection. The report inside was entitled:

*3.10.2002. Afghanistan: Ambush involving Lt. L. Jones, Sgt.
Z. Nathan and civilian Professor J. Huntington.*
 Sitting down, Gabriel began reading.

Carla swung around from her laptop. "I don't think you should
go. Or at least consider meeting somewhere neutral, like a
restaurant."

Klaus dropped a script down on the desk beside her.

"What kind of message does that give Julia? She's agreed
to talk about the house sale, she's congratulated us on the
pregnancy—I really think she's moved on."

"I'd still feel happier if you changed the location."

He kissed the top of her head. "Don't worry, it'll be okay."

Reassured, Carla reached up to meet his lips.

Chopping the peppers and folding the saffron into the rice
felt like a ritual. It was comforting, this precise series of gestures. It took Julia out of her body; an unequivocal dance, the
choreography predetermined.

After finishing the food preparations, she slipped candles
into the candelabra. She wanted to create a sense of occasion;
it seemed only fitting.

Their best cutlery—old-fashioned German silver, sent
from Belgium, solid, puritanical in its lack of ornamentation—
lay on either side of Wedgwood bone-china plates. The white
linen tablecloth had been another wedding gift; the crystal
wine glasses she'd purchased to celebrate her appointment
five years before.

The whole table was a glossary of memory: a coda for
their marriage. A perverse last supper, Julia observed, speculating about who the guests could be to make up the necessary thirteen: Carla, Naomi, Gabriel, her mother, her Belgian
mother-in-law—all the spectators of their relationship, some
participants, some not.

A bottle of Margaux 1990 stood breathing on the sideboard. Julia glanced at her watch. Klaus would be punctual; he always was.

She disconnected the doorbell, switched off her cell phone, then methodically walked through the house pulling the phone connections out of their jacks. Finally she stood in front of the full-length mirror in the hall to check her appearance. She was wearing the dress she had bought for their last anniversary, a purple long-sleeved evening gown with a low back.

She was thinner now and her ribs undulated up toward her collarbone, which curved out like a pale archery bow. She touched it; its skeletal nature brought her own mortality to mind. She would be the high priestess tonight. She would be Justice, impenetrable, powerful.

Julia returned to the dining room and slid open the sideboard drawer. The gun lay on top of the cutlery. Picking it up, she checked the chamber; the four bullets lay nestled snugly against the steel, waiting. She heard a car approaching and looked at her watch; it was exactly eight o'clock. As she had predicted, he was on time.

70

London, 1861

Samuel pushed his way through the crowded streets. Stunned citizens huddled on street corners, oblivious to the falling snow. Outside the palace gates, the crowd's mourning clothes transformed them into a black moving mass. It was as if the whole country had dipped itself in ink to stand weeping in the white frost. Some cried openly, while others simply stared incredulously at the paperboys, sooty-faced messengers, holding up the ha'penny gazettes as they shouted the grim news.

"Fourteenth of December, day to remember, the Prince Consort is dead!"

"The Queen grieves!"

It was the morning after Prince Albert had died suddenly, of typhoid fever, and Samuel had never seen the English surrender to such emotion. It was disorienting, and the whole city had taken on an apocalyptic atmosphere.

Stoically, he forced a path through the motley bunch of spectators lingering on the steps of the Old Bailey. It was the fourth day of the trial; and it had taken him that long to find out where the proceedings were taking place. He had discovered the information only through persistent questioning of the new coachman at the bereaved Huntington household.

"Where do you think you're going?" A policeman stopped him as he stepped into the warmth of the reception hall.

"The trial of Mrs. Lavinia Huntington and Aloysius O'Malley, sir. The public gallery is open now, is it not?"

The police officer, who wore a mourning band around his arm, hesitated. The Negro servant seemed courteous enough, but he didn't recognize the expensive livery the youth was wearing.

"I'm here on my master's business," Samuel lied, "the ambassador of the Confederate States of America, sir." He saluted for good measure. In truth, Samuel had told his owner an elaborate fiction about having to travel to the country to purchase some new horses—a trip that would take several days. It was a measure of the esteem in which the ambassador held the young slave that he had allowed him to go at all.

Reluctantly, the policeman stepped aside.

The court was still settling into position as Samuel found an empty seat in the balcony of the public gallery. He spied the two accused; separated, they sat in a row behind the lawyers, flanked by policemen. Aloysius's face was thinner than ever; misery had emptied his eyes and his nose had become pinched.

Lavinia Huntington looked slighter than Samuel remembered. Dressed in a plain prison dress, her hair scraped back in a simple bun, she looked scarcely older than a child. She was still beautiful, Samuel noted, marveling at the creature his friend had risked everything for; Aloysius's dream of escape and more than that, of the two of them transcending the confines of their existences had also launched Samuel's aspirations. During the Irishman's short employment with Lady Morgan the two men had spent evenings planning the manner by which Aloysius could rescue Lavinia Huntington; fantasizing how the coachman, once free of his station and with Lavinia as his wife, would flourish as an independent tradesman in France or even Holland. Some dream, Samuel thought to himself bitterly. Nevertheless he promised himself that, upon his master's return to America, he would escape his servitude and make his way to the North whatever the outcome of the war.

A murmur swept through the court and Samuel glanced down. The judge was shuffling in to take his chair; his potbelly seeming to balance on thin, spindly legs occasionally visible beneath his gown, his face a pockmarked mask below the powdered wig.

The hammering of his gavel brought the scraping of chairs, the clearing of throats, and the low murmuring of those who had congregated along the wooden rows to an end. A court official in black robes stood up.

"The fourth day of the trial of Mrs. Colonel Lavinia Huntington and Aloysius O'Malley, both of whom stand here today accused by the Crown of the murder of the late Colonel James Edwin Huntington on the sixteenth day of September in the year of Our Lord eighteen sixty-one." He glanced down at his notes. "The prosecution calls to the witness box

Doctor Jefferies, a noted phrenologist," he announced portentously.

Turning, Mr. Erasmus Elijah Cohen studied the pale young woman. She must have been a beauty once, he observed, but anxiety had etched her face and her skin was drawn. Mr. Cohen's forte was moral outrage: he was rumored to be able to make a martyr out of an assassin, as long as there was enough raw material for him to construct a heart-wrenching fiction, the basic requirements being that the accused was female, young, of pleasant demeanor, and preferably of genteel origin. Of Mrs. Huntington's innocence he had not a doubt, and if there was any ambiguity he had not allowed it to penetrate his reasoning—like all good defense barristers.

As for the Irishman, his was a harder case to prove. Aloysius O'Malley's sudden dismissal gave him some motive, as did the accusation that he was Mrs. Huntington's lover. However, four witnesses had placed him ten miles from the scene at the time of the murder.

Erasmus Cohen reached over and squeezed Lavinia's hand reassuringly. "Fear not."

"But he has examined me and will have damning evidence."

"Phrenology, my dear girl, is the science of absolute speculation. In other words, total tosh, and I intend to expose the charlatan."

Dr. Jefferies, several charts tucked under his arm, the shiny orb of his bald head looking particularly prominent, took his place in the witness box. The prosecutor, Mr. Abby, an ambitious zealot of some forty years with the unpleasant habit of finishing each sentence by poking the air with a long, sharp index finger, as if reiteration meant truth, strode to the front of the jury box. He waited until Dr. Jefferies had finished proclaiming the obligatory oath then launched into his examination of the witness.

"Is it true that on the fifteenth of April this year you assessed the accused at the request of her husband for symptoms of hysteria?"

"It is true."

"And this visit had been preceded by an act of violence committed by Mrs. Huntington upon her husband, unprompted by any provocation of his own."

Erasmus Cohen leapt to his feet. "Objection! Your Honor, unless Dr. Jefferies was witness to that act of violence, there is no way of verifying the statement."

"Objection sustained. Dr. Jefferies, pray continue."

The phrenologist nodded importantly. "Colonel Huntington, who himself was a respected expert on phrenology, had expressed a concern that because of the violent and unpredicted mood swings of his wife, which had culminated in an injury to his head, so he told me, and Mrs. Lavinia Huntington's physical restlessness and nervous disposition, which appeared to have worsened since the birth of her child, that she may possibly be suffering from hysteria. He requested that I examine her skull for such characteristics—"

"Which you did." Mr. Abby seemed disinclined to be left out of proceedings.

"Indeed." Dr. Jefferies unrolled two charts and a court clerk then hung them from a display stand for all the court to see.

The phrenologist pointed to the first chart. "This shows the skull of a normal woman—one, in fact, who displays a great facility for maternal warmth, indicated in the dip just here at the left of the cranium. The other chart shows Mrs. Lavinia Huntington's skull. Here is the equivalent area: note there is a slight rise—this would appear to indicate that Mrs. Huntington was, and is still, lacking in maternal love."

Again Erasmus leapt to his feet. "Objection, Your Honor.

This is irrelevant information. A lack of maternal affection does not make one a murderess."

"Objection sustained. Continue, Dr. Jefferies."

Dr. Jefferies shifted his finger to another area on the second chart. "But what we are concerned with today is this projection. Set firmly in the right lobe, it is a clear indication of severe hysteria—almost certainly untreatable."

The prosecutor, watching the jurors' reaction, waited until the phrenologist's words had taken effect, then turned to the judge. "Thank you, Your Honor. That is all for today."

Mr. Cohen stood. Posing with his chin in his hand, he seemed the embodiment of classical contemplation. After a long sigh, he turned to Dr. Jefferies.

"Tell me, why would Colonel Huntington, himself a minor authority on phrenology, allow his wife to continue to assist him if he thought she was mentally unstable?"

"That is a question that lies between a man and his wife. I suppose that he loved her."

"Would it not be that he trusted her?" The defense lawyer directed the question toward the twelve seated men, as if they were the great moral arbiters upon whom he depended.

"Dr. Jefferies, you are considered to be an impeccable authority in your field?" he continued.

"I am indeed."

"In that case, would you agree to a little test?"

"Objection, Your Honor," the prosecutor shouted to the bench.

The judge, after glancing at Erasmus, shrugged. "Objection denied. Continue, Mr. Cohen."

"Dr. Jefferies, I repeat, will you agree to have your professionalism put to a little harmless test?"

"I will."

Erasmus turned to his assistant, a thin dark Hebrew who looked as if he might be his son. At a nod from the barrister, the youth pulled the top half of a skull from a sack at his feet. There was a ripple of expectation throughout the courtroom. With a flourish, he handed it to Erasmus who then placed the skull on the witness stand before Dr. Jefferies.

"I wish you to diagnose the skull before you," he said, "from a phrenologist's point of view. That is, to describe in as much detail as you can deduct from the cavities and bumps of the skull the psychology of its original owner."

Picking up the skull, Dr. Jefferies, his eyes shut, ran his fingers across the white bone almost as if he were caressing it.

"It belonged to a Caucasian female, approximately thirty years of age at death," he pronounced. "She was affectionate, poetic, given to frugality. She had an overly developed penchant for spirituality—moreover, for any religious activity—but also was not unknown to suffer occasional fits of rage. In fact, I would venture to say that she might have been an artist of some kind."

"Indeed, Dr. Jefferies, she was an artist of some kind."

The spectators gasped at the prophetic skills of the esteemed scientist. Acknowledging the faint applause, Dr. Jefferies smiled smugly. Erasmus raised his arms to silence them.

"She was an artist of some kind, sir, because the skull belonged to Bobo, a deceased member of the troupe of performing chimpanzees with Monsieur Flaubert's traveling circus."

The spectators' admiration swung instantly to ridicule and the courtroom was filled with loud laughter. Banging his gavel, the judge tried in vain to regain order, while Erasmus shouted over the commotion.

"I put it to you, sir, that the art of phrenology is an unproven science! It is mere conjuncture, open to manipulation of the most unethical kind!"

Dr. Jefferies, flushed, spun around in the witness box. "How dare you, sir! I have it on the utmost authority that Colonel

Huntington was indeed attacked by his wife, and indeed she did, and still does, suffer from hysteria!"

"While you, sir, suffer from a surplus of imagination!" the barrister fired back.

His eyes glued to the two accused, Samuel observed Lavinia's glance toward the rows behind him. He turned to see a cleric sitting there, a man in his late fifties with an air of anguish about him that isolated him from those around him. Lavinia faltered as she met the man's eyes, and she seemed to shrink further into her prison smock. The cleric soberly indicated his heart, then the leather-bound Bible he held in his left hand, and Samuel realized this must be Lavinia Huntington's father, of whom Aloysius had spoken.

71

Los Angeles, 2002

Gabriel stretched across the bed. He'd been back from the laboratory for a hour, but the contents of the envelope kept skipping across his mind like an unsolved puzzle. His mother was at the back of the apartment preparing coursework; through the wall he could hear the muffled sound of his neighbor arguing with his wife; the day's research lay filed and finished in the briefcase at his feet; the shifting planes of normalcy that constructed Gabriel's world seemed more or less intact. Except for Julia; except for the niggling thought that beat just under his consciousness.

He switched on his favorite Death Metal album and lay there as the music bored its way through his brain; a pounding rhythm that lulled him into a torpor. Then he reached for a spliff he'd rolled that morning. Still with the headphones on, he went to the window and pulled it open. It was a classic California fall afternoon; there was the faint smell of wood fires on the breeze, and a hummingbird suddenly appeared, wings whirling invisibly as it hovered over a late-blossoming bird-of-paradise plant. Gabriel switched off his Walkman, thinking the barely audible beat might scare it away. They were magical, he thought, these creatures, part-bird, part-insect—an example of the wonder of evolution, adaptation by default.

The colors of the small overgrown yard intensified by a couple of notches and he exhaled. The anxiety was still there, but this time he could see it clearly. And the shape of it was Julia—Julia and her ex-husband. With his hands on the windowsill, Gabriel leaned out, closed his eyes and sucked in all of the horizon with one breath. The scents, sounds, and the warmth of the sunlight jangled in his mind, a myriad of sensation, and the restlessness and energy of youth shot down to his heels.

It was then that he remembered Julia's face the last time he saw her—her forced laughter, her fingers twisting the phone cable as she talked to Klaus. Apprehensive, Gabriel reached for his cell phone and rang both her numbers—first her cell, then the land-line. Both rang, unanswered.

"It seems sensible, you know, to put the house on the market, get the best price we can, then go fifty-fifty," Klaus said, scooping up a forkful of rice.

"Despite the fact that it was my inheritance and my income that paid for most of it."

"I'm not responsible for the divorce laws in this state. But I am leaving you most of the furniture."

Julia's fury rose, uncomfortably like bile. She stared at her plate; her food was almost untouched. Hoping Klaus wouldn't notice, she poured them both another glass of wine. It was still their first bottle. She planned to get him drunk; that way it would be easier. Oblivious, Klaus cheerfully helped himself to another serving of paella.

"I'm so glad we can be civilized about this, and that we can be friends. I mean, you have to understand that my feelings might have changed but the depth of them hasn't."

Julia looked down at the knife, resting across her dish stained with the saffron of the paella. It was sharp, razor-sharp.

"In fact, both Carla and I are looking forward to having you in our lives. And, of course, our child's . . ." It was then that he noticed her trembling hand.

"Are you okay?"

"Sure. I'd like that."

Klaus reached out and rested his fingers over hers. His touch was completely neutral, almost paternal.

"What you have to comprehend is that some events are out of our control, Julia."

Julia pulled her hand away and stood suddenly, the chair shrieking as it scraped back across the wooden floor. "I think it's time I opened another bottle."

"Really? But we've only just finished this—"

"Ahh, but this one's special. A Margaux."

"You sure? I mean, you might want to open it when you've finished the report, or maybe have someone more deserving to celebrate with?"

"Believe me, I regard this as enough of a celebration."

Julia moved into the adjoining kitchen, where she leaned against the wall, her will momentarily wavering as she struggled with a pervading sense of predetermination. What was the sequence of events that had led her to this juncture? Did it matter? Klaus had betrayed her, had betrayed their child and their marriage. How could he sit there now, indifferent to the terrible destruction he was responsible for? What did she have left?

* * *

Gabriel's calf muscles burned as he labored up the hill, the bicycle wheels flattening against the tarmac with his weight. He reached the crest and freewheeled wildly down the other side. Nothing could halt the instinctive momentum propelling him toward Julia's house.

72

London, 1861

Mr. Hamish Campbell took the witness stand. Despite a certain gauntness, the young man appeared composed. In fact, his grieving reverberated far deeper than he could have possibly imagined. This had been his only solace: that their affection had made him conscious that he was capable of such a depth of emotion. After the Colonel's death, he had retreated to the sanctuary of his parents' house in the North country; his father's unquestioning joy and pride at the return of the prodigal son a balm to the terrible absence Hamish would now carry forever.

The student had not forgotten his own ambitions, but his mentor's death had given him cause to reconsider both his studies and his future plans. He had resolved to complete his lover's writings, continuing in the manner he imagined the Colonel would have wanted.

Under the scrutiny of the whole court he tried to stop his legs shaking. Thankfully, they were hidden by the high podium. He was there after much persuasion by the prosecution, but he also wanted justice. Had James accidentally killed himself? Why had he chosen Lavinia to assist at the ritual and not himself, even after Hamish had tried to warn him of the dangers?

He could not know the Colonel's mind—least of all now—but he did know that James Huntington had deserved to live a full life. Pouring his grief into a public crusade, which had involved letters to *The Times*, a lecture at the Institute for the Advancement of Science, as well as several more private campaigns at the Carlton, Hamish Campbell had convinced himself that Lavinia was guilty.

Up in the public gallery, a tall, once-handsome, red-headed woman dressed in a tight-fitting day dress, slipped through the door and wound her way to an empty seat next to the Reverend Kane. The cleric sat with his Bible clutched in one hand, his jaw set tightly against the indignity of the circumstances. Turning to acknowledge the woman's presence, he startled and dropped his Bible.

"Meredith?" he said aloud, only to be hushed by the surrounding spectators.

Meredith Murphy bent down and retrieved his Bible. "The devil herself, back from the grave," she replied as she handed the sacred book back.

In the witness box, Hamish Campbell was giving evidence about the rite the Colonel had been engaged in at the time of his death. He sensed a wave of support from the jurors, a gleam of friendly recognition for a well-dressed gentleman of refined appearance, someone from their own class, someone for whom they felt some natural empathy.

"Colonel Huntington had informed me that he intended to carry out the ritual, which was based on a similar experience he had undergone when living with the Bakairi tribe in the Amazon jungle," the student's voice rang out confident.

"And had he also informed you that he had asked his wife to assist him in this instance?" Erasmus encased his question with a polite, nonaccusatory tone.

Hamish hesitated, then glanced over at Lavinia, who looked

back at him blankly. This was the first time he had seen her since the constable had banged on his door to inform him of the terrible event.

"He had."

"And why, do you think, he chose her and not you, his associate, to assist him?"

"I can only surmise it was because she had been preparing a pamphlet, under his instruction, on the hallucinogenic flora involved in the preparation of the brew used in the ritual. I believe he wanted her to bear witness as a scientific observer."

"Surely it was because he trusted her? Because he trusted her with his life?"

"If so, it was a trust ill-placed," Hamish retorted passionately.

The court broke out into a commotion and the judge was forced to bang his mallet furiously. "Order! Order!" he cried.

The room quieted. Erasmus paced up and down in front of the jury.

"Tell me, would it not be true to say that the deceased and yourself had a close . . . a very close friendship?" he asked Hamish.

"As is appropriate between a mentor and his protégé."

"Protégé. A grand word, Mr. Campbell. Is it not also true that Colonel Huntington was known to indulge frequently in the consumption of opium, and that you joined him on these occasions?"

"I don't see how that is relevant."

"It is relevant, Mr. Campbell, because it may be possible that Colonel Huntington suffered an accidental death at his own hands."

"Colonel Huntington was experienced in these matters."

"I see. Is it also not true that Colonel Huntington and yourself were discovered on the night of July twenty-fourth at Feng's Oriental Palladium, otherwise known as a notorious opium den in Mincing Lane, and that Colonel Huntington was so intoxicated he had to be carried out of the building?"

"It would not be the first time two city gentlemen were guilty of a little overindulgence," Hamish replied wryly.

The gallery and several members of the jury broke into laughter.

Smash! The judge's mallet resounded. "Mr. Cohen, will you please desist from attacking the victim's reputation."

"I apologize, Your Honor." Erasmus swung back to Hamish. "Mr. Campbell, would you say that Colonel Huntington might have been in a fragile state of mind at the time of his death?"

"I cannot answer that. I was not privy to his psychology."

"No, but you were privy to a rather generous stipend, which included an apartment rented for you by your 'mentor.' Pray tell me what kind of 'research' required the use of . . ." He pulled a list from his pocket and, lifting his spectacles to his face, read aloud: "Two Louis V sofas, a Napoleon III ebony and brass-inlaid bedstead with mattress, a piano, the use of a butler and maid . . . oh, and several opium pipes?"

Flummoxed, Hamish Campbell looked over at Mr. Abby, the prosecutor, who lifted his brows quizzically. Sensing support slipping away, the young student faltered. "I cannot say."

"I have no more questions."

After glancing at the jury, Hamish stepped down from the witness box. Erasmus sat back down and reaching over to the next row leaned to whisper in Lavinia's ear.

"I do believe the jury may be swinging our way, my dear."

73

Los Angeles, 2002

Klaus reached for his wine glass. "I know it must have come as a huge shock to you," he said, "but that wasn't my experience. It was like a pressure had been building for months. I just couldn't deal with it anymore. You must understand that."

"Can we just talk about practicalities?"

"If that's what you want."

Julia watched as he swallowed a mouthful of wine.

"Do you mind if I make a quick phone call?" she said. "It's work." She indicated the phone that sat on the sideboard.

"Not at all."

She stepped behind him, slid open the drawer and took out the gun, then aimed it at his head. Klaus, his back to her, continued to sip his wine. Julia stood there, paralyzed, her finger curled around the trigger.

As Gabriel careered down the hill, he saw there was a car in Julia's driveway that he didn't recognize: a red Golf Volkswagen with a miniature Belgian flag in the corner of the rear window. His instinct had been right.

The road flattened out and he skidded into Julia's front yard, dropping the bike on the lawn. He pelted to the front door and rang the bell.

Open, open, he prayed, even as he realized, to his horror, that the doorbell had made no sound inside the house.

74

Old Bailey, 1861

Lavinia stood in the witness box, her hands gripping the rails. This moment, imagined, had terrified her, but now, in its actual execution, terror had detached her from her body. The weeks in custody had thrown her into an examination of her behavior and psychology: she knew she was guilty and must face her judges, both now and after her death. But here, standing before the rows of curious spectators, completely exposed, all she could think of was her son and how she should try to preserve her life for his sake.

Mr. Abby stepped forward.

"Mrs. Huntington, is it true your husband asked you to assist him in this ritual?"

"It is."

"So you were witness to his preparation and, how shall I put it, his *transportation* . . ."—his sardonic tone had the court laughing—" . . . on the evening of September sixteenth, and, I might add, to his horrific death the same evening."

"I was, sir."

"And you did nothing to save him from dying?"

"Objection, Your Honor," Erasmus cried. "That is a blatant accusation!"

"Objection noted. Please answer the question, Mrs. Huntington."

"I was rendered immobile by a great fear, sir."

"A great fear or a great indifference?"

Lavinia hung her head. "I do not know."

Mr. Abby, fueled by what he perceived as a minor victory, strolled along the row of jurors, studying their faces as if to say *I told you so*. At the end of the row, he spun back around to the witness box with great dramatic effect.

"Did you love your husband, Mrs. Huntington?"

The direct nature of the question floored Lavinia. Staring at the prosecutor—his eyebrows raised in query, his whole face a parody of disingenuous bewilderment, as if the very question astounded him—Lavinia suddenly found that she could not lie—neither to protect herself nor her child. I am my father's daughter, she thought; I cannot utter falsehoods after swearing an oath upon the Bible. Paralyzed by this knowledge, she faltered.

"Will you answer the question?"

Lifting her chin, she tried to blank out the leering faces beyond the prosecutor: some expectant; some already closed in judgment; others appearing to be willing her to defend herself—or so she imagined.

"I did, sir, perhaps too much so."

A ripple ran through the court. Lavinia stayed focused on the prosecutor.

"I believe now that I might have had unnatural and un-realistic expectations of such an emotion," she said. "As a younger person, I read novels and was much influenced by their romantic notions. My husband was a great deal older than I; in the early days of our marriage, he was both mentor and husband to me, and we enjoyed much intellectual discourse. Then later . . ."

"Later, you quarreled. About what, Mrs. Huntington?"

"I cannot say."

"Come now, we have already heard how Colonel Huntington received bruises about the head due to your hysteria—"

"Objection!"

"Dismissed, Mr. Cohen. Continue, Mr. Abby."

"Did you engage in a relationship with Mr. Aloysius O'Malley while he was in the employment of your husband?"

Condemn me if you must, but not Aloysius, she prayed. During the cold of the prison nights, she had imagined her execution a thousand times over. Exhausted, she now wished only for the charade to finish. They had worn her out with their questioning. Every day when she entered that court, she had to suffer the hysteria of the newspaper men and a crowd of screaming women holding placards. The letters she had received in the last month had not helped: impassioned notes from wronged women; letters from young girls trapped in arranged marriages who had elected Lavinia as their champion, death threats from cuckolded husbands. But the most terrible deprivation they had imposed upon her was not being able to see her son Aidan. She had not seen him since her arrest and the unbearable absence widened with each passing day.

She turned to Aloysius. The coachman had been in the dock for the past three days and Lavinia had longed for the chance to speak with him. But at the end of each session she was bustled away to her cell. *Aloysius*: just the sounding of his name gave her strength. *Aloysius*. She stared at his helmet of dark hair, his green eyes now conveying a sensibility that stretched across the courtroom like a rope to a foundering vessel.

"Will you please answer the question." The prosecutor's harsh voice jolted her back.

"We had a brief liaison, initiated by myself."

So there it is, I have condemned myself: the realization ran like a shudder throughout her whole body. But now that she had actually said the words, a great calm followed—a sense of disconnection, as if she floated high above the proceedings.

The court seemed to voice a collective gasp, then broke into shocked murmuring. The judge slammed down his gavel and the murmuring ceased.

Determined to be heard, Lavinia continued. "You have to understand that I was driven by loneliness. He had come from the same county, from my homeland. He is innocent of murder! He is merely guilty of succumbing to my seduction."

"So you admit there was a murder?"

"I do not know. I only know that at the time of my husband's death, I was possessed by a great jealousy and a great despair. I believed I would never have my marriage back, nor ever have the freedom to love another. At twenty years of age, one's life yawns before one like an eternity—"

"Jealous of whom, Mrs. Huntington? Surely not of the friendship between Colonel Huntington and Mr. Hamish Campbell?"

"I repeat, I cannot say. But I do not believe myself responsible for my own actions at the time of my husband's death."

"That will be all, Your Honor." Mr. Abby bowed briefly to the judge who then indicated that Lavinia should take her seat.

75

Los Angeles, 2002

Julia stood there for what seemed an eternity, wanting to kill him, knowing she had the capacity.

"Aren't you going to make your call?" Still eating, Klaus didn't bother to turn around.

Julia didn't answer. Every atom of her being was focused on the .44 Magnum, heavy in her hand, pointed at the back of his skull. It became fused with her skin, an organic extension of her anger.

Klaus caught her reflection in the window opposite—a wisp of an outline, but clear enough. He swung around.

"Don't move!" Julia said, her voice, furious and urgent, sounded out as violent as Klaus's surprised expression.

He turned back, his hands frozen to the table.

"Julia—"

"I want you to hear what you did to the three of us—you, me, and our son—"

"Julia, you're not being rational—"

"This isn't about rationality! It's about betrayal."

Klaus's cell phone started ringing in his jacket pocket.

"Don't answer it!"

Somewhere in the room, a fly began to buzz. Then there came a sudden banging on the front door. The noise almost shocked Julia into pulling the trigger.

❧

Gabriel stood at the front door smashing his fists against the wood. Nobody answered, yet the lights were burning inside. He climbed the fence and ran around to the back of the house, to the bathroom window. To his relief it was ajar. He slipped his fingers under the frame, hoisted it up, and climbed inside.

The sound of a gun being fired and glass shattering rang through the house.

"Julia!" Gabriel screamed, and scrambled over the bathtub toward the door.

76

Old Bailey, 1861

"The prosecution calls Dolly Copper to the stand!"

The maid, dressed in a pretty bonnet as if for church, smiled at the assembly as she climbed the short staircase to the witness box. In a defiant and confident voice, she swore her oath on the Bible.

Erasmus turned to Lavinia, who had paled. "Mr. Abby has us caught on a back foot with a surprise witness. Who is she, Mrs. Huntington? Will she be the source of some aggravation?"

"I am afraid, sir, that she will."

The defense lawyer turned back to the witness stand, his demeanor grave as he examined the extreme youth of the woman. Her feminine frailty and the open honesty of her face would no doubt appeal to the jury.

Mr. Abby stood.

"You have been in the employment of the Huntington household for three years, is this correct?"

"Yes, sir, and I have been very happy there."

"Tell the court what you witnessed on the evening of September fifteenth."

Dolly Copper glanced quickly at Lavinia then averted her eyes.

"I was in the library after the men had been there. I was just tidying up and doing my usual dusting—Mrs. Beetle likes to inspect the house last thing at night and everything must be in its proper order—"

"Get to the nub of the matter, Miss Copper. We adjourn for

lunch in half an hour and brevity is essential," the judge interjected, stifling a yawn.

"Yes, sir. Well, it was like this, the mistress came in and dismissed me, telling me she would replace the master's cognac as he was particular about it. I remember thinking at the time that it was an odd thing to say, as it were always Mr. Poole's job to look after the wine and such. Knowing that it would be my head on the chopping block if the room wasn't proper, I hung around the door—"

Eramus leapt to his feet. "In other words, you were spying!"

"I was not!"

"Order in court!" the judge commanded. "Pray continue, Miss Copper."

"Anyhow, that's when I saw the mistress tipping something into the Colonel's snuffbox. I knows what I saw 'cause I'd checked earlier to see whether the snuff needed topping up, and the box was full. I'm telling you, it weren't snuff she was mixing in with the master's tobacco, that's for certain."

An audible gasp ran through the court. Lavinia gazed straight ahead, her face deliberately emotionless.

❧

The judge glanced sternly around the murmuring spectators as the jurors filed in. Lavinia dared not look at the twelve men who had been in discussion for over four hours behind closed doors. Whatever the verdict, she was determined to consider herself free—free of the burden of guilt, free spiritually.

She looked across at Aloysius. The two of them were locked into this dreadful moment of waiting; her growing anxiety smashing against the court walls with each passing minute. She closed her eyes, imagining a different future: a small bridge over a river somewhere on the other side of the world, with the three of them standing together on it— Aloysius, Aidan, and herself.

"Has the jury reached a verdict?" the judge asked.

A short man with a handlebar moustache whose edges reached to the winged tips of his collar, and who looked as if he'd be more comfortable behind the desk of a counting house, stood. "We have, Your Honor."

The juror handed a slip of paper to the clerk, who passed it to the judge. A terrible silence fell upon the room as the judge opened the slip then began reading.

"In the case of Aloysius O'Malley, accused of conspiring with Mrs. Lavinia Huntington to murder her husband, the jury finds the accused not guilty."

Up in the public gallery, Samuel sounded a solitary cheer. The exclamation echoed around the hushed space, as, their breath held as one, the rest of the spectators waited on the next verdict.

The judge cleared his throat.

"In the case of Mrs. Lavinia Elspeth Huntington, the jury finds her guilty of murder—"

Uproar broke out amongst the onlookers. While members of the press, anxious to be the first to reach the printing room, pushed past the young American coachman who was now holding his head in horror. The Reverend Kane, in a sea of shouting people, began muttering the Lord's Prayer. Meanwhile, the two accused stared at each other, motionless.

The judge placed the black cap on his head.

"The condemned will be taken from these premises and shall be hung by the neck until pronounced dead."

A great roar rose up in Lavinia's head and the world ran away from her into sudden darkness.

Upon seeing her daughter collapse, Meredith Murphy pushed her way to the front of the court.

Lavinia's face was chalk against the gray of her flannel dress. Mr. Cohen and his clerk crouched beside her. Kneeling, Meredith reached into a pocket and placed a vial of smelling salts under Lavinia's nose.

"I am most dreadfully sorry, Mrs. Murphy." The defense lawyer laid his hand gently upon the Irishwoman's shoulder. "The jury and the whole of England was set against her from the start."

"You did your best, Erasmus, but even you cannot change the ways of the land, nor the travesty that often passes for marriage." She looked down at her daughter's gaunt face, now resting upon her knee. "Sir, I have not wept for fifteen years, and I'll be damned if I give them the satisfaction of seeing me weep now."

She reached into her purse and pulled out a small cloth bag filled with guineas. "You'll be wanting this."

The barrister handed the money back.

"Dear woman, I will be as saddened as you to see her hang."

77

Los Angeles, 2002

Gabriel rushed into the dining room. Julia stood holding a gun, staring at the shattered window opposite. Klaus was sitting in front of her, cowering, his hands covering his head.

"I shot to miss, deliberately. I stopped myself," Julia murmured, amazed. Gabriel pulled the gun out of her hand.

Klaus stood slowly and dabbed pointlessly at his wine-stained shirt. Then, as the full realization of what had happened rushed through him, he swung around to Julia and started yelling.

"You're fucking crazy! I'm going to press charges—this will be the end of your career!"

Lifting an arm, he moved to hit her. Gabriel blocked him.

For a moment the two men stared at each other, then Klaus backed off.

"You're Naomi's son, aren't you?"

"Are you okay?"

"What do you fucking think?! She tried to kill me! I want that gun confiscated and I will be pressing charges! You can testify for me."

"Testify? I saw nothing." Gabriel turned to Julia, still pressed against the sideboard in shock. "Julia?"

Julia looked at Klaus—he was just an ordinary fallible man in his early forties, with bad skin and a receding hairline. She thought about his inability to be honest, his fatal need to please to the detriment of his own personality, his lack of professional discipline. He was a chameleon, a victim of his own moral and emotional weakness. And, for the first time, she pitied Carla.

"You know what? I think we're all finished now." She pushed her way past the two men and went into the kitchen. Leaning against the sink, she began to shake uncontrollably.

"I had this sudden feeling that you were in danger. That sample you gave me to test . . ." Gabriel stood in the doorway, only dimly aware that he was shouting. He was angry, angry with the horror of it all, and his voice boomed out, full of questions. "It tested positive! I checked it three times, and it came up positive every time. It's definitely that sequence, Julia, but what's really odd is that it's female DNA."

Sweat ran in rivulets down Gabriel's forehead, plastering his hair to his skin. In that moment she saw the man he would become.

"It's you, isn't it? It was your blood."

"I made a decision," Julia said, her voice deceptive in its calmness. "I guess you could say that nurture triumphed over nature."

Later that night, Julia sat in the lounge room, the tape cassette player on the coffee table before her. After she'd promised to see a psychiatrist, Klaus had finally agreed not to press charges.

She glanced up at the portrait of Lavinia Huntington, then, her finger pressed down on the erase button; she wiped all the cassettes to Klaus. At last her anger had begun to fade.

78

Newgate Prison, 1862

Lavinia sat in the corner of the prison cell, on the narrow wooden bench that ran alongside the scarred and uneven wall. A tin bucket filled with water stood in the opposite corner; a small barred window, framing her last afternoon, set high into the wall above her. Blindly, her fingers traced the initials carved into the wooden surface she was sitting on: initials of the women who had been hanged before her. Shivering, she felt all of them in the room with her, a profound mass terror seeping up through the stone floor. Where would she find redemption now, except in the memory of those who would live on?

"Lavinia."

He stood on the other side of the bars, smaller than she remembered, his hair now grayer. There was no judgment in his eyes, only a weighty sadness.

"Father!" She was at the bars in a moment. Their hands intertwined; weeping, she lifted them to her face.

"Child, I should have taken you in when you asked me. This I shall regret until my dying day. Now compose yourself, I have Aidan waiting outside."

As the jailer went to fetch her son, Lavinia wiped her eyes

on the burlap skirt, then smoothed down her unruly hair. Somewhere in the shadowy corridor there was the creak of a heavy door.

Bewildered and wide-eyed, the child was carried in by a matronly prison officer. As they drew nearer, Lavinia could see Aidan was close to tears. Her cell door was unlocked and her father stepped inside.

"I shall collect him shortly," the prison guard announced before delivering the child into Lavinia's arms.

"Mama." Aidan wrapped his arms tightly around her neck. She buried her face in his ringlets, the tiny weight of him dissolving all that lay before her.

"Mama's going away, but you will see her again soon, I promise," she whispered.

She looked at her father. "He will come into his inheritance when he is eighteen. My will is with Mr. Cohen. I have left instructions as to who will be his ward after your death."

"Until then I shall take him back to Ireland, and I promise you he shall have the best care and education a child could wish for."

"Thank you, Dada."

Hearing the childish name, the Reverend broke down weeping.

❧

It is almost dawn. I thank God that my stay in this formidable hell has been brief, only days since my sentencing. In a few hours I shall no longer be of this world; it has been a short life—a mere twenty years—and although my act was calculated, I have known since I was a child that I was capable of such deeds. I am guilty of loving passionately; I am guilty of jealousy and romantic ideals. I am also guilty of murder, but I pray that you, my invisible and silent companion, will be humane in your judgment.

In the distance, Lavinia could hear the rattling of the prison guards' keys and their footfalls as they approached the cell. Trying to control her violent trembling, she closed the whispering box for the last time.

79

Los Angeles, 2003

Julia looked around the table at the four Defense Department representatives. Along with Colonel Smith-Royston, she also recognized a military psychologist from the Psych Division, but there were two others she had never seen before: General Burt Jennings, a muscular gray-haired patrician in his sixties; and the Head of Personnel, Amanda Jane, an African–American woman in her late forties. Flinty and angular, she appeared the most suspicious of the geneticist. Clicking a pen impatiently, she scanned the report in front of her and occasionally peered over her bifocals at Julia with forensic appraisal.

Behind the table a photograph of the President hung above the imitation fireplace; his closely set eyes held a faint gleam of incredulous bewilderment, as if even he could not entirely fathom the chaos he had inherited.

Only the crackle of turning pages broke the tense silence as the four officials finished reading Julia's report.

Feeling anxious, Julia poured herself a glass of water. The general looked up.

"Let me get this straight. What you're suggesting is that there may be several genetic factors involved in the individuals of interest, but you haven't been able to separate those factors from external influences."

"Sometimes genetic traits require external circumstances to launch them. In this case, an individual may have this particular mutant gene function, but if something in their environmental experience—call it 'nurture,' if you like—doesn't encourage the gene to detonate, then it'll just stay dormant on the DNA."

Amanda Jane leaned forward, her chin jutting out. "In plain English, Professor Huntington, you're telling us it would be a waste of time and resources to genetically profile potential frontline combat troops?"

Hesitating, Julia focused on a point somewhere between Amanda Jane's eyebrows. Knowing that she was being less than honest, and risking both her career and reputation, Julia swallowed before speaking. "It's complicated."

"Then simplify, Professor Huntington. It's what we pay you for."

"In plain English, it would not be ethical of me to suggest that, even with the required genetic profile, any particular man could kill in close combat without some later regret or remorse. In the course of my research I discovered that I simply couldn't isolate this propensity from other factors."

"Such as?" asked the general.

"Free will, sir."

Leaving the conference room, Julia felt as vulnerable as a target on a shooting range. On the way down to the main entrance, she noticed a campaign poster for the Candidate, offering wonderfully inarticulate platitudes instead of policy. He seemed an ironically apt choice for the current apocalyptic times.

Leaving the Defense Department building, she stepped out into the sun.

80

Life, confession, and
EXECUTION
of
Lavinia Elspeth Huntington
For the MURDER of her husband
Colonel James Edwin Huntington
by
The Honorable Stanley Taylor Williams Esquire

Old Bailey, this cold morning of January tenth, in the year of Our Lord eighteen sixty-two. The sheriff, with his attendants, arrived at the prison and proceeded to the condemned cell, where he found the condemned's father, the Reverend Kane of Anascaul, County Kerry, engaged in prayer with his daughter. After the usual formalities, Mrs. Lavinia Huntington was conducted into the press room where her hair was cut short. The executioner and his assistants then commenced pinioning her arms, which operation they skillfully and quickly dispatched. The condemned uttered not another word.

At a quarter of an hour before eight, the arrangements having being completed, the bell of the prison commenced tolling and the melancholy procession was formed, the prison chaplain preceding the culprit on her way to the fatal drop, and reading the burial service for the dead. No sound, if we except the deep sighs of the unhappy woman, interrupted the clergyman as the procession moved along the subterranean passage.

Outside, the gallows were surrounded by a great multitude of people, some of whom had traveled from as far afield as Lancaster to view the hanging of the creature who has been dubbed the Snuff Murderess. A great proportion of the onlookers were female, the fairer sex taking a particular pleasure in the execution of one of its kind, and there was all manner of heckling as the unfortunate woman arrived by prison cart.

Before the scaffold, Mrs. Huntington was seen tremulously to thank the sheriff and the worthy governor of the prison for their kind attention to her during her confinement. Then, perilously, her knees shaking, she ascended the scaffold and was placed in the necessary position. While the executioner was adjusting the fatal apparatus of death, the accused appeared deeply absorbed in prayer. The executioner, having drawn the cap over the accused's face, retired from the scaffold. On the signal being given, the bolt was withdrawn and the unhappy woman was launched into eternity. A few convulsive struggles were perceptible, and she ceased to exist. After a time, the body was cut down and conveyed into the prison.

Aloysius, staring at the broadsheet, recognized only the name "Lavinia."

"You know I can't read a word, Samuel."

Samuel put his hand on his friend's shoulder. "I thought you should have it anyway. It was quickly done, and afterwards a great quantity of birds rose up into the sky. Aloysius, I believe it were her soul breaking free at last."

Aloysius turned away, his shoulders shaking as he silently fought his emotions.

"I'll pray for her, and for the child left behind," Samuel said.

In lieu of an answer, the Irishman reached out and grasped the great calloused hand of his young friend.

81

California, 2003

Tom Donohue had picked her up outside the Defense Department building. She'd asked him to drive her out to the Joshua Tree reserve, and now, with the desert laid out before them, the cacti standing like silent sentries, the occasional cricket rasp breaking the air, Julia opened a bottle of champagne and filled two plastic cups.

She leaned over to kiss him. It had been four weeks since their first date, and two months since the encounter with Klaus. She had rung him the day after, determined to return his gun, and they had been seeing each other ever since.

"So what exactly are we celebrating?" Tom ventured. He put his head back and breathed in the atmosphere; it was fragrant with the scent of heat from the fading day.

Before completing her report, Julia had deliberately destroyed all evidence of the heightened activity that indicated ANG–1. Although she knew it was only a question of time before other geneticists made the same discovery, she had reached her personal decision. In any case, would they ever really be able to separate nature from nurture and then calculate in that other crucial factor, free will? Surely it was possible that whatever one's genetic inheritance, one could still evolve consciously beyond the genetic propensities of one's ancestors? The willingness to take moral responsibility was an immeasurable factor.

Either way, Julia was convinced Tom had been right: there were at least two propensities linked to the same mutant gene function—a capacity to kill, and a capacity to carry out that killing without emotional consequences.

"It's signed, sealed, and delivered," she said.

"And?"

She looked at him, marveling at the ease with which she'd found herself trusting the former Delta Force soldier.

"Come on," he persisted, "I need to know the official verdict."

"Officially, my findings were inconclusive."

"The unofficial version?"

"I pried open Pandora's box then decided to slam the lid shut again. Although you do realize that some other geneticist is going to discover it all over again in a nanosecond?"

"Thank you." He looked at his watch. "A nanosecond—I think that gives us enough time." He kissed her, then pulled her down onto the blanket.

The four Defense Department officials waited until they knew Professor Huntington had left the building, then General Burt Jennings nodded to Amanda Jane, who picked up a telephone. A moment later, Matt Leman, the representative from Xandox, was ushered in.

Colonel Smith-Royston pulled out a chair for the newcomer.

"Now, Mr. Leman, I believe Xandox has some information to share—or perhaps sell?"

82

Cork, 1875

The photographer steadied the legs of his tripod. The wind whipped up the camera cloth and sent Aidan's cap flying. Behind them, the ship's horns blared.

"Now I know it's mighty breezy, and any minute we will have cloud, but Master Huntington, if you could just look a little cheerful about taking this momentous trip to the land of the brave and the free."

Pulling himself up to his full height, Aidan stared at the seagulls that soared above the dock in a cackling spiral. He wondered if he'd ever see the Irish sky again.

The photographer disappeared beneath the cloth. Next to him, Aloysius played the buffoon until he finally got the youth's stern face to break into a shy smile.

Beyond them, way out to the horizon, the ocean continued its timeless pounding.

BIBLIOGRAPHY

The following are a selection of books and articles I read during my research for *Soul*.

Davidoff, Leonore. *The Best Circles: Society, Etiquette, and the Season*. London: Cresset Library, 1986.

Duncan, David Ewing. *The Geneticist Who Played Hoops with My DNA*. London: HarperCollins, 2005.

Dyos, H. J., and Michael Wolff (eds). *The Victorian City: Images and Reality* (Vol 1). London, Boston: Routledge & Kegan Paul, 1976.

Gould, Stephen Jay. *The Mismeasure of Man*. New York: W. W. Norton, 1981.

Grossman, Lt. Col. Dave. *On Killing: The Psychological Cost of Learning to Kill in War and Society*. Boston: Little, Brown, 1995.

Hartman, Mary S. *Victorian Murderesses: A True History of Thirteen Respectable French and English Women Accused of Unspeakable Crimes*. New York: Schocken Books, 1976.

Knelman, Judith. *Twisting in the Wind: The Murderess and the English Press*. Toronto: University of Toronto Press, 1998.

Picchi, Debra. *The Bakairí Indians of Brazil: Politics, Ecology, and Change*. Prospect Heights, Ill.: Waveland Press, 2000.

Pool, Daniel. *What Jane Austen Ate and Charles Dickens Knew*. New York: Simon and Schuster, 1993.

Ridley, Matt. *Genome: The Autobiography of a Species in 23 Chapters*. London: HarperCollins, 1999.

————. *Nature via Nurture: Genes, Experience and What Makes Us Human*. New York: HarperCollins, 2003.

Sweet, Matthew. *Inventing the Victorians*. London: Faber and Faber, 2001.

The Illustrated London News (Feb. 1861–Dec. 1861).

Welsh, Alexander. *The City of Dickens*. Oxford: Clarendon Press, 1971.

ACKNOWLEDGMENTS

My thanks go to Professor Marilyn Monk, Dr. Tim Newsome, Jennifer Bostock, Professor Nelson Freimer of the Center for Neurobehavioral Genes, Los Angeles; Dr. Ainsley J. Newson, Paul Schutze, Jeremy Asher, Viv Neary, Japhet Asher, Adam Learner, Nina Learner, Maggie Rosen, Maeolisha Stafford, Dr. Alistair Owen, Eduardo Sanchez, and Matthew Ollerton. Thanks also to my publisher Linda Funnell and editors Julia Stiles, Nicola O'Shea, and Lydia Papandrea; and my literary agents, Rachel Skinner (Australia), Catherine Drayton and Kimberly Witherspoon (U.S.), and Julian Alexander (U.K.).

READER'S GUIDE

SOUL
TOBSHA LEARNER

QUESTIONS FOR DISCUSSION

1. Learner draws a historical comparison between phrenology and genetics, Darwin and creationism, the onset of the American Civil War and the fallout of contemporary American foreign policy. Do you think by raising such comparisons she is commenting on the nature of progress or suggesting history in some ways merely repeats itself?

2. *Soul* is very much a story about power. What are the greatest differences between Julia and Lavinia in terms of the types of power that they have, or lack, in the world—intellectual, familial, social, economic, professional, and maternal?

3. The prison of Lavinia's marriage has its basis in the consolidation of economic power solely in the hands of a man. What have been the most important elements in the establishment of women's independence in the western world over the last century? What commodities, abilities, and freedoms do we take for granted that Lavinia could never gain access to?

4. Learner's characters talk frequently about nature versus nurture, about genetic imperatives versus free will and moral responsibility. Is Lavinia a moral person? What code of ethics does she follow? What are her strongest priorities?

5. Why do you think that Julia is able to avoid killing Klaus—and therefore avoid either going to jail or losing her

own life—while Lavinia is compelled to kill James? Do you think that Lavinia's decision was the right one, either morally or in terms of her struggle for survival? Does Julia represent a more evolved version of her great-grandmother, or does she simply have more choices?

6. Genetic propensities are triggered or not triggered by external factors such as stress, physical environment, and even diet. How do the external circumstances that trigger the propensity to kill without remorse in both women differ?

7. Post-traumatic Stress Disorder has a huge impact not only on combat soldiers but also their families and friends. The notion of genetically profiling men who would not suffer from it is morally complex. How does Learner address this issue?

8. Learner portrays Klaus as someone who has frequently failed to stand up for himself, yet when he leaves Julia, he does so in an aggressive and self-centered way. Is he actually a narcissist, or simply someone who took years to learn how to prioritize his own needs? Is he a modern-day cad? How does he compare with James, his parallel in Lavinia's story?

9. What do you think of Julia's decision, early on in the book, to accept the Defense Department contract? Is she ethical in her thinking about her work? Can you envision situations in which her super-soldiers could be essential to public safety or national security? How do you feel about her decisions at the book's end?

10. Gabriel is an enigmatic character. Do you think that he loves Julia, or does he seduce her for professional gain? Given their age difference, what do you make of the fact that he genuinely seems to care about her well-being? How does this relate to his own upbringing?

11. Much of Lavinia's story revolves around differences between culture and manners in Ireland and England. Are these always differences of class? What other factors go into creating the rift that Lavinia so often feels as an Irishwoman in Mayfair?

12. How do you think Julia's story would have unfolded had she not miscarried? Would Klaus have come back to her? Would Carla's pregnancy have influenced his decision? Do you think that having a child would have altered Julia's anger toward Klaus or her decisions about harming him?

13. The Irish Famine was one of the great crimes perpetuated by an indifferent England. In what way was the English aristocracy implicated?

14. The ambassador for the Confederate States did indeed have an embassy in Mayfair and the Confederacy was active in campaigning for support in Britain. What economic hold did they have over the manufacturing industry in England?

15. The genetic imprint that Julia, Lavinia, and Julia's soldiers share begs the question of whether war—the use of lethal conflict to settle differences—is inherent in our nature. Is war a necessary part of life? Can you envision a society—a town, state, or nation—that could function entirely without internal armed conflict? Do such societies already exist?